Praise for *Brief Gaudy Hour*

"Margaret Campbell Barnes, author of *My Lady of Cleves* and *The Passionate Brood*, has done it again. In *Brief Gaudy Hour* she has not only struck it rich as far as an historical subject is concerned, but she has also handled the subject, in her own particular way, with the dexterity of a veteran in the field of historical fiction." – *Philadelphia Inquirer*

". . . an immensely entertaining and absorbing novel . . . In a day when so many cheap historical novels are being written, one should be all the more grateful for those books which combine a thorough knowledge of backgrounds with a just assessment of life and character. Mrs. Barnes' are among the best." – *Chicago Tribune*

"Despite its well-known details, the story of Anne Boleyn takes on a new excitement. This is due to the author's skill in depicting her heroine as a real woman. Somehow, by the end of the story, she has convinced you that, in spite of her faults, Anne was a sensitive and lovable person." –*Toronto Globe and Mail*

"Anne is presented sympathetically, but not always as an admirable person . . . A well-written, romantic novel." – *Library Journal*

"Margaret Campbell Barnes has established herself firmly in the front rank of historical novelists." – *Sunday Empire News*

Brief Gaudy Hour

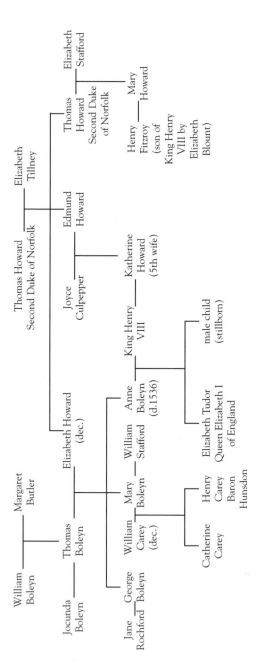

House of Howard

House of Boleyn

House of Tudor

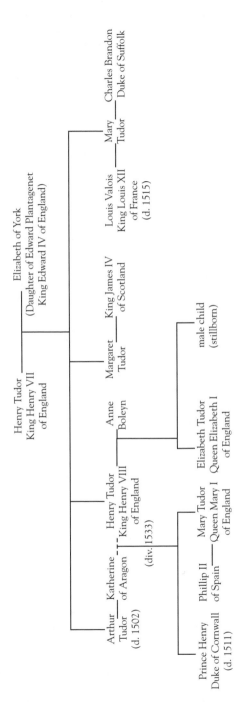

The names and personages represented by this chart serve only to clarify relationships between the characters in this book. Ordering of names does not represent birth order, and in some cases may provide incomplete birth and death records. The purpose of this chart is to enhance the story presented on the pages that follow.

Brief Gaudy Hour

A Novel of Anne Boleyn

MARGARET CAMPBELL BARNES

SOURCEBOOKS LANDMARK™
AN IMPRINT OF SOURCEBOOKS, INC.®
NAPERVILLE, ILLINOIS

Published by Sourcebooks Landmark, an imprint of Sourcebooks, Inc.
P.O. Box 4410, Naperville, Illinois 60567-4410
(630) 961-3900
Fax: (630) 961-2168
www.sourcebooks.com

Originally published in 1949 by Macdonald & Co., London.

Library of Congress Cataloging-in-Publication Data

Barnes, Margaret Campbell.
  Brief gaudy hour : a novel of Anne Boleyn / Margaret Campbell Barnes.
      p. cm.
  ISBN 978-1-4022-1175-1 (trade pbk.)
  1. Anne Boleyn, Queen, consort of Henry VIII, King of England,
1507–1536—Fiction. 2. Great Britain—History—Henry VIII,
1509–1547—Fiction. 3. Henry VIII, King of England, 1491–1547—Fiction.
4. Queens—Great Britain—Fiction. I. Title.

PR6003.A72B75 2008
823.'91--dc22

                                                                    2007037523

              Printed and bound in the United States of America.
                  CH 10 9 8 7 6 5 4 3 2 1

To

MY HUSBAND

"Verily,
I swear, 'tis better to be lowly born,
And range with humble livers in content,
Than to be perk'd up in a glist'ring grief
And wear a golden sorrow."

Anne Bullen in Act II, Scene III, of Shakespeare's *King Henry the Eighth*

Author's Note

In Tudor times so many parents called their children after royal personages that it gave rise to a confusing repetition of such names as Henry and Mary. In order to avoid this, it has seemed advisable to alter the Christian names of one or two minor characters in this book.

Wellow, Isle of Wight,
1947–48

Chapter One

"NAN! NAN! COME IN and be fitted for your new dresses to go to Court!"

"Nan! Come and answer your father's letter."

"Nan, child, don't stand *toute égarée* in the garden. Your turn has come."

Simonette's sharp French voice shrilled first from one open casement and then from another as she bustled through the Castle rooms stirring up waves of preparation for the launching of her pupil on the chancy sea of life. Simonette, in the Boleyns' service, was the perfect governess. For her, this day, years of exasperation and devotion were terminated in triumph. Tears might come after. But here was the proud moment in which to produce the young thing she had made.

Yet the girl to whom she called still lingered on the terrace watching the giddy flight of butterflies above the drowsing knott garden. For her, as for them, the gaudy hour of life was being born. Bright as their painted wings, heady as the hot perfume of the flowers. Full of golden promise, and transient as the summer day.

All that was spirited in Anne Boleyn thrilled to the prospect of the brilliant future; but, being intelligent and sensitive beyond her years, she spared an ungrasping moment for a savouring of the past. The happy, innocent past—so wisely filled with graceful pursuits and the joy of burgeoning appreciations. Before the flurry of dressmakers and the glitter of courts obsessed her, she must look her fill upon this Kentish garden, stamping the impress of its happy recollections upon her heart. The lovely lawns where she had been wont to play with her brother and sister, the stately trees beneath which her father walked, the yew arbours cunningly devised for dalliance where her cousin, Thomas Wyatt, read aloud his poems and made love to her.

To Anne the gardens of Hever meant more than all the stately ancestral pleasances of Blickling Hall, or her late mother's home at Rochford. They would be as a salve when she went forth into the unknown, and something beautiful to come back to. She would sit sometimes and remember them when she was in France.

For Anne was fiercely sure now that she would go to France.

In his letter from London, her father did not actually promise it. He merely summoned her to Court, saying that Queen Katherine would be graciously pleased to receive her. But when he was last home he had hinted that he was striving for this honour to be granted her—the honour of being chosen to go to Paris in the train of the King's sister, who was betrothed to Louis the Twelfth. It seemed an incredible thing to happen when one was barely eighteen. But Sir Thomas Boleyn was Henry Tudor's ambassador to the French Court, and ambitious for his children. And, of them all, Anne had his heart.

Goaded by the urgency of her governess's voice, Anne turned at last. Her dark eyes were starry with excitement, and her right hand clutched the Ambassador's parchment to her bosom. But her left hand lay quietly hidden in the green folds of her gown.

As she went up the wide steps and through the great hall, the older servants smiled at her indulgently. Already there was a great carrying hither and thither of chests and coffers for her journey. George Boleyn, her brother, brushing aside a welter of hounds, caught her boyishly by the shoulders and hugged her. "Your turn at last!" he exulted, just as Simonette had done. "And I am to take you to London."

That was the keystone to her happiness. At present there would be no pain of parting from her youthful circle, no loneliness to mar her good fortune. Of all creatures in the world, this brother, but a few years older than herself, was dearest. His was the laughter, the crazy gaiety that had leavened the cultured companionship of their mutual friends. They would all be there; not in the gardens at Hever, but at Greenwich, Windsor, or Westminster. For a little while longer they would be together—with their swift wit, their shared passion for music, their versifying, their dancing, and their endless discussions. Thomas Wyatt and George and their friends who already had places about the King, Wyatt's sister Margaret, and her own sister Mary, who was more beautiful, if a little more stolid, than the rest.

"Why should Mary, who is younger, have gone first?" demanded George, following the trend of her unspoken thought.

Anne shrugged. She knew that the same resentment had been smouldering in her governess's breast during these last few months of quiet preparation. But now, today, it mattered nothing. "Mary went first," she said. "But I may go farther."

"You mean with the royal bride to France?"

To save her face in case of any future contretemps, Anne laughed a gay denial of her hopes. "Oh, I have been promised nothing!" she temporized.

The glances of brother and sister met and held with that intimate understanding which was between them. Then the young man's eyes shifted and were momentarily hooded. "Mary has blossomed out. She has been noticed at Court," he remarked uneasily.

But Anne's thoughts were centred on her own destiny. She took little heed of his unwonted gravity. "It is scarcely surprising. Our mother was accounted one of the loveliest women present when the Queen first came from Aragon," she reminded him lightly, a little enviously perhaps. For although Anne was by far the more accomplished of the Ambassador's two daughters, Mary was the acknowledged beauty.

Back in the room where she worked at her books, Anne unrolled the letter which had so suddenly changed her quiet life. "May I answer it myself, Simonette?" she asked gravely of her waiting governess.

"*Bien sûr, ma chère.*"

"In French or English?"

"They say that the Princess Mary, although but a child, writes equally well in either, as well as in Spanish. The Tudors like their women to be educated. And you know which his Excellency, your father, would prefer."

Anne assimilated the hint that, with an eye to advancement, her letter might be shown in higher circles. "And you think my French is good enough?" she enquired anxiously.

The tall, shrewd woman standing by the writing desk smiled with the assurance of one whose task has been conscientiously performed. "I have every confidence in your ability, Nan. And who knows but what one day you may have to write to yet more important people?"

With a deft movement of her right hand Anne jerked the blank waiting parchment towards her and took up a quill. Seated with the sunshine illuminating her dutifully bent head, she poured out her filial gratitude, understanding fully for the first time why Sir Thomas and Simonette had made her work so hard at music and at languages. In her letter she expressed eager appreciation of the promised privilege of conversing with so great a queen as Katherine of Aragon. And, mindful of the difficulties and temptations that bestrew a young girl's path in such exalted places, she made a spontaneous promise to her father. "I am resolved to lead as holy a life as you may please to desire of me," she wrote. "Indeed, my love for you is founded on so firm a basis it can never be impaired."

It never occurred to her to question what he might desire of her nor what vast forces might shake the basis of that love, and little did she realize, as her quill moved on, the solace her naïve promise would be to an affectionate man caught in the net of his own worldly ambitions. A man who already knew parental qualms for his younger daughter.

When the letter was sealed and dispatched, Anne delivered herself up to the chattering seamstresses. Half-basted dresses had already been cut from materials far finer than any she had previously possessed. Brocades and velvets had been reverently lifted from the dower chests of her Howard ancestors, and refashioned to the full, flamboyant mode. Anne thought they made her look taller and her waist yet more slender. They seemed to lend her a sombre dignity, accentuating the wealth of her raven hair, the delicate high moulding of her cheekbones, and the pallor of her skin. But she herself knew that once she began to talk and laugh with people, something would come to life in her, lending animation to the pale oval of her face; and the thing which Thomas Wyatt called witchery would take possession of her slanting, almond-shaped eyes.

The seamstresses went on working by candlelight, but when Anne became weary, Simonette sent her to bed. And when her tiring maid had turned down the covers and pulled the embroidered shift from over her head, Anne knew that like that—with the alabaster of her body half hidden in the warm night of her hair—she was lovelier than she would ever be in any dress.

Only now there was nowhere to hide her left hand.

Anne looked down at it, as she always did, with reluctance. Upon her little finger grew a second nail, almost a second finger, an abnormality from birth. Something of which she was ever conscious.

And the consciousness was like a secret sting, often goading her sensitiveness to sharpness and ill-humour, sometimes to a kind of competitive zeal. It seemed to set her apart from other girls. So that always she must excel in everything in order to outweigh this one imperfection.

She could not bear people to speak of it. Here at home everybody knew and understood. But now that she was going out into the world she must learn to be clever about it. She must not let her new friends twit her. With so many things that she could do well, she must not let it spoil her chances of preferment. Or of love.

Anne paused to study the reflection of her nude body in a long metal mirror. Thank God, it was exquisite enough for the most exacting lover. She was glad that her parents, through some freakish caution or ambition, had omitted to arrange a betrothal for her in infancy. Unlike her sister and her girl friends, she was still free. Free to choose her own lover.

She clambered lightly into her four-poster and pulled the covers up to her little, pointed chin. Absently, she bade the fresh cheeked country wench good night and watched her snuff the candles. But by the pale glimmer of the peeping moon the long dreams of youth went on. She would meet this lover in France perhaps. Meet him suddenly, as like as not. One day she would rise and dress and go out, the same as on any other day; and then suddenly she would see him coming towards her, and she would know. He would be tall, of course, and fair like George. Or dark, perhaps, like Thomas Wyatt? Never, she felt, could he be as charming as Thomas or as dear as George; but he must be stronger, more masterful than either. A soldier perhaps. The kind of man who wouldn't stop to write a sonnet to one's eyes, but who would sweep one into compelling arms and stop all protests with a kiss. She was certain about that. But his colouring? In God's name, should he be dark or fair?

The door opened and Anne's stepmother came into the quiet room, carrying a candle. A domestic figure, dispelling romantic dreams. And quite suddenly Anne realized that in a day or two she would be leaving all the dear familiar things of home.

Jocunda Boleyn was not blue-blooded like Anne's mother. She never went to Court. She was just a country gentlewoman of Norfolk whom Sir Thomas had married, as widowers left with growing children will. She was incapable of sparkling or saying witty things or of looking arrestingly handsome like the rest of them. But it was Jocunda who, for all the family, made Hever home.

She put down her candle and came and sat on the edge of the bed, and Anne threw both arms about her. "God save me, I do not really want to go! I had forgotten that you will not be coming too!" she stammered, shaken by unexpected sobs.

"Hush, poppet! It's only that you are tired out with all the day's fuss." Jocunda held the immature body to her comfortable, childless breast. "Why, you, of all of them, would eat your heart out here! You are just the kind of wench to whom wonderful things will happen. Imagine, going to attend the Queen!" The mistress of Hever appeared to be searching a little helplessly for some panacea for her own approaching loneliness. "She is a God-fearing woman, our Queen."

Anne sat up, still sniffling forlornly.

"Everyone will like your singing, and your father will make a brilliant match for you," prophesied Jocunda. "Only sometimes I cannot forebear from wishing—"

"You wish I would marry Thomas Wyatt, don't you, you soft-hearted creature?" smiled Anne, wiping away her tears with both hands; for only before this one woman, who had loved her tenderly since childhood, would she use her left hand naturally and without embarrassment.

"Were you to travel the whole world you would not find a man of more beautiful character," submitted Jocunda.

"I know."

"And you would settle down at Allington a few miles away, and I should have no need to lose you."

"But I am not in love with Thomas," objected Anne. "The dear Lord knows I should be sore put to it to do without him, Madame; but I do not want to marry him."

"Are you sure, Nan?"

"Quite sure."

Jocunda regarded her speculatively. Somehow she had more qualms about letting this fledgling go than about either of the other two. "You are so young, and somehow I have the feeling that marriage with a man like that would give your whole future security."

"If there be one thing of which I *am* sure it is that I do not want a dull security," said Anne, in that clipped, decisive way of hers. "Verses and gallant speeches make a lovely background, like harmonious tapestries, but they are not the viands of a feast. And sometimes I grow tired of being treated as if I were a breakable Madonna. I want something more—more exciting than that. Something harder to attain, like the way I have worked for Simonette. Something with a spice of danger even." The beating of warm blood was animating Anne's face. In the shifting candlelight her eyes looked almost green, and she laughed through thick lashes from the corners of their narrowed lids—a fascinating, hussy's trick which her stepmother had always deplored. "When I love a man, my sweet, I shall love him with every pulse in my body," she declared. "Through adversity, sin, or danger."

"Nan!"

The second Lady Boleyn was often scandalized by the things her predecessor's brilliant children said; but Anne only nodded her sleek head. With her calm assumption of worldly wisdom, she might at that moment have been the older of the two. "You will see, Madame; now that my great chance has come I shall meet him, here or in France. It will be a love match; but he will be rich and powerful as well, so that I shall have all the music and jewels and wonderful dresses I want. And I shall have my dear, attractive father to thank for it all!"

Jocunda rose and wandered restlessly about the room. "I'm not so sure," she said, straightening Anne's comb and ribbons and a disarray of pins. And then, as if she must unburden her mind to *someone*, she added bitterly, "I would to the dear Mother of Christ it were so!"

Anne watched her unwonted restlessness from the curtained stillness of her bed. It was so seldom placid Jocunda spoke like that. "Whom then should I thank, Madame?" she asked, wide-eyed.

"I am afraid, in part, your sister Mary," answered her stepmother without turning.

"Mary? But that is fantastic! She is even younger than I."

"But very beautiful. She has been noticed at Court."

"That is what George said. How splendid, Madame! All our Howard women are beautiful, are they not? But still I do not see—"

"Splendid, yes; but dangerous." Jocunda laid down Anne's simple, unjewelled comb, and came and stood at the foot of the bed. She looked baffled, distressed, and rather as if she had been losing sleep. "It is the King himself who has noticed her," she said.

The King! Henry the Eighth of England and untitled, country-bred Mary Boleyn! For an unthinking moment it seemed dazzling. "But surely Queen Katherine—" stammered Anne, in her young half-innocence.

"The Queen has been sick for months now, ever since she was brought to bed of her last stillborn son," sighed Jocunda. "In London, now, they think we Boleyns are to be courted, complimented. Your father never was in such high favour. He is entrusted with all the negotiations for this French wedding. There are places made for George and you and for all your friends. But to me—oh, I know I am but a plain Norfolk woman, and it is not for me to meddle—but, oh, Nan, Nan, it is all wrong! King or no King, it is sin. And your sister so nearly betrothed to Sir William Carey!"

Anne's eyes were dark with amazement. "You mean my sister Mary is the King's mistress?" she asked, with the unsparing directness of youth.

"Not yet, I pray the Blessed Saints! But how to prevent it?"

"Surely my father—"

Jocunda was quick in his defence. "What can he *do*, Nan? The Tudors made us. The knighthood and everything. As you know, your father is partly of wealthy merchant stock. All that we have and are could be shorn from us."

"You mean that he would *sell* her?" The ugly thought was incompatible with the distinguished bearing of Sir Thomas Boleyn and the careful way in which he had had them instructed in theology.

Jocunda stood sadly, her capable hands folded against the dark material of her dress. "When you get to Court, dear child, you will find that men live or die by favour of the King."

"Then why doesn't Mary herself—" All that was virginal in Anne—all that had been reared in a gracious home and grown accustomed to a budding poet's respectful expressions of love—was rudely shocked. "Surely," she cried, "*she* can refuse?"

But unversed as Jocunda was in fashionable ways, she knew a good deal about human nature. "Haply her head is turned," she suggested. "He is said to have sought her out and sent her jewels. It is a great honour, men say."

"Honour!" echoed Anne scornfully.

"I pray you, judge her not too harshly, Nan. Even if she would remain chaste—you know what King Henry is like."

Certainly, Anne knew what King Henry was like. Didn't everyone know? Even people like herself who had never seen him. All men talked of him, and there was the copy of Van Cleef's portrait hanging in the great hall downstairs. A great, ruddy, good-looking giant of a man, gorgeously dressed. A godlike person, swaggering through life, beating wrestlers and musicians at their own game. Challenging everybody. Dominating everybody.

"Who would dare to refuse?" sighed the harassed chatelaine of Hever.

"I would," boasted Anne Boleyn, with all the fiery pride of untried youth.

Jocunda laughed indulgently and bent to kiss her good night. "God knows, I shouldn't have talked to a child like you about it!" she chided herself. "But you must learn soon enough if you go to Court. And I would not have that sharp tongue of yours spitting out anything that might add to the burden of your poor father's driven conscience."

She put a hand to the hangings embroidered with little white falcons, and drew them gently about her stepdaughter's bed. "Sleep well against the journey, Nan!" she adjured. And took up her candle and departed.

But long after Jocunda's footsteps had died away along the gallery, Anne lay wide awake in the darkness thinking about her sister Mary. Mary who used to deck herself with daisy chains upon the lawn, and who never could construe her Latin verbs. Pondering about Mary, who always looked like a golden-haired stained glass saint kneeling at her prayers. And trying to picture Mary in Henry Tudor's bed.

Chapter Two

B Y THE TIME AUTUMN had carpeted the lawns with beech
leaves Anne had travelled far from Hever. Not so far in miles
as in experience and thought. She had met with fine modes
and manners, and assimilated ideas widely divergent from
Jocunda's. Humbly, receptively, she had assisted at the glittering
functions of the great. For a few awe-inspiring weeks she had lived
at Court in the household of Katherine of Aragon. And she had
seen the King.

The Queen had been kind but—dare one admit the truth?—a
little dull. Her conversation had been well informed, her manners
perfect; but except with her own friends, she was habitually
restrained and formal. And once one became a little less awed by
the stiff grandeur of her Spanish entourage, not all her fortitude
could hide the fact that she was in reality a sick and weary woman.
Such attractiveness as she may once have possessed had been spent
in a series of miscarriages for, conscientiously, with almost religious
fervour, Katherine had submitted her thickening body to all too
frequent attempts to bear a living Tudor son. And privately Anne
considered that the only time she looked interesting was when she
was talking to her little daughter Mary.

But Anne had the sense to look upon those difficult, homesick
weeks at Westminster as a useful initiation. Her reward came when
she was chosen to go to France as maid-of-honour to the King's

younger sister, Mary Tudor, who was the merriest and most popular princess in Christendom.

Sir Thomas himself brought her the list of appointments. True, her name came fourth and last. But then she was only a knight's daughter; whereas Anne and Elizabeth Grey were the King's own cousins, and the Dacre girl had been sired by a lord. Probably it had been thought that her fluency in French would prove useful.

The wonderful thing was that her name should be there at all! Young Nan Boleyn of Hever, whom no one had ever heard of outside Kent. Clearly, it was another Boleyn triumph. Astute Sir Thomas, elated a little above his usual composure, had beamed upon her. "I always said you had my brains, even if your sister Mary has the Howard beauty," he chuckled. "What more can we desire?"

"What more indeed," agreed Anne. An ambassador, a gentleman-of-the-King's-bedchamber, and a maid-of-honour all in one family. And Mary.

Anne had thanked him prettily; but her thoughts had winged back to Hever. To Jocunda, who alone of them all had never achieved anything spectacular. Grateful to her father and to her governess she would always be. But in her heart she recognized the greater value of something which her stepmother had put into her—the clear moral sense which made her capable of sharing Jocunda's hatred of the debt to Mary. And besides hating the way people smirked when they spoke of her sister, some new streak of fierce self-sufficiency growing in Anne made her resent the steppingstones laid down for her light, climbing feet, and preferred to find her own.

To be young and ambitious was to inherit the earth. To cull its sweets without incurring any of its responsibilities. Great events in the lives of her betters formed but a glittering background to her own inconsequent enjoyment. Of the passionate strivings which actuated them she recked nothing. The drawn-out bitterness of a proud, deserted queen was but the shadow against which to experiment with the substance of an admiring dance partner or a becoming dress; the diplomatic sale of a princess's body but a vaguely realized tragedy necessary to a new maid-of-honour's small success.

And now the illustrious bridal party was held up by the weather at Dover. Though Henry himself had come to see his favourite sister safely embarked, and Louis of Valois, with so little vigour left to enjoy a bride, waited impatiently in Paris, human plans and passions must wait until the autumnal gales had lashed themselves out.

In spite of the constant round of gaiety with which the King and his crony, Suffolk, filled the grim old castle, there was plenty of time for an unimportant maid-of-honour to daydream and write in her diary. Curled up on a window seat in the Princess's anteroom, Anne committed to her tablets a vivid description of her mistress's proxy wedding at Greenwich. The bride had looked adorable, Henry Tudor resplendent, and the French guests had been the last word in elegance. And instead of being partly bald like Louis, the proxy bridegroom had been young and personable.

"Are you not cold over there by the window?" asked Anne Grey, drawing her embroidery frame closer to the leaping fire.

"What do you find to write about, Nan Boleyn?" badgered her bored sister Elizabeth.

"About the royal proxy wedding."

"The State recorders will do all that," they told her.

"But they may forget about the piteous paleness of milady's face and the way the sun shone through the windows spilling a kind of gossamer gold all over her gown," murmured Anne. Only people in her own bright circle, like Thomas Wyatt, understood the joy of painting pictures with words, she supposed; and, laying down her pen, sat there wool-gathering in the growing dusk.

Dear Thomas, with whom she had so much in common and with whom she would have to part so soon! Was he, perhaps, the reason why her father had as yet arranged no marriage for her? He was so eligible, so constant, and their neighbour. And Jocunda wanted her to marry him.

Anne began picturing a wedding at Allington or Hever. Something like the Greenwich one, only less grand, of course. Her father grave and distinguished, with his dark, greying hair. Jocunda in one of her sober-coloured gowns, with deep contentment in her eyes. And she, herself, in a white pearled dress like the Princess's, with a man standing beside her making solemn vows. Only somehow the man was not Thomas. Her dream bridegroom was as yet a stranger. A girl's fancy still wrought upon him, peering through rosy mists of the future, trying to mould features as yet unseen. All Anne knew was that he must be tall and ardent. But, when the time came, would he be dark or fair? She never could make up her mind.

As if summoned by her vagrant thoughts, her cousin Wyatt came hurrying into the room, accompanied by her brother. "The wind has dropped," they announced. "So it may be you will all sail tomorrow."

Wyatt's glance went straight to her, though he stopped to make polite conversation with the King's cousins; but George, with his usual impulsiveness, came across to the window seat. "Suffolk is to escort the Princess and stay until after the wedding in Paris. I have it direct from the King," he said, boasting a little.

"I don't much care for the Duke of Suffolk," said Anne, drawing aside the fullness of her velvet skirt so that he might sit beside her.

"He apes the King too much, but he plays a good game of tennis. And whoever is in charge of the party, I wager you will be a credit to us, Nan." Sobered by the thought of parting, he threw an arm about her shoulders and appealed to their cousin. "She is conducting herself with marvellous success, isn't she, Tom?"

"A new Diana in the field!" smiled Wyatt, coming to join them. He spoke with a polished raillery which made him seem much older than George, and snatched teasingly at the tablets on her knee. "And here, if I mistake not, we may find interesting impressions of her new hunting ground!"

Anne clutched at them protectingly, and a small friendly scuffle ensued.

"I must see who my rivals are!" insisted Wyatt.

"You can't read a woman's secrets!" protested George, joining in the fray.

But Wyatt only laughed. "Once there is something secret in her life, our Nan will cease to keep a diary," he prophesied.

"Go and write a sonnet to the bride," Anne bade him, aware that the two senior maids-of-honour were regarding them with disapproval.

"Wouldn't it be more fitting to write a dirge?" suggested George. "She, so full of laughter, condemned to bed with an old death's-head like that!"

"I think it is cruel!" broke out Anne.

But even in this off duty hour it was dangerous to talk so freely.

"Our cousin was obliged to arrange the marriage for diplomatic reasons," observed the elder Grey sister, adopting the proprietory tone with which she was wont to put the flighty Boleyn girl in her place. "And at least the weather has been kind and given her a month's reprieve," she added, beckoning the handsome Wyatt to pick up some dropped silks.

"Perhaps it has been a reprieve for the King, too," giggled her younger sister.

The two Boleyns looked up sharply. With the spiteful little jabs of Elizabeth Grey's tongue one could never be sure. She might have meant only that it was dull these days at Westminster, with a sick Queen surrounded by priests and doctors. But no one could help noticing that Henry had twice gone out hawking here with their sister. They were young, touchy, half-shamed, and proud.

"Is it true that Mary is the King's mistress?" Anne whispered to George, while the servants were lighting the candles against the growing dusk.

Young Boleyn shrugged uncomfortably. "You should know best. She shares your room."

"She is always singing to herself."

"It would be for William Carey. She is supposed to marry him next summer."

"Pooh! She scarcely knows him. And that new necklace she wears! I asked her who gave it to her—"

"And she said 'Henry Tudor.'" A new, clipped hardness seemed momentarily to have eclipsed George's boyish charm.

"You know?"

"I saw the goldsmith bring it to his bedside."

"But, George, Jocunda says it is sin."

"Jocunda doesn't live at Court," pointed out her stepson cynically.

"And you mean that neither our father nor you will speak to her about it or do anything?"

"What can we do?" he asked, just as Jocunda herself had done. "One doesn't thrust one's head into the lion's jaw."

He would have gone to join the others by the fire, but Anne tugged at his modish slashed sleeve. She looked perplexed and childish, much as she used to look when he taught her to read the leaden figures on the sundial at Hever. All her early concepts were lying shattered about her, and she was trying to apply some painfully acquired new ones to herself. "But suppose it were I?" she asked, in a small scared voice.

George turned sharply. "God forbid!" he ejaculated.

"But where lies the difference?" she persisted.

He looked at her with puzzled tenderness, smiling at himself as well as at her. "Only in the degree of my affection, I suppose," he admitted.

They were talking in whispers. It was unmannerly, unpardonable. They went to warm themselves at the fire and the conversation became general; but although the King's cousins were so much more important, both the attractive young men hovered about Anne. She was pleasantly aware of it, and her strange, elusive beauty bloomed.

Presently Lord Dacre's daughter came from the inner room to fetch her. "The Princess needs you, Nan," she said, with weary friendliness. "To read French with her, I think. And will you take your lute."

A warm feeling of triumph tingled through Anne's veins. Officially, her spell of duty was finished, and she was the youngest and most obscure of them all. But the King's sister had sent for her. She glanced towards the plain, resentful faces of his cousins. Neither of them had any particular ear for music nor a good French accent.

Anne forgot all about her sister Mary. She rose and shook out the folds of her new green velvet. She knew that at least four pairs of eyes were upon her. She gathered up book and lute. Unhurriedly, with that peculiar grace of hers, she walked towards the Princess's private room. Soon, when they had crossed the Channel, it would be, "Nan, the Queen of France wants you!"

Chapter Three

THE PRINCESS MARY'S YOUNGEST lady came into her presence with a brave attempt at assurance. But just inside the door she paused, the book pressed to her bosom and the gaily beribboned lute dangling against her skirt.

Mary Tudor sat alone in the dusk. She had laid aside her heavy, gold beaded cap. Her chair was set before the window as if she had been watching the sunset, and the last streak of its stormy glory seemed caught in the curly bronze mass of her hair.

"Will your Grace have the candles lit?" asked Anne timidly.

Mary did not move. "No, child," she said listlessly. It was her last night in England.

Anne advanced uncertainly and laid the leather-bound book on a table. Deftly, the slender fingers of her right hand found the place. "Will your Grace have me finish the 'Roman de la Rose'?" she suggested.

"Not tonight, after all, I think."

It was then that Anne saw the tears on her mistress's cheek. She stood very still, trying to assimilate a depth of grief she had never experienced. Humbly, she recalled how it had felt, parting from Jocunda; but this was something more. And her young heart hurt with sudden generosity beneath the tightness of her bodice.

"You had better have someone to pack your trunks, Anne Boleyn. The wind abates, though it still looks very rough." Mary turned her head and smiled bleakly, without trying to hide her tears. "Shall you be sick, do you think?"

"I have never had occasion to know, Madame," stammered Anne. Queen Katherine of Aragon would never have asked one of her younger women so homely a question. Nor let them see her weep.

Anne closed the French book. She had ceased to be the clever new maid-of-honour, dramatizing herself. By thinking of someone else, she was bringing the background of her life into reality. "May I play to you, Madame?" she ventured presently. Above everything, music was the thing these half-Welsh Tudors loved, and it was the one kind of consolation which she, in her insignificance, could offer.

"Play that thing the King composed about 'Adieu, mine own lady,'" Mary bade her.

Anne was glad that Thomas Wyatt had taught her the song at Hever. She needed neither lights nor score. Indeed, she was happier thus, because of her deformed finger. She took the lute into sensitive hands and played, sometimes softly singing the words. In the informality of the hour self-consciousness fell from her, so that a new tenderness informed her tutored skill. She realized that her mistress was bidding a wordless farewell not only to a beloved brother and to England, but to all her dreams. For her there could be no splendid lover, only a grotesque travesty. She went on playing softly until approaching footsteps intruded on their shared mood. Footsteps, voices, the tail-end of one of George's audacious jests, and then a deep, boisterous laugh. The King's laugh.

Mary roused herself instantly and stood up, dabbing at her eyes with a gay silk handkerchief, and motioning to her inexperienced maid-of-honour to withdraw a little.

Anne laid aside her lute and went to stand dutifully in attendance near the door, as she supposed Jane Dacre or even the Greys would have done. She saw the Princess reach for her headdress and wondered if she should have helped her put it on. But before anything could be done about it, the door swung open and the room was stabbed with a pathway of light, warm, golden light from upheld torches, momentarily illuminating a group of courtiers waiting outside. And through the pathway of light came Henry Tudor.

"What, all in the dark!" he exclaimed, in his hearty way.

Charles Brandon of Suffolk followed him, and a brace of servants sidled hurriedly past them to light some of the candles on the table and poke the fire to a blaze. They did not stop to set tapers to the wall sconces, and when they were gone and the door was shut again the centre of the room was lighted like a stage.

Henry moved with a quick, light tread surprising in one so powerfully built. His hugely puffed sleeve brushed Anne's arm as he passed. Although her black dress was as one with the shadows, for the briefest moment his light, observant eyes appeared to be aware of her, so that she wondered hopefully if he had heard her singing his song or if he recognized her as Mary's sister. But he was so accustomed to a fringe of lesser people waiting upon his occasions that their presence meant no more to him than the lifelike figures embroidered on the wall tapestries behind them. Even within his family circle, a waiting woman more or less neither concerned nor curbed him. He went straight to Mary and clipped her in a brotherly embrace; while she, who was short and inclined to plumpness, reached on tiptoe to kiss him, French fashion, on either cheek.

"Milord Admiral tells me if this lull continues he will be able to set sail tomorrow," he said, still holding her before him by a hand on either forearm. "You'll not be afraid?"

And Mary Tudor's candid eyes had looked back fearlessly into his quizzing ones. "No," she said, with that air of almost boyish gallantry that so became her.

Anne Boleyn kept very still, watching the intimate scene from her humble stance against the arras. Never before had she seen the King away from Court functions, quite closely, like this—closely enough to catch each inflection in his voice and to watch the least flicker of his sandy lashes. He was everything that people had said, and more. More powerful, more ruddy, more dynamic. The Duke of Suffolk was handsomer, to be sure, and almost as tall. And he was probably the most important man in the kingdom, except Wolsey and her uncle of Norfolk. Yet somehow even he served only as a foil to his friend. For like all redheads, these vivid Tudors had a way of making other people look drab and colourless.

Anne watched them with profound interest—but not, of course, in the same way that she often watched their squires and young attendants, picking out possibilities of romance. To Anne, at eighteen, the King and Suffolk were just two important people approaching middle age. Public characters, of whom one stood vastly in awe.

"As I came through the anterooms I told your wardrobe women to have everything packed overnight," announced Henry briskly. And in spite of his regal gorgeousness, Anne was surprised to recognize a kind of forthright homeliness about the man.

"Can you be ready before dawn?" asked Suffolk, more gently.

The King had gone to warm himself before the fire, and Charles Brandon's brown eyes were bent solicitously on Mary. But she did not look at him; only at her brother's broad, unrelenting back. "I can do anything that is required of me," she said.

If Henry noticed the tension in her voice, he gave no sign. Possibly he felt that if he turned his back on suffering it would not—for him, at any rate—be there. Or preferred to steer the conversation towards suffering which he could by no means have prevented. "The reports have come in about those two ships wrecked against the jetty," he was saying, with a gusty sigh. "Sixty of my sailors were drowned. I must tell that competent secretary of Wolsey's to send some money to their widows."

"You have pity enough for them," said Mary.

The rebellious words seemed to be dragged from her; and suddenly the room was charged with emotion.

The King swung round like a gilded vane slapped by the wind. It was so unlike this even-tempered sister of his to speak with bitterness. If it had been sharp-tongued Margaret of Scotland now . . . "What can I *do?*" he demanded, angrily. And yet one could see that he, too, was deeply moved.

Pressing further into the shadows Anne Boleyn held her breath. It wasn't every day one heard someone taunt the King.

But there was to be no quarrel. Perhaps the Princess knew that this was really the best way to treat him, if one dared. "You know that I was obliged to arrange this marriage for the sake of an alliance with France," he protested, with dignified restraint. "You don't suppose it's easy for any of us to part with you, do you?"

"Greenwich will be deadly without you this Christmas," said Suffolk.

"It's always deadly now," complained Henry. And then, as if the thought of a sick wife reminded him of his own grievances, he added plaintively, "I, too, had to marry where I was bid—only it was Spain that time."

"Oh, Harry, I know!" Mary was all warmly human at once. "But Katherine used to play with us. She was already our loving sister-in-law. And Louis is so *old*."

"The sooner he will die!" snapped Henry, strolling to the table to pick up the book of French poems.

"And then we shall have you back again," soothed Suffolk, quick to cover up the brutality of the words. Again he tried to attract her attention, and this time a long look passed between them. They must have known each other intimately for many years, and it was almost as if he were willing her to do something. Mary glanced at her brother, who stood browsing through the pages, his appreciation already half caught by the beauty of some well-known line. She held her head high. One could almost see her taking her courage in both hands. "Harry!" she began tentatively.

At the urgency in her voice he looked up, a finger still marking his place. "Well?"

"I hate leaving you. You've always been more to me than the others. And I do know you had to arrange this marriage. But there is just one boon I would ask before we part."

He put down the book and came towards her. "Anything, my dear."

But her eyes still implored him, "As you love me, Harry—"

The words were scarcely audible, and he stood staring at her in perplexity. And presently she went down on her knees, her brocaded skirts billowing out about her, and caught at his hand. "You know that I will do this if I must, for you and for England. And that I will go through with it proudly, in a manner which will never shame you. I will do everything to please Louis. Tomorrow I will obey you. Only give me this one hope to take with me. That when he dies and when I marry again, I beseech you, Harry, let it be someone to please myself."

It was a long time before the King answered, and still she clung to his hand. Anne fancied there were tears in his eyes. "What do you think, Charles?" he asked at length.

Suffolk started a little, as though he had expected to be the last person to be consulted. "It seems reasonable," he stammered, the words half smothered in his fashionable spade-shaped beard.

"Holy Mother in Heaven, make them let her!" prayed Anne, trying to imagine what it must mean to a woman to be bartered twice.

To her relief the King bent down and raised his sister to her feet. "Very well, you minx, I promise," he said. And then, because he couldn't bear to do things by halves, he laughed boisterously and bade Charles be witness to it.

"You hear, Charles, how generous he is?" echoed Mary, between laughter and tears. "Oh, Harry, it will be so much easier to be kind to Louis now!"

She ran to a little side table and poured three glasses of wine. Charmingly, she handed a glass to each of them. And gallantly they drank to *la nouvelle reine Marie*.

"And if you are bored by an old husband, I pray you, don't beguile the time by making eyes at his handsome young nephew, the Dauphin," teased Henry.

It was almost dark and the chapel bell began to ring for Vespers. "Well, we must be up betimes," he said, setting down his empty glass with a yawn. "And for all friend Louis' infirmities, I should advise you to get some sleep while you can, sweet sister!" He tweaked her lovely hair in passing and dug Suffolk in the ribs. "I know if I were your bridegroom you'd have need of it, eh, Charles?"

He chuckled, well-pleased with his own magnanimity, and waited while Suffolk bent courteously over her hand. "I shall come aboard to see you both off," he promised, laying an affectionate arm about his friend's shoulder as they went out together.

Almost before they were gone Anne noticed that the Duke had left his fine fur-lined cloak lying over the back of a chair, but she did not dare to call out or run after him. Majesty had too lately left the scene. Even Mary herself still stood in the middle of the room, staring a little dazedly after them, as if there were more she would have said. The tall candles on the table made a ravishing picture of her ruddy hair and creamy skin. And suddenly a swift, wordless drama was enacted before her maid-of-honour's astonished gaze.

The door opened hurriedly and, with a word of apology to someone outside, Charles Brandon strode back into the room and gathered up his cloak. Mary Tudor did not move, and as he passed her he pulled her close against himself and, with one wary glance towards the half-open door, kissed her passionately on the lips.

Taken off her guard, Mary tried to push him from her—to warn him that they were not alone. Not a word was spoken, but he turned to follow the direction of her warning glance. His hands dropped from her waist. "Mary Boleyn's sister!" he muttered with an oath, when his eyes had had time to pierce the gloom.

Seeing their dismayed faces, Anne wanted to cry out. To swear that never would she betray their love, no matter how near the King her sister was. But instead she stood waiting, dumbly, as if it were herself who was in fault. For the first time since she came to Court her wits deserted her and as he passed her, Charles Brandon looked straight into her frightened face. His own was full of malevolence. He brushed her aside brusquely as if she stood between him and something he strove for. Even after the door closed behind him, Anne felt cold with his suspicious anger.

She went slowly to her mistress.

Mary stood twisting her rings. "What you have seen, child, is nothing evil. I would not have you think that, for your own sake as well as mine," she said, picking her words with care. "The Duke and I have always known each other, and I have always cared. When I was even younger than you I used to hide letters for him in all sorts of places about the Palace. It was exciting and a little dangerous. And now—" Mary raised her eyes and looked straight at Anne. "I love him, but we have never sinned."

To see her was to believe. Her quiet statement had more weight than any protestations.

All the opportunist in Anne Boleyn ran hand in hand with her affection. She kissed her mistress's hand impulsively. "What I have seen, Madame, is none of my business," she said.

Right from the outset, it seemed, the new Queen of France would have need of her and of her silence.

Chapter Four

ANNE'S GAUDIEST HOURS BEGAN in France. Louis' Court was a dazzling parterre of pleasures for her delectation. Like the bright butterflies at Hever, she had emerged from her chrysalis of adolescence to sip heady essence from them all, and to flutter her wings awhile in the warm sunshine of success.

All the splendour and wit of Paris scintillated about her, and she served a Queen whose love of gaiety matched her own, and Mary had shown her special favour. Not merely calculated favour for her silence, but favour with affection.

It was Anne who had helped her to bear the Duke of Suffolk's departure, since she alone knew what it meant to her. And when the jealousy of his own people forced Louis to send most of his new Queen's women home again, he suffered Anne to stay. Because of her fluent French, Sir Thomas Boleyn told her. Father and daughter had both called down further blessings on the diligence of Simonette, and though Mary raged at finding herself waited on by foreign strangers, Anne was secretly glad. All those impressionable French gallants, she thought—and just one English maid-of-honour!

And apart from that one arbitrary act, Louis had been exceedingly kind. Not only had he loaded his "fair Tudor rose" with costly gifts, but for her sake he had pinned all sorts of belated reformations upon the remnant of his misspent years. He adored her, and merely by being her lovable self she quelled the brutish in any man who cared for her. She never indulged in tedious religious discourses, as so many modern women did to advertise their learning; and she seldom appeared shocked. In a land of light love affairs, she laughed merrily at most of the lewd jests told at Court, but herself remained un-smirched. And Anne Boleyn was clever enough to take her cue from one who seemed to have solved the problem of being both irresistible and chaste.

There were few restrictions in Queen Mary's household, yet those who served her knew the grief it would occasion if they erred. Besides which, Anne had the grace to remember that she was daughter to the Ambassador from the Court of St. James. All that she did could bring fame or shame to England. And blithely as she enjoyed the sophistication of Paris, the quiet gardens of Hever had helped to mould her heart.

She was very careful not to err. But it was not always easy. She was too talented, too quick of wit not to draw attention. Even, at times, the Dauphin's dangerous attention. And with each conquest her strange beauty bloomed less fitfully. When ardent young men forsook acknowledged beauties and pressed about her for favours, Anne began to understand that there was something which bewitched them more than classic colouring and features. Some elusive charm which stirred their sex upon the briefest encounter. Something which she possessed and must learn to wield adroitly. When some enamoured courtier presumed too far, she would glance at him with that devastating sidelong look of hers, provoking him to desire, yet keeping him uncertain of fulfilment. But there were those, more bold or more experienced, who soon taught her the necessity of hiding her own too warm response beneath a deceptive show of coldness. Not just to tantalize, but to save herself from shame.

Life in France was teaching country-bred Anne many things. Among them, the quickness of her own desires. But she was shrewd enough to recognize them as a weakness—a mortal enemy which might at any moment betray her, undoing all the carefully built up perfections of her other parts. So she bound her sexual impulses with strong cords of fear and prayer and self-interest, and pushed them, like a caged beast, into some limbo of her being, so that no one would guess at their exuberance and so that her own pride could usually forget their power.

For Anne was beginning to know herself, although as yet she did not recognize the elements that warred in her. It had not occurred to her that the cultural urges which Simonette had implanted, the suave vaulting ambition of her father and her step-mother's good middle-class moral code were elements that made her character more complex than it need have been. That they had made her a prude, capable of being consumed by passion. That because of her father's diplomacy she was growing into a woman who might lie to others, but on account of Simonette's clarity of vision she was already incapable of deceiving herself. Always she would be sure of her own motives, so that the comfort of sinning unwittingly was forever denied her.

Among the lesser things that France taught Anne was how to dress. Beneath her mistress's amused, indulgent eye Anne began to experiment. Cautiously, with small details, at first. Intriguing little gold bells tinkling at the points of her velvet cape, so that everywhere men's eyes followed her. Or a headdress of plaited gauze, costing more in ingenuity than in money. A headdress which looked like a gossamer halo above her shining dark hair, and drove richer women with heavier features to distraction.

And then, becoming more daring, she discovered that a graceful girl can wear anything, and that fashionable women are but sheep.

A pert French girl, grudging her an admirer, had remarked too audibly that it was amazing how a man of breeding could desire to kiss a foreigner with a deformed hand and an ugly mole upon her neck. Actually, Anne's mole was small; but her sensitiveness was great. Floods of tears soaked her pillow that night, but not for worlds would she have let her rivals see her mortification. After much thought she rose and went to her duties and, while putting away the Queen's jewels, asked humbly if she might borrow a deep pearled collar that Mary seldom wore. The pearls were set on tiny bands of black velvet and it suited Anne's long, slender neck to perfection, making her look more mature and adding to the lustre of her eyes. Quite effectively, it hid the offending mole and deprived quite a number of other French girls of their dance partners. And then two important duchesses began to grace the Palace in high, jewelled collars, and half the Court followed suit. "Why, Nan, you have set the fashion with my poor little trinket! You had better keep it," laughed her mistress generously.

With such encouragement, Anne's courage soared. At last she dared to do what she had always wanted to. With the help of her sewing woman she designed a full, hanging sleeve which afforded cover for her blemished left hand. Lined with silver taffeta, such sleeves were immensely effective against her gown of midnight blue. Burning with self-consciousness, she took her place at supper and braved the barrage of her rivals' titters. And it was that night the Dauphin Francis asked her to lead the dance with him. And because Anne was as skilled in the dance as she was about clothes, a new French fashion was born. The Boleyn sleeve.

Anne would have been scarcely human had she not been elated. Even the Queen complimented her, and right from girlhood Wyatt's polished love-making had accustomed her to lap up adulation. Oddly enough, it was her father who was not so pleased. He drew her aside and warned her, gently, to be careful. "We want no breath of scandal to touch you here. Who knows but what it might spoil your chances hereafter in England?" he said. And Anne wondered what was in his farseeing mind. She had supposed that he was waiting to see what matrimonial chances offered for her in France, where she had already met several men who could stir her senses, but as yet none who could touch her heart. But she rejoiced that she was still free. Free to distribute her favours lightly, to read fine French poetry, to learn to play a variety of musical instruments, and to invent new dance steps for her friends.

In the froth of light flirtations, Anne had almost forgotten the splendid lover of girlhood's dreams. Life was so glittering, so gay.

And then, suddenly, Louis of France died. Quite effortlessly, it seemed, like a withered leaf falling into its bright parterre of perfumed flowers.

Instantly, all the colours and the music ceased. The Court became a world of sombre black. Dirges and requiems were the only sounds. *Le roi est mort.* And with the sad words, Mary ceased to be Queen of France. She was just a widow. A widow with real tears in her eyes. For it was impossible for one so affectionate not to feel gratitude for her husband's many kindnesses, and not least, perhaps, for the last boon of all.

"Louis was always kind. And, after all, it wasn't very *long*," she said.

"Shall we be going home?" asked Anne. Now that all the dancing was done, Hever was beginning to tear at her heart again.

"Sir Thomas tells me that if we do my brother will be sending milord of Suffolk to fetch me thither," answered the comely dowager Queen, with a little secret smile.

Her women were assisting at her *levée* after the week of strict mourning during which etiquette required a royal widow to keep her bed; but when they had changed her white weeds for unbecoming black ones, she sent them all away except Anne. "It is rumoured that some of the French Council are urging Francis to marry me," she said. "The Dauphin! The new King, I mean!"

Anne stared aghast. "But you are—"

"His aunt by marriage? Yes." The little humorous dimple dented Mary's cheek. "And not really old enough to be *that*!"

"You mean they want it because it would continue the alliance?"

"I suppose so."

"But it would be almost incest!"

Mary Tudor shrugged dolefully. "If the Pope granted a dispensation when King Henry had to marry our elder brother's widow, in all likelihood his Holiness could be persuaded about this. Particularly now we have an English Cardinal."

"But the King promised that you should choose. That day at Dover—"

"Yes, the King promised. I must pin my faith to that." Mary got up from her dressing stool and began pacing the room, drawing a dismal trail of black draperies behind her. "Oh, if only I *knew*! If only I could *see* Henry."

"At least you will see milord the Duke," Anne reminded her. She, herself, had no particular desire to see him; but if it comforted her mistress—Anne put down on a chair again all the scattered garments she had so absent-mindedly gathered up. Automatically she went to fetch Mary's jewel coffer, her mind searching for further comfort as she went. "Madame, I remember one evening when the Dauphin did me the honour to dance with me," she began impulsively, carrying the richly inlaid box across the room. "That is, when he was urging me to—to be more kind—" She stopped abruptly, with burning cheeks.

Mary watched the girl's reflection in her mirror. "Yes, Nan? I can imagine he did. You know you can speak quite openly," she encouraged, smiling a little.

Anne set down the jewels before her. "I expect he was trying to make me sorry for him," she explained apologetically. "He told me he supposed he would soon have to marry King Louis' daughter. His sex-dry, sanctimonious cousin Claude, he called her. For his sins, he said, and to strengthen the succession."

Mary could so easily imagine Francis saying it. In spite of her own anxieties, she had to laugh. "I hope it may prove true," she said, selecting the earrings she wanted and clipping them on. She jerked up her russet head, so that they swung like defiant stars. "But whether it be true or not, I will not marry him!" she declared.

Girls often talked like that in the privacy of their own rooms; and then meekly obeyed their menfolk. "But if King Henry insists?" murmured Anne, regarding her with admiration.

Mary sprang up, closing her jewel case with a snap. "Am I not a Tudor, too?" she boasted. "And quicker, being a woman?" In this whirlwind mood she was a small replica of her brother, and even in her unbecoming weeds she managed to look most inappropriately radiant—a ripe woman with all her warm capacity for love running riot. "After all," she excused herself, half laughing, "he shouldn't be such a fool as to put temptation in my way!"

Full comprehension of her words left Anne breathless. It had not occurred to her that a woman could really disobey about marriage. "You mean that you will marry the Duke when he comes? Without waiting for permission? Here in Paris?"

Chapter Five

WHEN THE DUKE AND temptation came, it was to take Mary back to England. Beyond that, Henry had said nothing. And it was not for a commoner, hankering after a Princess of the royal blood, to ask. Probably Henry had never even thought of him as a suitor, or perceived the danger of sending him. The Brandons were *nouveaux riches*, even more so than the usurping Tudors. No royal favour could make Charles' lineage like that of the Duke of Norfolk, Anne's maternal uncle, whose family had often intermarried with the Plantagenets and whose quarterings were prouder than the King's.

Out of respect for Louis, Mary lived in seclusion for some weeks. She and Suffolk rode and hawked together in the parklands whenever they dared. But all too soon came a letter from England full of welcome and brotherly affection; and an envoy primed with instructions regarding their return.

It was the following morning that Anne was summoned early from her bed. She shivered as she drew her fur-lined cape about her and hurried through deserted, draughty passages. Although none of the other women had been roused, she found her mistress already dressed, and Suffolk standing by the window in her bedroom. Mary had discarded her black and put on rose brocade. They both looked bright-eyed and pale, almost like children bent on some unlawful enterprise, and the Duke was snapping his long loose fingers as he always did in moments of stress. Beyond them, through a low arch, Anne could see a priest moving about in the little private oratory.

"We want you to be a witness to our marriage," said Mary, without preamble.

Anne felt cold with excitement and fear. "Does my father know?" she asked.

Mary shook her head.

"Better that he be not involved," said Suffolk courteously. But they all knew that somehow her father would have prevented it.

The candles were lighted and the young priest stood waiting in the archway, his frayed vestments no whiter than his face. He was no celebrated French prelate, fit to marry royalty; only a humble English monk who had done nothing more conspicuous all his life than fear God.

"But now he fears Henry Tudor more," thought Anne.

The sea might flow between, but Henry Tudor was in the minds of all of them, and his presence seemed to dominate the room. Somehow they all found themselves talking in whispers. Anne turned appealingly to Mary, formalities forgotten. "Wouldn't it be safer to wait?" she suggested.

As if in answer, Mary went buoyantly to her lover's side and pushed open a casement. Spring sunshine streamed over her gown and on her eager hands, making her the most romantic thing Anne had ever seen. Outside, the Seine was sparkling through thin morning mists, and the great city was coming to life. Birds were singing in the garden trees, and the heavy scent of lilac caught at one's senses. "I have waited so long," breathed Mary, betraying herself to a suspicion that fear of being forced to marry the Dauphin had had nothing to do with it.

Suffolk took her into his arms carefully, as if afraid of crushing her beautiful dress.

Anne realized that in his present situation he must be afraid of a good many things. But mostly, at the moment, her mind was crit-icizing him as a lover. Had he been *her* lover, she would not have minded about any rose brocade. Only that the man for whom she risked so much should be ardent. Ardent enough to match her courage, and to satisfy that denied, ravening desire that was hidden in her. Anne felt the flame of it rising, suffocating her, so that she put a hand to her slender throat. On a magic morning like this, while lovers were still young, the fusion of two such forces should indeed have power to jettison fear and tradition and common sense. How right, she thought, to snatch at real love when one met it! To escape the ugly obscenity of bartered sex. How thrilling to be married secretly in Paris, in the spring!

But common sense had a way of outliving sentiment. "W-what will become of me, Madame?" she asked, when that unadorned, brief sacrament was over, the frightened priest gone, and when the thought of what her father would say was very present.

"You know that there will always be a place for you wherever we live," Mary assured her.

"Will that be in England?" asked Anne.

The Duke himself handed her a glass of wine. "I am afraid not, Mistress Boleyn. Not for awhile, at least," he said gravely.

"Dear Nan, it may mean hardship and even ignominy," prophesied Mary, too honest to persuade. "Living quietly away from Court until we hear whether my brother will receive us. My husband," Mary Tudor smiled at him and blushed adorably. "My husband is going to write to Cardinal Wolsey to plead for us to the King."

That seemed a very sensible thing to do. Anne conjured up a picture of the rich, scarlet-clad Cardinal who, more than any man in England, had the King's ear. "Is he kind?" she asked, ingenuously.

"He has always been kind to *me*," answered Mary, as simply.

Then surely the King must forgive them. And if he didn't? Mary, at least, would never suffer at his hands. Living with her might mean giving up for a time all the fun and fashion and flattery of palaces, all the excitement of this newfound power with men, all her success. Anne's mind ranged regretfully over these hard-won things that had come to mean so much to her. In any other mood the thought of losing them would have swayed her more. But today it was not her head, but her heart, that was involved. The primal part of her that loved Jocunda and stirred to the beauty of a Kentish garden. Anne did not love easily. The circle of her dear ones was small; but she had learned to love with loyalty. And, essentially, she was a gambler. After all, everything might turn out well. Caught in the right mood, Henry might possibly have granted them permission to marry anyway. If one had the courage, it was always worthwhile challenging life. Anne kissed Mary's hand, made her obeisance to the Duke, and said she would stay.

All day she went about with a vast sense of importance and primly sealed lips. But all this romantic pother had made her forget that staying or going did not rest with her.

After supper her father sent for her. It was rarely that she saw him in the sombre panelled room where he worked and talked with important people about international affairs. "It is known all over Paris that the Duke of Suffolk has abused the trust our master placed in him, so it is time I made other plans for you," he said, still writing the last sentence of his dispatches.

In this setting he seemed like some stranger, and Anne tried to speak as if she were at ease. "I know about it. I was there," she admitted. "And I have promised to stay in milady's household."

"Don't talk like a fool, Anne!" he said, without looking up.

She stared down at his neat, greying head in dismay. She knew that he only called her Anne on formal occasions, or when he was very much displeased. "You mean you will not let me?"

Sir Thomas appeared to be reading over what he had written. "Mary Tudor is no longer Queen of France," he observed.

Anne stood before him feeling very young and unsure of herself. "No. I suppose she is just the Duchess of Suffolk now, but I know how much she has always wanted to be Charles Brandon's wife. And when a woman—"

"She may not long be anybody's wife," interrupted Sir Thomas grimly. "She may be widowed again."

"Then the Duke is a very brave man," said Anne, grudgingly.

"Or plays for very high stakes. Without the King's mercy this sudden lunacy could be accounted treason."

She remembered how unimpassioned he had been, and that any children of the union would stand very near the succession. Traitors who coveted the crown were beheaded on the block. For the first time a faint impact of tragedy impinged upon Anne's carefree life. The possibility of it for someone she had actually spoken to—someone she knew. And thinking of the morning's ecstasy, she realized what a different degree of widowhood such tragic loss would mean to Mary. Anne's new-born selflessness made a last desperate flutter. "But do you not see, sir, she would want me all the more. It has always been, 'Nan, Nan, the Queen has need of you!'"

"You did well in her service," conceded her father, more mildly. "But we must wait and see whether the King will pardon them."

Anne watched him seal and roll his parchments. "Is it true that they would have made her marry the new French king?" she asked.

"No. There was a minority for it in the Council. But he is going to marry his cousin Claude."

Sir Thomas dismissed the matter as irrelevant, and Anne felt sure that Mary had seized upon the scare as an excuse. She sat down slowly by the hearth. It had all been rather a shock, and her father had never insisted upon his children standing upon ceremony.

He came now and stood with a hand on the back of her chair. "My dear Nan, it is not like you to be unreasonable. We are all devoted to her Grace. But surely you don't suppose I would risk offending the King for a matter of womanish sentiment? I have your brother's career to consider. And then there is my claim to your great-grandfather's estates and the earldom of Ormonde which is still in dispute. We must all move cautiously until we know how the King takes this outrage."

Anne began to feel afraid. She wished he hadn't talked about treason. It was a terrible word. "Do you think, sir, that he will hold it against me that I was a witness at their marriage?" she asked.

Sir Thomas Boleyn fingered his gold chain of office consideringly. "You are very young, and I shall do my best to persuade him that being in the Princess' service you had no option but to obey. But if you go on doing such impulsively foolish things I shall begin to think that, after all, the admirable Simonette did not quite finish your education." He went back to a final sorting of the dispatches on his table. "And in that case, there are plenty of good convents in France," he added.

It was the usual threat to insubordination—the accepted retreat from any family *impasse*. And Anne had no desire for *la vie religieuse*. "What do you propose doing with me, sir?" she enquired docilely.

"I see no reason to change my original plans for the present," said her father, suavely. "You have always wished to be in the household of the Queen of France."

Anne sprang up. "You mean Claude?" All that Francis had said about his cousin came back to her. "But she is so *strict*!"

"She is a very God-fearing woman."

Anne seemed to have heard someone say those very words about Katherine of Aragon. Incontestably, it was true of both exalted ladies. But why, oh why, couldn't some of the good people it was her lot to live with be less dull? It had been a long day, and Anne felt older and wiser for its happenings. Perhaps this new worldly wisdom was one of the last and most useful things which France would teach her.

Chapter Six

THE RIGID MONOTONY OF service with Queen Claude might have been enlivened by attending one of the biggest events of the decade, when Henry Tudor crossed the Channel to meet Francis of Valois on the plains of Andres. Each monarch took his entire Court with him, and a veritable town of pavilions and tents sprang up for their reception. Such feasting, revelling, and jousting had never been seen. Such outward display of fellowship, such secret rivalry! Each nation tried to outdo the other in the splendour of their mounts, their equipment, and their clothes. Women stripped the family presses of velvets and brocades, and many a man well-nigh ruined himself sooner than be outdone by his fellows. For days the plain was ablaze with pennants and heraldry.

The Field of the Cloth of Gold, men called it.

All spring, Paris had been in a turmoil. For weeks beforehand men visited their tailors, and women talked of nothing but clothes. Anne would have given anything to go. All the more so because her entire family would be there. Even, for once, Jocunda. And because she had designed for herself a dress of spangled silk more breathtaking than any of her companions'.

But even in this, Claude cheated her maids-of-honour of their pleasure. Of all dates in the calendar she must needs terminate her first pregnancy towards the momentous week in June. Only when all the sport at Andres was over—either as a special concession or because she was so useless in a sickroom—was Anne allowed to make the journey to see her relatives. She travelled with the messenger who carried Francis news of his wife's health. And if she entertained any hopes of catching that gallant Frenchman's eye again with her spangled dress, she was doomed to disappointment; for by the time she arrived servants and baggagemen were in the throes of packing up, some of the tents had already been taken down, and most of the more important nobles and their families were on the point of departure.

But it was wonderful to sup with her family again, to exchange news, and to laugh and jest with George. Time flew so quickly, talking of old familiar things and receiving messages from home, that it was already time for bed before she began to feel aggrieved at her sister's absence from the party.

"Mary had a migraine and went early to the tent which you are to share with her," Jocunda told her.

Anne embraced them all and went there gaily. It was all part of the adventure to sleep in a tent as her uncles had done campaigning in Scotland, and even if she had missed all the fun her brother had been describing, it was like Heaven to get away from the discipline of the French Queen's household. But Anne paused with the tent flap in her hand, arrested by the unexpected sound of sobbing. She peered within. The servants had either forgotten, or been too busy, to light the hanging lantern. But in the long May evening it was not yet dark. She could discern a half-packed travelling chest, some hastily discarded finery trailing from a stool, a shining pool of jewellery thrown down before a mirror, and her sister lying face downwards across the low camp bed.

"Mary!" she exclaimed softly. Somehow the sobbing sounded all the more incongruous among such trappings of pleasure with the subdued flush of a sunset gilding the gaily striped sides of the tent.

Stumbling over a pair of silver shoes, Anne went to the low camp bed and bent down to shake her sister gently by the shoulder. "Are you not glad to see me?" she asked, resentful of such a greeting.

But Mary Boleyn only sobbed the more, throwing one bare white arm across the pillow.

Anne jerked forward the stool and sat down beside her. "What distresses you so?" she asked more gently. But she already knew.

"It is all over," moaned Mary, lifting a face reddened and blotched with tears.

"You mean between you and the King?"

Anne regarded her younger sister with curiosity and awe. It was two years or more since she had last seen her, and it was difficult to imagine that this girl with whom she had eaten, played, and slept could be the King's mistress. But then Mary was so sleekly beautiful. Anne put out a hand and lifted a tress of the soft fair hair which she had always envied. It seemed to her like living gold, and the tendrils of it curled instantly, confidingly, round her slender fingers. Soft, confiding as Mary's nature.

"Do you care so much?" asked Anne.

"I w-wish I were d-dead!"

But then Mary had always cried easily. George had been wont to twit her for it. Whereas with herself such abandonment of grief would have betokened a broken heart. If she were ever fool enough to break her heart over a man!

"But you didn't love him?" she expostulated.

Mary's blue eyes, awash with tears, regarded her reproachfully.

"You couldn't have!" persisted Anne.

"No. Not *love* perhaps."

"I know that you must feel angry, and a fool, and hate to meet people," said Anne, groping for what her own reactions would have been. "But you can go home for awhile. Until people have something else to talk about." Her gaze, accustoming itself to the dim and fading light, wandered round the disordered tent until it came to rest upon a richly enamelled necklace which would have looked well against her own white throat. "And, of course, you will miss all the dresses and the jewels," she sighed.

"That is the least of it," lamented Mary, who could look just as delectable in a dairymaid's smock. "It was the cruel way he did it. Urging me to come to France in his train, flattering me, and then, when I had given him everything, just dropping me like a worn-out glove."

It was the old story. How could Mary be so simple? What had she expected, wondered Anne, feeling infinitely more worldly-wise.

"Did he tell you himself?" she asked, curiously.

In spite of her grief, Mary gave vent to a little splutter of laughter at the bare suggestion. "Kings don't have to deal with unpleasant details of life like that," she explained bitterly.

"How then—"

Mary sat up dabbing at her eyes and pulling her expensive miniver wrap about her. "He just didn't come any more," she said drearily. "I used to lie awake waiting. And when he was well on his way to Calais, our father told me he had orders to conclude my marriage with Sir William Carey immediately."

"Are you with child?" asked Anne.

"How should I know yet?"

How strange to bear a child who, but for a bar sinister, might have ruled England! Another Fitzroy, like Bess Blount's handsome boy. But evidently Henry did not mean to acknowledge this one. It would be inconvenient, perhaps, at a time when the Pope was being approached about a divorce. Anne wondered irrelevantly if her first niece or nephew would look like the King. She tried to think of something comforting to say. But it was a long time since she had lived with her sister, and they never had been as close companions as herself and George. "You were to have married Will Carey anyway," she reminded Mary. "Perhaps you will grow fond of him. He is quite a pleasant sort of person."

"But only a knight. Considering that I gave his Grace the flower of my womanhood, he might have done something better for me!"

Coming from someone heartbroken it seemed so small a grievance. "It is really only her self-love that is hurt," decided Anne. "It could not be her heart."

She sat for awhile in the gathering gloom imagining how she herself would have behaved in her sister's place. Never, surely, could she have been so meek and tearful about it all!

"Mary," she essayed presently.

"Yes?"

"What is it like to be the King's mistress?"

Mary answered almost dreamily, "It is exciting. The way people watch when he speaks to you in public, and knowing how some of the women envy you. The covert glance, the thrill of a passing touch, and everybody really knowing. It is much more exciting than marriage."

Mary was smiling now and turning the King's opal on her finger. Her face was flushed, and there was a warm reminiscent quality in her voice which made Anne feel uncomfortable. But the gloom lent itself to confidences.

"I meant what is *he* like as a lover?"

"Oh, of course he is not *young*, if that is what you mean. But he has wit and poise. He is always master of the situation. Being wanted by him makes one feel surrounded by luxury and importance." Mary drew up her knees beneath the coverlet and sat hugging them. "And you know, Nan, I think even if Henry Tudor were not royal at all, there is something about him that would make other men's love-making seem tame."

"It could be," admitted Anne doubtfully. But it was all beyond her comprehension. Her mind had strayed to poor Will Carey, who would be forced to take the King's leavings. Probably Mary had not sufficient imagination to be sorry for him.

But why should she bother? She had her own way to make—her own life to live. She was confident that she could do well enough for herself. She never had wanted to be beholden to her sister. And Jocunda would be glad. Dear, single-minded Jocunda.

"I am so sleepy after my journey and all the talking," she yawned. "Come and bathe your face and let us get to bed. It must be amusing sleeping in a tent!"

But, of course, it hadn't been amusing for Mary, lying awake waiting for a lover who didn't come.

Chapter Seven

I T WAS AS BAD as living in a convent. Walking in procession to
Mass with a string of *jeunes filles*, and having Queen Claude
read dull religious books while we worked at our everlasting
embroidery frames!"

Anne was back at Hever, and Thomas Wyatt and her brother
had ridden over from Greenwich with the King. They were sitting
in the kitchen garden because Henry, himself, deep in discussion
with Sir Thomas Boleyn, was pacing back and forth across the
lawns. As in earlier summers the three of them had wandered there
in hope of pilfering old Hodges' fruit, and had stayed because the
high brick walls against which he trained it lent an added intimacy
to the brief hour of their reunion.

Listening to her tale of woe, Anne's audience made suitable
sounds of commiseration. "No dancing?" George was understood
to enquire, between bites at a juicy medlar.

"Her Majesty thought it an enticement of the devil. Sometimes
in the middle of her solemn functions it was all I could do not to
leap up and clap and twirl in a morris dance, just to see what all
the old French dowagers would do!"

"Had you no music either?" asked Wyatt, who would sooner
have gone without food.

Anne fostered his sympathy with a dramatic sigh. "Only chants
and dirges. And we were not allowed to converse with men."

George hooted with ribald laughter and nearly choked over his fruit. "A sister of mine without any *men*!" he spluttered.

"Had I known that, I might have slept better o' nights," grinned Wyatt. "I shall always feel beholden to the virtuous Queen Claude."

Anne flipped a cherry at him and put another into her mouth. She was swinging idly on the low bough of an old apple tree, while he leaned against the trunk. Her brother, in all his court finery, sat cross-legged before her upon a bed of thyme.

"There is something about virtuous women that starves me," said Anne, with a vindictive little grimace. "If it *be* virtuous to avoid the delights you have no stomach for!"

Wyatt laughed, but watched her appraisingly. In some indefinite way, she had changed. She had grown up, of course, but not quite in the way he had expected. "You must have hated leaving our own Princess's household," he said gently.

Anne stopped swinging and turned to him at once with the sincerity she so often concealed nowadays with levity. "I never minded anything so much, Thomas. I would have stayed with her, but my father would not let me. And I was so *afraid* for her."

"You need not worry any more, my sweet. Now that they are both home and forgiven. It was very generous of the King. Did you know that he spent Shrove-tide with them in Suffolk? It is thought that he will invite both her and the Duke back to Court."

"It wasn't wholly generosity. He missed them woefully," pointed out George. "Nothing we could do was right, and there was no one to take their place. The Queen was sick at Windsor and he had tired of—" Whatever George was going to say trailed off into an inaudible mumble as he bent to detach a burr from his scarlet hose. Anne guessed that Wyatt had frowned him to silence.

Idly, she selected two pairs of cherries from the little heap in her lap, and hung them round her ears. "And he was getting tired of Mary," she concluded for him. She hated being treated as if she were a child or a cloistered nun. After a small silence, broken only by the blackbirds, she added casually, "I haven't seen her since she married Will Carey. But Jocunda says, when it came to the point, she took it very well."

They went on eating their fruit contemplatively. "There is Jocunda," said Anne suddenly, as a bustling figure crossed their line of vision from the direction of the house, followed by Simonette and servants bearing flagons and refreshments. "Do go and help her, George! You know how flustered she always gets when the King comes."

The son of the house rose at once from the sweet, crushed thyme. He, too, adored Jocunda. Anne knew that he would tease her and set her laughing, and keep everybody else in the best possible humour. She watched him run blithely after their step-mother, tossing back his fair hair as he went.

"He is one of those precious people who will never really grow up," she laughed.

But Wyatt hadn't bribed a colleague and changed his turn to attend the King in order to look at Anne's brother. He had all the hours at Court in which to do that. And here, of Anne's own making, was the one brief chance he had hoped for. Dared he believe that she had purposely manoeuvred it?

"The months you were in France seemed a lifetime, Nan," he said. "I've bitten my pen trying to tell you how I wanted you."

"I was glad of your letters, Thomas."

"How glad?"

Anne looked straight before her at the familiar trees, the court-yards and the high, twisted chimneys of her home. "There were times when I used to shut my eyes and picture us here in this beloved garden."

"And any when you thought but of me?"

"Why, of course." She knew what was coming and tried to fend it off. "And I loved your Italian sonnets."

Wyatt came and knelt beside her. "I have given you more than sonnets, Nan. I have given you my heart."

"My dear!"

"And nothing can ever change it. I've so little time to talk to you alone." He was no longer stringing pretty phrases. He was putting the longing of a lifetime into a few fleeting minutes. He glanced back along the path, even while he seized her hand. "Nan, if I can get your father's consent—now, today, before I have to go—will you marry me?"

Anne searched her heart. It was so lovely to have him again. "I want your love, Thomas. I scarcely know how I could live without it. I've had it so long, haven't I?" She turned her hand in his, fondling it, with a little diffident laugh. "But as for marriage, truly, dear friend, I do not know."

"There is no one else?" he whispered urgently.

"No, no, I promise you. But I am so lately come home from abroad. Give me a little while to think."

Anne was in quiescent mood, caught between two phases of her life. If he had pulled her into his arms and kissed reluctance from her lips, he might perhaps have had her. Might have kept her safely all her life. But, in his chivalry, he took her at her word. "I will try to ride over next week, alone," he promised.

There were voices calling across the garden. Simonette's, and her father's. It sounded as if his conference with the King were over. At any moment their privacy might be invaded. Wyatt got up hurriedly, dusting his knees; and Anne took the lute she had brought and began playing something at random.

"Let us see if we can set that new ballad of yours to music," he suggested, trying for her sake to recapture their former nonchalance. "How does it go? 'Fair shines the sun on youth's short day'."

On the other side of the wall Simonette had been hurrying to warn Lady Boleyn that Sir Thomas had gone into the house to seal some documents, and that the King would soon be ready to depart. But the King himself had left the stone bench where he had been sitting and was strolling towards her, admiring his host's flowers. "Where are those two young men of mine?" he called amiably, pausing to sniff at a rose bush.

Simonette supposed them both to be with Jocunda. By all rules of etiquette she should have offered to go and fetch them. But as she curtsied to the ground her quick eye espied the flutter of a green skirt in the kitchen garden, and a more venturesome idea came to her. Whatever the King's business at Hever, it must have been settled satisfactorily. He seemed in jovial mood. Simonette had always been zealous in the Boleyns' service; and if Mary had not proved clever enough to make the most of her chances, well—Mary was not her only pupil. "If it please your Grace, I last saw them going through that open archway into the kitchen garden," she said, without apparent guile.

"An odd place, surely." Graciously, Henry motioned her to rise. But it pleased him very well to look across Sir Thomas's bowling green and see branches laden with ripe medlars swaying beyond an invitingly open door in a mellow brick wall. Kitchen garden or not, it looked a delectable place. And just at that moment, sounds of music and laughter were borne faintly thence on the summer breeze.

Music, medlars, and laughter. Henry Tudor loved them all. Until the horses were brought round he had time on his hands. And he, too, had caught a glimpse of the green skirt. He nodded to Simonette with a kind of conspiring bonhomie and went briskly down the path between trim box-bordered flower beds.

In the doorway he paused a moment to appreciate the unexpected scene. The elegant Sir Thomas Wyatt, in slashed silver, leaning over a dark girl in green. Picking out tunes beneath an apple tree. So this was how his gentlemen spent their time while their betters were in conference. And, by Heaven, the young dog had taste! Who was she, now? A slender creature, dappled in sunshine spilling through the quivering leaves. But, of course, she must be the elder Boleyn girl. The *other* one. The one Sir Thomas had just been talking about.

Henry regarded her with less impersonal interest. He must have seen her before about the Court, he supposed. But some time ago; and always as one of those shadowy females in someone's entourage; subservient, mute, withdrawn. Never laughing out loud like this in the sunlight. All vivacity and enticement; not a bit like pretty, placid Mary Boleyn.

And she could improvise, too.

Amused, intrigued, Henry walked on towards the thyme bed with that light tread of his. Wyatt, with his back to him, was pattering scraps of verse as the girl composed a tune for them. Neither of them was aware of him until his shadow fell across them.

The girl saw him first. Caught unawares, hostility flamed in her, to be followed by a revealing flush of embarrassment. Instantly, Henry knew her to be virgin. The hostility was for past misuse of her sister, not for present interruption. But she was too quick-witted to leave an awkward situation unmended. With a movement of extraordinary grace, she was down in a billow of green silk at his feet. "God save your Grace!" she breathed. And Henry, standing over her, saw that her body was even lovelier than her face.

"Wyatt, you dog in the manger, why haven't you presented this lady instead of hiding her under an apple tree?" he bullied pleasantly.

Even that budding statesman's *savoir-faire* was taxed. Proudly, yet reluctantly, he did as he was bid, and would have abandoned their pastime politely. But apparently his Grace wished to participate. His excellent memory was beginning to function. "I have heard my sister say you could sing," he said, motioning Anne to rise.

"Like Orpheus!" murmured her admirer.

"I pray you, how does milady fare?" asked Anne eagerly.

Henry laughed comfortably as he seated himself on a short pruning stool Wyatt had brought. "Like a nesting bird. I saw her at Westropp and she is already big with child." He helped himself to a medlar, and bit at it appreciatively. "Whose words are those you were trying over? Yours, Wyatt?"

"No, sir. They are the lady's own."

Henry was obviously surprised. He himself was no mean versifier. He motioned Anne back to her bough and handed her the discarded lute. There was nothing for it but to play. Improvising a tune for her own poor little ballad before a sovereign who had composed anthems which were sung in all the royal chapels of England! Anne wished Hodges' well-raked ground would open and swallow her up. But presently they were as happily absorbed in their occupation as they had been before, and Henry was joining in. Experimenting with a note, suggesting a cadence—only most of his suggestions were a good deal better than their own. Once he reached over and took the instrument out of Anne's hands. If he noticed the little finger she always tried to tuck away, he made no sign. "Try it in B flat," he said, and picked out the same notes in a minor key. "I believe the whole thing would sound more plaintive and quite charming."

Henry pretended to no proficiency on the lute, but his ear was trained and perfect. And he understood harmony. He was enjoying himself. He loved music as they did. He had forgotten all about his host and horses, and his young companions had paid him the supreme compliment of forgetting momentarily that he was a King.

He sang the simple ditty through, while Anne, watching his time-beating hand, essayed to play it as he wished. The result was delightful.

"You must play it for my sister sometime," he said.

He began talking about the effect of the Italian sonnet on English poetry, and questioning Anne about French composers; and it was not until harassed scurryings and alarms made it apparent that half the household was searching for him that he got up reluctantly. "Do they have to make all this hullabaloo? Could not that fool of a governess have told them where I was?" he complained, filling his mouth with another medlar before leaving.

Sir Thomas and Lady Boleyn escorted him to the courtyard; Wyatt and George became courtiers on duty again, and Anne followed meekly behind. She was still dazed from her unexpected experience, and not a little impressed. She had always worked hard at her music and relied upon such accomplishments for social success. Yet here was someone who picked up an unknown ballad and a half-made air and perfected them casually, in an odd half hour—besides being a redoubtable sportsman, a fine Latin scholar, and a King.

Henry mounted flamboyantly, well aware of his horsemanship and the splendid figure he cut. It was only when his mind was set on bigger issues that he did spectacular things with that easy lack of self-consciousness which he secretly envied in trueborn Plantagenets, like the old Countess of Salisbury. "You must bring your daughter to Court," he told his host kindly, at parting. But as soon as his broad back was turned, Anne threw Thomas Wyatt a rose.

She stood on the terrace watching the gay cavalcade until it had passed from sight through the gatehouse. After the rest of the household had gone in again, she still stood there, looking at the peacocks and the flowers and the butterflies. Just as she had done that first day she had been invited to Court. But now the thrill had gone, and her thoughts were touched with some indefinable sadness. Perhaps, after all, it would be pleasanter to live quietly in Kent. To be a country gentlewoman like Jocunda. To live in one's own house, without competition. To be content, and stop climbing. There would always be books and music and cultured friends at Allington. And loyalty and kindness.

Once again Simonette was calling her. But this time it was her father who wanted her. Anne went slowly indoors. She walked thoughtfully with down-bent head, indecision on her mind, and a tender smile on her lips. It was not until she was halfway across the Great Hall that she realized that her father and stepmother were waiting for her. It seemed that Jocunda had been arguing about something and had broken off suddenly in mid-sentence.

'Where have you been, Anne? I sent for you as soon as the King left," said Sir Thomas, from the dais.

Anne lifted her head and stood stock still, like a startled doe scenting danger. She noticed the rolls of legal-looking deeds spread on the table beside him, and saw Jocunda pull a chair to the light of an oriel window and take up some needlework, as if to disassociate herself from whatever he was going to say. A strange foreboding seized her, weighting mind and limbs. And the foreboding was somehow associated with her momentary sadness in the garden.

"You will be glad to hear that this long dispute with the Butler branch of the family is being settled at last," Sir Thomas told her, tapping one of the documents. "By the good offices of your uncle of Norfolk it is mutually agreed that the Irish estates are to be shared. That is, when one or two matters are satisfactorily cleared up."

There was nothing remarkable about that. Anne was his elder daughter, and he often spoke to her about family affairs. "You will be Earl of Ormonde then?" she asked, knowing that the title had been one of the main causes of dispute.

"No," he admitted regretfully. "But my grandson may be."

Anne stared at him uncomprehendingly. She turned to Jocunda for enlightenment, but her stepmother avoided meeting her eyes. "Your grandson?" she repeated. "But why not George?"

"Naturally, I should have preferred it that way. But we had to give way about something. That is where Thomas Howard has been so clever." He came down from the dais and seated himself near her. He looked pleased and genial, but Anne felt that he was trying to wrap up something unpleasant in smooth words. "You may have wondered, my dear Nan, why I had you fetched home from France?" he asked conversationally.

After a year of Queen Claude's austerity, Anne's relief had left little room for curiosity about the reason. "I supposed it was because of the strained relations since our new alliance with Austria," she said, such matters being but daily bread in an ambassador's household.

"That certainly furnished an official excuse." Sir Thomas placed his long, immaculate fingertips together as he frequently did when announcing the outcome of debates. "But on your uncle's suggestion we are settling these family differences by offering you in marriage to your cousin Sir James Butler, who is, as you know, the Earl of Ormonde's heir. I was speaking to the King about it only this morning, and he has been gracious pleased to approve."

Anne's dreams of a love match died within her as she stood. So *this* was why her father had left her free so long. Allowing her an extra hour to try her wings; and then bartering her, like all the rest, in the end.

"James Butler," she repeated, scarcely above a whisper. She remembered him vaguely as a quarrelsome, redheaded little man, with a sword cut over one eye. He lived somewhere in Ireland, and she and George had made fun of him as children. In a detached sort of way, she was grateful to Jocunda for not poking consolation at her by suggesting that he had a nice disposition or wasn't quite as old as he looked.

She still stood there in the middle of the familiar hall. She had walked in a free woman and now, suddenly, found herself trapped. She knew now what a rabbit must feel like, scuttling busily across a thyme-scented hill and suddenly caught by its soft foot in an iron gin. Not killed outright. But with all future excursions just blotted out by pain. She opened her mouth to speak. To remonstrate. To let loose all the uprising, clamouring rights that filled her. But

Jocunda looked up at last and shook her head, and Anne knew that the dear, peaceable woman had already said all there was to say. And that it had been of no avail. How could it be, sneered some savage fury in Anne's mind, when the Boleyn trap had been baited with an earldom?

But like a foolish rabbit before it learns there is no hope of escape, she made a last bid for freedom. "Thomas Wyatt has just asked me to marry him," she said, in a voice which sounded too flat and expressionless to be her own.

"You should feel honoured, my dear," approved her father. "Thomas is a very personable young man and our very good neighbour. He should go far."

Anne turned to him, her control broken. "The King likes him. He certainly will go far. Will you not let me marry him instead?" she begged desperately.

"Not now. It is too late," said Jocunda.

Anne found herself down by her father's chair. Shaking his arm, looking close into his inscrutable face. "But you have always encouraged me to be friends with him, both of you. And you said just now that he is—"

"He is not the heir to an earldom," concluded Sir Thomas quietly. "But I assure you I have always kept him in mind as a *reserve*, shall we say?"

Anne watched him smooth out the sleeve of his best doublet which her despairing fingers had crumpled. For the first time she almost hated him.

Chapter Eight

B ECAUSE THE KING HAD invited her, and because her father wished it, Anne resumed her position in Queen Katherine's household. Court life no longer dazzled or intimidated her. Experience abroad and careful cultivation of her talents made personal success almost too easy. The spur of ambition had gone. Why strive for advancement when life as a maid-of-honour was but a temporary state, and all the hours of every day led to the dull future of undesired matrimony?

She began to spend her talents thriftlessly on present pleasures, seeking popularity among her equals, even neglecting her duties. Living for the moment, and making the most of the months that were left. The precious months while she was still Anne Boleyn, the attractive unmarried daughter of the Ambassador to France. Only her closest friends guessed at those spells of solitary depression hidden between her bursts of reckless gaiety.

"If only they would have let you marry my brother, we could have gone on being together always—you and Thomas and George and I," sighed Margaret Wyatt, whose presence at Court was Anne's constant solace.

Margaret took it for granted that her friend was as broken-hearted over Thomas as she herself was because George had been betrothed to Jane Rochford. But in her heart Anne knew that she had never really wanted to marry him. That she had only grasped belatedly at the comfort of his charm and loyalty in the hope that it might save her from the boorishness of James Butler.

She knew that arrangements were being made for her forth-coming marriage, and that tedious litigation would probably insure the earldom to some unborn son of hers and James'. She tried to shut out the thought of him from her mind. Yet there were times when she was obliged to face it. Sitting at her embroidery, afraid to make a sound, while the ailing Queen dozed; and at night, lying awake after the rushlight had flickered out, she would imagine James' harsh face, close up, making lusty inarticulate love to her, demanding his conjugal rights. She would have to live in an isolated Irish manor where nobody cared two pins whether she could dance or sing, so long as she could renew the family tapestries and breed. In an orgy of self-pity, Anne pictured herself down a vista of years. Always cumbersome with pregnancy, like Katherine. Growing rustic in mind and less lissom of limb, until all that strange sweet power she had over men was wiped out, unfulfilled.

With a man one loved, she supposed, it would be different. The Duchess of Suffolk was delighted with her new baby daughter; and Margaret Wyatt would give her pretty eyes for a chance to produce a small replica of George. But Anne did not want children. The maternal urges of most women were not in her. She knew herself to be capable of lavish giving in some *grande affaire*; but her nature was not made for the endless, self-effacing sacrifices of motherhood. She often wondered if this were a sin in her, but shrank from confessing it.

Willingly, out of gratitude, she would have given Wyatt children. But that employment of her better nature was denied her. And never had she appreciated him more than in his dignified acceptance of bitter disappointment. Although he saw her frequently in the performance of their several duties, he strove not to pester her with protestations which she was no longer free to accept, yet never ceased to make her feel precious with proofs of his constant regard.

But it was George who understood her best. He knew she had not half the virtues with which Wyatt's adoration endowed her.

And shared experience had taught him that she grieved less for what she must accept through a loveless marriage, than for what she must forego.

"Take heart, my poor sweet," he whispered, one morning when he came to visit her in the Queen's apartments at Greenwich. "You see that it has happened to me, too. Imagine having to live with Jane after knowing Margot Wyatt all one's life."

"Why could not the Fates decree that James and Jane marry each other, and so leave us free?" lamented Anne. "But at least Jane *wants* to marry you."

"And at least through her I shall get back our mother's Rochford estates," jibed George flippantly. People waiting upon the Queen's pleasure in the crowded anteroom began pushing past them, hurrying towards the windows. "Well, let us be merry while we may," he suggested, leading her towards a group of friends who were watching something going on down in the courtyard. "Judging by the commotion, the great Wolsey has arrived."

They joined Margaret and a handful of courtiers, most of whom had been appointed to the royal household since Anne went to France. Among them were three of her new admirers. Handsome Hal Norreys, whose cultured mind and charming manners especially commended him to the King; and two gentlemen of the privy chamber, Francis Weston and William Brereton. They all turned to welcome the Boleyns, for both had that indefinable quality which made them the light of any circle in which they moved. And if of late there was a new feverishness about their gaiety, a streak of cynicism in their sparkling wit, it but served to make them the more modish and sought after.

"Quick, Nan! Here comes the Cardinal!" called Margaret Wyatt, and as usual they all crowded to the open casements as if his coming were the event of the day.

And a fine sight it was in the morning sunlight. The imposing figure in scarlet riding upon a tall, snow-white mule, beneath the wide, tasselled hat which had brought such prestige to England. The long retinue of priests and wealthy pupils and well-fed henchmen. The Palace grooms and baying hounds running out to welcome them. And all the importunate hangers-on who invariably followed the most powerful representative of church and state, filling his legal courts with their pleas or seeking the pontific blessing of his uplifted hand.

"How diverting to see the way half the great families in the country send their sons to be trained in his household now he is both Chancellor and Cardinal," mused George, looking down upon a veritable colour box of plumed velvet caps and richly hued doublets following immediately behind the display of scarlet.

"It amazes me how he can find time to instruct them," said Margaret, waving discreetly to some of the young gallants whose eyes boldly raked the casements of the maids-of-honour.

"Besides building a fine new college at Oxford," added dapper little Francis Weston.

"One day he may go too far and outbuild the King," prophesied Will Brereton lazily.

"Well anyhow it would be amusing to know whether our wealthy nobility pay for their precious offspring down there to grow up in the odour of sanctity or success," speculated Anne. "If they did but know it, our young men here in the royal household are lambs of innocence compared with milord Cardinal's. Are they not, Margot?"

"You should know best, my love," teased her friend.

"Lambs, are we?" bridled Weston, who was given to bragging about his amatory conquests. "After the dance tonight, Nan Boleyn, I will make you eat your words!"

"In the meantime we appear to have some new rivals among the sophisticated wolf pack," observed Hal Norreys, drawing Brereton closer to the window. "That strong-looking fellow in the leather doublet, for example."

"You have no need to fear *him*," laughed Anne. "See, he is so wrapped in his own importance that he takes not the least notice of us!"

"Let us go down," suggested Margaret, knowing very well that the moment Wolsey was closeted with the King most of his lay escort would find their way into the walled garden where the Queen's ladies took the air.

"What if her Grace calls for me? I am supposed to be in attendance," objected Anne. But she went just the same. It was better
than staying indoors alone to think. One day was much like another
now. One rose and dressed and went out, or waited on the aging
Queen. And every day marriage loomed closer, like a dungeon door
through which even one's imagination dared not pass.

She lingered for awhile with the others under the elm trees.
As usual, Wolsey's protégés crowded round her when she sang,
and vied with each other in composing complimentary verses in
very poor imitation of Thomas Wyatt's. They laid bets on the
other girls' pet spaniels and set them racing after a ball. But Anne
found them callow and uninteresting after some of the distinguished men she had met in France. She was not altogether sorry
when someone came out from the Palace and told them that the
King was in no humour for business and had challenged Charles
Brandon to a game of tennis, and most of her companions drifted
away to watch.

"Are you not coming, Nan?" urged Margaret, linking her arm
in George's.

But hearing that the Suffolks were there, Anne had a great
longing to see her erstwhile mistress again. To talk to someone who
knew all about facing a repulsive marriage, and whose grief she
herself had helped to assuage. Perhaps now, while everyone was at
the tennis court, would be a good time. Better to risk a severe reprimand from Queen Katherine than to miss seeing Mary Tudor.

Humming softly to herself, preoccupied, Anne crossed the
daisy-strewn grass in the direction of the Duchess' apartments.
She took a short cut along by the chapel. It was cool after the
swooning heat of the garden; but sunlight fell in shafts between
the pillars so that the long, deserted cloister was half golden and
half grey. Her heels tapping along the flagstones broke the
drowsing stillness; and presently she became aware that their brisk
little echo was being answered by a louder, firmer one. She looked
up and saw a man coming towards her. At a turn of the cloister he
came out of the vaulted gloom into full sunlight. He was tall,
slender of hip and broad of shoulder, more strongly built than

either Wyatt or her brother. She recognized him as the young man in the leather doublet who had had no mind for wenching. He, too, was hurrying in a purposeful sort of way; but within a few paces he stopped as if he had changed his mind. Almost as if he had come to meet her.

And suddenly Anne knew who he really was. Her heart beat tumultuously in her breast, so that she put up a hand to still it, and all Heaven sang.

She, too, stopped—unaware that she did so. Or that there was anything strange or unmaidenly in so doing. They were within a few paces of each other, and for the first time she looked upon the features her girlhood's dreams had tried to formulate. They were more rugged than handsome, and his skin was wholesomely tanned. He had attractive eyes, boldly flecked with brown. He was the man she had always wanted for a lover—wanted and waited for. And she let out a little ripple of laughter because, after all, his hair was neither fair nor dark. It was ruddy, like the Tudors'.

"Why do you laugh?" he asked resentfully.

"Because you are so different." she answered breathlessly, as if she had come a long way to find him and had been running.

He glanced down at his plain soldierly doublet. "If you mean that I don't wear my sleeves stuffed like bolsters and all slashed about like a woman's—"

She guessed at once that beneath his truculent air he was unduly sensitive, and that he had been recently mocked. "No, no," she assured him. "It is just that you yourself are different."

"But you have never seen me before."

Anne stood silent—she, who always had an apt answer for anyone. For how could she explain?

"And I have never seen anyone like you," he added, more boyishly.

"What am I like?" she asked eagerly, wanting to see herself through his exploring eyes.

He fumbled a little, quite unable to express how appealingly lovely she was with that newly awakened look softening her eyes, and one white hand pressed to her black velvet bodice. "You are so slender. As if you might break in my hands," he stammered.

Although she had expected the usual compliments, she was wholly satisfied. And when he held out his hands before him to show how strong and clumsy they were, a tenderness that most women keep for children welled up in her.

To hide this new sweetness of emotion, and because it was so ridiculous to be standing there, she turned aside and seated herself on the sunlit wall between two pillars. "You didn't come with the others and hear me sing," she reproached, for something to say.

"*Do* you sing?" he asked negligently, seating himself beside her. "I don't much care for music."

Anne gasped. Even the most tuneless bore at Court would scarcely have dared to say so. But because he was the only man she could love, it was as if he stripped her in a sentence of half her worth. And there was worse to come.

"And it is all some of those popinjays seem to think about, music and making ill-gaited ballads. And boasting about seducing maids-of-honour," he complained, heartlessly snapping off a jasmine branch that nodded through the aperture between them.

"It is mostly boasting," proffered Anne, on behalf of her friends.

"Then it is all the more waste of time."

Whereby Anne gathered that he had not had enough of his ruggedness knocked off to mix easily with his fellowmen. "How then do you spend *your* time?" she asked, in a small voice.

He laughed then, more tolerantly. A little apologetically, perhaps, as if in reality he envied opportunity to learn some of the accomplishments he affected to despise. "Where I live it takes us all our time to keep our sword arm nimbler than our neighbour's," he explained. "Not just fancy tilting with heralds telling you when the other man is going to start."

"Where do you live?" asked Anne.

"Up north. And you?" He looked her over from her pearled headdress to her elegant little brodekin shoes. "Always here at Court, I suppose?"

There was the slightest pause before Anne answered. For the first time since meeting him she remembered that she was about to be married; but she could in no wise bring herself to spoil this new joy. "My home is in Kent," she said noncommittally; and hurried on to another subject. "Would you like to come and watch the King play tennis?"

"I scarcely understand the game so it would give me little pleasure," he said.

"People don't always watch for pleasure."

"Why? Does he play so ill?"

Anne gave a little shriek of laughter. She did not usually suffer fools gladly. But this strange young man, with his direct manner of speech, was so new to her world. "He still plays extraordinarily well," she explained patiently. "But most men swell his audience out of policy. And, as a newcomer, it would be wise for you to do so. That is, if you want to get on at Court."

"I don't particularly. I only want to get away from it."

"You don't approve of us very much, do you?" she sighed. "What *do* you want to do?"

He grinned then, disarmingly. "Sit here and talk to you."

"That you cannot do, for it seems milord Cardinal is going. There are the horses being taken round. And all your friends are coming this way."

He got up to look for himself, and the smothered profanity on his lips was sweet to her ears. But she was far too experienced to prolong the occasion. It must seem to him that it was she who sent him away. She stood up, too, smiling a little, her hands folded before her so that the fingers of her left hand did not show.

His gaze came back to her, and he seemed half-angered at his own reluctance to leave her—like a man with his own plans urgently before him, who finds himself caught unexpectedly in the binding tendrils of some thicket. "No woman has a *right* to look so—so fragile that a man could break her in his two hands," he reiterated.

Her smile turned to laughter. "But I am not in your hands," she said.

He took up the challenge at once. He gripped her by either forearm, the strength of his fingers biting unwittingly into her tender flesh. And Anne's whole body remained quiescent, willing him to hold her so.

"I am quite strong, really. I can pull a bow with anyone," she protested in a flurry, all normal poise forsaking her. She was speaking at random, like a squawking captured bird, deliciously nervous as a silly child of sixteen who has never been touched by a man before. And he knew it. Whatever else he might be slow about, he was no fool about sex. His firm, hard lips parted in a grin of enjoyment. "All the same, you couldn't pull yourself out of my arms if I chose to hold you," he told her.

But voices were already calling him. Footsteps were echoing along the cloister. Anne gave him a little friendly push. "Quick! The Cardinal is going," she whispered. He laughed and released her, and ran swiftly to join his comrades.

Too late, she put out an arm to stay him. "I don't even know your name!" she called after him. But he only waved and ran on.

She followed more slowly, savouring her newfound joy. Out in the courtyard, where Wolsey's party was moving off, she mingled with her friends again. "Who is that man?" she asked, of no one in particular.

"Which man?" asked Margaret Wyatt, just as if a girl could look dispassionately upon a courtyard full of men and see any other.

"The one with hair like beaten copper, of course. The one whose horse is still waiting."

"Don't you know?" said Francis Weston, who always had all the latest gossip. "He is Lord Harry Percy, the Duke of Northumberland's eldest son."

Lord Harry Percy. Anne stood staring after him. She saw him vault into the saddle, catch the reins from his grooms, and break into a canter to catch up with the departing cavalcade. She was no mean horsewoman herself, but he seemed to do it all in one fluid movement. She could imagine him riding furiously, in some border-land feud, without any saddle at all.

"I see they are still wearing last year's jerkins up north," sniggered some wit at her elbow.

"Seeing that they become him so well, perhaps he prefers them," snapped Anne.

"Well, if he doesn't employ a London tailor it certainly isn't because he can't afford to," observed Hal Norreys tolerantly. "I suppose in their particular wilds the Northumberlands are as important as any King or Cardinal."

Anne thanked him gently, as if he had defended her personally. Harry Percy.

She murmured the words to herself. Of course, she had heard of him. But she was committing the name to her heart, rather than to her memory. She turned and retraced her steps abstractedly across the daisy-strewn lawn. She had quite forgotten that she had been on her way to see Mary, Duchess of Suffolk, to talk about James Butler.

Chapter Nine

ANNE LIVED IN A dream until she saw Percy again. She no longer lay awake dreading matrimony. Her mind was too full of the sweets of present courtship. The Queen rated her for being absent-minded, and her friends chaffed her about being in love. But she went her way and answered nothing. "This time I will use all the enchantment that is in me to make him mine," she vowed, when next Cardinal Wolsey's gorgeous cavalcade came to Greenwich.

Purposely, she waited apart from the others. But when she saw Percy come into the Queen's garden, all wiles deserted her, driven out by an overwhelming simplicity of love. And there was no need for them. He came straight to her and took her hands. He had had a fine slashed doublet made for himself, and his hair had been smoothed until it shone. He wasted no time on social formalities. "His Eminence is inviting the King and Queen to visit the new manor he has had built at Hampton. When we all go thither tomorrow, will you ride with me?" he demanded.

Anne laughed with sheer happiness. "In that case wouldn't it be more convenient if you knew my name?" she suggested, mocking him from beneath long, dark lashes.

"I know what I call you," he said.

"Tell me!"

He glanced round impatiently at the chattering groups of courtiers. "Not here," he said. "What *is* your name?"

"I am Anne, daughter of Sir Thomas Boleyn."

A look of more wary interest came into his face. "So you are Anne Boleyn? I have already heard several men speak of you."

"Pleasantly, I hope?"

"By the things they said I supposed you must be either an angel or a witch."

"For you I will be either," she promised gaily. "And my friends call me Nan."

"Then, Nan, will you ride with me tomorrow?"

"It can only be if my mistress, the Queen, has no need of me."

He seemed to remember at last that they were still holding hands. "Could she not have another lying-in or something?" he suggested heartlessly, drawing Anne towards a grassy bank and throwing his cloak upon it.

"Then I shouldn't be able to come at all." Anne sat down upon the new grandeur of his garment, and he threw himself down beside her. "Besides, I had forgotten," she added, pulling at a handful of green blades. "Sir Thomas Wyatt has already asked me."

"He is the poet everybody thinks so highly of, isn't he? And in love with you, I suppose?"

With any other man, Anne would have used so flattering a conquest to fan the flames of jealousy. But with this blunt north-countryman she found herself being completely candid. "I suppose so, since he once asked me to marry him," she said.

"Why didn't you, since he is so popular?" Percy asked savagely.

"Because my father forbade it."

"And you were brokenhearted?"

"No. I have always loved Thomas Wyatt, but more as a friend. To know him is to love him, I think."

The scowl left Percy's features. "Then perhaps he won't want to break my head."

"I can scarcely imagine his wanting to do anything so uncivilized." Seeing him redden, Anne knew that her shaft had pierced that unexpected sensitiveness of his. "Nor do I suppose he could," she added quickly, glancing down at his muscular perfection.

"Then that is settled," he said, rolling over onto his stomach the better to observe her face. "I have bought you a horse," he added, almost casually.

Anne could scarcely believe her ears. "You bought me a horse? And you had seen me only once? And did not know my name," she gasped. But, of course, Hal Norreys had said how rich the Northumberlands were. Probably giving a girl a horse was no more to them than giving her a ribbon or an embroidered cap.

Percy smiled at her eagerness, happy at having pleased her. "He is a roan. With a white star on his forehead. And quite gentle."

Anne sprang up, wild with excitement. "Since I have been here I have never owned a horse of my own. All we maids-of-honour are allowed to keep at Court is a spaniel. May I see him?"

"I was hoping that you would want to. Then we can get away from all these people. My groom is walking him round by the stables."

It meant a few precious moments alone. They talked as they went. The roan was glossy as silk, and nuzzled at Anne's caressing hand. She was delighted with him. "How clever of you! He is just up to my weight. But you need not have worried about his being gentle. I have been used to hunting with my brother since I was small."

He looked at her approvingly. To be a good horsewoman, and fearless, meant more to him in a woman than all the gifts of the Muses. "It would matter to me supremely if you were hurt," he told her quietly.

"I shall call him Bon Ami," said Anne.

"Have you anywhere to keep him?"

They glanced at the full rows of stalls. She knew quite well that only lords' daughters were allowed to have their own mounts. But nothing, nothing must prevent her from keeping this first wonderful gift. "My father is away," she said, thankful that he was in France. "But I am sure my brother will arrange something. Put him for the moment in Sir Thomas Boleyn's empty stall, and tomorrow I will ride him." She turned in a flurry from efficient groom to exultant master. "There is the chapel bell. I must fly to attend her Grace to Mass."

"And tomorrow you will make sure that someone else attends her in her stuffy coach," he insisted.

"Poor Margaret! And poor Thomas!" giggled Anne, picking up her skirts above dainty ankles and scurrying back towards the Palace.

But what was a girl to do when an excitingly persistent young man not only plagued her to ride, but also brought her a horse?

And so on the morrow it was Margaret who was being jolted, back of the horses, in the coach, holding cold compresses to the Queen's aching head, while she, Anne, rode with her new admirer in the morning sunlight. "Someday I will make it up to poor Margot!" she vowed.

The September day was perfect. Little wisps of mist pegged themselves like shining cobwebs about the hedges, making the familiar Thames meadows a land of fantasy. The tops of the oaks were turning to autumnal gold, and every now and then startled swans flapped furiously along the surface of the water.

"And God knows how few such perfect days are left to me," thought Anne.

Bon Ami went faultlessly along the soft earth of riverside lanes. By the time the walled silhouette of London was lost to view, she and Harry Percy were lingering as far behind the royal cortege as they dared. And as they rode they told each other precious small things about the years before they met, exploring each other's minds, and building a foundation for their love. Utterly wrapped in the wonder of attraction and dissimilitude. Until they came to Hampton.

Henry Tudor himself drew rein then, involuntarily. Russet, his horse, flicked away the flies and cooled his fetlocks in the clear shallows where, mirrored on the river's sparkling bosom, stood the fairest domestic building imaginable. Moat and walls were but a gesture to the dangers of a bygone age. Behind them all was peace and comfort. Roofs and pinnacles and towers rose in a kind of harmonious jumble, homely yet dignified. A jewel set in green gardens and sprawling to a gleaming watergate. "It is the loveliest manor I have even seen!" exclaimed Henry, above the ecstatic comments of his followers. His delight exceeded anything that Wolsey, in his proud complacency, could have hoped, and when the King, guiding his great horse across the drawbridge, added pensively, "It is big enough to be a summer palace," such excess of appreciation may well have occasioned the wealthy prelate's first faint feelings of uneasiness.

From the moment Henry was inside the courtyards, the beauty of the place had him in thrall. Great hall, chapel, kitchens, fish ponds—he insisted upon seeing them all. While the Queen rested, his sister Mary accompanied him, inflaming his gusty Tudor enthusiasm with her own. And by the time the fat Cardinal finally showed them his own workroom he found himself quite breathless, and for once uncertain of his own wisdom; for Henry touched the exquisite linen-fold panelling with expert fingers, and stood for a long time before the stone fireplace with its splendid carving of a cardinal's hat. "I could work here myself," he said, enviously. And it was too late then for Wolsey to regret his ostentation and to recall with misgiving the story of Naboth's vineyard.

But work was for neither of them that day. There was good cheer and rare wine, with service and entertainment unrivalled even at Windsor. Wolsey was an incomparable host. And Thomas Cromwell, his plain indefatigable secretary—plunging hither and thither seeing to the comfort of their guests—acted as a complete foil to his master's leisurely graciousness.

All afternoon Anne relieved Margaret Wyatt in the Queen's apartments, catching only a distant view of the archery contests at which she longed to compete. But afterwards there was supper, with all manner of tempting dishes and minstrels playing the King's own music. Lord Harry Percy, it appeared, had distinguished himself at the butts; and the King, in his bluff sportsman's way, made much of him and invited him to the royal table, both in consideration of his prowess and his father's rank. Although Anne was not near enough to talk to him, they could at least exchange glances; and afterwards, while the laced cloths were being drawn and the trestles pushed back to make room for games and dancing, he drew her aside through a little door to give her the prize he had won. Thrilled as she was, Anne dared not wear it openly because everybody knew that she was betrothed to James Butler. She tried to summon enough moral courage to tell Percy so, but was afraid to lose him. And to her surprise, when she tucked the jewelled cloak clasp into her bodice, he made no protest.

"The King draws a marvellous fine bow, and he was not the only one," he said, secretly marvelling to find that for all their fiddling and versifying, most of these southerners about Court had preserved their hardihood.

"But his wrestling days are over. Whereas, you—" Anne's eyes rested upon a troupe of acrobats and wrestlers who were waiting to take the floor, and noticed that not one of them was more finely built than he. "Will you not try a throw?" she urged, ambitious for him to win yet more praise.

But it seemed he did not want to leave her.

"There will be dancing later," she told him, hoping that he would ask her to partner him.

"I am afraid I know more about defending the northern Marches than dancing," he confessed.

She tucked an encouraging hand through his arm, and would have shown him some of the steps had not George Boleyn appeared at her elbow, scowling uncertainly at the man who had enticed her from more august company. "Nan! Nan!" he summoned in an urgent whisper. "The King is calling for you."

Anne let go of Percy's arm. "The *King*!" she repeated, in surprise.

"Oh, don't imagine he's luring you to his bed," said George, with brotherly candour. "He wants you to sing that ballad of yours to the Duchess."

Anne followed him, surprised and elated. In spite of the rich tapestries and the finely dressed company how pleasantly domestic was the scene!

The King was sitting by the hearth, with his sister beside him and Suffolk leaning over the back of his chair. Queen and Cardinal were talking together. The Queen looked rested and happy, flattered no doubt by her host's suave attentions. She was evidently enjoying the family party. Every now and then her gaze strayed to her little daughter, who was dancing with a tall boy of about fourteen. And if everybody knew that young Henry Fitzroy was her husband's bastard—well, it had all been a long time ago and most kings had more than one. Taken on the whole, Henry had been a good husband to her.

The light of kindness softened all the company's faces as they watched the young people dancing. At ten, young Mary Tudor was entrancing. Affectionate and unspoiled, with all the cultural advantages of her exalted background. "In a few years she will dance as well as I do," thought Anne, with an odd antagonism stirring in her. And when her glance rested on the child's well-set-up partner, Elizabeth Blount's by-blow, she knew momentary pity for their father. How hard it must be for a king to have just one son to whom he was devoted, to whom he could leave nothing save his own personal estate of Richmond! And no more chance of any legitimate sons.

But the fiddlers had stopped and amid a gust of delighted applause Henry's daughter ran laughing to the shelter of his outstretched arm. The beloved aunt, after whom she had been named, set a box of comfits on his knee for the child to pick at. Then, seeing Anne standing waiting, she beckoned to her kindly. "Here is my exile's solace, Anne Boleyn, to sing to us," she said.

Henry turned his thickening body, his face benign and florid in the firelight. His small, lascivious eyes flickered over her admiringly. "Well, Mistress Anne, where have you been since I found you and Tom Wyatt hiding under an apple tree?" he asked, in high good humour, setting everybody laughing.

Anne borrowed a lute from one of the royal musicians and sang as she was bid, her clear high voice filling Wolsey's guest chamber with as sweet melody as ever was heard there. It was the second time she had sung for the King, and this time she knew no nervousness; only that the song was perfected and that she had the power to please. She was aware of her brother's pride in her, and of Wyatt's appreciation. Of the high honour paid her. Of Mary Tudor's pleasure and the King's interest, which she felt sure was not wholly on account of her voice. But most of all she was glad of the good fortune which had given her a chance to shine before Harry Percy. Perhaps, after this, he would speak less slightingly of music. If only she could make him really love it, as all the others did.

In the moment of their generous applause life was for Anne a golden bubble of enjoyment, bright with excitement and success. A little space of time detached from the past and without concern for the future. Intoxicating enough to be sufficient unto itself.

But, alas! It was the wrestlers' turn next and she must make way for them. The Duchess invited her to a stool at her side. "You must sing for us again presently," she invited.

But Anne's golden bubble of success was soon pricked.

She looked up, past the King's surreptitious ogle and saw the Queen's protuberant eyes watching her. Katherine turned away almost at once, and was in conversation again with her scarlet-clad host. But presently she said a few words to Donna da Salinas, who in turn beckoned to Anne. Katherine, always completely mistress of any situation, had chosen the moment when some mummers were entering to an accompaniment of shrieks and giggles, so that neither the King nor his sister noticed. And there was nothing for it but to obey.

Anne stood resentfully before her mistress and the Cardinal. And the Aragon woman kept her standing there. Only when she had finished what she was saying and the mummers were just about to begin did she turn and say negligently, "My new spaniel, girl. Donna da Salinas left him asleep on her bed. He may waken and be frightened in a strange place. I pray you, go and bear him company."

Go and bear a spoiled lap dog company! When her highly trained voice had just given pleasure to a King. To fetch the spoiled little beast, which any page could have done would have been bad enough. But to stay up there in the cold, away from all the admiration and the fun! She, the daughter of one of the King's ambassadors, who had once refused the kisses of the new King of France.

All Anne's vanity was outraged. If anyone else had asked her she would have flounced with disdain. But those hard, protruding eyes were upon her, and she dared not disobey. She would not be asked to sing again. She would offend Mary Tudor. And she would miss the dancing.

Shaking with rage, half-blinded by tears of disappointment, Anne stumbled along the unfamiliar passages. Twice she lost her way; and when she had climbed the backstairs there was no one to direct her to the Queen's apartments. No one even to bring her a light. Stairs and galleries were deserted. Even the servants must be downstairs, listening and goggling at the buttery hatch.

At last Anne found the Spanish woman's room. A rising moon spilled silver through the latticed windows. The Queen's spaniel lay in a snuffling, silken ball, fast asleep on the bed. Anne looked at it with loathing. Then crossed the narrow room and leaned her hot forehead against the cooling horn of the window. "I hate her! How I hate her!" she muttered, rolling her damp kerchief into a tight, hard ball.

There were footsteps following her. There must have been some of the backstairs pages about after all. The door was still wide open. Anne straightened up, instinctively trying to hide her anger and distress. But to her joy it was Harry Percy who stood there, hesitating until his eyes grew accustomed to the gloom. As soon as he was sure that she was alone, he crossed the room in a few strides and took her in his arms.

"I followed you," he whispered, searching her tear-marred face. "Why did the old hag send you away?"

Anne clung to him and he held her gently, letting her cry against his costly new doublet. And presently, between sobs, she tried to explain. "She didn't want me to sing again. I suppose the King looked at me too long. Or she thinks there have been too many Boleyns in his life. Always she has been twice as strict with me as with the other girls."

"My poor sweet!"

"I have never let anyone see me weep like this except my step-mother. Not even when they said hateful things about my hand."

"I am not anyone."

Anne blew her nose with vigour. "It was foolish, I know. But I hoped they would ask me to sing again, and I wanted you to see how well I dance," she confessed, with the intimate candour which she usually kept to herself.

"It was a sweet foolishness and I love you the more for it." He searched for his own handkerchief and dried her face.

"Well, since the wretched dog sleeps and we cannot dance," she sighed, withdrawing herself from the consolation of his arms and making as if to leave the Spanish woman's room.

"Why wait in a draughty corridor?" he asked reasonably.

Anne hesitated, afraid but sorely tempted. "I should be disgraced forever if they found you here."

"The door is open and we should hear anyone on the stairs. Besides, they will go on frolicking down there for hours yet."

Half capitulating, Anne sank back against the window seat. "There is no need for *you* to miss all the merriment," she pointed out, halfheartedly.

"Can you suppose I do not *want* to stay?" he whispered; and there was something so exciting in his urgency that, deep in love as she was, Anne sought to defend herself from it a little longer. She pushed open a small square casement so that a reach of swift running river and the sleeping gardens lay before them in the moonlight. "How lovely it is," she murmured. "George tells me Cardinal Wolsey had the manor from the Knights Hospitallers, and enlarged it. I would rather live here than in any house I have seen."

But Percy had eyes only for the loveliness of her profile. "You haven't seen Wressell yet," he reminded her.

She looked up and smiled. Already he had talked much of his father's Northumbrian stronghold. "Is it very grim?" she asked.

"I suppose you would find it so. After Paris, and these southern unfortified places."

"But to you it is what Hever is to me."

"My father keeps almost regal state there, and one day it will be mine. It seems strange, but until now that has always sufficed me."

"And now?" she asked, fiddling with the dagger at his belt. Almost pressed against him, too close for safety, in that narrow room.

"Now it must have a woman in it."

"What sort of a woman?"

"One with hair like the night, and a face the shape of my heart and lovely hands."

Carefully, Anne sheathed the murderous blade and spread them both before her. "Only one is lovely, Harry," she said, sad that she was not all perfection.

He turned her left hand over carefully so that the ugly blemish did not show, and kissed the palm. "It is a specially vulnerable part of you for me to cherish—just as you have defended my boorish ways against ridicule," he said.

There was a part of him, vaunting and aggressive, for the world, and another, all young tenderness, for her. Anne's dark eyes adored him in the moonlight. "*Il faut toujours lutter pour les choses que l'on tient les plus precieuses,*" she said softly.

With their eyes they drank deeply of each other before ever their bodies touched. He had only to reach out his arms to pull her against his thudding heart. And this time it was in no mood of tender consolation. To his joy her whole exquisite body responded to his passion. He felt her arms reach up eagerly about his neck. And when his hard young mouth came down on hers, her hands but drew him the closer. Only when at last he ceased kissing her, did she stir reluctantly in his arms, breathing a small sigh of utter completion.

"I should have told you. I am to marry my Irish cousin, James Butler, because of the family title," she said, knowing that nothing could part them now.

"I will kill him first," he promised, close against her lips. And then, more soberly, "There are plans for me, too. But from the moment I saw you they had no meaning."

Anne pressed herself back against the moonlit wall. It seemed necessary to move away from him in order to think. "What shall we do, Harry?"

But how to think in that ecstatic hour? He only laughed in all the deep fullness of possessive manhood. "After all, anything may happen," he decided, with superb optimism.

Utterly absorbed in each other, they had not heard the quick approaching footsteps. The hurrying figure of a man in a white doublet passed the open doorway. "Nan, where are you? If you are not alone, for God's sake be careful! The Queen is leaving early."

The words came in urgent undertones, and he was gone. They were not even sure if he had seen them.

"It is Thomas Wyatt," said Anne, aghast. "No one else would take such a risk for me."

"God in Heaven, he must have seen me follow you! I was standing next to him," muttered Percy.

It could have been their undoing—would certainly have been, with any other out-rivalled suitor. Anne laid a hand on Percy's wrist to allay his consternation. "Thomas must be hurt to the quick," she said regretfully. "But he would never betray me."

For a moment they both listened intently. "He is right. She is at the turn of the stairs. You can hear her women chattering."

"Harry! What will you do?"

He took a quick look round the room. To leave by the door was to risk being seen before reaching the end of the gallery. Wyatt, in his conspicuous white satin, could only just have made the turn in time. He pushed open the casement and looked down. A mulberry tree still flourished beneath the wall. Swiftly, silently—blessing the bygone Knights Hospitallers—he swung a leg across the sill. "Fasten the casement after me," he whispered, beginning to let himself down.

While he sought a foothold among the branches, his hands and face were still level with the sill. Anne bent over him, radiant and laughing. A woman to grace a Border castle. A woman to share any adventure with. "Heaven send all spaniels pleasant dreams," she laughed back, her nimble hand already on the latch.

Chapter Ten

T HE QUEEN'S INFLUENCE WAS waning. It had been a good
influence during those halcyon days when she had first
married Henry. But she was considerably older than he, and
had never been a beauty. She must always have wanted him, Anne
supposed, even during the few short months when she had been
married to Arthur Tudor, his sickly elder brother. Even before
Arthur died, Henry must always have been there, radiant and vital.
And once the Pope had granted a dispensation for Katherine to
marry him she had, as everybody knew, been faithful to him with
every fibre of her stumpy body and every thought of her straight-
forward, inflexible mind. But now, what with her righteous obstinacy and his disappointment about an heir, Henry's affection was
almost wiped out with irritation.

Whereas the influence of Wolsey waxed rather than waned. He,
too, was older than the King. He had been the athletic, colourful
personality who had caught at Henry's warm imagination when first
he came to the throne. And still, by dint of prodigious industry and
expenditure, he excited admiration in his master's mind. If his tall
figure had grown too portly with good living to excel in worldly
sports, it looked all the more spectacular in pontific scarlet. Henry
himself was never indolent. He busied himself with state affairs.
But he never had need to worry. Wolsey gave him security. So far
did the man's grasp of world affairs overtop that of his fellows that

no dissentient voice was ever raised in Council. There was no need for money passing through his capable hands to be dissipated in trying out the whims of smaller men. It was there to be poured out without delay or question upon whatever project he had persuaded Henry to pursue. By keeping balanced all other power in Europe, England became more powerful and more feared than she had ever been. Wolsey saw to it that that fine soldier, Francis of France, and Katherine's nephew, Charles of Spain, were forever titubating at either end of the seesaw, while the massive figure of Henry Tudor, straddling the centre, could control their rise or fall by shifting the weight of his favour first to one side and then to the other. Wolsey had made him Arbiter of Europe.

No wonder that the great Cardinal came almost daily to Westminster or Greenwich, and was closeted for hours with the King!

Anne Boleyn was no longer a heedless girl. Public events no longer formed merely a background for her own small pleasures and successes. With maturer vision she began to behold the important personages around her, not only as forces affecting her own life, but as human beings working out their own designs and destinies. She judged the direction of their desires and their hopes of success. She became aware of them as diverse characters. She was aware of the Queen's stupidity in relying upon argument instead of wiles, of Suffolk's gradual ascendency over Mary Tudor's unselfishness, and of the special significance of being in part a Howard because of one's Plantagenet blood. And because, for all her butterfly gaiety, she had been brought up to think astutely, she was even aware that although Henry Tudor dominated men's minds, it was Thomas Wolsey who really ruled England.

"When I first came here the Cardinal used to say 'The King desires this or that'," said Henry Percy, speaking privately within the circle of Anne's friends at Greenwich. "But now, when he is off his guard in his own house, he often says, 'The King and I'."

"Or, more often, just 'I'," laughed his friend and colleague, Cavendish.

George Boleyn frowned. "The state he keeps and his overbearing ways give great offence to men like my uncle and the Duke of Suffolk," he said.

"And to many others," confirmed Will Brereton, whose family had leanings towards the simplicity of the new Lutheran religion.

"And yet he can afford to be courteous to shopkeepers, and the poorer sort of people flock to him for justice," observed Margaret Wyatt, pondering on the inscrutable ways of greatness.

"Perhaps it is just that he cannot afford to have equals," suggested Anne.

But what mattered it whether the Cardinal were loved or hated so long as he came—and brought the young men of his household with him?

All through that winter the Duke of Northumberland's heir was to be seen about the Queen's apartments; and whenever Anne could escape from her duties she was with him. The Queen's senior ladies were too much concerned about their mistress's ill health to notice. Anne and Percy lived in a daze of happiness, making little effort to hide their mutual passion. And as time went on it was taken for granted even by the gossips.

"What, in God's name, will be the end of it, Nan?" asked George anxiously at Christmas time. He had twirled her off into a new French measure lest she should make herself too conspicuous by dancing throughout the revels with Percy.

Anne suffered his loving interference patiently. "It is an honest love," she pleaded. "Something utterly different from all the light, worthless affairs I have known before. Something that makes me for the first time the kind of woman God meant me to be. And you, yourself, admit that you like Harry, now you have come to know him."

"True," admitted George, considering how lovable she had become. "And it is a thousand pities you cannot marry him. But what will happen when our father comes home?"

"Oh, George, I dare not think!" sighed Anne, acknowledging the King's smile almost absently as they passed the dais. "But surely, apart from the enduring quality of our love, he would consider an alliance with the mighty Northumberland worth more than the Ormonde title?"

"Even if he did, is it not true that Percy himself is contracted to the Earl of Shrewsbury's daughter?"

"He hates the sight of her. Mary Talbot has a body like a brood mare. He swears that whatever happens he will never marry her," declared Anne, speaking in a series of triumphant sentences as the dance ended in leaps and twirls. But as her brother led her to a window seat, she added in a fierce undertone, "Are we cattle to be sold like this for the fattening of the family estates?"

George was less revolutionary, and had taken no part in Mary Tudor's daring matrimonial defiance. "It seems we are. And for my own part I see no way out of the market pen," he answered bitterly, his eyes on the sweet face of Wyatt's sister as she passed with William Brereton.

Anne looked up in swift contrition and pressed his arm, *"Mon cher,* I am sorry! I had forgotten," she murmured. "I loathe your Jane."

But dislikes touched her lightly when all the world was filled with this new radiance of love. Anne's whole nature was softened and her tongue grown more kind. Even when her future sister-in-law showed jealousy of her happy comradeship with George, she evaded all contest; and when people asked pointedly if Mary Carey's new baby had Tudor-coloured hair she refrained from the repartee of which she was so capable. She wrote to Jocunda of her lover, and was very gentle with Thomas Wyatt. Patiently, she taught Harry Percy the newest dance steps and even trained his passable baritone to the lute. When he was inclined to be awkward or farouche, she smoothed out resentment and turned the conversation so that he might shine in the world into which she had coaxed him. For the first time she knew what it was to be more ambitious for another's accomplishments than for her own.

"What can she see in the fellow?" demanded the polished Wyatt, alone with his friend.

"He is no courtier, but I like him," said George. "Only—"

"Only what?"

"Only sometimes I can't help wondering whether, with all his toughness and contempt for poets, he would in a crisis have more endurance than you or I."

They would glance across the room to some alcove where the dark head of Anne and the Northumbrian's flaming one were sure to be in close proximity over her embroidery frame, which was usually but a screen for dalliance. "Now she is to marry Ormonde's son, he has no more right to her than I, who have loved her faithfully all my life," Wyatt would mutter.

For the first time, out of sheer misery, he began to pester her, using his nimble wits to pay her compliments beyond the limited powers of her lover, and infuriating him by referring casually to mutually remembered incidents from which Percy was excluded. He would hug his knees on a cushion at Anne's feet or lean over the back of her chair, emphasizing the familiarity of their youth and indulging in friendly scuffling as they had been wont to do. "That chain, Nan. Did I not give it to you upon your fifteenth birthday?" he teased, one morning in the Queen's gallery. He lifted a slender gold pomander chain that hung from her girdle and inspected the small jewelled mirror at the end of it. "I am amazed and gratified that you still wear the thing."

"I still value it, Thomas," said Anne gravely.

"But scarcely as you did then, I fear. I well remember how you raced across the lawn at Hever and tiptoed up to kiss me when I brought it. You were not so tall then, my sweet."

Both of them were aware of Percy, ousted momentarily from her side, leaning against the window with folded arms. Of his scowls, and of the covert amusement of their watching friends. "A girl must have a mirror," pointed out Anne, as lightly as she could.

"I see no necessity when she had the mirror of men's eyes," said Wyatt. He glanced mockingly at her resentful lover and proceeded to hold the thing this way and that, admiring the reflection of his newly grown brown beard—a small, pointed adornment which was all the latest craze at Court. "It is I who need it to watch the advance of fashion."

"Put it down, Thomas, and don't be so conceited!" laughed Anne, making a grab at her property.

"But it must seem such a worthless trifle to Mistress Boleyn, who sings for the Princess and dances before the King! Who keeps her own blood horse at Court, and whose dress is fastened by a jewel from a Duke's son's cloak."

Avoiding her defensive hand, he suddenly jerked the chain from her girdle, bending to plant a light kiss on the back of her shaven neck as he did so, then holding the stolen trinket aloft in laughing triumph.

Percy's hand flew to his dirk. And, knowing his hot temper, men marvelled that he did not use it. They could not know that gratitude restrained him. That Wyatt, slim, debonair, and unarmed, could provoke the lovely Boleyn's fierce northern lover with impunity because he had once warned her of the Queen's approach, and had not betrayed them.

Anne herself was well aware of this; but, all the same, a warm spark of triumph flamed in her because two men were hating each other on her account.

Wolsey stayed longer that day, discussing some secret matter with the King. "What do these statesmen find to talk about all this time?" grumbled Percy rudely, after his rival had gone.

"I thought you had been wont to find the time all too short," retorted Anne.

"When we leave this time, I shall not come again perhaps for weeks."

That had shaken Anne. She looked up, needle suspended and all social subtlety driven from her face. "Not come again for weeks?" she echoed, in dismay.

"Milord Cardinal is going to France."

"To France? But my father is on the point of returning thither. Harry, what *is* all this secret business of the King's?"

Lord Percy shrugged. It was true that his friend, Cavendish, who sometimes assisted the Cardinal's secretary, had hinted things in confidence. But he wasn't much interested. "Some say that it is to promote a French marriage."

"You mean the King's?"

"Hist, Nan! It would be death to speak of it."

Yet it was such tremendous news. One *must* speak of it. "But the Queen?" whispered Anne.

"If she had given him sons it would be different, I suppose."

Anne's mind flew back to her mistress, whose solid body she had helped to dress that very morning. Self-assured Katherine, whose very rooms were full of dignified security. The Queen whom scandal had never touched, whose gracious kindness the people venerated and who had been part of England for twenty years or more. It was simply unthinkable. "But how will he get rid of her?" she asked.

The Northumbrian shrugged. All he wanted was to get Anne alone and show her that he would not share her. "Everybody knows he would do anything to get a legitimate son."

Well, it could be true. And now Anne came to think about it, had she not seen a painting of the French king's sister being carefully unpacked when her father sent a messenger from France?

She thrust her needle into the canvas of her embroidery and rose. She was still shocked by the rumour Percy had passed on to her but she pushed it to the back of her mind, anxious only to give him the opportunity for privacy which they both desired. "I will walk with you to the garden gate," she said, and sent a page for her cloak.

They left the anteroom and went down the backstairs and out into the early March sunshine. A stiff breeze was blowing up from the river and the Queen's garden was deserted. When they were come nearly to the gate they paused, as if by mutual consent, between a great briar bush and the garden wall. The bush, as they knew well, hid them from all prying eyes at Palace windows. But for once Percy did not take her hungrily in his arms. "What will Wyatt do with that chain?" he asked sulkily.

"Wear it, I suppose, to plague me," laughed Anne, plucking an over-blown rose and letting a small shower of pink petals fall from one palm to another.

"And pretend that you gave it to him."

"And what if I did? Are we not cousins?"

"To boast that you were his before you were mine."

The charge was ridiculous, but his jealous caring was sweet. Anne shrugged, and went on shredding petals.

Percy came a step closer. He seized her by the arms and almost shook her. His eyes searched her enchanting face. "And you do love him. You said so. He has had all the precious years of you that I have lost, because I didn't come and find you sooner. He has made love to you a hundred times with that glib tongue of his—and kissed you."

She looked up, smiling and tender, with complete candour in her eyes. "Oh, Harry, haven't we been over all that before? Haven't I told you that you are the only man I have ever loved, or ever could love, with all of me? Haven't I forsworn my poor pride enough and shown you my desire enough to convince even an ill-tempered Northumbrian?" She laughed, adorably, and flipped a stiff-stemmed bud against his freshly shaven cheek. "Do I not risk my uncle's wrath every day by flaunting your great jewelled cloak clasp on my breast?"

He bent and kissed her passionately. "I know, I know, my love. But it is not enough. Any man can give you a brooch to wear." He let go of her and stood there, comely and virile in the sunlight, tugging at the heavy signet ring on his finger. "Here," he said roughly, "take this."

He forced it into her hand. A heavy jewelled thing of chased gold which must have been in his family for generations. "But it is your father's seal, as Warden of the Marches. How will you sign your documents or enforce your orders?"

"By the point of my sword," he said curtly.

Anne still held the thing as if she were afraid of it.

"Put it on," he ordered.

She burst out laughing because when she slid it onto her finger it dangled like a hoop. "I pray you, be not so absurd, Harry! How could I wear it even if I would?"

"I will have it made smaller. At least it will show all other men that you belong to me."

Joy surged through Anne's whole being. "You mean that we shall be betrothed?"

"In spite of everything, we shall be betrothed," he promised gravely, looking into her eyes.

It was like some wonderful game, pretending that they *could* be. And yet was it not true that one day he would virtually rule half England? That her father might be dazzled by the prospect. A pre-contract was a solemn thing. Almost as solemn as marriage. Standing together in the sunlight, with the hopeful green of spring about them, Anne almost felt that this *was* their marriage. It was quite different from Mary Tudor's, which once she had dreamed about. But somehow pearled dresses and proud ceremony mattered little now. All Anne's world was centred in the man before her. Her ambitions whittled down to the right to share his bed and board. If he had been but an archer in her uncle's guard, she would have wanted him just the same. Wanted him, and gloried in his physical strength. Her hand closed tightly over the ring. With all her heart she wanted to keep it. "My father is expected any day from France," she managed to say.

"Because we love greatly we must have courage to defy convention," he encouraged her.

"When he tries to force me into marriage with this Irish cousin I will plead our pre-contract," promised Anne. "And you?"

"Nothing, nothing will ever make me deny it."

He had hurried her then and there to the armourer's, and before the Cardinal left for France the ring had been beaten to the size of her finger. During the days of her lover's absence Anne flaunted it as if it were the wealth of all the newly discovered Indies. She would have worn it proudly all the days of her life.

Chapter Eleven

BECAUSE THE LOVE OF Anne Boleyn and Harry Percy was so precarious, it was all the more precious. Because at any moment they might have to fight for it against parental authority, it assumed the grandeur of a cause. The marvel was that as yet no busybody had talked about it in high places.

"If only my sister could have been the one to marry James Butler," Anne would sigh. "So long as she has her infant, she would care little whether the father were Will Carey or another."

"There would still be Mary Talbot," Percy reminded her, with a grimace. They had recently been sorely troubled by a letter he had received on the subject from the Earl of Shrewsbury's chaplain.

"Is it possible that Cardinal Wolsey would help us?" suggested Anne. "The Duchess of Suffolk told me he was kind."

"Kind to the poor, and to Thomas Wolsey!" scoffed Percy, who lived in his household.

"But he interceded with the King when she married her duke."

"And see how Suffolk is beholden to him! Debts of that kind pay good dividends. And, after all, Wolsey risked but little. He was sure of the King's ultimate affection for them both."

"Sometimes I think the King is more kind than the Cardinal," mused Anne.

And, although she never spoke of it to Percy, she even toyed with the idea of appealing to the King himself. He was so charming to her these days. Far more approachable than her cold-hearted uncle, or even her father. So genuinely interested in her music. Often, on his way to chapel or tennis court, he would stop and talk to her. He wasn't so terrifying really—not if one just talked to him gaily. It was so stupid of people to bow and scrape and stammer, as if he were an ogre. He was only a man after all, and responded as readily as any other to a glance or a jest. Too readily, perhaps, thought Anne, with a lilting laugh and heightened colour. Perhaps that was why she couldn't discuss her idea with Harry. For, in fact, Henry Tudor was quite exciting to talk to with his infectious laugh and that wicked look in his eye. And when he was pleased he retained quite a measure of his amazing good looks.

The sobs of her sister, Mary, had almost faded from Anne's mind.

But then she would overhear Henry speaking sarcastically to the Queen or snapping at Wolsey's lumpish secretary. And her courage would fail her.

And so the weeks went by, and the first month of summer brought her father home from France. She and George met him warily. He was affectionate and affable, and mightily set up because new honours awaited him. His travelling days were done and he was to be created Comptroller of the King's household. George and Anne perceived sadly that their days of liberty were done, too. He would always be at hand, controlling their lives. Almost the first thing he did was to arrange a grand wedding for his son and Jane Rochford. But oddly enough, although he must have needed his share of the Ormonde estates to go with his new position at Court, he said nothing more about Anne's marriage.

"Perhaps your Irish cousin has had the bad taste to prefer someone else, and your father puts off telling you," suggested Percy, deceived by Sir Thomas Boleyn's suave manner into crediting him with a compassion which Anne was beginning to learn that he did not possess.

"It could be," she admitted doubtfully.

"And then my father might repudiate this contract with Shrewsbury's daughter in view of the fact that your mother was a Howard."

It sounded more than ever like clever bidding at a cattle fair.

"Anything may happen," agreed Anne, echoing her lover's optimism without conviction. But whatever happened now would be too late to rid her brother of Jane. And it was Jane who ultimately betrayed them.

It happened at Greenwich, during that idle hour of a summer afternoon when people talked in desultory groups or strolled about the gardens. The young Princess Mary and Henry Fitzroy were playing hide and seek among the bushes, and several of the younger courtiers had been inveigled into the game. Margaret Wyatt and George Boleyn, who both adored children, had joined in with zest; Thomas Wyatt had been pressed into acting as umpire. Anne and Percy stood talking by the sundial. Only the new bride, Jane Rochford, feeling piqued and neglected, beheld their happy absorption with an envious eye and noted how, after awhile, they wandered away down the river path towards a little grotto where a lewd stone cupid spouted water into a lily pond.

The children's excited shrieks and George's ready laughter rent the drowsy hours. The aged Countess of Salisbury, that authentic Plantagenet to whose care Mary had always been entrusted, sat watching them, surrounded by her ladies and her dogs. And presently at the height of the fun, the King and Wolsey came across the lawn from the Council Chamber, followed by the new Comptroller, a pack of solemn councillors, the Dukes of Norfolk and Suffolk—everybody, in fact, who mattered. But there was no need, it seemed, to stop the game. Henry was in benign humour and he, too, loved playing with children. He stopped, with all his splendid entourage spread out like a peacock's tail behind him. "Run, Harry! Catch the wench!" he exhorted his handsome, misbegotten son.

But the royal wench was too quick for him. With a flash of pale blue satin she emerged from behind a fat dowager's skirts and touched "home" at the sundial. Everybody laughed and clapped, and Wolsey, who was Mary's godfather, made his master a graceful compliment. "Now it's Fitzroy's turn to hide," decreed Wyatt. And, guided by some spiteful imp of fate, the lad must needs make his way down the grassy path towards the grotto.

Mary Tudor counted twenty, lifted her flushed face from the beloved Countess's lap, and listened. Unerringly, she followed the direction from whence came her playmate's whistle. Grownups who were taller than she could see him dodge from behind the bush she was making for and double further down the river path. George Boleyn stopped laughing and moved, as if by accident, to block her way. Casually, Thomas Wyatt and Norreys joined him. Together they formed a brightly hued group almost screening the little grotto from the King's vision. Supposing them to be on her side, the child would have allowed herself to be quietly headed off.

"Keep your hounds to the right scent! The stag's at bay!" rallied the King.

"I can't find him anywhere!" panted Mary.

Jane Rochford caught at her flying sleeve and pointed.

"Quiet, little fool!" muttered her husband, trying to glare her into obedience. Even then it did not occur to him that anyone would betray his sister intentionally for spite.

But Jane only showed him the tip of her pink, contemptuous tongue. She would teach him to neglect her, spending all his time with his proud sister and that soft lovesick piece, Margaret Wyatt! "Look, your Grace! Up there by the Cupid grotto. Can't you see the bushes move?" she whispered.

It was too late to warn the lovers then. Straight down the path ran Mary. Fitzroy escaped unseen, but she pulled up triumphantly at the grotto, thinking she had found him. With eager arms she pushed aside the sheltering branches of a yew tree. "Nan Boleyn!" she squealed in surprise. "Oh, Mistress Anne, I've caught you instead!"

She had indeed.

At first she had not noticed Lord Percy, standing there beside her mother's embarrassed maid-of-honour. And, as far as she knew, there was no particular reason why he should *not* be there. But a sudden silence must have warned her. She was a singularly intelligent child and not vindictive. In her half-understanding of the situation, she would have turned away and gone on searching for her playmate.

But the King had looked up quickly when she called Anne's name. He had seen her standing there and thought it part of the game, admiring her lifelike assumption of dismay. But then Nan Boleyn was a clever girl! "You've run a pretty quarry to earth this time, poppet!" he called out, with his hearty laugh. "But your stag seems to have turned into a startled fawn."

No one seemed to echo his laughter. Only Cromwell gave vent to a nervous, ill-timed snicker. And as Mary turned away Henry caught sight of Northumberland's redheaded son. In the confined space of the grotto he was perforce almost touching Anne. His face reflected her abashed dismay, and his whole bearing had all the possessive protectiveness of a lover. Henry's own face darkened like clouds before an approaching thunderclap. His fair skin reddened as if someone had made a bad joke at his expense. He turned abruptly from the afternoon's merriment and walked on towards his private apartments, leaving his daughter disappointed and amazed. The countenances of the Duke of Norfolk and Sir Thomas Boleyn were a study as they tried to keep up with him.

As their ways parted, Henry bade the Cardinal a curt good-bye. "The young fool is of your household," he barked. "Look into it, milord."

And before going on to the Watergate, Wolsey turned and said something to Cavendish.

Anne, herself, scarcely knew how it had all happened. One moment she had been in her lover's arms, enjoying a few stolen moments in the seclusion of the grotto. All around her had been shouts and careless laughter. And then quite suddenly the King's daughter had pulled the branches aside. Mary had stood there, with a bramble scratch on her face, panting and friendly. And in her surprise the silly minx had called her name. Called it aloud so that the King could hear. And then there had been an awful silence, and people staring. Someone had giggled; and Anne had felt like a kitchen slut taken with some scullion. She had seen the King glaring at them, and had wanted to call out that in the midst of so much greed and intrigue their love was the one clean, beautiful thing. And when he had turned away without a word, she had been desperately afraid.

She had caught sight of her father's face—white, angry, and contained. Of her brother and sister-in-law glaring at each other as if they had quarrelled. Then everybody seemed to melt away. The fragile Plantagenet countess had gathered together her ladies and her dogs. And the children, aware of one of those inexplicable blights which grown-up people sometimes bring, had suddenly tired of play and gone off together to watch the watermen turning Wolsey's barge against the tide.

And here was Percy's friend, whispering something to him and hurrying him away. He must follow the Cardinal, and leave in that barge for London. At the moment of parting Percy had pulled her to him, warming her with passionate lips. But he had looked grave, and dared not stay. "Keep up your heart, for it is mine," he had said. And then he and Cavendish were gone, too. Everyone was gone.

Anne would have hurried along the path to follow him. But dread dragged at her feet. When she came to the sundial, she stood alone and hesitant where so much gay company had lately been. The sun was already slanting westward behind the pinnacles of the Palace towers and their long pointed shadows lay across the grass. She shivered as their chill pierced her sun-warmed body. If Wolsey had sent for Harry Percy because the King had ordered it, she would indeed have need to keep up her heart.

Chapter Twelve

WHEN THE CARDINAL CAME again Anne looked in vain for Harry Percy. All morning the Queen kept her in attendance while she dictated letters to her secretary. She was more exacting than usual, and obviously worried. Ever since Wolsey's visit to France she had been writing privately to her nephew, the Emperor. Whether Katherine knew about the French Princess' portrait or not, she must have felt that the diplomatic visit boded her ill. And with the uncanny swiftness of such rumours, words dropped in the Cardinal's household about some secret matter of the King's had already become whispered gossip in the Queen's apartments.

Her own entourage were horrified and indignant. Even people who did not particularly like her heard hints of her downfall with pity. But Anne Boleyn, longing to be free from her orders, knew only irritation. Her own plight was so much more pressing, so desperate with the egoistic urgency of youth. A dozen times or more she ran surreptitiously to the windows overlooking the garden. Other gallants from York House dallied with other maids-of-honour, but nowhere could she see her own. They would all be leaving presently, and if the old harridan kept her much longer she would know nothing of what was happening to him. And all her future happiness might depend upon it.

"If he be not there, seek out George Cavendish," she had

managed once to call down to Margaret Wyatt, who was keeping watch for her in the garden.

And at last Margaret had come to relieve her. "Say that you have a migraine. Say anything," she whispered, taking the Queen's box of wafers from her friend's hands. "Cavendish has at last got away from that taskmaster Cromwell. He is by the garden gate."

Anne hated malingering to a mistress whom she had seen many a time attending public functions whilst in direst pain. But her strained white face was a sure advocate. Instead of going to her room, as the Queen had given her leave, she crept down the back stairs. People were coming and going through the gate, and Cavendish drew her into the herb garden. "I promised Percy I would try to have speech with you," he said.

"What news have you?" she asked breathlessly.

"None that is good, I fear. But he sent you his undying love."

The words had an ominous suggestion of finality. "He cannot come again?" she stammered.

"The Cardinal has forbidden him to see you. He is virtually under arrest."

"Oh, God have mercy on us!"

They had to speak in whispers because Donna Maria da Salinas and the Queen's confessor were strolling in the garden. Anne strove her utmost to be calm. "I beseech you, Master Cavendish, tell me everything."

"That afternoon when the King saw you in the grotto, we had scarcely stepped ashore from the barge at York House before Wolsey sent for Percy and told him that he had given offence to his Grace."

"How did he take such interference?"

"Proudly, so that I was glad to be his friend. He held up his head, and although he spoke respectfully he showed defiance."

"He would! He would! But how do you know?"

"Wolsey rated him before us all. It is a way he has."

"How Harry must have hated that!"

"His Eminence says it makes for humility."

"Which he has not himself!"

"Yet loses no opportunity to point out to us how he, who once rode the proudest chargers, now bestrides a mule like any parish priest."

"A mule that cost as much as most men's horses and looks well against his scarlet vestments! It is all part of his showmanship," scoffed Anne, forgetting that she had once believed him to be kind. "But go on, my dear one's friend. What did this swollen upstart say next?"

Cavendish stubbed at an unoffending root of marjoram with a fashionably shod toe. "It will not please you," he warned.

"No matter. I must know."

"He said that Percy had demeaned his state as heir to one of the noblest earldoms in the Kingdom by dallying with 'that foolish wench yonder in the Court'."

Anne's pale face flushed scarlet. "Wolsey, the upstart son of a butcher, dared to say that? God in Heaven, give me patience!"

"You asked me, Mistress Anne."

"I know. I know. Forgive me."

"I do assure you that although some think Percy haughty and too quick with his blade, most of us could have struck his Eminence for that." Cavendish stepped out from their retreat for a moment to make sure that the Queen's friends were out of earshot, and then took up the tale. "His Eminence went on to say that the King had previously been very well disposed to Percy, and would have advanced him. But that now, by the King's orders, he would be obliged to send for his father out of Northumberland."

"Send for the Earl!" gasped Anne, who had come to cherish a secret terror of that almost mythically fierce personality.

"And that, if that didn't bring him to reason, the King would have him punished."

Anne moaned and covered her face with her hands. They now had the herb garden to themselves, and her companion drew her compassionately to a nearby seat. "It appears that the King and your father have some other man in mind for you," he said.

"That will be my cousin, James Butler," agreed Anne drearily.

"I make no doubt of it. Percy knew of it almost from the first, didn't he?"

Anne nodded, and sat staring at the sweet-scented parterre of thyme and rue and fennel before her. "Did Wolsey say how soon it was to be?"

"It appears that the King had declared himself almost on the point of bringing the matter to a conclusion, and that for some reason he himself intended to advise you of it. In such a way, he said, that you would be glad and agreeable to it."

"Glad and agreeable to marry James Butler!" cried Anne bitterly. "What sort of man-starved frappet does he take me for?"

"Percy answered right arrogantly then. You know that way he has of standing with his hand on his dagger and tossing back his hair? 'Am I not a man grown?' he demanded, almost baring that blade that has killed a mort of lawless men in the keeping of the King's Marches. 'Old enough to fight his Grace's enemies and my father's, and fit to take a wife of my own choosing.'

"'But she is already chosen for you, as you well know,' says milord Cardinal. 'Was not Allen, milord Shrewsbury's chaplain, sent to you but a few days since to talk of this matter?'

"Percy fairly snorted at him, 'Chosen! And what a choice! After Mistress Anne, who is straight and slender as a birch tree, with skin and hair like ivory and moonlight—though she be no earl's daughter, but a simple maid.'"

Anne's dark eyes glowed with joy. "He said *that* to the great Cardinal? Before you all!"

"Yes, and milord Cardinal sneered in that smooth way he has. 'Simple maid, prithee!' he said. 'The simplest thing about her is that she has but a knight to her father.'"

"Oh, Master Cavendish! How I hate him!"

"But Percy was quick to defend you. 'What, is her lineage less than mine, even when I come into my full estate?' he cried. 'Was not her mother of Howard blood, own sister to the Duke? And is not her father heir general to the Earl of Ormonde?'"

"And then I suppose Thomas Wolsey began prating about my paternal grandfather being but a mercer, and Lord Mayor of London," raged Anne, who had many a time had to bear the spiteful taunts of the blue-blooded Grey sisters and of Jane Rochford.

"So he did," admitted Cavendish. "And then shifted his line of attack and said that in any case your father had already promised you, and that the King was privy to it."

It was all past bearing. Anne sprang up impatiently. "But Harry Percy and I—Surely Harry told the Cardinal that we two—"

"Of a truth, Harry told him." Cavendish rose and faced her. He had seen the incredible thing happen. "It is not easy to tell so haughty a man as the Cardinal anything. He does not wait to listen to the opinions of others. But Percy stopped him, almost standing in his way as he would have swept out of the chamber. 'Sir,' he persisted, 'How was I to know the King's mind in this? And, not knowing that his Grace was interested in the matrimonial affairs of Sir Thomas Boleyn's daughter, I have already contracted myself to her. We have for weeks past sought each other's company before witnesses as promised man and wife. I have already gone too far to be forsworn.'"

Anne hugged her arms across her heart, almost dancing in her proud delight. To be loved like this, by a man of Percy's high temper, was worth everything. His love was like a golden cloak about her, making her impervious to other men's anger. "He said it before you all! In spite of our both being betrothed elsewhere, he had the courage to claim me!" she cried. "Did not that shake milord Cardinal?"

Cavendish hated to damp down the flame of her precarious joy. "But little, I fear. Only as the irritation of a fly that can be beaten off, or squashed. 'Foolish boy!' he said contemptuously, brushing him out of his way with a swish of Italian silk. 'Do you suppose that the King and I know not means to deal with such matters?'"

"Always 'the King and I!'"

"And his final word, before he went to his oratory, was, 'Tonight I will send for milord of Northumberland . . .'"

"Oh, *mihi beati Martin*!" moaned Anne.

"The messenger must already be spurring his way north. And though I am loath to say it, Mistress Anne, I wager the three of them together will bend even Percy's fierce will before their own." From the quiet of the herb garden they could already hear a great clattering of horses in the courtyard. His master's audience with the King was finished, and he must go. He gathered up his cloak and bent hastily to kiss Anne's hand. "What I, and most of us, cannot understand," he said, "is why your father should be so set on keeping you for someone else when he might have had for you the wealth and prestige of Northumberland's eldest son."

Anne scarcely heard him. She caught desperately at his arm. "But shall I not see him again?" she implored.

Cavendish had kept that crumb of comfort till the last. "If he can possibly elude the vigilance of the guards, he will come tonight. I have bribed a waterman to leave a skiff drawn up on the strand. The tide should serve and he will climb the wall here by the water-gate." Seeing Anne's white-faced grief so suddenly transformed into a transport of joy, he feared for her caution. "Speak of it to no one. Not even to your friend, Mistress Wyatt," he insisted. "For he carries his life in his hand." Truth to tell, Cavendish thought his friend crazy to attempt it, but looking at the strange beauty flaming in Anne's radiant face, he was not so sure. "He says that he would as soon die as not see you again," he added gently.

He was already halfway to the garden gate before either of them remembered the most important thing of all. "But where, Master Cavendish, where?" called Anne, pursuing him.

He turned and grinned. "There is always Cupid's grotto," he whispered back, and was gone.

Anne nearly swooned with the suddenness of her delight. If the Fates were kind she would see her lover this very night. She would be in his arms again. She ought to have trusted him to bring it about. She might have known that a young man who had led fierce border forays would make light of guards and walls. A young man whose hot blood was on fire for her. And he had called on *her* courage, too. It was no easy thing for one of the Queen's maids-of-honour to climb through a window and enter the garden o' nights. But he had belittled her with no persuasions or instructions. He had trusted to her head and heart to find a way. And not if the Queen should call a hundred times would she fail him!

Chapter Thirteen

THE REST OF THE day passed in a daze of unreality. Vespers and supper seemed unending. Never had the King's musicians and mummers been more tedious. But mercifully the evenings were drawing in, and the tapers were lighted early in the Queen's bedroom. Moved the hourglass ever so slowly, there came a time when the royal jewels were put away, the pet dogs fed, and the purple bed hangings drawn. At last a maid-of-honour could call her soul her own. At last she could gaze out into the moonless, starless night; and risk danger and her own fair name to answer its enticing call.

In the gloom of the grotto Anne awaited her lover. The laggard hours crept by. "I have been waiting for him, like this, all my life," she thought. It seemed an age since she had dodged the sentry by the moat and sped like thistledown across the lawn. One by one the lights of Greenwich Palace had gone out, and she was growing cold. Beneath the scudding cloud rack that obscured the stars the fat little cupid looked less friendly. The stillness was broken only by small scurryings of unseen creatures and the occasional shrill screech of an owl. At any other time Anne would have been terrified. But her whole being was set upon one thing, tense with suspense, listening and waiting. Faintly, from the corner of the stone bench, she could hear the Thames lapping her banks, and the familiar shivering of dipping willows and the rustling of reeds. It seemed an eternity before she heard the muffled sound of oars.

Percy's wary footsteps made no sound upon the grass. Standing with thudding heart, Anne guessed that he was coming; but neither saw nor heard him until the moment when his tall form blocked out the lesser darkness of the cloudy sky.

And then time itself stood still.

She was sustained by the strength of his arms—engulfed in the glad mingling of their mutual love. Speechless in their hunger for each other, they clung together and kissed. In those first ecstatic moments all sense of despair and danger was blotted out. Anxiety melted in delight. All coherent thought was drowned in passion. Long frustrated passion, matured but unassuaged.

"Your forehead is all hot with sweat," Anne murmured at last, feeling it wet beneath her hands.

"I had to row part of the way against the tide. And you, my love, you are cold." He gathered her hands to his breast and kissed them back to warmth.

"Not now!" she laughed.

"No one has chided you, or made you suffer?" he asked anxiously.

"My father still says nothing. I cannot understand it. I know that he was angered that day he saw us here together. But no one can part us now."

Percy had no words to praise her steadfast courage, but only drew her body yet closer to his own.

Anne tilted her head back against his arm, surveying the dim outline of his face adoringly. "Harry, you were wonderful confronting the Cardinal like that. Cavendish told me how you acknowledged me yours before them all."

"And not a man but must have envied me!"

But even his most extravagant caresses could not quell their dire need to discuss reality. "If you stood up to the Cardinal, you can defy your father when he comes," said Anne.

He did not answer immediately, but, divesting himself of his coat, threw it across the seat for her. "You have not seen my father, sweet," he said, grimly, drawing her down beside him and taking her in his arms again.

Anne traced his half-seen features with a tender finger. "You said once that he is old and suffers increasingly from some wound."

"Old, but very tough," smiled Percy, guessing at her half-exposed hope.

Anne shivered in the darkness. "How I would that he might die!"

Percy rocked her laughingly in his arms. "My exquisite little Borgia, I admit that my father is not a man whom it is easy to love. But he is still my father. It was he who first showed me how to use a sword."

"I know, Harry. It is wickedness of me to think of it. Although they use us as pawns for their ambitions, there is still *something*. But if only you were earl now, and had all those castles and men—"

"It would be one's life's dream come true. To be uncurbed by his mastery, with you and the family estates. My ancestors built Wressel Castle. Shed their blood for it. And I love every stone."

"And if it came to choosing between the hateful old place and me?"

He silenced her pouting lips with his own. "The Court Beauty being jealous?" he teased.

Anne laughed up at him, all tenderness at once. "In part, Harry. Yet I would go there with you tomorrow and give up all the pleasures and compliments of Court life. What are they but hollow baubles compared with the full, secret sweetness there can be between a man and a woman?"

"At least you will never have cause to feel jealousy of any other woman," he assured her; and fell to thinking of what their life would be like together. Mentally, artistically, she was far above him. But patiently she would instruct and humbly he would learn, because he loved her. On every other plane they met, well-matched in courage and vitality, in love of horses, outdoor life, and sport. If he could not rhyme or make music like her other admirers, he could always keep her his by the strength of his manhood. Serve her utterly, yet remain her master. In the perfection of their union, lust was the smallest part. "As soon as I inherit we will live up there, and

I will fill the place with all the books and musical instruments money can buy," he went on, speaking out of wishful fancy. "I will send to Paris for rare stuffs for your dresses. We have horses in our stables fleeter and more mettlesome than any I have seen here. You will be like a queen there, but far more dearly loved. Nan, my sweet, for you I swear I will even learn to play upon the virginals."

"Heaven forbid!" Anne gave a little hastily suppressed shriek of laughter, and then became deadly serious again. "We are only spinning dreams like happy children. But we must weave them into reality."

"But how, with the King himself promising you to another?" asked Percy, knowing the odds against them and more intent upon enjoying to the full the moments they were sure of.

He would have lulled her with the sweets of present love; but, womanlike, Anne wanted assurance for the future. "The Princess Mary and her duke risked everything and were forgiven," she murmured, her mind still clinging to the daring example of their secret wedding.

"The Cardinal was on their side. But for that Suffolk might have lost his head," Percy reminded her, not unmindful of his own.

But clear thinking was well-nigh impossible with Anne's arms stealing persuasively about his neck and her head resting against the thin silk of his doublet. "There is a way," she whispered.

"Nan?" The name was no more than a glad, breathless questioning. He did not pretend to misunderstand. He slid a finger beneath her little pointed chin, lifting it until her lips were level with his own. They sat knee to knee, looking deeply into the shadowed mystery of each other's eyes.

"Take me now while there is yet time," she urged.

Hers was all the warmth and enchantment man ever dreamed of, and she offered it to him alone. Harry Percy held himself rigid, fighting his hot desires, her perfect body already surrendered in his arms. All these weeks he had restrained himself, honouring her, hoping to make her his wife. And now, goaded by frustration, the maelstrom of undammed passion bore him on its dangerous tide. She was bewitching, altogether exciting, although with him she used no conscious wiles. Different from other women, complimented by kings, desired incurably by all men who came beneath her spell.

"Beloved," she whispered, "don't you see that if I tell James Butler I am no longer virgin he will not marry me? That even my father could not force him to it."

Percy knew that she spoke the truth. "But, Nan, my dear, my very dear, the shame," he reminded her unsteadily, for conscience's sake.

"Oh, you have no need to tell me! Don't you think I have counted it? My stepmother in tears, Norfolk thundering, my new cat of a sister-in-law lapping it up like cream!"

"And you would have to bear it all."

"Dear fool, do you suppose I should suffer nothing if James Butler used me for his pleasure and the procreation of his heirs?"

He crushed her to him. "Nan, Nan, be quiet! I tell you no man shall have you—"

"It is separation I cannot bear." Anne could have won him easily with that strange power she had over men's senses, but she was too proud. Because she loved him with all of her, body and soul, she had to persuade his reason. "When will you understand, Harry, that I love you utterly?" she pleaded. "That nothing life has ever given me, nothing that it can yet offer, can weigh against a moment of your approval, against your most casual touch or smile. That I would lose the whole world to keep your love."

Already she was his past saving. "You make me very humble, Nan," he muttered, against her breast.

"Then I am cleverer than the Cardinal," laughed Anne, caressing the bright disorder of his hair.

Love like this was a rebirth. It burned away all cruelty and bitterness, running over in a measure of human kindness that made the world a lovely place. Crushed against her lover's heart, all the long disciplined desire in her rose to its consummation. Metamorphosed by love, she knew it to be no longer something evil—some snare, some super-abundant force to be feared—but something natural, sane, and good. In Percy's arms that night Anne lived the brief rich transport of her life. Throwing aside security and favour, she made the reckless surrender which could have kept her sweet.

He held her to the uttermost moment, risking his life to do so. By his ardour he stripped the future of each of them of any real satisfaction in any lesser loves.

Dawn was breaking before they parted. A faint streak of pink across the Essex marshes heralded the unwanted day. Anne stepped from the grotto to the grassy river path, stretching ecstatic arms to a late-risen sickle moon. "Whatever happens, my love, we shall have this night to remember," she said softly. "And even if we must pay for it with all our lives it will be no price at all." She turned to him suddenly, earnestly, as if she had just made some momentous discovery. "You will always remember that, Harry, won't you?"

He stood watching her, a few yards apart. "Why do you speak like that? Almost as if something terrible and unborn in our minds?"

"I don't know." A new, portentous gravity was upon her. "Only if the future should hold only sorrow for us and you saw me suffering, you must say to yourself, 'She chose it so. Together we lived that night.' Promise me, Harry!"

"I could not see you suffer!"

"Jocunda says we must all suffer for our sins, in this world or the next." Anne broke off, trying to laugh lightly. But laughter would not come. "Yet this is no sin," she tried to reassure him. "The sin lies in parting us and selling our young bodies for prestige and power. Neither is there any shame in love like ours," she declared, standing before her lover in the silvery sable of a still shadowy world. "All the shame is in the bartered beds our parents bound us to."

Either he was more conventional than she, or still too bemused with the wonder of her to pay attention. "Your little shoes are soaked with dew," he observed irrelevantly, kneeling to wipe them tenderly upon his cloak.

She, too, came back to concern for present reality. "Go quickly or someone will see your boat!" she cried, almost pushing him from her in a sudden panic for his safety.

"Not until I have seen you back at your window," he said, perceiving that the Palace servants would soon be astir. And when she proved mutinous, he was the more masterful. "No accident must befall you. You are mine now," he told her.

Anne's face burned, but she met his gaze with bravely shining eyes. "That is what I will tell them," she promised, with returning optimism. "I am happier than I have ever been, Harry! They cannot marry me to anyone else now. And if I should bear your child, my father may be glad for you to take me." She looked around at the beauty of the brightening world, wondering why such cruel interference and recriminations must be suffered. "And perhaps, who knows, by the time he is born they will forgive us," she added softly.

In his saner moments Percy had never shared her optimism. There was still Mary Talbot. And in his heart he knew how he, and all his brothers, feared their father. He pulled Anne to him and kissed her farewell. Because of his uncertainty and his sense of unwilling guilt towards her, his parting words were weighty with sincerity. "Remember, Nan, since the first day I saw you I have wanted you to be my wife. I shall always want it."

"And remember, Harry Percy, whatever happens I would rather be your wife than Queen of England!" Gaily, heedlessly, Anne Boleyn threw the words back to him as she sped, with lifted skirts, towards Henry Tudor's splendid Palace.

Chapter Fourteen

WHEN ANNE HEARD THAT the Earl of Northumberland had waited upon the King and then gone immediately to York House she scarcely knew how to bear the suspense. The Court was back at Westminster, and the Cardinal's fine town residence only a few yards further down the river. From the royal wharf she could see the barge that had borne him thence still bobbing, moored, upon the slapping tide. Sturdy watermen in the Northumberland livery sat about her thwarts, chatting casually, as if the purport of their master's visit were of no particular moment. Yet within the Episcopal Palace he must even now be closeted with Wolsey, discussing his eldest son's unsanctioned love affair.

Anne leaned over the river wall, gazing downstream at the un-revealing windows of milord Cardinal's private apartments. Had they sent for Percy yet? Would he hold out firmly against his father's wrath as he had done against Wolsey's? And would either of them listen to his arguments? It was intolerable to stand waiting like a pawn, knowing nothing of the next move. Somehow or other she must see for herself and know what was going on.

People jostled against her as she stood unheeding, the stiff breeze whipping at her skirts. The Spanish Ambassador and Sir Thomas More were put ashore to see the Queen, a hay wherry was being unladen for the stables, minor state officials and their clerks kept coming and going. A woman who looked like some sort of seamstress stood chaffering with a waterman, and was finally rowed to the steps of York House. And then a carpenter, with his bag of tools. Anyone could go except herself, it seemed. Yet her whole future was being decided there—now, at this very moment, perhaps. Unable to bear inactivity, Anne began to pace up and down. Who was there to whom she could appeal for help? Whom could she trust? Even Margaret Wyatt knew nothing of the surrender which had made her Harry Percy's beyond all question of formal contract.

Someone was calling to her gaily from the Watergate. She looked up in annoyance. But it was only young Arabella Savile, who had recently joined the Queen's household. When she had first come, Anne, remembering her own homesickness, had been kind to her. And already the girl's cheerful good nature had made her a general favourite with gentlefolk and servants alike. She had a merry round face, blue eyes, and a tip-tilted nose. The thought occurred to Anne that one could trust Arabella.

"Come down and feed the swans!" she called, throwing a groat or two onto the tray of a pieman patronized by the ferrymen. But as soon as she and Arabella were leaning over the wall throwing crumbs of pastry to a hungry family of cygnets, she lowered her voice. "You have an aunt who is in charge of the maids at York House, haven't you?" she asked.

Arabella nodded, flattered that the fêted Boleyn should take so much interest in her.

"And you get permission to visit her sometimes?"

"Whenever I am not on duty."

Anne threw the last of her crumbs upon the water. "Bella, could you go now?" she asked.

The Queen's youngest lady looked amazed at the urgency in her companion's voice. "I suppose that I could. I have only to ask Donna da Salinas."

To her surprise she felt this strangely attractive girl whom all men quarrelled over tugging desperately at her arm. "Go now! And take me with you," she was entreating. "It means everything to me. You probably know that milord Percy's father is there."

There were people passing all the time, and Arabella Savile caught only part of what Anne was whispering. But to her Nan Boleyn was a glamourous personality, whose casual kindness she had long been waiting to repay with some acceptable service. And here was the opportunity. It promised an amusing adventure with just that spice of danger which appealed to her. "Right willingly," she agreed, her blue eyes sparkling. "But how will you—"

"That serving wench of yours. She is about my height. You could, perhaps, make some pretext to borrow her cloak?"

Together they hurried back to the private apartments. And when Mistress Savile reappeared and called for a waterman to row her to York House it excited no surprise. As usual she took her woman with her. A tall, slender wench muffled against the wind in a hooded cloak and bearing a basket of gifts upon her arm.

"I will learn all I can from my aunt," whispered Arabella, as they disembarked. "But while I am with her I am afraid you will have to stay with the servants and tradespeople at the end of the hall for fear she might recognize you."

Anne had scarcely bargained for that. But maybe it was the best place to pick up gossip. Avoiding the unwelcome attentions of some pages who had probably seen her at Greenwich, she went and seated herself on a form between a group of shaveling clerks and an aging priest who scarcely looked up from his beads. As she sat there, with her borrowed hood held close as though she suffered from a toothache, she noticed that all manner of people kept drifting in either through the open door from the courtyard or from behind the serving screens. Carpenters, upper servants, scullions, they all had an air of expectancy—as if they knew not what they waited for but, by being about, would make sure of missing nothing.

Anne felt certain that the group of clerks beside her, with their shiny tonsured heads together, were discussing the Percys.

"His father is in the long gallery now with milord Cardinal," announced a passing usher, confirming her suspicion. And a buzz of good-natured jesting arose from the pages clustered round the door.

Anne hated them all for knowing about the love which made her very life.

"Hist! They're coming this way!" warned a man whom she recognized as George Cavendish's groom.

A rich brocaded curtain was held aside and Cardinal Wolsey came into the upper end of the hall with his guest, and together they stood talking beneath the great oriel window on the dais.

Anne's heart beat wildly.

So this was Percy's father. This tall, dark-visaged, sinister-looking man, with the keen eyes and sharp hawk nose, and a red riding cloak which jarred horribly against his host's scarlet.

He turned and looked at the crowded lower end of the hall as if planning some campaign. "Where is the young fool?" he asked, without troubling to lower his voice.

"I will have him sent for," said Wolsey suavely.

And while they waited, the earl called for a noggin of good strong wine to fortify himself for the interview, so that his cheekbones were almost as red as his cloak by the time Percy came hurrying in at the open door.

Anne could almost have touched him as he strode past the form where she sat. She wanted to call out, to sustain his courage, but dared do nothing to show him that she was there. His head was held high as if he were well aware that the hour of his manhood's assertion was upon him, and there was that air of arrogance about him which she loved. Seeing his father on the dais, he would have gone straight up the hall to greet him, but the earl made an impatient gesture and snarled at him to stay where he was. With a brief "by your leave" to his host, and throwing back his trailing oversleeves as if he were about to wash or to wrestle, Northumberland came swiftly down the shallow step to confront his son. His very rage seemed to bear him along. And, seeing him closer like that, Anne perceived with chilling heart how little chance of clemency there was for either of them. Hatred of a younger man who would one day lay him to rest and inherit his estate had ousted all natural affection from his close-set eyes.

"You always were a proud, licentious, unthinking waster!" he accused, clipping his words harshly between clenched teeth. "And now that I am brought hot-foot like this because you have already incurred the King's displeasure, what comfort can I hope for from you in my age?"

Percy pulled the jaunty cap from his head and sketched a hurried obeisance. Faced with such an embarrassing situation, he looked surprisingly gauche and young. "Not here, sir," he entreated, glancing round him at the groups of goggle-eyed underlings.

But even decent family pride could not restrain the earl from seizing the opportunity to inflict humiliation. "And where better?" he demanded. "Have you not demeaned yourself to the level of a lackey? Misusing your time when you might have been learning from milord Cardinal's wisdom, and abusing my trust by dallying with a wench who is none of yours."

"She *is* mine!" countered Percy. But somehow the protest seemed puerile, as if such a burst of parental authority had already dwarfed his manhood; and Northumberland, in full spate, ignored it. "Prodigally spending money on her which I and my father have laboured to amass," he complained.

"The hateful old niggard," thought Anne, wondering if he would want back his ring and her horse.

"Milord Cardinal tells me that you have even been wanton enough to enter into some sort of contract with this Boleyn girl," went on Northumberland.

Avidly, every person in the hall listened. Wolsey himself sat in collusive silence. Not a potboy shuffled his foot, and Anne's whole being hung upon her lover's answer. From her humble bench by the screens she could see but a part of his profile, and the way his hands twisted at the gold-quilled cap behind his back. "It is true. I have," he said. But his voice was less defiant than when he had acknowledged her his before the Cardinal and had had the backing of his friends.

The veinous red patches on Northumberland's cheeks deepened to purple. "Have you no regard for me or for our liege the King, to whom we are more beholden than your light head can, seemingly, imagine?" he shouted. "Do you not see that because of your willfulness the King in his indignation might have ruined me and my posterity utterly? Do you take no thought even for your own estate, in your hot hunt for the things of the flesh?"

How little they chose to understand, these middle-aged materialists! Had they no lovely memories of their own youth whereby to gauge how clean and uncalculating first love could be? "You don't understand, sir. This is no light affair," Percy was striving to explain. "Anne Boleyn is the Duke of Norfolk's niece and would bring honour to our house. And with all my heart I love her."

To young lovers it seemed argument enough. To their betters, who took their appointments and rent rolls from the King, honourable affections seemed as nothing compared with his displeasure. But why, oh why, need Henry Tudor have condescended to concern himself with the Boleyns' affairs, wondered Anne, wishing that her family had made themselves less conspicuous.

"You will obey me in this and marry where I say or, by God in Heaven, I will disinherit you!" bellowed Northumberland. "Have I not other sons to leave my title to?"

Of course, a man so insufferably competent would have! It gave him so much more power over each. Anne could imagine a row of dutifully kneeling sons carven round his tomb; and Northumberland, in his lifetime, bullying his wife into producing them. Until she, poor thing, had so gladly predeceased him.

To be disinherited meant to lose Wressel and the grim border mastery and all the things Harry Percy loved—to lose them for her sake. Anne saw him draw himself rigid as the parental shaft went home. "I have never liked Mary Talbot. I should go mad with her always at bed and board. How then shall I beget you heirs?" he was muttering desperately, hating to discuss these things in public.

"The same way as better men have done before you, taking the wives arranged for them, no matter where their lusts have strayed," snarled his father. "Do you suppose that when I first married—"

Percy's sword hand stopped crushing the cap and flew to his dagger. He had adored his overburdened mother. Even Northumberland turned aside, shamefaced, and let the half-formed sentence die. "I pray God this may be a sufficient admonition to you, and that you will be suitably beholden to his Grace and to milord Cardinal in that they lament your folly rather than malign me for the same," he said more mildly.

He moved closer to his son, so that the unwilling resemblance between their features was more marked. Although the gesture intimated that, once he got his way, the breach would be closed between them, yet he still intimidated Percy with those gimlet eyes of his, enforcing all he said with powerful hand beat on open palm. "You will give me your word not to try to see this Anne Boleyn again, and as milord Cardinal is witness I will see to it that you are married to Shrewsbury's daughter before the month be out."

Percy blanched before him. He was giving way. It was inevitable. Piled high behind all present parental arguments was the wearing force of all those brought to bear throughout remembered years. Anne understood. All that was maternal in her looked back and saw her lover as a small child being brought into that overbearing presence. A presence which must have been to him as awful as God's, but less benign. She knew how the habit of instant obedience could undermine one's courage. But never, never would she let it subdue her own in this matter of her love.

Northumberland's cruelty was not yet done. To crown all he turned to the half-cowed, half-tittering menials of Wolsey's household. "Mark my words, all of you," he ordered, "and for the short time that my son will yet be with you see that he goes not forth unknown to your master, and be not sparing in telling him of his faults."

No proud young noble's humiliation could have been more complete. Northumberland returned to the dais. He had done what he came to do, and been quick about it. Beaten down the insubordination of this arrogant cub of his, and obeyed the King. And what else mattered? He could go up river now to his half-deserted town house, and leave the Cardinal to deal with the young fool's sulks and all this modern sentimental nonsense about breaking up a love match. After all, his Eminence was well paid for it! And as for that wretched Boleyn wench, no doubt her father would behave as efficiently, and see that she married her Ormonde cousin immediately and ceased running wild and making havoc of other parents' plans.

Anne sat, white faced, and watched her lover go. A lover who had betrayed her more deeply than any but themselves knew. It was not fear that held her still. Even then she would have risked all shame and scandal to follow him out into the sunlight. To comfort and reassure him. To ease his desperate unhappiness. But how could she add to his humiliation by letting him know that she had witnessed it. That would be the hardest thing of all for him to bear. Though the nails dug into her palms she would not stir until Arabella Savile came. She must spare him the shame.

Chapter Fifteen

SOMEHOW THE DAY DRAGGED to a close. That evening Anne begged an audience of her father. Since he had neither reproved her nor made any further pronouncement about her marriage, she would not wait to be sent for. There was one card still in her hand. If she confessed her surrender to Percy, her Ormonde cousin would have none of her; and, furious as her father would be, he might even then intervene and appeal to Northumberland. In the depth of her misery Anne felt that no shame could hurt like separation. Even if Percy were disinherited, all she asked was to be with him. She would bring every gift of mind and body to compensate him for material loss. She would know how to make him happy.

So emotionally spent was she with the day's anxiety and grief that she could scarcely push open the heavy door of her father's room. She must steel herself to meet yet more parental anger. She had caught a glimpse of herself in the Queen's mirror as she came. She knew that her eyes were dark pits in the pallor of her face. She cared not what she looked like and hoped she was with child.

But in the quietness of the new Comptroller's household there was only genial comfort. Sir Thomas held a glass in his hand and seemed well pleased. "You look ill, child," he exclaimed, with concern, and led her to the warmth of a crackling fire.

He was kind. He put the untouched glass of wine into her hand and bade her drink it. It was the King's best vintage and warmed her shivering nerves. Tears of reaction stung her eyes. Why had she not confided in him before? Why had she thought him hard when he had told her about her betrothal? Compared with the blustering of the unspeakable Northumberland he had been gentle and humane. Perhaps, after all, he would help her?

As she set down the glass she noticed for the first time that they were not alone. Her uncle, Thomas Howard of Norfolk, stood by the window watching her. A dark, forbidding figure with a hatchet-shaped face. He, too, held a wine glass; and, with the return of her swooning faculties, Anne gathered that the two of them must have been about to drink a toast to someone or something at the moment of her entry. She rose immediately and apologized. The Duke seemed in no wise annoyed and even smiled that rare, thin-lipped smile of his. But in his presence the oft-prepared words died on her lips.

"You wanted to see me, Nan? To ask my advice, perhaps?" prompted her father. "Your importunate messenger said your matter must be spoken of without delay."

Anne clutched at her courage. "Before milord Northumberland leaves London," she managed to say.

"Ah, that unfortunate affair." Clearly they knew all about it. Everybody must know by now, she supposed wearily. But still nobody scolded her.

"Perhaps, my dear Thomas, it was not after all so unfortunate," suggested his ducal brother-in-law. "You know the old adage, 'The value of a commodity lies only in the demand'."

In her troubled state Anne took in nothing of his meaning. But she felt that he was watching her with a new, amused interest. That they both were. She wished that she had stopped to put on a better gown. She hated appearing like a poor relation, and if she had not felt herself to be looking so plain she would have had more confidence to talk with them. After all, they were her menfolk, her own flesh and blood. They must care for her and for her good name. And probably the powerful duke could help her if he would.

"I pray you tell me, sir, is it only because of my contract with the Ormonde family that the King was so displeased to find me with milord Percy?" she ventured to ask him.

"I scarcely imagine that he would mind vastly whom Percy marries, so be it that he marries quickly," answered Norfolk sardonically.

"Then if, for any reason, I had been free to marry him, his Grace would not mind about Mary Talbot?"

"Whomsover his son marries is Northumberland's business," said Sir Thomas Boleyn.

Anne rose from her chair. "Then I entreat you, good uncle, speak for me to the King!"

"Have I not always been ready to do you any possible service for your mother's sake?" said Norfolk, with unwonted courtesy.

He had never done her any that she could recall. Since his sister's death he had never visited Hever. So that it was odd of him to speak so now, when for once he had cause for anger. But Anne's mind and will were occupied with the difficult words which might free her from a travesty of wedlock. "This marriage with James Butler—" she began. It was more difficult even than she had imagined to say this thing before her uncle. But perhaps it was better that he should be there. Once the thing was said, for very shame of each other's knowledge, neither of them could wittingly force her to make a cuckold of her cousin. And her father surely must urge Northumberland to let his son marry her.

She looked from one to the other of them—two calm, considerate men. But in a moment now, when she had told them that her body was already Percy's, they would be livid with rage. The words stuck in her throat. Her tongue felt dry as leather. She closed her eyes so that she might seem but to be saying this wonderful thing over to herself. She conjured up the attractive image of Harry Percy and her longing for him gave her strength. "No one can force me to marry James now. Not even the King himself," she began bravely.

The truth was launched at last. Now, nothing could stop her from telling them. She opened her eyes to confront them, and to her surprise found them still listening calmly. Seeing her so tense with nerves, her father pushed her gently back into the chair. "No one is going to force you into any marriage, his Grace least of all," he said comfortably.

"There is a reason, and you must know it," went on Anne, supposing that she had not heard aright or that he said it to soothe her.

"Certainly, there is a reason, a good reason. And you can spare yourself the embarrassment of telling it to us. For naturally, my dear child, we already know."

Anne sat up straight and stared at him. "You *know*," she faltered, wondering why he did not strike her instead of standing there with that smug, secret smile on his face. Could it be that someone had seen them enter the grotto that night? And that, after all, her father was secretly glad, since Percy was the better match?

"I warrant that most people about the Court know, or at any rate conjecture. Your family appears to attract publicity," remarked Norfolk bluntly. "Let us hope you will play your cards better than your fool of a sister!"

Regardless of her deformed finger, Anne gripped the arms of her chair, her eyes on Thomas Howard's face. "Play my cards better than Mary?" she echoed faintly. "I don't understand."

Norfolk laughed and came to warm his back at the fire. "There is no need to play the innocent here *en famille*," he told her. "We have all seen you, often enough, laughing with the King on his way from chapel or sharpening your wit for him in hall."

Slowly realization came to Anne; and with it dismay, panic, and fury at her own blindness. It was second nature to her to please and to attract men, and her vanity had been tickled. But she had not wanted Henry Tudor's attentions. They could only endanger the thing she *did* want. She had been so deep in love that for once her perceptions must have been dulled.

"It isn't true!" she burst out incredulously, the hot blood suffusing brow and face and neck. But she knew that it *was* true. And that the thing she had come to say would never now be said. She would never dare to utter it. "How do you know?" she asked, with terror in her voice.

"Months ago, last summer, his Grace came riding back from Hever. He'd been to see your father about the possibility of a divorce, and about sending him to Paris to sound King Francis with regard to his sister, the Duchess d'Alençon. And your father, ever an opportunist, had improved the occasion by speaking to him about the Ormonde title and my suggestion that you should marry the heir. But you, it seems, had improved the shining hour still more. You'd been playing for his Grace in the orchard or something. He has noticed you ever since, hasn't he? Always benign and affable. And the other afternoon when he caught you in that absurd grotto with Harry Percy, who is of much the same build and colouring as he was at that age, I suppose he felt sharply that he was missing something."

With horror, rather than triumph, Anne saw it all. A man at variance with his wife, worried over the succession and his secret endeavours to obtain a divorce—her own light-hearted habit of flirtation—and the Queen's dignified animosity.

Her uncle stood changing his balance from toe to heel before the blaze, an irritating, cocksure trick he had. He had not so betrayed his natural taciturnity with women for a long time. "They say the King hasn't slept with his wife these three years," he remarked, examining a fine piece of goldsmith's work above the chimney breast. "It must be a cold bed for a man like Henry Tudor!"

And now he wanted her, Nan Boleyn, to warm it. A young virgin for the amusement of his maturity. But she was no longer virgin. She was a woman fresh from the satisfying passion of her lover. It was unthinkable. It was sacrilege. Her body was not hers to give.

Anne turned upon her father. "And would you have *both* your daughters the King's playthings?" she demanded.

And seeing that he did not answer, she took his silence for assent. "Why then did you have us carefully nurtured in the Scriptures, taught to keep ourselves chaste? I have always supposed that were I to tell you I had given myself to some lover of my own age you would have me beaten or shut up in a convent!"

"The King is different. In every Court in Europe—" began Sir Thomas. But he stood shifting a sheaf of the household accounts and would not meet her eyes.

"I can assure you that it is a much sought honour!" jibed Norfolk.

"And usually a short-lived one!" jibed back Anne, remembering her sister's plight. Despising them, seeing through their hypocrisy, she found herself no longer afraid.

"You are cleverer," Sir Thomas hastened to reassure her. "Simonette agrees with me. I always said you have my brains."

"And what do you want me to do with them? What can you want for the family more than you already have?" flamed Anne.

Sir Thomas passed a hand over his brow. A climber's path is beset with snares. "Royal favours beget animosity," he admitted. "Already Wolsey and the Spanish faction hate me. We must stand together, we Howards and Boleyns. Create a party."

Anne began to regard him with pity, rather than with anger. Although she had, in the family tradition, used her wits and gifts to set herself well on the road to success, she could still look back and see life's original values; whereas, he had already travelled so far along its tortuous ways as to be caught in the thicket of self-deception from which there is no return.

"You need not fear that his Grace will soon tire of you as he did of Mary," he reiterated. "You have a way with men. You will know how to keep him."

"I do not want to keep him. Nor any splendour that being his mistress might bring me. I will not give myself to this obscenity!" cried Anne passionately. "I have learned what true love is and no matter how Henry Tudor may tempt or you coerce me, I will not let ambition pull me down from the stars into the mud."

"This is the mere moonshine of a lovesick wench!" shouted Norfolk, glaring at her with his close-set eyes. "Have you no sense, girl? If not for us, then for your own advancement?"

"I tell you I would rather live like some petty squire's wife in a grim, bare manor, and never feel the warm triumph of power, nor ever hear music again."

Emotional strain was taking its toll. Anne was becoming hysterical. Weeping to be spared all that her sister had wept to lose. Her father knew only too well how ill and lifeless this could make her. When Norfolk would have cursed her roundly for a fool, he made a sign to him to let her be. "I had meant to give her time," he said.

"But as this calf love fades, his Grace will know how to make his will acceptable, so that she will take her good fortune gladly. It is a pity we spoke of it."

"I am glad you spoke of it," countered Anne sharply. "For at least I am warned. What I must say, and not say." But for the warning she would by now have told them that she was no virgin. And all to no purpose. Save to endanger Percy's life. Since the King wanted her for himself, she would never dare to speak of it now. No one but she and her lover must ever know.

She tried to control her trembling limbs and get up to go. The shadow of Henry Tudor loomed over her. And some other vague shadow which she could not discern.

"I would that your stepmother were here! You need a woman with you," complained Sir Thomas, torn between concern and exasperation. "But I can assure you that if you do not put this foolish young man from your mind and receive the King's favours with seemly gratitude, his Grace will dismiss you from Court."

Anne stopped in her tracks. To be dismissed from Queen Katherine's service for no willing offence! She, who had served the Queen of France with such distinction, who had set the Paris fashions. It laid her vanity in the dust. "What have I d-done that I should be so punished and disgraced before my friends?" she stammered indignantly.

"You will have offered Henry Tudor an affront which no sovereign could brook," said Norfolk.

"Then let me go tomorrow," she entreated, curtsying herself from their presence as best she could. "There is no longer anything here that gives me joy."

Her father went with her to the door, disturbed by the pinched pallor of her face. "What will you do, Nan? You will make yourself sick with this obstinacy," he said with compunction.

But Anne drew herself fastidiously from the comfort of his supporting arm. "I will go home," she murmured. "Home to Hever."

Jocunda pushed open a casement so that sunlight lay in golden patches across the broad oak floor boards and the stillness of Anne's bedroom was pierced by the mounting ecstasy of larks and the distant notes of a hunting horn.

"It is a beautiful day, Nan. Will you not get up?" she urged.

"What is there to get up for?" countered Anne, who had so loved the sunlit garden and the sound of sport.

There was something frightening to Jocunda in the still, flat way she lay there. It was true that Anne had been very ill. So ill that her father had ceased to reproach or goad her. Soon after coming home from Court she had caught a chill while hunting recklessly in the rain, and all winter sharp attacks of coughing had worn her to a shadow. But now the girl was out of danger and should really make some effort.

But Anne only lay there brooding about the past and remembering the morning when Harry Percy had ridden away. There had been no more swaggering buoyancy about him then. All his movements had repeated her own hopeless lassitude and it had been difficult to believe that his set, unsmiling lips had kissed the heart out of her body. Shaken with sobs, uncaring how she looked, she had watched him from an upper window at Westminster. "Now, this moment, he is riding out of my life," she had said aloud; striving to impress the realization of years of emptiness upon her stunned consciousness.

And now Westminster and Greenwich were bright memories of the past and it was springtime at Hever with lovers lingering in the lanes, and Anne Boleyn, dismissed from the Queen's service, lying late abed, listening disinterestedly to the cheerful sound of some huntsman's horn, and Jocunda bringing her a bowl of steaming broth.

"Your father has been at his desk this hour past. You must eat if you would grow strong again."

"I am not hungry, Madame."

But Jocunda plumped up the pillows and put the bowl into her hands. "My poor sweet, it is nearly a year now—"

"Say rather a lifetime!"

"And milord Percy married to that cross-grained wench, Mary Talbot these nine months or more."

"And his damned father dead these six months. Had he but gone to hell three months sooner, I would be Harry Percy's wife by now!"

"Child! Child! Don't talk like that. Don't *look* like that. It grieves me to the heart."

"I am sorry, Jocunda. And you so good to me! So good to all of us. I remember how you were with Mary." Anne caught at her step-mother's hand and kissed it. To please her she sat up and tried to swallow the broth. But after a mouthful or two she stopped, with tragic eyes and suspended spoon. "Have they—has Mary Talbot—is she going to bear him a child?"

Soothingly, Jocunda began to brush back the long raven tresses that always seemed too heavy for Anne's small, sleek head. "There is no word of it," she said. "By all accounts Wressel is a bear pit. The new earl cold as the dairy floor and his lady hot with resentment."

Glad yet pitiful, Anne pictured Percy going unwillingly to his ill-shared bed, and thought what joy might have been theirs had he kept his defiance longer. Deploring his unwilling betrayal, she yet forgave him. For, when it came to more than words, how could anyone defy the King, Northumberland, and Wolsey? They held all the power in their hands. Beaten, one could only hate them.

"There are other men," Jocunda reminded her, setting down both brush and half-empty bowl.

"But only one who has ever lit anything in me," asserted Anne, more reasonably. "In years to come there may be men who can stir my body, as some have done in the past. But never again can I love like that—so that it made me pitiful, generous, without spite." Some of her animation had come back as she leaned forward with clasped hands. "Dear Mother of God, how different I was then! I was the sort of woman you have always wanted me to be, Jocunda. For to love and to be loved like that is a burning away of trivialities—a cleansing, a dedication, a gratitude to Heaven!" But presently she drew her wrap of miniver about her, and with it old memories and resentments. "Ah, well, Harry is

Earl of Northumberland now. And his beloved Wressel is his, and Mary Talbot's crooked body, and his memories of mine! I hope they burn him!"

"Nan! Nan! You will make yourself ill again."

"Oh, I know, I know! You can see, Madame, the wickedness that is in me. But they planted it there, Wolsey and the King between them. Would I could make the King suffer and humiliate the Cardinal as he humiliated my love that day!" Wracked with a nervous headache, Anne covered her ears with frenzied palms. "Oh, for pity's sake, will that accursed huntsman stop winding his horn!"

But the hubbub was coming nearer. Hounds were baying across the parkland. "Heaven help us, it is the King!" exclaimed Jocunda.

In a second, breathless and barefoot, Anne was beside her at the window. And, sure enough, there was Henry Tudor, laughing all over his good-looking face. Laughing because he was catching people unawares again, laughing as if nothing cruel enough to finish life had ever happened. A dark wave of hatred and fear swept over her.

"Perhaps he has come only to discuss state affairs with your father," flustered Jocunda, hurrying from the room to receive him.

For months past all Anne's thoughts had been turned morbidly inward. Except for passionate resentment, she had thought little of Henry Tudor. She had been too heartbroken to be touched by the smaller satisfactions of vanity. And in any case she had supposed his flattering preference to be wiped out by displeasure, and the whole episode to be over.

But now there were hurrying footsteps and excited voices and Jocunda was back in her room again followed by Simonette and Matty, Anne's own tiring woman, bearing her best Court dress across spread arms.

"Your father bids you come down," said Lady Boleyn.

"I am too sick," hedged Anne, climbing back into bed.

"You were well enough to be downstairs playing with your wolfhound yesterday," said Simonette sharply.

But Anne ignored her. "Do you wish me to become a wanton like Mary?" she challenged, cruelly pushing the issue at her God-fearing stepmother.

There were tears in Jocunda Boleyn's eyes, and her hands were at the rosary hanging against her skirts. "You know that I would give anything to prevent it," she said.

"Then tell Matty to take that dress away."

"No one can prevent it, Madame, since the King wills it," pointed out Simonette triumphantly. "Have you not made trouble enough for your poor father already, Nan?"

But Anne had passed beyond her tutelage. "This is between milady and me," she told her curtly.

Jocunda waved the disappointed waiting-woman from the room. "Never before have I defied my husband; but I will help you if I can," she promised.

"But the King is waiting," protested Simonette.

"It will be a new pastime for him," said Anne, trying to compose herself against her pillows.

Sir Thomas did not send again. Driven either by his own anxiety or by the impatience of his master, he came in person. "In God's name, what is the meaning of this?" he demanded, seeing his daughter still abed and the other two women idle. "Get up and dress, you lazy, ingrate hussy, and have them rub some colour on your cheeks! And see you lose no time, the three of you—putting me out of countenance in my own house before the King!"

"Would you not have our daughter use the reasonable excuse of sickness, knowing what shame this portends?" ventured Jocunda courageously.

Her husband glared at her as if she had gone mad. "Shame?" he repeated. "Say rather the honour. Did you not hear his Grace promise me the wardenship of Penshurst and all the royal chases hereabouts?"

In spite of her thumping heart, Anne steeled herself to defy him. "The King ruined my life, and I will not give my body for his pleasure!" she declared. "Not even were he to make you Chancellor of England!"

The master of Hever was too deeply shocked for speech. For the first time in his family life he was confronted by a will strong enough to pit itself against his own. He would have struck Anne and dragged her forcibly from her bed had not Simonette, who was subtler than any of them, touched him deferentially on the arm so that he swung round on her instead.

"And you, whom I have housed all these years, why have you not taught her obedience?" he demanded, his voice half-strangled in his throat.

"Might it not be that your other daughter obeyed too readily?" she had the temerity to suggest.

Her eyes were intelligent and compelling, so that curiosity began to cool his rage. "What is in your tortuous mind?" he asked slowly.

"Only a proverb we have in our country, sir. '*Reculer pour mieux sauter*'."

"Or 'Easy come, easy go', eh?" he muttered, capping it with a sound English one.

Finding the tension relaxed, Simonette shrugged and laughed. "We all know how being kept waiting for a meal whets the appetite," she said.

Sir Thomas stood irresolute, baffled by his womenfolk. Anne was behaving like an obstinate brat. But Simonette was no fool. She had always been properly ambitious for her pupils, and she at least was not trying to restrain him out of any mawkish sentiment.

Now that he came to look at Anne more carefully, she certainly did look deathly ill—and ordinarily he was very proud of her. He took a turn or two about the room, worrying absently at his beard like a man making up his mind to lay a risky stake; and then went out in silence, bracing himself to gainsay the mighty Tudor.

As the door closed behind him, Anne sank back, her small reserve of strength all burned up. A fit of coughing shook her body so cruelly that she could not get her breath. Her heart stopped its violence and her lips went blue, so that Jocunda feared for a moment that she would die then and there in her arms.

It would have been a quick and easy death, without notoriety or the searing of condemning years.

But Anne was young and strong.

A week later she was out of doors standing by the sundial with Henry's letter in her hand. "I and my heart put ourselves in your hands, begging you to recommend us to your favour," he wrote.

Since he had been denied the pleasure of seeing her, he had written humbly, like any ordinary, sighing lover.

So Simonette had been right.

Reading her first royal love letter, Anne felt a warm sense of power rising in her. "The King of England wants me for his mistress," she told herself softly, taking the flowers into her confidence and flouncing a little to the gaudy butterflies. And then, drawing her well-marked brows together, she crumpled the parchment in her hand. "How I hate him!" she said out loud.

She said it, perhaps, to reassure herself. Because the fierceness of her antagonism to Henry and his Cardinal had become a symbol of her loyalty to Percy. But even then she must have been aware of a difference in the quality of her resentment towards the two of them. For the Cardinal, who was older and looked at her coldly, hatred was unrelieved, implacable, whereas with Henry Tudor, the man of hot desires, all sorts of possibilities crept in. Shared tastes, mutual sources of enjoyment, a certain amount of liking—and fear that she would not always be able to hate him wholly.

She must walk warily.

In the meantime, there was the letter to be answered. But as she turned to re-enter the house, she saw Thomas Wyatt coming through the garden towards her. He must have ridden over from Allington. He looked freshly shaven, modish, eager. Of course, Jocunda had been right. Now that neither James Butler nor Harry Percy claimed her, there would be other men.

"I had thought to find you surrounded by half the swains of Kent," he said, holding both her hands and looking at her with warm brown eyes. He stood close beside her in the sunlight and told her that she was more bewitching than ever, and that sickness had but etherealized her beauty. And, whether he paid her compliments or not, it was altogether good to have him.

Instinctively, she transferred the King's letter to her left hand and hid it in the fullness of her sleeve. "Come and tell me all the latest gossip from Court," she coaxed, drawing him beyond range of an excited household's prying to their favourite seat among the yew alleys. For although she had fiercely forsworn the old false life, she found herself, after so much seclusion, avid to hear the doings of the fashionable world.

Wyatt rejoiced at her eagerness, recognizing it as a sign of returning health. "The thing that everyone talks of is still this 'secret matter' of the King's remarrying for the sake of the succession," he told her. "But it seems the Pope has no heart to offend Spain."

"Why must his Grace make such a mystery of it? The Queen herself has known for months," said Anne.

"Before you left Court?"

"Yes. He came to her room one morning as soon as we had finished dressing her, and they were closeted there talking for an hour or more. They say he was trying to persuade her that his conscience had been afflicted for years, and that their having no living sons was a judgment on him for taking his deceased brother's wife. I know that he came out looking distressed and sheepish, and that he left her in floods of tears. It was the first time I had ever seen her cry. But she is far too obstinate to give him his freedom by admitting that her marriage with Prince Arthur was really consummated."

"To know her is to trust her word. There never was a woman more honest," said Wyatt thoughtfully. "But life would probably be much pleasanter for her if she would. And for all of us. We all know that his Grace would see her honourably provided for."

"But it would mean giving up being Queen of England."

"She is probably standing out more for her daughter's legitimacy. There is such tender love between them."

"And even though the King is trying to get his freedom, she seems to love him, too," mused Anne, guiltily aware of Henry's letter hot in her hand.

"Is that so marvellous?" said Wyatt. "After all, they have lived together in amity for eighteen years."

Anne dismissed the matter with a shrug. She did not like the Queen. Katherine of Aragon always tried to be fair to her, but could scarcely be expected to show a Boleyn favour. And a young French queen would probably be much more amusing to work for. "How is my brother?" she asked, abruptly changing the subject.

"Plunging more recklessly than ever into every sport and mummery about the Palace," smiled Wyatt, reminiscently. "To make up for his home life, no doubt."

Anne suddenly wanted to be there, too, to laugh with George and relieve the hurt at her heart in a spate of bitter brilliance. To stand with him in mutual defence against the world, warmed by the balm of his ready understanding. "I suppose his Jane has nurtured all manner of rumours about me?" she enquired.

"At least time gives the lie to some of them! I believe that George abjures her bed because he caught her telling one of the Grey girls you were with child by Harry Percy. She has a poisonous tongue."

"And a lively imagination," added Anne lightly. Not to a soul would she ever speak of that ecstatic night now, since her lover had been driven to deny her.

"She must be the only one of us who has enjoyed your absence," said Wyatt, secretly reassured. "She was always jealous of you, Nan. And particularly of her husband's unshakable affection for you."

He drew her closer and because Anne was not yet wholly strong, she allowed herself the cousinly comfort of leaning against his shoulder. "And what about you, Thomas? What have you been doing all these months?"

"I have been to France on a mission for the King. I have written some more doggerel. And now I have come to Allington to set my affairs in order. And to see you," he told her. "George tells me that your father is no longer pressing the Ormonde suit, and now that you are free again—"

"Never again free in heart, Thomas."

He took possession of the hand lying idly in her lap. "I know how you have suffered. But it will pass with the years, dear Nan," he said gently. "And who should know better than I how to comfort you?"

"A man needs more than that."

"A semblance of marriage with you would mean more to me than the undesired reality with any other woman. I have waited so long, Nan."

"And you still wear my trinket!" she sighed, espying about his neck a link or two of the chain he had pilfered from her to annoy Percy. "You are very dear and faithful, Thomas."

"I would give my life for you, Nan."

She drew back a little, her mind already back with Percy. "I have heard men say that before," she murmured forlornly.

The hot, aromatic scent of sun-drenched yew and the drowsy hum of bees were like a warm mantle about them. Wyatt got up and moved a pace or two away lest her nearness should conquer common sense. "It is true that I shall love you till I die, Nan; but I am a man and no lap dog, and Allington must pass to my sons," he managed to tell her.

Anne made an involuntary little gesture of dissent. Somehow she had never even imagined him married to anyone but herself.

But he stood there picking at the stiff, shiny sprigs of shrub. "We are no longer irresponsible children, sweet," he said gravely. "The golden days when we sucked life for our own pleasure are passed and such obligations must be planned for. But I beg you to consider well before, of necessity, I ask some other woman to be mistress of Allington. For both our sakes, Nan. For, although you are not in love with me, you might do so much worse than take me."

"Oh, *mon cher ami*, so much, *much* worse!" she cried, touched to the heart by the wryness of his smile. "But now I dare not."

"Dare not?" he repeated. "But your father has never shown himself averse to me."

"It is not that," Anne hastened to assure him, drawing the King's letter from her sleeve and deliberately letting it roll across her lap.

"So it is true," he muttered, whitening to the lips at sight of the imposing seal.

"Did Jane omit to say *that* of me?" she asked bitterly.

"A year ago I grieved because it was on all men's tongues," he admitted with a stricken look. "But then the King was angry about Percy, and you were dismissed from Court. And so the rumour died."

"Well, now it has come to life again," said Anne, staring straight before her.

Suddenly she found herself swept into Thomas Wyatt's desperate arms. He was crushing her protectively, while the King's letter rolled to their feet. "Oh, Nan, my beautiful, my incomparable, don't give in to him! Do always as your own heart dictates!" he was imploring. "Whether you take me or another. Were you my sister, I would say the same thing. I have been so close to him at Court."

"But I thought you were devoted to him?" argued Anne, staring into the beauty of his anxious eyes.

"Yes, yes. There are things about him—his music and ability and a good comradeship which charms men's affections. But he has changed so much of late, since this accursed divorce business."

Anne knew that Wyatt was thinking only of her. Because he was so precious in the losing she released herself very gently. "He can *order* me to come to Court," she pointed out, stooping to retrieve her letter.

"If he does you must remember what happened—"

"To my sister? Yes, I will remember. But you must see, Thomas, that it would mean death to marry me now."

Chapter Sixteen

J OCUNDA CONSIDERED THAT THOMAS had behaved beautifully. And Anne, ostensibly reading poetry in the long gallery, was thinking how much she would hate to see some stranger mistress of Allington. "All my life," she thought, turning a scarce-read page, "I seem to have been on the point of marrying Thomas." And even now, for his sweet constancy, she might have married him, had it not been for Henry Tudor.

But life had never withheld anything from Henry Tudor. And no one else's desires had ever mattered in comparison with his own. And consequently Anne's silence only whetted his appetite. Far from being displeased, he was intrigued by her having the courage to commit such an enormity. It showed that she was not easy game, and needed to be wooed. Well, he liked his women that way. Spirited, like his horses. It provided better sport, breaking them in.

Being no backward lover, he came in person. It made him feel adventurous and young. There were a dozen good reasons why he might choose to ride to Hever any fine morning to see his house-hold Comptroller, without setting people talking. Sir Thomas Boleyn had always been accommodating, and this time Henry caught Anne unawares.

She did not hear him pull aside the door arras. She looked up from her book and saw him standing there, and knew by the lustful look in his eyes that he must have been watching her for some minutes. Like a stoat before it strikes, she thought.

Her heart missed a beat as she rose. She laid aside the leather-bound poems to curtsy. She had not meant to be caught like this, with not so much as a servant about; but she would be no silly, fascinated rabbit for his kill.

She was so graceful in every movement, and he so susceptible and self-assured.

"What are you reading this sunny forenoon, Mistress Anne?" he asked, in that mellow voice of his.

His air of gallantry made her nervous. Because she was not too sure of controlling her own voice, she held out the book to him respectfully. He came and took it from her, turning over the fine, illuminated pages with appreciative fingers. Seeing the title, his sandy brows shot up in surprised amusement. "'Troilus and Criseyde'? Strong meat for a virgin, isn't it?"

"I like it," said Anne.

"So do I," he chuckled. "Do you know those words at the end of this lovely verse?

> '—my royal estate here I resign
> Into her hand, and with full humble cheer
> Become her man, as to my lady dear'?"

With the closed book in his hands and his quizzing, libidinous eyes on her face, he quoted them softly. Too softly.

Furious with herself for providing the trap, Anne felt herself flushing like any simpering chamber wench. But she would not let him discompose her. "Sir Thomas More considers them fine poetry," she said, holding her dark head proudly.

"He is right. And I should like to set them to music and hear you sing them." Responding at once to the dignity of her breeding, he ceased to ogle her. He laid aside the book and sat down on a curved music stool beside her. "It is high time we had you back at Court, adding your beauty and accomplishments to your brother's beguiling levity," he invited.

Anne's lips set themselves into a rigid line. "With so many matters of real import to think upon, your Grace could scarcely be aware that I have been grievously sick," she said frigidly.

"Could I not?" he chaffed. "Have I not those about me who are nearest to you in blood? And do you suppose that I have never enquired for your health?"

His reproachful sincerity made her feel a clumsy ingrate. "Your Majesty is magnanimous," she murmured.

"Not magnanimous, and you know it," he contradicted brusquely. "I have missed you, Nan."

She looked up in genuine surprise. "Yet you dismissed me." She would have added "without good reason" had she dared.

"Was it not best for a time?"

His words seemed to imply some interrupted understanding between them, which Anne resented. But she knew that it *had* been best. Even had she not been ill, she could not have lived at Court away from the kindness of Jocunda, through the desolation of these past months.

"And now you will come back," Henry was saying pleasantly. He rose and wandered to an open window, admiring an enchanting vista of trees and lawns. His words were less a question than a command.

Anne rose meekly, since she could not sit while he stood. "I am still not strong," she prevaricated stubbornly.

He swung round with a flurry of jewelled velvet. Masterfully, standing close before her, he put out a hand and lifted her small, pointed chin the better to examine her face. "Still resentful, you mean, my jade!" he corrected her, with a short, brutal laugh. "What did you expect me to do? Stand aside and let any hot-blooded young redhead fondle you first, once I had marked you for my own?"

Agonizingly, his words brought it all back. The silks and scents, the sunny lawn, young Mary Tudor's voice, the warm strength of her lover's arms. Anne felt like a half-broken filly, kicking furiously against a master who knows every trick of the animal he handles. Nothing, nothing would make her obey him. "Since for no fault the Queen gave me my *congé*—" she began.

But he only grinned. "You need bear no resentment against my wife. I make no doubt she was glad to see the back of you, but it was I who told her to send you packing."

Anne's dark eyes glared back hatingly into his amused light ones. She knew that he was enjoying himself immensely. "Well, what do you say now, my beauty?" he asked more gently, bending to taste her parted lips with an experimental kiss.

"That her Grace may not want me back," argued Anne, still forcing herself to defiance although her limbs were as water.

"She may not want you, but she shall send for you. And soon."

Anne's breath was coming short and fast. It was not fair, being held so close to him. Between anger and desperation, she felt a sob catch painfully in her throat. "I still need my stepmother," she protested faintly.

Seeing her genuinely distressed, Henry let her go. He stood for awhile by her music table, fingering the fine lute and rebec she had brought from France. And Anne, struggling in a welter of conflicting emotions, stood staring at his broad shoulders and the back of his ruddy, close-cropped head. She waited with her left hand hidden in her sleeve and her right hand pressed to her slender neck, as she so often did in moments of stress. But for once, it seemed he was not really concerned with the rare instruments he handled, and by the time he turned back to her all trace of mockery and mastery was gone. "Listen, Nan," he said, his voice husky with earnestness. "I care not how or with whom you come, so be it you come. You have my leave to bring Lady Boleyn an' you will. I am a lonely man these days, and have need of you."

They stood measuring each other like two protagonists about to enter the ring, and presently the fine, high moulding of Anne's cheeks softened to a smile. She knew that after all she had won the first round and could afford to be generous. Tactfully, she tried to hide her triumph. "Would you then have me come back as before— as the Queen's maid-of-honour?" she asked.

"I would sooner it were as the King's," grinned Henry ruefully.

But Anne shook her head. "That would be dishonour," she said primly.

He stood looking at her, as if determining something within himself. "You speak truth. You are as yet too thin and pale," he conceded. "I will tell Lady Boleyn to cherish you here awhile and bring you when you are ready to come."

"You are generous, sir," she admitted, curtsying to the floor. "I realize that your Grace could command me."

He tweaked her cheek kindly as she rose. "And what should I gain by it, my pretty Nan? A frown from those black eyes of yours, a sulky answer from lips made for passion?" He made no further attempt to touch her. "Believe me, I would rather take away from this pleasant room the recollection of one spontaneous laugh, your glance enjoined with mine. Of one verse read, so you have in some measure enjoyed my company. And so I will stalk you patiently," he promised, moving towards the door, "in order to catch you the more securely."

But there was that spark of coquetry in Anne which would not suffer her to leave well alone. "Are you so sure that you *will* catch me?" she asked, challenging him with that devastating sideways glance from beneath her lowered lashes.

He stood, enslaved, with the arras already lifted in his hand. He made a gorgeous figure in the morning sunlight. He was King of England and, of all the lovely women who preened themselves at his approach, he had sought her out.

But it was neither his gorgeousness nor the signal honour shown her which moved Anne. It was something about the man himself. A warmth and vitality that made her wonder why so short a time ago, as an inexperienced girl, she had thought him middle-aged. Something which, in spite of her angry resentment, made her think how exciting it might be to be loved by him, a momentary thought for which she held herself in swift contempt.

"Do I usually let my quarry escape me?" he countered boastfully. "Ask those who hunt with me!"

And his self-confident laughter seemed to enrich the walls of Hever as he let the arras drop behind him and encountered Sir Thomas Boleyn waiting to escort him down the stairs.

Chapter Seventeen

"I T MUST HAVE TAKEN a deal of courage, Nan's not answering the
King's first letter," mused Jocunda, eying the second one as if it
were some bargain from the Devil.

"She has plenty of that," agreed her father complacently.

"More than Mary."

"And more intelligence, too!" The better to examine the royal
missive, Thomas Boleyn swept aside the designs for the Ormonde
hatchment with which his table had been strewn; for why concern
himself about a mere Irish title now? A year or so ago he would have
broken the royal seal as a matter of course and told his daughter how
to deal with the contents. But now the King's continued attentions
had put Anne upon a different footing, and there were moments
when Sir Thomas was secretly afraid of her sharp tongue. She was
so temperamental and yet so clear thinking—so much more imperious than Mary. "Here, take the letter to her, good wife," he ordered.

"It is past believing," complained the lady of Hever, taking it
reluctantly. "Messengers from the Palace every few days. Freshly
killed buck, supposed to fatten her, but more to show off the Tudor's
skill. And 'Cherish her, dear Lady Boleyn,' he tells me—as though
I need *his* orders to look after mine own!"

"Jocunda! I would have you remember it is the King you speak of."

"And how I would it were not! If only it were young Wyatt or
some other honest lover who could marry her! I've a mind to

burn the temptation here and now before it burns the wench's body in hell."

Her husband's face reddened uncomfortably. "It is different, I tell you, with a King!"

But Jocunda realized what honest love had done to beautify Anne's nature, and how—thwarted, turned back upon itself—it might sour her. "'Thou shalt not commit adultery' it says," she quoted at him from the only book she knew. "But nothing, as far as I know, about cohabiting with kings." And was told, for her pains, that such foolish talk came of the iniquitous Lutheran idea of letting women read the Scriptures for themselves.

So there was nothing for it but to take the letter to her step-daughter; and because Jocunda never poked or pried, Anne pulled her down beside her on the oak chest where she sat, and read it aloud.

"*To my mistress,*" Henry had begun romantically. "*As the time seems very long since I heard from you, or concerning your health, the great love I have for you has constrained me to send this.*"

"The great love," murmured Jocunda, half-awed in spite of herself that such words should come from Westminster to Hever.

"If so be that he knows what a great love is," scoffed Anne. "*Since my last parting with you, I have been told that you have entirely changed the mind in which I left you, and that you neither mean to come to Court with your mother, nor any other way.*"

"It is true, Nan, that we have made every possible delay and excuse."

"*Which report, if true, I cannot but marvel at,*" went on Anne, "*being persuaded in my own mind that I have never committed any offence against you. Dear God, was it no offence to destroy my life's happiness?*"

"Here, let me finish it," offered Jocunda, seeing the tears starting to the girl's eyes. And stretching out an exasperated hand she skimmed it over, stressing the more important parts. "*It seems hard, in return for the great love I bear you—* You see, Nan, he says it again!—*to be kept at a distance from the presence of the woman in the world I value the most. Consider, my mistress, how greatly your absence afflicts me. I hope it is not your will that it should be so; but if I heard for certain that you yourself desired it, I could but mourn my ill fortune, and strive by degrees to abate my folly."* Jocunda hurried through the formal phrases of salutation. *"Written by the hand of your entire servant, H.R."*

The portentous words seemed almost unbelievable in the quiet of the homely, familiar room. "Well, I suppose it is something to have the King of England for one's servant!" laughed Anne in a strained sort of way, succumbing to a surge of triumphant excitement.

"And his Grace certainly writes a lovely letter, as if he really loves you. I had expected it to be more gross."

"Gross or fine, this time I shall have to answer it."

"Your Father hopes that it will wake you from calf-love whimsies to the reality of a splendid future," reported Jocunda reluctantly.

"It is not the future of which I am thinking, but the past," answered Anne slowly. "My beautiful past. One short summer of ecstasy and hopes, trodden into the dust like a morning puff ball by his uncaring feet!" She went to the window, but her great dark eyes saw nothing of the familiar view. They were staring back into time, seeing again the sunlit river meadows, the daisy-strewn lawns in the Queen's garden at Greenwich, the tender smile of her young lover. "How dare the King hope that I shall love him?" she cried. "How dare he presume to think that he can buy my devotion with glittering baubles? In spite of all the humble courtesy of his letter we know what he wants, and how can I give him my body after—after—" The words died in her throat, strangled by a sob. She threw herself down against the cushioned window seat, her head pillowed despairingly in her arms; though even in the wildness of her distress her movements appeared to be guided by a sense of drama.

Jocunda looked down at her pityingly. Having nursed her through delirium, she knew that the girl's surrender to Percy had been absolute and beyond time's healing; though never would she betray that accidentally acquired knowledge. "If you keep firm in your refusal to become the King's mistress, the dear Mother of

Christ will help you," she counselled simply. "Is it not written, 'Blessed are the pure in heart'?"

Anne rose and kissed her. "Yes, dear Jocunda. But it is also written, 'Thou shalt honour and obey thy father'," she answered, with a caustic smile. "And I suppose that if I go on disobeying him it can only end by their putting me in a convent."

"Most women must have felt at some time or another that there are worse places," murmured Jocunda.

But Anne was scarcely the type to serve impersonally with a community of cloistered women. In spite of everything, there were still plenty of worldly things she loved. Though her lover had been taken from her, she did not want that strange sex power of hers to be sealed up. She wanted to be free to use her talents and her charm in the open light of the world. To feel again and again the warm glow of applause and power. To see the hunger in men's eyes.

Her whole nature swung away from the thought of conventual life and back to Henry Tudor. She had not supposed that a man of his age and importance could show himself so ardent a lover. How much easier it would all be if, as Jocunda had expected, his approach had been completely gross. And he himself without attraction.

Signing himself her humble servant was a polite figure of speech, of course. Yet surely, as a woman, she was still free to yield or to refuse?

But she would not suffer herself to think of him.

When she went to bed that night her fingers sought beneath the pillows as usual for the jewelled miniature of Harry Percy. It was all she had of him. She could not see it in the darkness, but she could hold it—and go to sleep, as usual, thinking of him and praying for him. But for the first time a shade of resentment lay across her thoughts. Why could she not be free to live and love carefree as other girls? Why, why must the two of them make of her tired heart a perpetual tilting ground?

And when next the King came to Hever he intimated that he would lodge the night. This time there would be no calling for horses and hurrying away.

Supper was a gay and gracious meal, followed by good music, good talk, and all the pleasures of a cultured home. And afterwards Sir Thomas and Lady Boleyn withdrew from the parlour and left him alone with their daughter. As obviously as though he were an accepted suitor and his object marriage.

Anne looked up in anxious embarrassment. She saw that Henry was standing before the fireplace, outlined warmly against the leaping flames, and that he was no longer jesting.

"I have been revolving in my mind your answer to my last letters," he said, turning the great signet ring on his finger. "And I have put myself into great agony not knowing how to interpret it—whether to my advantage or not."

Anne had not intended him to. She had written cleverly, ambiguously. Not daring to refuse him, she had been playing for time. But now, tonight, she realized that she would be forced to give him a definite answer, and because he was a king the issue was so big. She could neither forgive him, nor bring herself definitely to lose him.

Hurt as he was by her reluctance, it was Henry himself who helped her. Laying aside all air of authority, he came and sat near her. He took her poor, malformed hand in his as she stood beside him. "I beseech you earnestly to let me know your mind as to the love between us two," he entreated simply.

Touched and grateful, she turned towards him, the fingers of her other hand picking nervously at the pearls that trimmed the padded shoulder of his sleeve. "It seems so fantastic," she said, in a low voice. "I sometimes think your Grace speaks these words in mirth, to prove me."

"By all the Saints, Nan, do I look as if I were jesting?" he protested, torn between anger and amusement. "Does a man placed as I am, with all the fierce light of publicity beating upon his every movement, invent excuses, write pleading letters, and ride fifty miles or more to see a woman unless he wants her?"

"In doing so, your Grace does but demean himself," murmured Anne, in a rare access of modesty.

"Have not you, too, Plantagenet blood?" he countered.

It was true enough. Each of them had it equally, through their mothers. And she knew that with him it was an obsession. Anne wondered if that had inclined his eyes to light upon her sister. If it had been Mary's blood, rather than her celebrated beauty. But that was a subject she dared not touch upon. "It seems so strange that you, who have only to hold up your finger—" She floundered a little, uncertain how to address him in such intimate circumstances. "Why, you could have almost any woman you choose."

"Apparently not!" pointed out Henry ruefully. "And I want none other than you. That is why I need desperately to know whether I shall succeed in finding a place in your heart."

Anne judged it discreet to move away putting half the room between them. To Henry her graceful movements were reminiscent of the timid deer he was wont to stalk. And never had he known such delicious ardour in the chase. Her very alternation between friendly candour and frigid formality drew him on. "Your Majesty knows that we Boleyns have good cause to hold you in affection," she began. But he sprang to his feet, goaded to exasperation. "Nan! Nan! How can you talk as if I were a stranger and you some silly, simpering sycophant? When you know I have been thus wounded by the dart of love for a whole year."

Recognizing the controlled passion in his voice, she did not deliberately set out to inflame him further. It was the inherent coquetry in her that always made her look back over her shoulder with that slow, enticing smile. "What then would you have of me?" she asked, knowing the inevitable answer.

"Have I not already written it? Do you want me to tell you as well?" In a stride or two he was beside her, pulling her into the crushing strength of his arms. Holding her head against his heart, roughly, so that the jewels on his doublet hurt her breasts, while his hands explored her exquisite body. "Nan, you hot hypocrite, you are trembling!" he laughed exultantly. "Is it because, for all your pretended coldness, you want the thrill of having a man put it into words?"

He jerked up her chin so that she could breathe again, forcing her to meet the demanding admiration in his eyes. "I want you to be my mistress and my friend," he told her. "I am tired of pretending that I come to hunt a stag or see your father. More than anything I want to proclaim you mine before all men, so that they must envy me my jewel. But how can I do this until I be sure that I am not deluding myself and that you entertain for me a more than ordinary regard?"

Anne made no answer. She stood motionless, engulfed, half swooning with the unfamiliar scent and closeness of his body. She was helpless to resist his kisses. And when he had tasted the sweetness of her mouth, he made what was for him the supreme gesture. "Listen, Nan," he promised, looking down hungrily into her enchanting face, "if you will do the duty of a true and loyal mistress, giving up your heart and body to me, not only shall the name and place be given you, but I shall cast all other women out of my thoughts and my affections, serving you only. There will be no competition, Nan."

He released her so that she might the better answer him, holding her lightly at arm's length with his hands upon her shoulders. "*Now* do you know what I want, sweetheart? And what I can give?" he asked, more gently.

But still she did not answer him, and he flung away from her, ever and anon glancing at her downcast face as he paced tempestuously about the room. "Is it nothing to you that I, Henry Tudor, will be your devoted servant?" he shot at her. "That your least wish will be gratified? That everyone—even your high and mighty uncle—will defer to you?" It was a completely new experience, this pleading to a woman for something he could not get. Except for sons, and the divorce he craved in order to obtain them, life had never denied him anything. From sulky bewilderment to anger, his voice ran through the gamut of his reactions. Finally, as the incredible probability of refusal sank in, he fetched up by his host's table, picked up a drawing of the promised Ormonde arms, stared at it, and threw it down again. "Even if you do not love me," he said, with a kind of savage dignity, "you Boleyns are not usually so devoid of policy."

The shaft struck home. And Anne was no saint. The whole dazzling prospect opened like a shining pathway before her. Jewels, dresses, entertainments, envious glances—every pleasure life could give her, and herself the alluring centre of them all. Influence and riches to spend on those she loved. Power over those who had hitherto thwarted or disdained her. Small, apt revenges, that would be very sweet. But stronger, more compelling than all, was the excitement of the Tudor's insistent passion.

But because his touch could warm her to disloyalty to her lost love, once again Anne steeled herself resolutely against his persuasions. The flower-strewn pathway of ambition faded before a wave of God-fearing rectitude, and real fear beset her. As if some unfathomable gulf yawned suddenly before her, she recoiled with horror from his advances and fell upon her knees. "I think your Majesty degrades us both," she found courage to say. "And to ease you of the labour of asking me such questions again, I beseech your Highness, most earnestly, to desist. And to take it in good part when I say from the depth of my soul that I would rather lose my life than that virtue which is the best part of a woman's dowry."

Henry stood looking down at her, too much surprised, or too much moved, to speak. He did not move until her parents came back into the room, hoping to learn the outcome of the interview. "It was clumsy of me to urge you, Anne," he admitted, trying to save his face and drawing a little leather case from the wallet at his belt. "See, child, what I have brought you. I had Master Holbein paint a miniature of me, and the best craftsman in Goldsmiths' Row set it in a bracelet." He risked no refusal by seeking to fasten it on her wrist, but laid the lovely jewelled thing on her father's table. "Keep it and let it plead my love," he said, with a sigh of self-pity. "And when your virgin heart comes unfrozen a little, send me some answering token. In the meantime," he admitted, turning with a charming smile to his host and hostess, as though assured of their cooperation, "I perceive that I must needs possess my mind and body a little longer in patience."

Seeing the tears on Anne's cheeks, he would have raised her. But she was too quick for him. Evading his out-stretched hand, she stepped back defensively against the wall and faced him. Innocent, for once, of all studied effect she stood slim and proud between a window emblazoned with the arms of a house as regal as his own, and a painting of a Lord Mayor of London whose womenfolk had been trained in simple virtue. "I do not understand how your Grace can retain such hope," she said coldly, braving her father's anger. "Your wife I cannot be, both in respect of mine own unworthiness, and also because you have a queen already. Your mistress I will not be."

As the simple, unequivocal words fell into the hushed expectancy of the room, Jocunda crossed herself, grateful that nights of prayer were answered. Sir Thomas looked as if he might be taken of an apoplexy. And Henry Tudor had his answer.

After a year of evasion and disappointment, he was able to accept it with surprising dignity. There was that element of sportsmanship in him which could admire courage when he saw it. But unwittingly, Anne had revealed to him that it was not only her body he desired, but also her spirited companionship.

Chapter Eighteen

ANNE HAD BEEN SENT to her room in dire disgrace. Her father had rated her soundly. Jocunda had been forbidden to bid her good night. And behind those tall, lighted windows of the best bedchamber, Henry was probably even now working off his wrath on poor Norreys or Brereton, or whoever happened to be undressing him.

"Harry, my heart's love, have I not been true to you, giving up what most girls would have sold their virtue for?" Anne whispered, gazing out unseeingly upon the still, moon-bathed garden. But the happy days of their love-making seemed a lifetime ago. Her lips were already desecrated by another man's, and Harry Percy was perhaps abed with his complaining wife. Gradually the righteous exultation which had sustained her began to fade, giving place to the uncomfortable conviction that she had acted like a fool.

Everyone except Jocunda seemed to think so. And now Simonette must needs come to air *her* views. Anne could hear her brisk footsteps tip-tapping along the gallery, and presently she came into the room bearing a cup of hot milk. "My Lady would have you drink this," she said.

"And you were looking for an opportunity to come and tell me all I did amiss!"

"You behaved quite seemingly." Simonette's face was neat and noncommittal. But when she had given Anne the cup, her schoolroom manner changed abruptly to that woman-to-woman tone she often used now that Anne was past her tutelage. "But since you pretend to hate his Majesty—oh, la! la! what an opportunity for revenge!"

"Revenge?" repeated Anne, staring in questioning surprise.

The Frenchwoman needed no further encouragement. She came back and sank down upon the window seat, settling her stiff skirts around her. Against their shiny blackness her clever hands lay whitely one upon the other along the boniness of her knee. "*Ma chère Nanette*, when I was teaching you, you were not wont to be so dull," she protested, with a thin, affectionate smile. "Why not make him want you—as you have wanted that handsome lover of yours? And I wager the Tudor could want a woman to the exclusion of all decency and conscience! Make him go on wanting you!" Simonette's face and voice were informed with all the sadistic cruelty engendered by a decade of reluctant chastity, and as usual in her more human moments a trace of her native accent lent piquancy to her perfect English. "Not for a week or a month, *ma mie*," she hissed, "but for a ver-rie, ver-rie long time."

She had captured Anne's attention completely. Their glances were locked, almost as though the younger woman drank at some mental fount of nourishment. In their absorption, although each was unaware of it, they spoke in whispers. "But how could I do that," asked Anne, with an incredulous gasp, "once I had agreed to be his mistress?"

Simonette laughed reassuringly. "I am past my youth, *voie-tu—sèche et laide*. But I was young like you once. I had a middle-aged lord for my lover, and I kept him for years. I saw to it that he was never quite sure of me, nor quite satisfied. Had I had your beauty—" Simonette broke off with a shrug. "Well, who knows? I might never have entered your father's service and filled up my loneliness with Boleyns, or cared as I do for your advancement."

All that was worldly-wise in Anne realized that she might have suspected this sudden revelation, and that Jocunda suspected it instinctively. Avoiding comment, she opened up a fresh line of argument. "You know that I am not really beautiful."

Simonette relaxed against the leaded casement, her battle half won. "You have something much rarer than beauty. Something which men recognize instantly. You remember, Nan, the story I used to make you translate from the Greek. The story of Circe?"

"Circe was a sorceress."

"*Eh, bien?* Have not all women who hold a man in thrall something of the sorceress in them?"

Anne thought of her poor finger, and of how the King—who loathed all sickness and deformity—had held it lovingly, not caring for its ugliness. "You think that I could keep the passions of a King enthralled?" she asked slowly.

"If you can control your own," smiled Simonette.

"Why do you say that?" demanded Anne, her face burning in the gathering darkness.

The woman's glittering eyes mocked her. "Another redhead!" she jeered.

Anne knew that it was true. That none but a redhead had ever inflamed her own desires. A shamed silence hung between them, thick with the intimate things which had been half-expressed. Thirsty, Anne crossed to the bedside and drank her forgotten, tepid milk. She stood pondering awhile, looking down fastidiously at the creamy skimmings clinging to the bottom of the cup. "Simonette, he said my least wish would be gratified," she said presently. "Do you suppose he meant only jewels and the expensive things most women want? Or the sort of things men scheme for as well? More important things like—like power against other people?"

"A man in love is as wax," answered the Frenchwoman, thinking with dismay how childishly defenceless her favourite pupil looked standing there beside her virginal bed in a snowy shift.

But Anne was not really childlike nor defenceless. Her next words amazed her mentor. "You think then that I could persuade him against even Wolsey?"

Even crafty, ambitious Simonette was shocked. The bare idea brought her to her feet. "*Mon dieu*, child, you fly high," she expostulated. "Wolsey is sacrosanct. A Papal Legate, and the most influential man in Europe."

"But I hate him!" cried Anne.

Betrayed by the strange intimacy of the hour and kept in countenance by the evil evinced by her companion, Anne found herself giving voice at last to the corroding bitterness of her inmost and most shameful thoughts—the half-acknowledged thoughts upon which her frustration had fed all winter. "Simonette, I would almost sell my soul to be revenged upon that man. To pluck from him his state and his complacency. And if this chance be open to me still, I swear that I will use it to topple him from his smug security. And that when the time comes—however it comes, and whatever it may cost me—Harry Percy, my beautiful lover, shall be there to see it happen. So that he may forget the loveless hours in his forced marriage bed and wipe out the hurt of his own humiliation with the sight of upstart Wolsey's!"

"Step carefully, Nan! The King loves him," warned Simonette, noting the rising hysteria in Anne's voice.

But Anne began to pace the room, scornful of danger. "What do I care?" she cried, in wildly exulted mood. "The worst that could happen to me, if the King should tire, is to be cast aside like Mary. And who knows but what, when that times comes, I shall be glad? I shall still be young, Simonette."

"Young enough to marry, as she did?"

"Perhaps." Anne's thoughts flew regretfully to Thomas Wyatt—Wyatt who, for all his patient constancy, would take no man's leavings. And then, with more contempt than pity, back again to her sister. "But married or single, at least I shall not lie upon my bed and sob!"

"Then you mean to become the King's mistress after all?" probed Simonette, trying to hide her eagerness.

Anne went to the window. The lights in the King's bedroom had been snuffed, and the blankness of his casements seemed to shut her out. "If it be not too late," she answered, less confidently.

"Did his Grace leave you some loophole should you change your mind?"

"He said that when my virgin heart unfroze I was to send him some token."

Simonette was all competent activity at once. Ignoring Lady Boleyn's instructions that Anne was to get some sleep, she lit the candles and began searching among the girl's possessions for something suitable. "That bracelet the King brought you—I saw your father carrying it to his locked coffer. *Mon dieu*, how the rubies glowed!" she ejaculated, between her fervent rummagings. "Why do you laugh at me?"

"My incomparable Simonette! You remind me so much of that day my father's letter came, when first I went to Court. Routing through all the chests and cupboards as you did then. Laying out all my poor bits of jewellery. Starting me off in life!"

"We are a good bowshot further on now than then," grunted Simonette, opening yet another chest. "Ah, here we have something—God knows, we cannot compete with the King's gift in worth and workmanship! But here is a kind of medallion."

"Oh, *that*! A worthless trinket I had as a child."

"No matter. *Ne voie-tu*, Nan? A painted maiden all alone in a boat, tossed on a stormy sea, stretching out her arms to a gorgeous knight upon the shore. If Henry Tudor be as quick as I deem him, it should be rich at least in *meaning*."

Anne was quickly at her side. "And see, it bears my initials."

"If we could convey it to your brother at Westminster—"

"Hal Norreys will take it. He would do anything for me."

Simonette slipped the thing into her pocket lest Anne should sleep on the matter and change her mind. "Tomorrow George will find some quiet occasion and hand it to the King," she prophesied triumphantly.

"As you will, Simonette." Anne tried to speak indifferently, but her black eyes shone and her voice was bubbling with excited laughter. "Though if his Grace still be as burning eager as when he kissed me in the parlour, a button from my shift would serve well to bring him to heel!"

Chapter Nineteen

ALL THROUGH THE CRISP November day the King had been hunting in the Kentish woods. Relays of horses had been posted for him between Eltham and Allington and, as usual, he had tired out half a dozen of them, as well as most of his followers. And when at last he drew rein for the final kill it was on a grassy knoll but a few bowshots from Hever.

Before dismounting he grinned amiably at George Boleyn, who had followed him closely, and pointed at a peep of the Castle just visible through the thinning trees. Both of them were too blown for speech, but when Henry pulled off his glove, George noticed that he had had his sister's medallion made into a ring, and was wearing it ostentatiously on his little finger. And as soon as the King had recovered sufficient breath he lifted his hunting horn and wound it lustily for her. He had been in marvellous form all day, and he wanted Anne to see him at the peak of his triumph—first in the field and complete master of one of the many sports at which he excelled. From the terrace below, Anne recognized the imperious blast as a summons. She had been half expecting it all morning, and was already in her riding habit, and as she mounted Bon Ami and rode forth from her home, she knew that there would be no changing her mind again this time, however cleverly she might tread. She was not fool enough to suppose that it would be easy. There would be secret pangs of conscience, a price to pay for every royal favour and a whole world of envy, hatred, and malice. Although there were friendly greetings waiting for her at the summit of the hill, and Norreys, Brereton, and Weston vied with each other for the honour of helping her dismount, Anne saw the hatred in the eyes of many a man who had panted at Henry's heels.

Her glance passed them all by, friendly smiles and cold stares alike, and went straight to the King as he stood bare-headed beneath a great beech tree, dispatching a stricken buck. The wide, spreading boughs, smoothed flat underneath by the antlers of his deer, made a rich canopy above him. Their leaves were still thick and redder than the remote November sun which swam, detached as a painted bladder, in the mist grey sky. Their warm depth of colour cast a glow upon him, lighting up even the fine golden hairs upon the backs of his hands and accentuating every tensed muscle in his powerful body. Roughly, good-naturedly, he pushed down the slobbering, baying hounds that swirled about him for the smoking offal. At times one could scarcely see him for their tawny, leaping bodies and the snapping of savage jaws; and the next he was there, a solid, green-clad figure in the midst of them, dominating both man and beast.

Something primitive stirred in Anne at the sight of him. What he had done to her and whatever he might do, physically he was superlatively a man—and to his huntsmen, seemingly, a god! She knew that she would always remember him best like that, and guessed that he had timed his effective stance for the moment of her arrival.

Leaving hounds and carcass to the hunt servants, he turned and smiled at her, the sweat unheeded on his forehead and blood dripping in great gouts from his curved hunting knife. He threw the knife to a page to clean, and came straight to her before them all—with laughter on his lips and the dried twigs snapping crisply beneath his feet. "So you heard me wind my horn?" he called boyishly.

"The very souls in hell must have heard it!" Anne laughed back at him.

"I wanted you to know I was coming home," he said, turning to grin amiably at her brother, who had risked his neck all morning to follow more closely than the rest.

An air of youth informed Henry. He no longer sought her glance with circumspection, but openly—recklessly—laughing for sheer enjoyment and closing his hand over hers so that she must notice that he wore her token trinket as a ring.

He stood beside her while the servants laid out each man's kill. He was generous in praise of other men's skill, but naïvely delighted with his own. He had every right to be. He was in the prime of his manhood, and could draw a longer bow and tire a fleeter horse than any of them.

Anne knew that Simonette had been right, that in denying him she would sometimes have much ado to deny herself—and hated herself for the knowledge.

"We will ride down and dine with you, Thomas," he told her father graciously. "And Fortune send Lady Boleyn a well-stocked larder, for our appetites are sharp!"

Anne glowed with triumphant beauty as he waved aside a dozen eager admirers and himself lifted her to the saddle. And looking into each other's eyes as he did so, they both laughed unsteadily, for no better reason than because she was as thistledown in his arms.

At a casual lifting of his hand the whole company began to move wearily down towards the Castle after him. Even Suffolk and her uncle rode discreetly a few paces behind. But she, Anne Boleyn, rode by the King's side in her brave new Tudor green. It was all very heady after Percy's youth and Wyatt's gentleness.

And after supper, in the long gallery, Henry tried to claim his reward.

"I have been patient, Nan. God, what a fool of patience I have been," he pleaded, his hands fumbling at the tightness of her bodice. The man was brutish in his urgency, and Anne's stillness beneath his kisses was no longer swooning and quiescence of the senses, but reawakened desire. With the fiercely stormed defences of her mind she fought it desperately. To yield at the first assault would be to lose all. "Not in my father's house!" she protested.

By his baffled look of amazement she knew that no woman had ever before denied him. He would have taken her by force, but his very astonishment proved her safeguard and she was quick to take advantage of it. "Have I not promised you that I will come to Court?" she reproached, finding a relaxed moment in which to slip from his embrace.

"How soon?" he barked.

In her relief from fear of immediate surrender Anne assumed an unaccustomed meekness. "When your Grace wills."

"Without your stepmother?"

"Quite alone. To re-enter the Queen's service. Is not your Grace the very fountainhead of all Christian knighthood?"

He fancied she was mocking him, and was not yet sure of her surrender. And yet what girl in her senses would be reluctant? What girl ever *had* been? Tormented and intrigued by so new, so unexpected an experience, he stood scowling at her. "What makes you so stubborn, Nan? So aloof? If I thought that you were still mooning after that lanky redheaded Northumbrian—"

His tone was menacing. Her immediate thought was that no harm must come of this to Percy. She used the weapon that ever came readiest to her hand, glancing up provocatively at the King from beneath the lure of dark lashes. "Is it my fault if I have a *penchant* for the colour?" she asked impudently, her glance resting approvingly upon his own close-cropped head.

He caught at her hand and swung her to him again. "Then I am not abhorrent to you, you enchanting thing?"

"Would that you were!" breathed Anne, with all the conviction of truth in her voice.

"Then why all this pother for your virtue?"

"What you would have has always been preciously guarded. I wanted above everything to bring it to my husband."

The King was obviously touched. "I love you the better for it, Nan. And promise you that I will cherish it as if I were free to *be* your husband. There shall be no lights-of-love. I will keep myself to you only." Clearly, he saw himself above the laws of lesser men, and the position he offered her as one of honour, not of shame. "I had a good mother and have been blessed with a faithful wife," he went on, musingly. "Always I have loved good, dutiful, domesticated women. I do not like light women in my house." He spoke with sanctimonious sincerity; and Anne, knowing how she was tricking him, felt almost ashamed to see the effort he made to curb his baser parts.

He sat down and drew her onto his knee, and fell to caressing her hair. "Think, Nan, how interesting our lives can be," he urged, resting his cheek tenderly against her head. "You must not believe that I but lust after you. Have I not loved you for a year or more? There are things I covet besides your bewitching body. I want your gaiety, your wit, your youth—just as I enjoy the company of that young devil of a brother of yours and his friends. And there is your music. You have a rare gift, Nan. And then, thanks to your father or to that gaunt French maid of yours, you are well read beyond the wont of women. There are books and poems we can talk of, winter evenings, when we weary of the cards. You have been brought up to think—to have a mind of your own—so that a man may be the richer for your company."

"Do you not see that to have a mind of my own might be sometimes dangerous when your Grace likes dutiful women?" pointed out Anne, laughingly at his inconsistency.

But, being in love, he saw only the delicious dimple in her cheek.

"There is so much that you can give me, little Nan. And what man in all the world can give you more than I?"

"There is but one thing," began Anne, twisting her trinket upon his finger.

"You have but to ask, my darling."

Anne looked into the face so familiar to all Europe, so closely bent upon her own. She knew him to be erratically generous; but the time was not yet ripe to seek the boon that had become an obsession. One would need to have a man more deeply in thrall before trying to influence him against his best friend. She must content herself with something smaller. "There may be much venom to contend with when I return to Court," she said thoughtfully. "I can no longer share a bed with Blanche Dacre or some other maid-of-honour."

Henry tweaked her ear. "Have I not made it abundantly clear whose bed you can share?"

But Anne was not to be fondled into silence. One must have some official place. "Since I go there to please your Grace, I cannot expect the Queen to like me the better for it."

"Neither have you reason to expect Katherine to be unkind. But I will have milord Chancellor see to it."

"You mean that I may have lodgings of my own?" she persisted.

"As near to my own apartments as possible."

Anne thanked him charmingly. "As soon as your Grace sends me word that they are ready, I will come," she promised.

Henry pursed his lips. Was he still being stalled, he wondered. Was the artful baggage still creating difficulties. He bethought him of an expedient. "You will have your sister," he reminded her. "William Carey is at Court, and you could lodge temporarily with them."

"No!" expostulated Anne, vehemently. And Henry had the grace to redden, realizing that he had committed a blunder.

Anne knew that in his impatience to possess her he had momentarily forgotten the scandal, had not thought of the indecency of the arrangement. To him, it was as if Mary Boleyn had never been. "Mother of Heaven, will there ever come a time when his mind is as blank of *me*?" she wondered. "Please God, I have enough personality to leave more mark than that!"

Since she was going to him half against her will, violating the one love of her life to do so, she would see to it that she went openly, with the full light of public envy upon her. So that there could be no question of marrying her off quickly when he had had his way and then forgetting all about her. She would see to it that there was no confusion in men's minds between the petty, sordid scandal that had been Mary's, and the romantic blaze that would be hers. When she could hold her royal lover off no longer, all England should know that she was the King's mistress. And Thomas Wolsey, who had contemptuously spoken of her as "a foolish wench about the Court," would live to eat his words!

Chapter Twenty

A ND SO IT HAS really come to pass," said George Boleyn, looking round a pleasant, panelled room enriched with some of Cardinal Wolsey's best tapestries. "The Lady Anne's lodgings."

"And conveniently near to the King's privy staircase," observed his sister Mary, speaking no doubt out of her own brief experience.

"Does the Queen realize?" asked Margaret Wyatt, gathering up the yapping spaniel she had been feeding with sweetmeats.

Anne, radiant in a new pearled gown, nodded assent. "Last night after supper she sent for Jane and me to pass an hour at cards with her."

"I marvel at her Grace asking you," laughed George. "It must be so mortifying to know that whichever of you loses it is her husband who pays the gaming debt!"

"But last night I won! Did Jane tell you that when I turned up the winning card her Majesty said, 'Ah, nothing less than a King will do for Mistress Anne!'" The Queen's notorious maid-of-honour stopped twirling the King's ring on her finger and scowled like a reprimanded child. "She has a way of saying a thing, without apparent rancour, which cuts worse than other women's open scorn."

"Conscience, dear Nan," jibed George.

"No, just Katherine," grimaced Anne, tight-lipped. "The woman is always so insufferably right."

Since it seemed indecent to pursue the subject in Mary's silent presence, George sauntered to the open window in search of distraction. "There goes your brother on his way to the bowling alley," he called over his shoulder to Margaret.

"Why does the King always invite Tom, and not you, to play?" she asked, hurrying to join him.

"Probably because I play so ill, dear Margot," laughed George, pulling her gently to his side. "The King may like to win, but he is too good a sportsman to brook poor opponents."

While he thrust his head out of the casement to call down to his versatile cousin, Mary Boleyn rose and collected her possessions preparatory to some domestic excursion. She still looked virginal, with her flawless features and smoothly parted hair, and a wave of nostalgia for their happy childhood swept over Anne. "Are you happy in your marriage, Mary?" she asked, under cover of the gay, triangular conversation going on with Thomas Wyatt.

"Will Carey is kind to me, if that is what you mean," replied her sister placidly. "But, as you know, we are too poor to count for much at Court."

"I will try to make Henry give him some better appointment elsewhere," promised Anne, fully aware that it was sensitiveness to people's jests rather than kindness which prompted her offer. The old scandal, she felt, made her own position ludicrous. But Mary seemed to have forgotten those tearing sobs which had made so deep, so unfair, an impression upon an inexperienced sister. "Have a care not to prove too easy prey, as I did, dear Nan," she was whispering, in unresentful concern. "The moment he had satisfied his lust, my little power was gone."

The same old warning. And this time by one who surely knew. Anne longed to question her, but tossed her head, too proud to ask. How *could* Mary admit to such humiliation? She herself would know much better how to play the game. Quick to hear the King's voice down in the courtyard, and the usual stir attendant upon his appearance, she was already sure of her next move. And the moment Mary and their cousin Margaret were gone from the room she went to show herself at the window, waving a gay salutation to Wyatt and joining in her brother's badinage.

Out of the tail of her eye she could see Henry laughing and talking with his brother-in-law Suffolk and another kinsman of hers, Sir Francis Brian, while a posse of pages carried their gear to the bowling alley. But, pretending to be unaware of them, she smiled down beguilingly upon her girlhood's lover. It was mean, she knew, to bring him beneath the royal displeasure, but how amusing to see what a little jealousy could do! "Come up, dear Thomas," she invited, "and take a cooling drink with George and me before you play."

She knew very well that at the sound of her voice the King had stopped talking and was watching them. Equally well she knew that nothing would induce Wyatt to cross the threshold of rooms which another man kept for her. And a few weeks ago she herself would not have dared to pit the one against the other.

But Wyatt's savoir-faire was equal to the situation. "His Grace and milord of Suffolk await me," he excused himself. Cool and immaculate, he bowed to her and, crossing the sunny courtyard, attached himself to the waiting group of players.

"Surely you know that no man presumes to touch what is Caesar's," grinned George; and Anne noticed that he said it with a new complacency.

With sudden concession to weariness she sank down upon the window seat. "How we have both changed," she sighed, recalling how vehemently he had once hated the idea of her name being coupled with the King's as Mary's was.

"Time has thrust the change upon us, my sweet," he assured her, with a shrug and a yawn. "You remember the good old tag '*tempora mutantur nos et mutamur in illis*'?"

Anne watched him with affectionate envy as he ranged appreciatively about her room, living from moment to moment, from enthusiasm to enthusiasm, guiltless of cunning and untroubled by her morbid stabs of conscience. Never, she supposed, would he quite lose that spark of spontaneous boyishness which made him so attractive.

"Since our father has schemed so successfully for our advancement we must accept our griefs along with the mundane glitter. I suppose, like you and Percy, I could have found happiness beyond words with Margot," he said, his fair youthful face momentarily clouded by a sorrow of which he seldom spoke. "But I do not deny that I find quite a deal of unworthy satisfaction in finding myself, unexpectedly, the Viscount Rochford—just as you must find enjoyment in these splendid rooms."

"The Lady Anne's lodgings," Anne repeated pensively. "Yet I have no title. Is that how people speak of me, George?"

He chose a walnut from a golden dish and, drawing his elegant dagger, began whittling the shell into a little boat for Mary's boy. "It is how the King has given orders that all the servants and Court officials shall speak of you," he answered.

But even his evasions were significant to her. "You mean there are others who—?"

"Naturally, there are people of the Queen's party."

Anne gave vent to a little spurt of excited laughter. "Am I already important enough to split the state into parties?"

"It would seem so."

"And what do these others call me? These enemies?"

"The Concubine," he told her bluntly. Since she must needs know it, George spoke derisively. But his dagger dug savagely into the hold of the little boat, and when Anne sprang to her feet he forbore to look at her.

"I do not care!" she declared, a shade too stridently. "I could have crept back to Court quietly, could I not? But I persuaded Henry to give me separate lodgings so that everybody should know by whose favour I am here."

"So why *should* we mind?" agreed George quietly, ranging himself beside her in her gorgeous shame.

Anne flashed him a glance of gratitude.

"After all, anyone but a simpleton must know that I am given the Rochford title because the King's passion for you cheated us out of the Irish one. So there seems no reason why they should not call you—"

"Except that it isn't true," flamed Anne.

"Not true?" George fumbled his dagger back into its sheath. With the ridiculous little barque still in his other hand, he stared at her wide-eyed. At her proudly held head, her lissom, pearl-decked body and all the seductive grace of her. "With all this—this sumptuousness?" he objected. "And the King supping here almost every night?"

"Yes, he sups."

"And you would have me believe—? Nan, you must be crazy!"

"Surely, as a gentleman of his bedchamber—"

"But we all supposed—"

From the step of the window embrasure Anne challenged his incredulity. "Though I grow hard enough to lie to all the world—though I still love Harry Percy and my whole life is become a lie—have I ever lied to *you*, George Boleyn?"

Relief that she had not paid for his title overwhelmed him. "Then how—?" he stammered.

Anne's laugh was low and full of self-contempt. "It is not easy," she admitted.

He had always adored her. And now, with this new enchantment about her, he could see how a man in love with her might be hopelessly enslaved. "If you can hold off a man like Henry Tudor, and he a King—if you can do that to him all these weeks—you can do anything," he breathed respectfully. "By Heaven, Nan, you must be a witch!"

She laughed more easily then. Stepping down from the window, she kissed him on the cheek, flattered that even a brother could see something of her Circe fascination. "If I am," she boasted lightly, "it is Henry who will do the burning."

She would have passed him with a careless trail of perfume and a swish of silk; but suddenly he caught her by the wrist. He was white beneath his sunburn, and awe sat upon his face. And something Anne had never before seen there. Some fleeting look of fear. "Then perhaps, after all, it could be true the thing Jane said last night," he muttered, standing close to search the unfathomable darkness of her eyes.

"And what did your hell-cat Jane say?" she jeered curiously.

Instinctively, he glanced over his shoulder and lowered his voice. "That Katherine of Aragon had been nearer the mark had she said, 'Nothing less than a *Queen* will do for Mistress Anne!'"

The two of them stood silent, locked by his hold upon her wrist, even their awed gazes locked. Anne's face changed and aged as the full meaning of Jane's daring words sank into her consciousness. Breathless, arrested, motionless as a statue, she stood absorbing the dazzling new thought. And, though she still seemed to stare into her brother's eyes, a whole series of wishful fantasies passed like pictures before her mind. She saw herself in some yet more gorgeous setting, swaying statesmen and courtiers beneath the King's fond smile—saw her proud, sardonic uncle and the Cardinal crawling for her favour. She heard her own laughter as a beaten Wolsey rode away forever on his sleek white mule, with Harry Percy watching him. And then the bells of London were ringing, and the crowds cheering, as black-eyed Nan of Hever—that "foolish wench about the Court"—rode through their streets with a golden crown on her head, and her white throat decked with the splendid jewels she had so often held, kneeling, for Queen Katherine. But beyond the great Abbey doors the pictures faded. All was solemn, candle-lit gloom, so hazy with incense that one could in no wise tell what came after. It was too dark to be sure whether Henry was still smiling or not, and very cold. And fat Katherine's jewels lay too heavy on her slender neck.

As George released her hand Anne raised it, in the familiar gesture, to her throat; almost believing them to be really there choking her.

"It could be, if he gets his divorce," she heard herself saying, in a voice that sounded dazed and unfamiliar.

And then Jane Rochford was in the room, with Hal Norreys and Margaret Wyatt, and a chattering bevy of people urging them to come and watch some of the best bowling ever seen.

Anne pulled herself back firmly into the present. She knew that Henry had sent for her. That he was childish enough, and jealous enough, to want her to see him score over Thomas Wyatt in a game of skill.

Chapter Twenty-One

I T WAS MIDSUMMER AND the game was on the green. "Always so
much pleasanter than when they play in the closed alley," said
Anne, settling herself in the chair Hal Norreys had set for her
by the gallery window.

Before taking it she had looked round cautiously to make sure
that the Queen was not present. But Katherine seldom came to
watch her husband play these days. She and her ladies were at
their devotions, no doubt. And Wolsey, instead of plaguing the
King with state affairs, was holding his Chancery court at
Westminster.

At the stir of Anne's arrival, Henry looked up and waved. His
broad face flushed with pleasure, and she noted the way he settled
the jewelled belt more snugly about his hips, and strutted more
confidently than ever. Preening himself, like one of the gorgeous
peacocks on the terrace. But soon the players had changed ends
and he had forgotten her in his keenness for the sport. Or rather, by
her presence she had provided just that fillip of feminine adulation
necessary for his fine performance. Like one of the patient peahens,
she supposed, suppressing a desire to giggle.

The gallery lattices stood wide and a cool breeze blew in from
the Thames, carrying the fragrance of closely shaven turf which
hung upon the noontide air. And the groups of players and pages
down on the sward looked like gaily coloured tapestry figures

worked on a bright green background, squarely framed by a rectangle of chapel cloisters and a piece of the tilt yard wall.

"One day I must work the scene in silks, with everyone watching while Henry stoops to cast a bowl. It will please him enormously," she thought. She was sure that Katherine, in eighteen years, had never thought of anything so novel. Yet Henry loved ingeniously contrived surprises, and if one must live with him how well worthwhile to please him! Perhaps Katherine had begun that way, and tired. For Anne had to admit that her own agile brain sometimes found it exhausting; and when she was not called upon to be either enticing or restraining him, she was glad enough to relax.

So now she let the peace and warmth of the scene lull her to a daydream, in which she imagined herself back at Hever with life at its carefree dawning again. The short, hard clack of the biassed wooden bowls as they knocked against each other, or kissed the small white jack towards which they were aimed, might have come from some neighbourly game on her father's green at home. From time to time the voices of the players came up to her—friendly, chaffing, tense or laughing. And then there would be long silences while, with grotesquely held gestures, they watched the course of their own, or their opponents', bowls.

At first the friends about her talked in undertones, making frivolous comments and laying wagers, honouring their routine duties with long-drawn "Ohs" and "Ahs" whenever the King did anything particularly spectacular. But today the play grew too gripping for half attention. Spectators' minds and eyes soon became riveted on the green, for the best skill in England was theirs to bet on and enjoy. Each of the four men moving about the square below was an expert, and each at the zenith of his skill. But the play of Henry Tudor and Thomas Wyatt was positively scintillating. Each performed uncanny feats, as if driven by some devil to outshine the other. As the game wore on there was no need for perfunctory adulation. Each shot, upon its own merits, called forth a handclap or an almost painful groan of incredulity.

Anne sat up straight and watched each point. Like a shuttle-cock in play, her feminine interest flew back and forth between her two avowed lovers. She observed how Henry, who usually, prior to delivery of a shot, had no eyes for anything but the jack towards which his shot should draw, would pause to glance appraisingly at his deadliest opponent. It was as if, distracted, he noted Wyatt's good looks, his early manhood and the good taste of his sartorial perfection, rather than his play. And as if the game, nearing its final issue, had become a personal contest between the twain. She wondered if others besides herself were conscious of some drama being played out behind the normal tenseness of the contest.

"Sixteen all, and the last end!" called her uncle, Thomas Howard of Norfolk, noting the score on his tablets and skipping like a rather stiff goat from a stream of woods the pages were rolling down.

For the last time the gaily coloured figures crossed the green. Accustomed sportsmen, they walked together with easy badinage to hide their real anxiety for the issue so soon to be determined. When they turned beneath the lengthening shadow of the chapel wall, Francis Brian, having won the previous end in partnership with Wyatt, took the jack from the eager, unsteady hand of a sweating page. He stooped, and sent the small white ball speeding far along the green towards the spectators in the gallery, knowing well that the King and Charles Brandon of Suffolk preferred playing to a short jack.

"Last end, and the game might go equally well to either pair," gurgled George Boleyn, in ecstasy. "Double that last wager, Hal?"

One by one, from the cloister end, each man's wood curved down the green, Henry and Suffolk watching anxiously as Brian's sidled expertly to touch the jack.

All hung now upon the fortune of their second woods.

Francis Brian sent up a cunning bowl to protect his first, but Suffolk's second delivery disturbed the clustered head of woods, carried the jack a few inches and came to rest close by.

"Suffolk lies winning shot!" In the abnormal quiet Thomas Howard's harsh voice echoed sharp as the twang of a bowstring against the tilt yard wall.

With consummate skill Wyatt retrieved the position. Playing up on the backhand, he curled his wood round the two of them, to lie yet closer to the jack than Suffolk's.

"Oh, fine shot, Wyatt!" rang out Henry's voice.

"And last cast of the game," muttered Jane Rochford, within the gallery, having wagered more than she could afford.

As the cheering died down the King took Wyatt's place.

"And suppose, after all, he does *not* win?" thought Anne.

With all her heart she wanted Wyatt to win—Wyatt who was part of her life, dear almost as George. But now that she had driven them to this fierce rivalry, she was afraid. Afraid for herself, but far more for Wyatt. Any other day Henry would have lost gracefully and walked back to the Palace chuckling about what a wonderful game they had had. With an arm about his opponent's shoulder, as likely as not. Arranging some time in his busy life when he would be able to play again. But today he was there to show his woman that he could win. That he brooked no rivalry, either in sport or love. The intention was written in every masterful line of him.

Stooping, marvellously agile for his girth, he balanced the heavy, polished bowl upon his palm, sighting the jack. His hand was cool and strong. Dipping his right knee, he made his final cast. Sweetly the bowl rolled along the sward, turned inward by the bias, lost speed, rolled over and lay a few inches short, almost covering the jack. From where Henry stood at the far end it must have looked a winner.

His tensed features broke into relief, expanded into a grin. Turning, he hit his partner a congratulatory thwack on the shoulder. "Charles, we've done it! The end is ours! The final cast is mine!" he cried triumphantly.

But Brian and Wyatt, having delivered their shots first, were standing at the gallery and where all the woods lay clustered, and from whence, like the spectators, they had a more equal vision. And instead of a burst of applause there was an uncomfortable silence. Suffolk seemed uncertain how to answer, and Norfolk, the time server, gave no ruling.

Anne watched her cousin Thomas step swiftly towards the jack. On soft, heelless shoes, he picked his way between the other bowls, concentrating upon his own and the King's. He glanced up questioningly at Norfolk, and silently, reluctantly, Norfolk nodded.

"'Tis only a game, God send he keeps his mouth shut! For whatever comes of this will be my fault," prayed Anne, in panic.

She sprang up, her fingers clutching at the window sill, as Wyatt's voice cut the silence. "By your leave, sir, it is not," he said courteously, but without hesitation.

A gasp went up at his temerity and the heated pages stood all agog. Anne saw the frown gather on Henry's brow, saw him come striding towards the end beneath the gallery. It was significant that neither man appealed to the umpire, as they normally would have done. Clearly, it was a matter to be settled between themselves. And herself the reason. Even the most insensitive or casual onlooker must by now be aware of that fierce undercurrent of hostility between them.

Halfway across the green Henry stopped and pointed. "Wyatt, I tell you it is mine," he affirmed, with an attempt at conciliatory reasonableness.

But Wyatt stood in respectful silence, patently unconvinced.

Why, why must he be such a foolhardy idealist? Offering himself as her knight. Trying at this late hour to tilt against the attempt upon her virtue, or to shield her tarnished name!

And then Anne saw the sun sparkle on the ring on Henry's pointing ringer—*her* ring, which Wyatt must inevitably recognize, since he knew her trinkets much as he knew the jewels in his own verse. The small, private drama was played out immediately beneath her window, so that she could see the expression of their faces. She saw Henry point again. She saw him go slowly, calculatingly closer, until his outstretched finger was almost under his daring subject's handsome nose. "Wyatt, I tell you it is mine!" he repeated dangerously.

Anne knew it was not the game they cared about so passionately, but herself.

She sensed the exact moment when Wyatt's eye fell with realization upon the flashing thing—saw him go white and draw, himself suddenly erect, shivering a little like a thoroughbred, as he took the blow against his constant heart. What would he do? Or say? Any other man, she knew, he would have struck or challenged.

One could not strike the King.

Not a man moved. The whole assembly held their breath, aghast that one of their number should defy the Tudor, in such a mood, about what seemed so trivial a thing.

"Measure them, then!" snapped Henry.

But before Norfolk could do anything about it, Anne saw her cousin's hand go to the opening of his shirt and bring forth the gold pomander chain that he had once filched from her to stake his claim against another lover, and which he always wore. The jewelled initials, A.B., dangling from the end of it, flashed in the sunlight too. Ostentatiously, he stretched it to its full length, before the King's darkening gaze. "If it pleases your Majesty to give me leave to measure the cast with *this*, I have good hopes yet it will be mine," he said coolly.

Anne's whole heart cried out to him. "Oh, Thomas! Thomas! And I taunted you that you would not risk the King's displeasure for my sake!"

She felt Margaret Wyatt's hand clutch at hers, heard poor Margaret's frightened sob.

For a moment it looked to both of them as if Henry, in his jealous fury, would fell Thomas to the ground. But Wyatt looked him unflinchingly in the face, before turning with the chain taut between his hands to measure the relative distance of each wood from the jack.

"Mine is the nearer, an' it please your Grace, by two links' length," he announced quietly; and Norfolk could not, before so many bystanders, deny it.

Blind with fury, Henry found himself in the position of a taunted lover. Yet outwardly nothing had been done amiss. Wyatt had been too subtle for him. Upon Wyatt the gods had showered all their gifts, it seemed—wit, genius, beauty—and, most indubitably, courage. He had everything that would make a woman love him. And, above all, his body had not thickened, and he was on the right side of thirty!

He had known Anne Boleyn all her life. Had called her "pretty coz" and kissed her when he liked. Among those tempting yew arbours at Hever. "God knows what intimacies she has allowed him!" fumed Henry, in the coarseness of his uncomprehending heart and the frustration of the intimacies he was still denied.

Meeting his courtiers' covert stares, he made an effort to gather his public manner like a mummer's cloak about him. And to accept defeat decently. "It may be so," he allowed, haughtily to Wyatt. "But if you have the advantage of me, then have I been deceived."

Curtly, he thanked Thomas Howard for umpiring, and dismissed the pages. Spurning his offending wood with his shoe, he kicked it aside into the gulley. Then left the green and strode alone to his apartments. But not before he had lifted sheepish eyes to the window where Anne stood, and she had read in them miserable uncertainty as well as anger.

She knew exactly how he felt.

Instead of showing her what a fine fellow he was, he had been made to look an unsportsmanlike clod. By a subject who was less accommodating than the Blounts or the Boleyns.

It was the first time any of them had stood up to him when he, King Henry the Eighth of England, had wanted a woman from their family.

Chapter Twenty-Two

T HE VIANDS ON THE supper table grew cold and, for all her anxiety, Anne grew hungry. "The King will not come now," prophesied Margaret.

"I tell you he will!" snapped Anne. "Have them bring in some brushwood and light a fire."

Up and down her fine room she walked, the ivory beads of her rosary clicking and swinging from her girdle as she went, stopping only when Will Brereton found time to look in for a moment to tell her that his Majesty had supped with the Queen.

"And milord Cardinal, I suppose?" questioned Anne.

Brereton tarried just long enough to glance out at the swiftly flowing Thames. "Wolsey is not yet back from Westminster, and his bargemen will have still going against this tide. It is thought the King will not wait up for him." As a silvery clock chimed somewhere he hurried away. "It wants but a quarter to nine, and I should be on duty with Weston in the bedchamber," he excused himself.

"It was a terrible risk to take, trying to make his Grace jealous!" expostulated Margaret Wyatt, as soon as they were alone again.

"Those who take no risks arrive nowhere," Anne told her tersely.

"Please God, it bodes no ill for poor Thomas," murmured Margaret; and that was the nearest she ever came to recrimination.

Anne's friends were very loyal to her.

She stooped to warm her hands at the new, crackling blaze. "Don't fret so, Margot," she encouraged, with a confidence she was far from feeling. "Let me but see Henry for a moment and I will right the world for Thomas!"

"But how can you hope that he will come after this morning?"

Anne turned and laughed at her. "Because of this morning he will not be able to stay away," she prophesied.

And as if to prove the truth of her boast, the door was thrown open and Henry Tudor stood there, glaring in as if he expected to find her in Wyatt's arms.

"Mistress Margaret and I are honoured," mocked Anne, making obeisance. "And mercifully, since your Grace is so precipitate, not yet undressed."

Henry neither smiled nor apologized. And at a glance from her friend, Margaret sidled past him, thankful to close the door behind her.

As he moved across the room, Henry's searching eyes never left Anne's face. "I must talk with you before I sleep," he said abruptly. His rings and gold chain had been taken off. Obviously, he had been to his room, intending to go to bed in dudgeon, and the turmoil of his caring had in the end driven him back to her.

Anne could think of nothing to say. The relief of seeing him was so great. She had only *made* herself believe in her own power—made herself believe that he would come.

Her heart-shaped face had grown white with strain, and she passed a hand across her brow. "I will readily tell your Grace anything," she offered. "But I—oh, Henry, I am so *hungry!*"

None of her usual clear-cut, calculated phrases could have served her better. He almost pushed her into a chair, awkwardly patting her shoulder as if she were a starving child. "Eat then," he ordered, with exasperation. "You were a fool to wait."

"I hoped and prayed that you would come!"

He lifted the lid from some spiced lampreys, sniffed appreciatively, and helped her lavishly with his own hands. Then set a cold capon before her. "Carve it for me, Henry! Let's not call the servants," she entreated, seeing that the homely occupation was already beginning to make his heroics look foolish.

Silently, expertly, he obeyed. The last thing he wanted was to call the servants. Heaven knew, it was seldom enough he got her alone! And the spiced dish compote smelt so good he wished he hadn't supped. Katherine had been a bundle of injured self-righteousness, and the food, brought all the length of the great hall, half cold. Whereas here—Extravagant wench, to order a fire in June! But how homely it looked. With the one woman he wanted sitting there eating her supper like any squire's wife. He leaned across and poured her a glass of his own Burgundy. And when she had drunk it the colour came back into her cheeks, which was the one thing needful to make her ravishing.

When Anne judged that the edge of his anger was blunted, she rose and faced him across the table. "You were gravely displeased about the gold pomander chain," she stated, carrying the war into the enemy's camp.

"You must have given it to him," he accused, sullenly.

Anne moved the stem of the Venetian glass round and round, weaving patterns on the linen cloth. And Henry, fascinated, watched her tapering fingers. "He is my cousin," she explained, with a reminiscent smile. "As you know, we have always lived within a few miles of each other. He and Margaret played with us when we were children. We all loved each other so much that, when we were too young to have money, we were wont to *make* each other gifts."

"But not the kind of gift a man delights to wear against his naked skin," growled Henry.

Anne saw that she must pick her words more carefully. "In twenty-five years I must have given Thomas Wyatt a variety of things," she agreed. "But not that chain."

"I saw the initials. And the meaning way he held it to enrage me."

"Oh, I do not deny that it was mine. But he filched it from me one day at Greenwich."

"You mean, before I—"

Anne had an enchanting way of looking up suddenly at anyone she was talking to, and her eyes sparkled at him, warmly as the wine. "Before you noticed me. While I was busy at my embroidery frame he tweaked it from my belt—" She had been going to say "To tease me," but suddenly the bolder words slipped into her brain. Words which were difficult to say, but which would make the King trust her and draw his grudge from Wyatt. "To annoy another man whom I preferred," she substituted.

Henry pushed aside a chair unseeingly and came closer, his eyes hot on hers. "So you made Wyatt jealous, too, poor devil?"

Anne made no answer, content to observe that jealousy was veering from the particular to the general.

"There must always have been men here and in France."

Anne lowered her lashes and endured his persistence. "Could I help it?" she murmured modestly.

He stared down at the curve of her cheek and the white division of her breasts visible beneath the straight, low-cut bodice of her gown. "No, damn you!" he allowed at last.

He stamped angrily to the hearth and stood there, kicking a charred ember into a shower of sparks. Then swung round on her again, and caught her watching him. He could almost have sworn that he had detected a fleeting smile. "The man you baited *him* with—that was Northumberland's young whelp whom I caught you with at Greenwich, I suppose?"

Anne's head shot up, and all suspicion of amusement died. "Yes."

"And I dealt with him. He's out of the reach of your wiles. Bedded with Shrewsbury's daughter."

"Yes," said Anne again, without flinching, defending with a calm assumption of indifference the only man she had ever loved.

"But Wyatt," Henry began pacing back and forth again, goaded by miserable uncertainty. "He is still here, under the spell of those witch's eyes of yours, and he has always wanted you. Your step-mother favours him. He was always about at Hever. Playing 'Catch as catch can' about the staircases, winter evenings, no doubt. Reading you his cursed poems in the walled garden. He has had every opportunity. Did he—?" Quite suddenly Henry Tudor's jealous fury broke up, leaving him utterly vulnerable. He seized Anne's hands, kissing them again and again. "Oh, Nan, Nan, don't you see?" he pleaded. "You and he are both young and I am nearly middle-aged. You don't know what it is to lose one's youth and still love ardently."

Compassionately, because he was being sincere to the point of self-depreciation, Anne pressed the palm he had been caressing across his mouth. She would not hear his humiliation, nor did she make any pretence of misunderstanding what he wanted to know. "No, he never has," she said.

Henry caught her to him in a transport of gratitude. "Swear it, sweetheart! Ever since that game this forenoon I have feared that I have been deceived."

"I swear it, Henry."

He laughed a little, apologetically, already embarrassed by the crudity of his own behaviour. "You see, my heart's darling, I had to be sure. All the more, because I am King, I couldn't take another man's leavings."

Anne's left hand groped among the folds of her skirt for the feel of her rosary. "I am not forsworn! Though he be in truth deceived, I have not lied," she told her bargaining soul. God be thanked, he had put the question of her chastity only in that way! Seeking time to steady herself, she moved to a table by the window where her private casket stood. Lifting a key from the chain about her waist, she unlocked it, revealing a pile of letters.

And Henry, peering over her shoulder, had the satisfaction of seeing that they were his own. "Fond little fool! So you have kept them all," he chided, tweaking her ear, well pleased. But as Anne lifted them, searching for something else, the sight of his seal must have curbed his vanity with caution. Shrewd Welshman as he was, he glanced at her askance. "They are not for prying eyes," he warned her, recalling certain amorous passages. "Better burn them, poppet."

But Anne hugged them to her breast, and her laughter sounded quite spontaneous. "Oh, Henry, are all men so stupid? To destroy a girl's love letters so that she cannot nourish her love by rereading them."

"Do you reread them, Nan?"

"Over and over by candlelight in bed."

"Why waste your time?" guffawed Henry shamelessly. "I know of better ways to nourish love in bed."

But Anne had found what she wanted. It was not his letters she had meant to show him. She wanted to prove to him Wyatt's integrity beyond all future doubt. She, too, was loyal to her friends. "Thomas never comes here now. He knows that I am yours," she said. "But sometimes, as you should know, a man's jealousy overmasters him. You must forgive him, Henry. Here is his beautiful farewell to me."

She held out to him Wyatt's latest verses, letting him read them through in silence. And presently, touched and ashamed, he read parts of them aloud.

> "*Of such a truth as I have meant . . .*
>
> *Forget not, oh! forget not this,*
> *How long ago hath been and is*
> *The love that never meant amiss . . .*
>
> *Forget not yet thine own approved,*
> *The which so constant hath thee loved,*
> *Whose steadfast faith hath never moved . . .*
> *Forget not yet, forget not yet.*'

"Poor Wyatt!" he said. "It is the heartbreak of a man who wanted you as desperately as I do."

Anne drew her ripe mouth into a hard, purposeful line. "But he wanted to marry me. He is that sort of man," she said, locking parchment and letters away.

When she turned round the King was regarding her in a new, strange way. "Anne, I am that sort of man, too," he said, not to be outdone. But almost immediately he qualified it. "I would marry you tomorrow if I could."

Though her heart knocked in her breast, Anne was clever enough not to pursue the subject. But the seed was sown.

He seated himself before the fire and drew her onto his knee. After letting him fondle her in silence for a few minutes, she had the temerity to ask what had first made him think of divorcing the Queen.

"It was when our daughter was but a few years old and we were arranging a marriage for her with the little Dauphin. Morett, the French Ambassador, began making difficulties; and I found that France looked upon Mary as illegitimate because I had taken my deceased brother's wife. At first I was furiously angered. And then, as each son I begat upon her died at birth, I began to think they must be right. And that God was punishing me."

"And then?"

"When my conscience could no longer bear it I spoke to Wolsey about it, and to the bishops, and to learned men like Sir Thomas More. More would give no opinion, and there are evil-minded persons who suggest that it is because I would be rid of Katherine for the sake of my own light desires, because she is eight years older than I. But even Wolsey, who is devoted to the Queen, agrees that somehow I must get an heir for England."

Wolsey would agree to anything, at the easy expense of a woman's happiness, thought Anne.

"These last few years must have been grievous for you," she said, encouraging the King's self-pity. "But now that you have sent the Archbishop of Canterbury to plead with his Holiness in Rome, and milord Cardinal is going to see King Francis, surely you will soon be free."

"Free to marry a French princess!" grimaced Henry, who for months had been moving Heaven and earth to do so.

"And will your new bride have to live beneath the disapproving shadow of Spain as I do?" teased Anne.

Henry was only too pleased to speak of something which he had so far avoided discussing even with his Chancellor. Most people, he found, were so touchy about what happened to Katherine. "I have had it in mind to set up a separate establishment for the Queen at Richmond, where we both lived with my parents before she married my brother Arthur. It is, in a sense, our Tudor dower house."

"She will not go back to Aragon?"

"Nothing will persuade her to. And, in truth, I—" It sounded weakly inconsistent to say that, when it came to the point, he did not wish her to, that she had been his background and his sustaining companion for so long. "I must do everything possible to avoid war," he concluded, rather lamely.

"And your daughter, the lady Mary's grace?"

"Mary can visit her," said Henry, magnanimously.

Anne lay back against his encircling arm, but presently, realizing it was high time to put another distracting thought into his head, she began to giggle.

"Why do you laugh, sweetheart?" he asked, feeling the shaking of her body beneath his urgent hands.

"Oh, 'tis nothing," trilled Anne. "Only last night at cards her Grace said the oddest thing. About marriage and you, I mean."

"And what was it?" asked Henry, curious, but not much caring.

"After I had turned up the winning card, she said, 'Nothing less than a *Queen* will do for Mistress Anne!'"

Henry's ardour slackened. Katherine's opinion, it seemed, still counted for a good deal. "You mean *she* had considered it *possible?*"

"Oh, I did not hear her say it," answered Anne, playing for safety. "I but repeat what my sister-in-law told me."

Henry got up, almost pushing her from his knee. "But everybody knows that I must marry someone of royal blood," he muttered, in great perturbation of mind.

Anne drew herself up haughtily, and faced him across the hearth. Compared with kind-hearted, dumpy Katherine, she looked arrestingly regal. Merchant as her great-grandfather was, through her Howard mother, Bigods and Mowbrays, all of them part of England, had poured into her that pulsing blood, bequeathed her those tapering fingers, that proud carriage and that grace. "Is there any blood more royal than Plantagenet?" she asked quietly, reminding him of the lineage which each of them, through their mothers, shared.

Never had she looked more beautiful, more fit to be a queen. Even Katherine had acknowledged the possibility. And from the two attenuated streams of Plantagenet blood a future King of England might be born, wiping out the uneasy stain of a usurping house. Henry looked at her and knew that he must have her. As more than a mistress. As a wife and Queen.

But Anne was not yet sure of him. 'Reculer pour mieux sauter' was to be her watchword. "Your new French wife will not want me here when she comes," she teased.

"It will not be what she wants," frowned Henry.

"She may be less complacent than Queen Katherine. She may be young and clinging," went on Anne, passing so close to him that the French scent she used was a seduction in his nostrils. Her laughter was low and mocking, and her eyes deep and black as night. "I had best go back to Hever, Henry, for she will expect you in her bed every night."

He threw out an arm to intercept her, but she eluded him. "You jade, to taunt me!" he cried. "You, who have never yet been there yourself!"

Lissom as a waving branch, she escaped him. With all the glamour that was in her she was fighting some unknown woman in France. A little crazed, she caught up a lighted candle in its silver sconce. Holding it aloft with one hand, and her outspread skirt with the other, she began to dance—beckoning and billowing, as if weaving some fantastic incantation around him; so that he turned as she turned, and ever and anon grasped for her, as for some Fata Morgana, yet found her forever out of his reach. "Will your French wife dance as I do? Will she make you laugh? Will she sing your songs as I do, Henry?" she panted, as she whirled. And when he could stand her witchery no longer and caught her, candle and all, in his arms, she only laughed the more wildly, so sure of her power that she could afford to court danger. "And will all her clinging burn you as my lightest touch?" she demanded, straining from him as he kissed her white throat and half bare breasts.

He would have had her then, had she not held the naked flame between them.

"For God's sake, Nan, you will burn us both!" he cried. It was the first time he had had to struggle with a woman for his will. It booted him nothing that he was a King.

"Thomas Wyatt risked your wrath for me this forenoon," she taunted. "And you, the all-powerful Tudor, are afraid to marry the woman you want. Afraid of Wolsey and a pack of statesmen!"

Her cruel comparison caught him on the raw, wringing from him at last the promise she wanted. "By God, I am not! Let me but get my divorce, and I will marry you!"

With an oath and a yelp of pain, he clamped his hand to his chin, where his red-gold beard was singeing. And swift as a cat, Anne took advantage of the partial release.

"You will get me no other way!" she defied him, pulling her torn dress up about her shoulders, and running to the door.

Chapter Twenty-Three

WITHIN A FEW DAYS Henry was standing with Anne on the wide steps leading up to the great hall at Hampton, watching the preparations for the Cardinal's departure. They and the whole Court were the Cardinal's guests; and within the hour Wolsey would be setting forth to persuade King Francis to wring a divorce from the Pope with a marriage between Henry and the Duchess d'Alençon as the bait. His well-fed, restive horses and sleek, crimson-trapped mules made a brave show in the morning sunlight.

"Forty liverymen in crimson velvet. A score of handsome priests to escort his silver cross before him. Cavendish running hither and thither to assemble them. And God knows how many gentlemen of his household to follow after," counted Anne.

"They should impress the French," chuckled Henry, thrusting his hands into the jewelled belt that spanned his girth, and strutting importantly where he stood.

"And the hat!" breathed Anne, with a wicked similitude of reverence. "The scarlet, tasselled hat borne aloft and bowed to almost as if it were the Host!"

"That, too, should give us prestige," agreed Henry, without perceiving her malice.

Anne slipped a hand through his arm and lowered her voice. "It has always been in my mind to ask you, Henry—is it true that when the hat was first brought from Rome, Wolsey caused tapers to be lighted about it?"

The King laughed, and squeezed her hand against his side. Like her young rip of a brother, she always had some new amusing tale to tell. "If he did, I never heard of it," he answered, making a mental note to twit Wolsey with it. But he spoke a little absently, his mind more on the man's mission than on his headgear.

"Being a King, I suppose you do not always hear things," condoled Anne, assuming an engaging air of sympathy.

"Beshrew thee, girl, am I not in a position to hear more than most men?" snorted Henry, who had spent a tedious morning with his Council. But after a moment or two of her submissive silence, curiosity prevailed. "What manner of things do you mean?" he deigned to enquire.

"Oh, not matters of any import," she hastened to assure him. "Just small amusing things that are common knowledge, but which even people who enjoy your affection would scarcely think fit to repeat to you."

"Not fit? God's breath, girl, am I an ogre with no sense of humour?"

"Then I see I must be your harbinger." Anne began to hum a lively little tune, and glanced up at him mischievously. "Has *that* tune come to your Grace's ears?"

"It has a catchy air," allowed Henry, who hated to be baffled by a melody.

"'Tis a ridiculous little *rien du tout* the Londoners sing about the Cardinal's hat." Because her dancing feet could in no wise keep still where there was any sort of rhythm, she began tapping it out on the stone step, and with diabolical gift of mimicry caught the very accents of an Eastcheap 'prentice.

> '*While's the red hat both endure*
> *Proud Wolsey makes himself cocksure.*'

"They do not love him overmuch, do they, Henry?"

"They have every reason to love him, considering the hours he spends in their stinking courts striving to show even the smallest shopkeeper justice," reproved Henry, loving her all the same for her gamin gaiety.

"With a herb-stuffed orange held delicately to his fastidious nose against the plague."

"You should show more respect for your betters, sweetheart," laughed Henry.

As he bent to caress a pair of his favourite hounds recently uncoupled from the kennels, Anne's flexible voice took on a more serious tone. "But, of a truth, Henry, it irks me that they should so sharpen their envious wit on one whom you esteem so highly. My brother says there is some low rhymester who is forever railing against his Eminence in the streets and taverns."

"A jailbird, no doubt. When men bear a grudge like that it is usually found that the dignitary they deride has, at some time or other, had occasion to punish them," Henry told her.

"I doubt not your Grace is right," agreed Anne. "Else why should this poet be so envious of milord Cardinal's magnificence? He makes a kind of roundelay, so that the very potboys are singing it. 'Why come you not to Court?' he exhorts some imaginary sprigs of nobility. And then, mincingly, as if they had answered him in doubt, 'To which Court? To the King's Court? Or to Hampton Court?' And when people of the baser sort encourage his satire with their laughter he pretends to show how, by the richness of its treasures and its opportunities, Hampton eclipses Westminster."

Henry frowned, and his mouth pursed roundly. "You did right to tell me," he commended. "I will find out who he is and have the presumptuous fellow whipped naked through the streets so that the Londoners may see where such ignorant insinuations lead them."

Anne knew quite well who the poet was, and he had her esteem and sympathy; but she was enjoying the ease of her own guile. All the same, when Henry invited her to dine with their host before his departure, she hung back a little. There was something very impressive about Wolsey, and it would be the first time she had sat at the dais table with him.

"The Queen keeps her room," added Henry, misinterpreting the cause of her hesitation. "She has been high-stomached with me this last week because she mistrusts Wolsey's mission."

"Unless she were a complete fool, how could she *not* mistrust it?" thought Anne.

"Well, sweetheart, are you not coming to wish Thomas Wolsey Godspeed and a happy denoucement for both our sakes?"

But Anne still lingered, although the King held out a hand to escort her.

"When my father was Ambassador to France he was wont to say that the Cardinal enjoyed snaring foreign statesmen into an alliance as most men enjoy the chase." Anne lowered her voice, with a wary eye on the waiting pages. "Would it not be better to leave it at that? Might he not ply his wits the better were he in ignorance of our intent?"

The green Tudor eyes began to twinkle. "You mean let him exploit Francis in good faith? Believing that I mean to go through with this French marriage."

"Would it not be kinder to his ecclesiastic conscience?"

Seeing that Henry was beginning to bluster and knowing how he would hate to take advice from a woman, Anne hurried on with what she had to say. "All the more because he thinks but disparagingly of me. When you spoke flatteringly of me when you were first come from Hever, saying, in fond foolishness, that my wit and beauty were worthy of a crown, did he not look down that long nose of his and say, 'It is sufficient if your Majesty finds her worthy of your passing fancy!'"

Henry stared at her and reddened. After all this time, the irritation of having his enthusiasm pricked like a schoolboy's came back to him. "Yes, it is true," he admitted, "and very like a pedagogue he said it! Though I know not how you came by his words."

Being loyal to her friends, Anne did not enlighten him. "It is not for an inexperienced woman like me to meddle in such matters, but for your Grace to do as seems best," she apologized, knowing full well that she had meddled quite successfully enough for one morning.

As they entered their host's crowded hall Anne knew that all eyes were upon her; and that when the tall, portly Cardinal came from his canopy of state to meet them, Henry was as anxious as any young swain for her to make a good impression. For the first time he was producing her openly before the minister who ruled both church and state, whose opinion he had always valued. Producing her as his mistress. And as the King's mistress Wolsey received her, according her just that right degree of esteem which was consonant with his duty to the Queen, and enriching the occasion with all the tactful resources of his suave worldliness.

"As a plaything I am probably welcome—to keep Henry occupied while he, the master statesman of Europe, works out his own brilliant schemes," Anne concluded shrewdly, looking into the brown, probing eyes and listening with unwilling admiration to the assured, cultured voice. But he had not looked like this, standing in his London hall, watching with drooping eyelid and curling lip while Northumberland baited his son and heir. Although Wolsey had been serving the King then as now, Anne chose to ignore the fact, and threw Henry an approving, conspiratorial glance. "And for all butcher Wolsey's fine statesmanship, he does not know that this time it is *we* who are fooling *him*!" she thought.

And the thought restored her confidence.

If Henry had feared that she would be either gauche or over-haughty, he had underestimated her manners, which matched the Cardinal's own. With pretty deference she listened to the great prelate's words, pleasantly aware that her assumption of shyness was calling forth all Henry's protective chivalry. She praised the master cook's *chef d'oeuvre*, a sweetmeat confection fashioned in the form of a chessboard complete with bishops, knights and pawns; and admired the Cardinal's priceless tapestries, and gold plate. Particularly she admired the set of gold plate which, over and above the vessels in use at table, was set out in shining splendour upon the shelves of a great carved sideboard, catching the glint of heraldic glass so that the whole hall seemed ablaze with light. The gold plate was always set out for royalty. Habitués of Hampton noticed it only with a sort of shared, complacent pride and the King was accustomed to seeing it there. It was only now, for the first time, while the artless questions of a newly exalted maid-of-honour dwelt so persistently upon the value of each piece, that he began to realize that Wolsey's collection was more rare and costly than his own. Vexatiously lending point to that absurd roundelay she had been humming.

Usually, nothing pleased Wolsey more than to talk to someone intelligent about his treasures, enhancing his prestige by telling how everyone on the Continent, from the Doge of Venice to the rich Flemish merchants, had sent or sold him works of art to curry favour. But soon his keen social sense warned him of an uncomfortable restraint, and he fell to talking of the previous day's doings instead.

"A long day, I fear, my dear Thomas, since you were home so late," observed Henry.

"So diligent for the well-being of the realm," smiled Anne.

Shaking off some indefinable stirrings of anxiety, Wolsey plunged with relief into a witty account of some of the more interesting Chancery court proceedings. And like all astute men discussing their own calling, he was well worth listening to.

"'Twas but this very day his Grace remarked how well the Londoners should love you," encouraged Anne.

"At least they know I am no respecter of persons," smiled Wolsey, complacently.

"As was well proved when your Eminence passed sentence upon Sir Amyas Paulet, confining him within his own precincts for seven years, although he be Treasurer of the Middle Temple," offered an ill-advised but enthusiastic chaplain.

By the sharp way Wolsey frowned at him Anne gathered that this had been one of the cases he had *not* intended to discuss and Henry, who knew and liked the defendant, looked up with a chicken bone poised between his forefingers. "A severe sentence, surely," he commented. "What was the offence?"

"Oh, the usual heresy charge of encouraging Lutheran leanings. He was found to have a copy of Tyndale's Scriptures in his possession and to be lending it round among young law students," answered Wolsey, a shade too negligently; and excused himself dexterously from the conversation by giving some order to a passing servant.

"That must have pleased the rabble—all the more so because he is not a Londoner," said George Boleyn, whose tongue was nearly as privileged as that of Will Somers, the King's jester.

Anne asked where the unfortunate knight came from. She had a vague recollection of having heard something about him before.

"From Limington, in Somerset," answered Henry, who had an excellent memory for such things.

Sir Amyas Paulet of Limington. Anne's glance passed down the length of the table and rested consideringly upon Cavendish. And as if by some strange coincidence, Wolsey's gentleman usher looked up at her at the same moment. Clearly, the name had evoked some shared experience. Anne, too, had a long memory; and she was certain that Cavendish, himself a Somerset man, hoped she had not. For was it not he who, idling away an unconsidered hour at Greenwich, had regaled his friend, Harry Percy, with discreditable stories of their patron's less reputable days? Sir Amyas Paulet of Limington. No wonder the name had a familiar ring. For had she not last heard it on her lover's lips while he dug up everything of ill report about the man they both hated?

"For setting so bad an example to his flock your Eminence should have put him in the stocks," she said lightly. And had the satisfaction of seeing blood no less scarlet than his papal silk mount to the Cardinal's pendulous and sallow cheeks. With a charming little gesture of apology, she smiled back into his hard and anxious eyes. "But I had forgotten—of course you could not do that to a gentleman."

How right Henry had been! About people trying to get their own back when someone had once had occasion to punish them. And thus early in the game Chance had delivered a useful card into her expert hand. A shiver of excitement ran through her veins. She had little power as yet, but she had the King's ear,

But the horses were waiting, and the Cardinal had lifted his hand in blessing. "The sooner I reach Dover the better I can serve my King," he said, with an effective blend of efficiency and court-liness. And before moving to a window overlooking the inner courtyard, Henry slid a costly ring from his own finger to his host's, and embraced him. And Wolsey, on his side, made graceful acknowledgement of Anne's status. "I entreat your Grace to treat my manor as your own for as long as it may please your Grace and the lady to stay," were his parting words.

Already he was seeking to propitiate her, because she knew that when he was a young parish priest Sir Amyas Paulet had put him in the stocks for drunkenness.

And, with Hampton glistening in the sunshine and Queen Katherine glooming in her apartments, it pleased them very well to stay.

All afternoon Henry forgot his own prowess and took pleasure in instructing Anne at the archery butts; and after supper they strolled through the Cardinal's privy garden and beneath the pleached elms down to the river. To Anne it seemed the loveliest place, with the throstles warbling their evensong and the sweet-scented stocks glimmering in the trimly divided flower beds. A great harvest moon was rising over Moulsey meadows and the lanterns at the prows of barges made splashes of rippling light upon the water. And presently Henry drew her to a stone bench beside a sequestered lily pond.

"Of a truth, this is pleasanter than any of your own palaces," murmured Anne, nestling close against him.

"And finer," admitted Henry, looking back at the silhouette of towers and pinnacles and chimneys grouped in homely loveliness against a primrose evening sky.

"Two hundred and eighty bedrooms!" persisted Anne. "And you do not mind?"

"Mind?" he laughed carelessly. "Why should I mind? The place and Wolsey's lavish hospitality are the talk of European Courts. When foreign ambassadors arrive, they come straight here. It impresses them with our wealth and power, my little wench, so that we can make better terms. Good showmanship, Nan!"

"But would it not be more seemly if they came to Westminster or Greenwich and heard *your* wishes *first*?"

Anne guessed that she was only putting into words what Henry must sometimes, subconsciously, have felt. "As to that," he answered, a trifle testily, "Thomas and I understand each other."

"It was generous of him to lend his country home—all the more so because, with this new water supply he has had piped beneath the Thames, the place must be almost immune from plague," Anne hastened to agree. "And, ah me! it is so beautiful I should like to live here always."

"With me?"

"Is it not fit for a King?" she teased.

"Then you take back what you said in that fine tantrum last night? That I should get you in no other way than marriage."

Anne only shook her head.

"Is not everything here set for us, my love?" he urged.

"But how much wiser to wait until Francis and Wolsey between them have had time to persuade the Pope."

"You would always have me wait for something."

He withdrew his arm in anger and, freed, she stood before him, earnest and reasonable, outlined against the Palace he already coveted. "But do you not see, Henry, that if you really mean to marry me—to put me in so pious a woman's place—his Holiness will want to know something about me. The first thing all these solemn convocations of priests will ask will be 'Has this lady led a virtuous life?' The last thing they must suppose is that we are already living together in sin. It would destroy your arguments, about your conscience troubling you with regard to your first marriage and your only wanting a legitimate heir for the realm's sake."

Henry leaned forward and took her hands, grinning up at her ruefully. "For my own peace of mind I sometimes wish, my darling, that you were less beautiful and more stupid," he complained, half-jestingly.

And Anne laughed back at him fearlessly. "You know that you do not. You know that you enjoy my companionship," she challenged. "But surely it is beginning to be manifest, even to your impatience, that in order to gain our hearts' desire it may be worthwhile to wait?"

"So it is your heart's desire, too?"

He sprang up and drew her close. The gathering dusk dealt kindly with the grosser lines which had begun to mar his good looks. His ways were virile and possessive. And in this yielding mood and betrayed by the magic of the evening, Anne found herself answering his hot passion with her own. Half-conquered, she abandoned herself to the strength of his arms, allowing herself the luxury of his experienced kisses. Enjoying the ardour of a man again. But Anne was no fool. She knew that, though Henry might lavish on her the wealth of England, surrender was the one luxury she could not afford to enjoy. "If I give in to him now, he may never marry me at all," she thought, remembering her sister's discarding. She stirred uneasily, struggling against the clamouring of her senses. "Henry," she whispered, from beneath the pressure of his insatiable lips.

"What now, my sweet?"

She tilted back her head until her brilliant eyes could hold his own. "If we should have a son now, too soon to name him Tudor? Just another Fitzroy—"

Another Fitzroy was the last thing he desired. With her vivid imagination, Anne could guess at the tantalizing torment Elizabeth Blount's fine, upstanding boy must have been to him as the years passed and all his wife's male babes were stillborn. All except the poor little Prince of Wales. Anne could remember the splendid rejoicings there had been during the few weeks he had lived, the rejoicings, and then the heartbreak. Cleverly, she played upon Henry Tudor's misfortunes and his fears. For a legitimate son he would give anything, make almost any sacrifice. And he knew, perhaps, that for all his passion, potency was waning. Passion must be subdued, preserved against the day when Katherine should die, or Holy Church declare her daughter Mary bastard, and so give him this fierce, delectable woman with whom to breed an heir to carry on his line.

Gradually, his arms slackened. Even in the sweet moonlit privacy of Wolsey's garden, he suffered her to go unenjoyed.

Chapter Twenty-Four

I N SPITE OF ALL their herb pomanders and careful precautions, plague closed the Court. All through the hot summer it raged and ravaged through narrow, gable-hung London streets, festering in prurient privies and dried-up, garbage-rotten gutters. The dreadful sweating sickness.

A sharp pain in the head and heart, a profuse sweating, and, in three or four hours, Death—with scarce time for prayer or languishing.

All men feared it, and few were ashamed to show their fear. The poor, perforce, stayed in their stagnant streets; and the rich moved away. The King to his daughter's sequestered home at Hunsdon. Wolsey, with overworked constitution and weak stomach, to Hampton, where all messages from the outside world were blared through a trumpet from the far side of the moat. Katherine, not much caring except for her child, to Greenwich. And the Boleyns, who really caught the dread disease, to Hever.

George, who caught it first, went there because his wife had no mind to risk her skin nursing him; and Anne, who had been sent there by the King in order to escape it, had had it only mildly. They were two of the lucky ones who had lived. Or so they believed then. It was pleasant, having George home again, convalescing in the September sunshine. Sitting with him on the terrace, Anne lifted a mirror for the third time to scrutinize her transparent skin. "Not a blemish," she murmured. It mattered so supremely. "You see, my face is my fortune," she laughed apologetically.

"Say rather, *all* our fortunes, sweet," he corrected her. For had not their father been created Earl of Wiltshire?

They were not yet quite strong and their escape had sobered them. It was the first time the dark wings of Death had brushed near enough to make them aware of its irrevocable reality and of their own passionate attachment to life. Each of them felt older for the experience.

"It took poor Will Carey and scores of our friends and yet we have both been spared, thanks be to God," reiterated George. "And to Jocunda."

"And Dr. Butts." In sheer relief, because they were still here with the sun warm on their faces and not newly laid with their ancestors in the gloomy vault, they began to laugh, remembering the dignified physician and the pills and all the instructions Henry had sent to save them.

"The King has been very kind. You know, George, he really does *care*. Several times he has made real sacrifices for me."

"You may be sure that he has not left himself without other competent physicians. And, lest you should grow puffed up, my sweet, Jane tells me with gleeful spite that he sent the same pills and affectionate letters to Thomas Wolsey. And screeds of advice. 'Have only a small and clean company about you. Do not eat and drink too much at supper. Put apart fears and fantasies, and make as merry as you can at such a contagious season!'"

"And of course that fat spider Wolsey won't catch it at all. Oh, George, how wonderful it is being able to say anything that comes into our heads as we used to do, away from all the Court prying."

He looked down at her anxiously as she leaned against his shoulder. "You find that being the King's mistress is not the sinecure people suppose?"

"It is trying *not* to be his mistress."

"In other words, since we are both still alive, the plague has been a godsend?" he commented drily.

"I had come to the point where I could think of no more excuses. You know the warm colouring of the man!" But even in the midst of her languor she looked up, her face alight with wicked amusement. "In the heavy toils of his last embrace, I had the wit to mention lightly that one of my women was abed with a strange kind of sweating fever. I had thought to find *myself* in bed with Henry Tudor. But never has lover unhanded me so quickly! *Et me voici*—"

Once again, because it was so good to be alive, they both laughed immoderately. "And, for my sins, when he had sent me home I found that one of Jocunda's poor dairymaids really *was* dying of it. And I caught it." Suddenly grave, Anne stretched out a hand and laid it on his arm as if to assure herself that he really had been spared. "Tomorrow, while you are still with us, we must have a special Mass sung in thanksgiving."

They sat for a minute or two in companionable silence. And presently, after looking sharply round to make sure that no gardener was working within earshot, the young Earl of Rochford began to speak of something which had moved him deeply, and all the more so since he had come so close to death. "Nan, I have a printed copy of the Bible in English from the press of this man Tyndale."

Anne sat up, all interest at once. "Jocunda has seen one. Her friends read aloud from it. I would give anything to borrow it."

"If you will take the utmost care of it, I will lend you mine."

"Not here?"

"No. When you return to Court."

"It is meet that people *should* read and think for themselves, George, and not have just what is doled out to them by priests like Wolsey, who have lived no better than the rest of us. To read the very words of our Lord for ourselves—the whole story of His Life— must be thrilling."

"Indeed, I found it so. I could not put the Book down. It is more full of drama and humanity than anything I had ever imagined. It puts our puny plays and verses to shame. Even the translated words are more beautiful than anything we have ever read in any language. Listen, Nan. '*I will lift up mine eyes unto the hills from whence cometh my help.*' And then again, '*Greater love hath no man than this, that he lay down his life for his brother'*." Young Boleyn's gaze lingered lovingly upon the soft rounded hills and burnished beeches. His susceptible, searching soul had been almost stunned by the sudden impact of such incredible beauty, so that the life of flatteries and intrigue into which he had been born seemed but a tarnished thing to flee from.

"How did you come by it?" whispered Anne, eager as he.

"A man called Cranmer lent it to me."

"Cranmer? It is the first time that ever I heard the name."

"But I wager it will not be the last. It is true he is but now called to Court. But he is a remarkably fine scholar. It appears that when two of the bishops who had been up at Cambridge with him were regaling him with all the latest news the conversation, as usual, turned upon the perennial subject of the Spanish divorce. They must have told him of the King's impatience with the procrastinations of Rome. And this Thomas Cranmer, whose mind moves among the portals of learning, said straight out, 'Instead of pestering a Pope who cannot afford to offend Spain, why could not his Grace appeal to the Universities of Europe for a legal decision?'"

"Surely, that is an idea as sound as it is new."

"So the King himself thought. I was with him when Bishop Gardiner told him of it. His Grace slapped his thigh and looked more jubilant than any of us had seen him in months. 'That man has the right sow by the ear!' he shouted."

Anne, too, sprang up and clapped her hands. "It will make us independent of Popes and Cardinals!" she cried exultantly. "The Tudors are always advocates of learning and I believe that, with persuasion, Henry would even agree to a Bible being put in every church."

"But do you suppose he would dare to ignore the Pope completely?"

"I believe he would dare almost anything to get me legally." Anne shook back the weight of her hair with a haughty little gesture she was acquiring. "Did I not tell you that he is getting me the lease of Suffolk House so that he can visit me from the Palace without so much scandal? And having it hung with some of the Cardinal's best tapestries. I wheedled Henry into making Wolsey see to it himself, although he must have been burdened to his drooping eyelid over all the business of the divorce."

"Nan, you are implacable! I believe that pleases you as much as having a house of your own."

Anne did not deny it. She herself was momentarily aghast, not at her implacable enmity, but that she, of all people, should find herself speaking maliciously of another's physical blemish. That, she supposed, was what a long-drawn-out hatred did to one . . .

George was not unaware of the change in her. "That being so, my love, were you wise to boast of it last week before all and sundry?" he chided, disliking her new, vain airs. "It is not like you, Nan. And Jane, you may be sure, took care that the way his plans had leaked out got back to the King's ears. Norreys warned me that he was furious, Nan, as well he might be!"

"What else is there to talk of here?" countered Anne, who had once been so contented with the country quietness of her home. But she had the grace to look abashed. "And if he *were* furious he wrote me but gently about the matter. All he said was that 'lack of discreet handling must be the cause of our arrangements being bruited abroad in London!' And that he trusts our next meeting could be arranged, not through other people's light handling, but through my own." But resentment could not flourish long before Anne's ineptitude for self-deception. "He was trying to shift the blame from me, which is more than I deserve, although he knew it was mine," she admitted pensively.

"I sometimes think he is half afraid of you," laughed George.

Anne turned and regarded him speculatively. "Were not you and Mary, too, sometimes when I wanted my own way as a child?" she probed.

George did not answer, but he knew that it was true; although he had always hated to acknowledge it, even to himself. There had been something about Anne—some passionate urgency, some glitter in her unfathomable, dark eyes—which had half scared, half hypnotized him into doing whatever she had wanted. Something which had made him stuff his ears when the servants told fireside stories of witches being burned. It was absurd, of course, to have felt that even for a moment with someone who could be so lovable.

"I am not boasting now, dear George, but just telling you," she went on more gently. "Though, God knows, most women would find it something to boast about! Henry has promised that I shall have ladies-in-waiting and a train-bearer and a chaplain of my own. And that, even though his family be there, I shall lead the Christmas revels with him at Greenwich." Excitement had painted colour on her cheeks again, and although she stopped to cough more often than he liked, her husky voice was lashed with laughter. "Whom shall I choose for my ladies?" Gaily, as though inviting him to tread a measure, she held out a hand, and together they strolled back towards the house.

"Margot Wyatt, of course," he prompted.

"And that sprightly little Savile girl who helped me get into York House. And I suppose it would be only kind to ask for Mistress Gaynesford because my equerry, George Zouch, is so desperately in love with her." Anne let go of his hand to tick them off on her fingers as she walked. "And then, I suppose, Uncle Norfolk's prim daughter, Mary Howard. What fun to dispense favours to them when they never deigned to visit us during all those years! And who else, George?"

Her brother made a wry grimace. "I am afraid convention will not spare you my lady wife," he reminded her.

But the whole prospect was too pleasant for repining. "Oh, well," sighed Anne, "at least she excels at backgammon; and it is said that all royal favourites must put up with spies in their households. You had better take Dr. Butts back to London with you, George, and see that the dear man does not succumb to the sickness himself, for if ever I bear a child I should want him with me in preference to all others."

Pausing for a moment by the sundial, George laughed indulgently. But, dazzling as the future seemed, there were moments when Fate seemed to be bearing them along too fast. "If ever you bear a child and it is the King's, Nan Boleyn, your bedside will be black with physicians," he prophesied.

"I will see that I do not bear one until I am Queen," declared Anne, her mouth setting itself into that obstinate line which he knew so well. And then, as if one thought grew out of the other, "I pray you, George, show this Cranmer some friendship; and I will suggest to our ennobled father that the man be invited here into our household."

They looked up to find their erstwhile governess waiting, sharp-eared, in the Castle doorway. "Would he be safe, think you, with this hungry spinster always at hand?" teased George, setting all the keys and scissors rattling from her girdle as they joined her.

"Would who be safe?" demanded the outraged Frenchwoman.

"A very brilliant and accommodating scholar who may prove useful in the matter of the King's divorce," Anne told her.

"But a tonsured priest," warned George, ducking to avoid retaliation from a bony hand whose strength in chastisement he had good cause to know.

"Nevertheless," laughed Anne, "I am sure that our good Simonette will work upon him for my sake."

Chapter Twenty-Five

THE PLAIN, BLACK-BORDERED CAP—not that glittering piece of frivolity," ordered Anne, in exasperation. "Have I not told you twice this morning that I am going to the city to bless cramp rings for the poor, not to Greenwich for a masque?"

Anne was late for the ceremony as it was, and Thomas Cranmer and the whole procession must be waiting for her. Perhaps, after all, she had been ill-advised to take Druscilla Gaynesford into her fine new household to please her equerry. The girl had been good company at first, with her love of books and her passion for dancing; but these last few days she had grown as clumsy and forgetful as a zany.

"God in Heaven, girl, what is the matter with you?" she cried, as Druscilla, down on the floor sewing a loose pearl to the hem of her gown, snapped the needle in two.

Druscilla did not answer, but stayed there on her knees, her blue eyes awash with tears. And Anne, dragged from contemplation of her own annoyance, noticed for the first time that, except for dark shadows which betokened lack of sleep, the girl's face was as white as parchment.

Anne had not been a maid-of-honour all these years for nothing, and suddenly her annoyance mounted to sharp suspicion. She caught at Druscilla's wrist and jerked her to her feet, so that her searching gaze could the better run over the girl's full-skirted body.

"You are not going to tell me you are pregnant, are you?" she demanded. It was too bad, after she had put herself out to be so kind to the lovers!

But Druscilla shook her head in dumb denial.

Anne let go the unresisting wrist and breathed a sigh of relief. A household as precariously respectable as her own could not afford that kind of scandal at the outset. "What is it then?" she asked sharply.

With the relief of unavoidable confession, tears came in full spate, "Oh, Madame, the book you lent me—"

"The book?" It was with horror that Anne's mind absorbed her exact meaning. "You mean my brother's Bible? Mother of God! You have not lost it?"

"It is w-worse than that," gulped poor Druscilla.

With grim deliberation, Anne put down the mirror she had been holding. Here was a matter more important than any present engagement. "But I told you to read it in private and to take the utmost care of it. Stop wringing your hands, 'Cilla, and tell me instantly what you have done with it. You know that to possess one is forbidden!"

The girl stood motionless before her. "I lent it to my betrothed," she confessed, with a sort of forlorn dignity.

"You lent it to George Zouch. And *he* lost it, I suppose?"

"It was taken from him."

"Stolen, you mean?" This was worse and worse. Her beloved brother was involved, and heresy hunters were everywhere.

"It was the Dean, in the King's chapel, Madame." Knowing that her mistress did not suffer fools gladly, Druscilla made an effort to be more calmly coherent. A touch of colour came back into her frightened face. Her mistress was angry, and with monstrous reason, but one had a feeling that she would understand. "My—George Zouch was so carried away by it that he could not put it down. He was reading the story about Dives and Lazarus *about the next world!* He took it under his cloak to vespers and knelt reading it. And the Dean must have seen him. And afterwards, as the others were leaving, George was still so engrossed that he didn't even notice until he felt a hand on his shoulder and heard the Dean saying, 'What is it that so absorbs you during Holy Office, my son?' And it was too late to hide the book then."

"And the Dean took it from him?"

Druscilla nodded in shamed assent. "He seemed very angry, and yet somehow excited," she volunteered.

"I make no doubt he was excited," said Anne grimly. For what could better serve men who were always seeking a handle against her than to stumble upon heresy in her own household? When Margaret Wyatt and Arabella Savile would have come to remind her of the time, she waved them away. "Send George Zouch to me," she ordered.

It seemed that the young man had been waiting in the anteroom.

He came forward with manly promptitude and, seeing that Druscilla had been crying, he took her hand and held it. He was a plain young man, but likeable.

"Druscilla tells me that she disobeyed me and lent you milord Rochford's Bible," accused Anne.

"By your leave, Madame, she did *not*," denied Zouch stoutly. "I seized it from her lap in sport, and though she fought like a tigress and babbled of your displeasure, I would not let her have it back."

Anne looked from one to the other of them. The girl's face was red enough now. And presently the suspicion of a smile softened her own. "You took it only to tease her?" she suggested more gently, remembering how Wyatt had once snatched at her pomander chain.

"She had been wrapped up in it for days. I could get no word or smile out of her. So I took it. I did not know what it was." Zouch dropped Druscilla's hand and stepped closer. His eyes were bright and eager. Though he lowered his voice, he spoke with respectful urgency. "Back in my own room I began reading, and it gripped me to the exclusion of all companionship or duty. You must remember, Madame, how it made all of life seem different. But I would sooner have died than endanger one you love. You have been so good to us. You do believe me, Madame?"

"Yes, I believe you." Turning, Anne slid a finger beneath his betrothed's drooping chin and raised her troubled face. "You must love him very much to lie like that," she said, with a rarely tender smile. "And what has the reverend and excited Dean done with it, do you suppose, Zouch?' she enquired, beckoning Margaret to put the finishing touches to her sober grey gown.

"He carried it immediately to milord Cardinal, who has f-for-bidden it." Zouch was very young, and the enormity of what he had done tied up his tongue.

But Anne, ready at last, swept round in regal disdain. "And who is milord Cardinal, to forbid the word of God?" she demanded, withdrawing from them completely the focus of her wrath.

The door was flung back and all the retinue Henry had promised her stood outside waiting to escort her to the city. Incapable of bearing yet more suspense, Druscilla ran to catch and kiss her hand. "And what will you do, my lady?" she entreated.

Anne's quicksilver brain had only that moment decided, but she took prayer book and herbal nosegay from the Duke of Norfolk's daughter with an air. "I will mention it to the King when he comes to sup," she answered negligently.

"Tell the King!" the guilty pair echoed, aghast.

"Before Cardinal Wolsey does." Anne knew the value of thrusting first. She laughed lightly and brushed her equerry's smoothly shaven cheek with the stiff sprigs of lavender and rosemary in passing. "You will see," she promised. "It shall be the dearest book that ever Dean or Cardinal detained."

And after supper when the cloth was drawn and Henry asked her to sing for him, she leaned against him with a pretty air of languor and begged to be excused. The ceremony of the cramp rings had exhausted her, she said. "And weeks have passed since your Grace played to *us*," she reminded him, persuasively.

Henry was nothing loath. He moved to a stool before the hearth and drew her harp between his knees, and in the cheerful glow of firelight the lovely instrument looked no more golden than his close-cropped head. Softly, experimentally, his thick white fingers began to pluck at the strings until all the room was flooded with sweet melody. His young men and Anne's maidens at the far end of the room forgot their whispered flirtations to listen. Accustomed to good music as they were, their love-making and their wagering died on their lips as they drew near, not because the harpist was King of England, but because he was one of the finest musicians in the land.

Sensing the difference between appreciation and flattery, Henry was very happy. Happy in the wistful beauty of his own creation, and in the gentle mood of the strange, elusive woman with whom he was in love. And presently, in his happiness, he began to sing. A song of his own composing, popular in hall and guardroom alike. "*Oh, western wind, when wilt thou blow?*" And as the well-known words fell from his lips, Will Somers, forgetting his jester's tricks and misshapen little body, took up the alto line in harmony with his master.

"Lovely, lovely," murmured Anne, when the last sweet note had died away. "Now sing the one you made specially for me, Harry." For the first time the family name slipped out, the name which he liked to be called by, but which she never used except for her first redheaded lover. She lay back resting in her chair. "Just for a little while, dear God, let me enjoy the passing moment, as other women may, without bestirring my wits to profit by it," she prayed.

> "*As the holly groweth green and never changeth hue*
> *So I am—ever hath been—unto my lady true*
> *From all other only to her I me betake*
> *Who hath my heart truly, be sure, and ever shall*"

sang Henry, glad to do her bidding. And this time, because he sang for her alone, even Will Somers did not dare to embellish the harmony.

Keeping oneself for one only. If only life could have been like that, instead of calculating one's caresses and slowly selling one's body! Anne sat with closed eyes, feeling the hot tears scald beneath her lashes. It must be just because she really *was* tired, because those stiff-necked Londoners had shown their resentment at her assuming one of Katherine's queenly duties. But why look weakly back when success was hardening in her grasp? The future was going to be so splendid that all other women would envy her.

She was aware of the applause and of Henry's hand warm on hers. "It is your turn now, if you are rested," he was urging. And then, quite gently, with a sort of pleased wonder, "Why, sweetheart, you are crying!"

Anne opened her eyes and smiled at him, blinking away her tears. Let him think they were for him, if it gave him any pleasure! "Your Grace knows that I cannot compete in the making of verses—only with my voice," she answered, dragging her mind back to the necessity of juggling with the present. "But a while ago I read some words that haunt me with their beauty. Verses which are worthy of your skill. Could you set them to music for me, Henry?"

He grinned down at her with humourous indulgence. "To please you, I make no doubt I could, were I permitted to know them."

Anne sat up, narrowing her eyes in apparent effort. "'*Set me a seal upon thine heart, for love is strong as death; jealousy is cruel as the grave.*'"

"Go on!" he bade her.

"'*Rise up, my love, my fair one. For lo, the winter is past, the rain is over and gone; the flowers appear on the earth; the time of the singing birds is come.*'"

Henry clapped his thigh. "Why, this would make a marvellous part song," he exclaimed. "There is a young tenor, Mark Smeaton, in the choir at Windsor who could take those lines about the singing birds and flowers. How does it go on?"

"'*Let him kiss me with the kisses of his mouth, for thy love is sweeter than wine, I am my beloved's. His hair is as the most fine gold, and his desire—his desire—*,'" floundered Anne, with a convincing show of mortification. "Alas! I cannot now remember."

He got up briskly, twirling away the rush-topped stool with an impatient hand. "But you must remember!"

Anne spread raised palms in a little French gesture, expressive of despair.

"At least you must know who wrote it?" he persisted, pacing about before the fire.

"A king."

"Ah!"

"I told you the lines were worthy of your Grace's genius," she smiled at him.

"Which king?" He swung round upon her suddenly in an absurd spurt of jealousy. "Not Francis?"

In spite of her concentration upon diplomacy, Anne laughed outright. "No, not Francis," she assured him. "Someone who was dead and gone before ever you set eyes on me. King Solomon."

Henry came and stared down at her with puzzled seriousness. "Then they must be in the Bible," he deduced.

"Yes, the Bible," she admitted.

"But they are about a love like ours. And the Holy Scriptures are about God."

"If your Grace doubts me, you could read the translation for yourself."

"I will send to Tyndale for one." And at the bare mention of the daring printer's name there came sudden metamorphosis from man to monarch against which she must always school her courage. "There is no need to do that," she said, without apparent effort. "Cardinal Wolsey has one. In his house a few yards down the Strand."

Before the words were well past her lips she was aware of her equerry's sudden tenseness and of the sharply held breath of Margaret and Druscilla. And of Henry's slow surprise.

"Wolsey?" he scowled. "But he, of all men, disapproves of the English version."

"Nevertheless, I know that he has one." Anne rose from her chair with enticing grace, and stood before him so that her eyes compelled him. Just so had the watching Margaret seen their Kentish herdsmen master dangerous blood stock. "I pray you, Henry, let us not spoil our happy evening for lack of it. Send for it now. Send Zouch, my equerry. He will, I know, prove a swift and eager runner." For the briefest instant her glance shifted mischievously beneath guarded lashes to the young man in question, making him her slave for life. "So that I may refresh my memory and your Grace devise the tune."

Henry found himself in a quandary. "Hush, Nan! Speak not so openly of having read it. The matter is dangerous," he warned uncomfortably. Greatly as he desired to read those words, he had, ostensibly at least, always upheld the Cardinal against these new Lutheran tendencies. "Parts of the Gospels and the Prophets I have already read," he admitted, blustering a little because he would not be outdone in the matter of literature by a woman. "But to borrow the Cardinal's English version on so frivolous a pretext—"

Anne's brain worked twice as quickly as his. "You could write it as an anthem," she coaxed on a ripple of warm laughter. "There is nothing frivolous about an anthem." Already she was easing the signet ring from his little finger, her touch less of a theft than a caress. "Here, Zouch!" she was calling over her shoulder to that grinning young dog of an equerry. "Take the King's ring to milord Cardinal. And listen attentively to what his Grace wishes to say."

Not even his sister, Mary Tudor, could have managed him more effectively, since in the end he imagined it was he who gave the order. And he was allowed no time for considered thought. Almost immediately the young man was speeding gratefully on his errand to York House, and Anne was improving the occasion. Still fondling Henry's hand, she drew him down beside her. "While we are waiting, shall I entertain your Grace with an amusing story of how milord Cardinal stole the book?" she offered.

"*Stole* it?"

"Yes. From one you love."

"From one I love?"

"At least, you have given me good reason to suppose so."

"Nan, what things you say!"

Beguiled by her sparkling eyes, he drew her closer, and seeing that their attendants had tactfully withdrawn, she told him about the missing Bible, with disarming candour. Never once did she stress her own danger, or her brother's. She told the story simply, as the folly of two lovers to whom she had been kind.

"It was like my own darling to forgive them," he commended, kissing her. "But if you are to be mistress in your own household, you must enforce more discipline."

Anne had her answer ready. "Was not I myself once forgiven in similar circumstances, when my cousin Thomas filched my pomander chain, and used it indiscreetly? So that I had grateful cause to learn magnanimity at its source?"

Henry pinched her cheek and chuckled, feeling himself a god.

"And well I remember," she added, "how gently your Grace chided me for some inadvertent word which betrayed our love to London gossip. And, taking the words to heart, I had it in mind to safeguard us both from the Cardinal's indiscretion. For if it were his intention to make an example of my household, as I fear it was, what unwelcome attention it would indeed have given to your Grace's private affairs."

Henry frowned with annoyance. "I had given Wolsey credit for more sense!" he growled, grudgingly allowing himself to be jolted by a new aspect of the case. And, turning to take the great Bible, he opened it before them all and began to read.

Chapter Twenty-Six

ALL WINTER THE DIVORCE proceedings dragged on. Henry Tudor and Katharine's nephew, Charles of Spain, entreated, cajoled and even threatened the distracted Pope, who could ill afford to offend either of them. Wolsey professed himself diligent in his master's behalf, while still finessing with France. Anne found herself the figurehead of a party which opposed both the power of Rome and the dominance of Wolsey, and represented the personal ambitions of her father, her uncle, and the Duke of Suffolk.

And through it all Katherine of Aragon remained adamant.

Nothing would persuade her to make things easy for Henry or for herself. Although it was years since she had cohabited with him, she would not save herself distress and indignity by retiring, with royal honours, into a convent. Henry Tudor's wife she was, and his wife she would remain. And never would she acknowledge any other woman as Queen of England. Regally, without even acknowledging Anne's existence, she had taken her place beside him in public until he actually deserted her. And now, lonely at Greenwich, she still fought singlehanded for her daughter's legitimacy, consulting with the Spanish ambassador, sending an unending spate of letters to Spain and Rome, and even managing to obtain a copy of the Papal brief which had been sent to her parents authorizing her second marriage.

But finally, against her wishes, Pope Clement had been persuaded to send another Legate to support Wolsey and decide the matter in England.

Campeggio, the Italian Legate, was a gouty old man, quite lacking in the outer graces of his English colleague. First he had produced a formidable array of carefully prepared forensic arguments in an effort to dissuade Henry from the whole business, only to find that the King of England knew more about the subject than most of his lawyers. Then he flattered Katherine into using him as her Confessor, and gained nothing more helpful than her solemn assurance that she had slept only seven nights with young, ailing Arthur Tudor and that, in spite of the lad's boastful talk, she had kept her virginity. And, after that, he even went so far as to suggest that, since Henry professed to be clamouring for divorce mainly because he had no legitimate son to succeed him, the difficulty might be solved by marrying his daughter Mary to his illegitimate son, Fitzroy!

Finally, finding it impossible to shelve the dispute, he roused himself from his various ailments sufficiently to hold a Legatine court in London. The great hall of the Blackfriars was packed with bishops and lawyers, over whom he and Wolsey presided. Katherine herself swept into court. And when the herald called "Henry, King of England" and the Tudor was forced to face her, he managed to fulfil his role with dignity. Averring lifelong affection and admiration for his wife, he dwelt upon her virtues and swore that nothing but fear of living sinfully and anxiety for the succession could make him seek to divorce her.

"And how did the Queen answer?" Anne Boleyn asked eagerly, the moment the King's party was returned from Blackfriars. She had drawn Hal Norreys apart; for Henry himself, looking neither to the right nor to the left, had gone straight to his private apartments, and she dared not approach him.

"For a few moments she said nothing. Her Grace was obviously deeply moved," answered Norreys.

"He told me what he intended to say—it was all sanctimonious policy, of course," interrupted Anne, impatiently.

But clearly Norreys had been deeply moved, too. "She got up and crossed the court. With difficulty, because of her thickening infirmity. Somehow that seemed to make it all the more dignified. She was all in black, some trailing sort of stuff that rustled as she walked. Every eye was upon her." He broke off, seemingly lost in mental contemplation of the extraordinary scene.

"And then?" prompted Anne.

"And then she went down on her knees before him. Her English was all broken up with little Spanish expressions, the way it is when she is distressed. And she was crying. She was speaking to him personally, but the court was so still we could hear every word. About all their years of happy married love, their mutual tolerance. I think she must have been thinking about Lady Blount and your— your sister, and how she forgave him. She reminded him of her obedience and devotion, and of the Princess Mary in whom they had such mutual joy. Once she spoke about their little son whom God had taken. I swear there were tears in his eyes, too."

Eaten by shame, Anne hardened her heart. "Ah, perfidious one!" she muttered, in French.

"And then the Queen seemed to remember that she was not alone with her husband, but in a court of law. She got up and looked him straight in the eyes and, raising her voice, called upon God to witness that he knew her to have been virgin when he took her."

Norreys moved to the window and stood looking out at the grey, hurrying river, almost as if he had forgotten he was not alone. He was young and generous, and his own mother was about the Queen's age. To get any more out of him Anne had to follow him and shake him by the arm. "And the King—what did the King say?"

"Nothing."

"Nothing! You mean, he didn't use this heaven-sent chance to deny it before them all?"

Norreys turned and looked at her, seeing her for the first time as strained and hard. "Perhaps he could not," he suggested.

Anne gave a little indecisive moan and let her fingers drop from his sleeve. "But he must have said *something—done* something."

"No one did anything except the Queen. She beckoned to one of her gentlemen, and leaned upon his arm, and walked away."

"And no one stopped her?"

"The King tried to. I think he must have realized that all Christendom would condemn him if he allowed judgment to be passed against her, and she not there. He bade the usher recall her. She must have heard quite distinctly what he said. But she never even looked back. She, who had never in her life disobeyed him or accorded him anything but courtesy! 'Go on, it is of no consequence,' she said casually to the man whose arm she leaned on. 'This is no impartial court to me.' And in that moment she made us remember, suddenly, that she was no subject, but a daughter of Imperial Spain. Unhurriedly, with her ladies and her two bishops following, and no man daring to detain her, she walked towards those great doors that lead out into Bridewell Palace. And the doors closed behind her. It was as if she were walking, unbeaten, out of his life." Ever since he was a page, Hal Norreys had lived close to the King, admiring his prowess and enjoying his kindly favour. But he was shaken out of all formal discretion. He and Anne moved within the same circle of friends and he had to say what he thought. "Nan, I am sure that she still loves him," he assured her, out of the complication of his own feelings, "but when she appealed to him about a thing like that and he didn't answer, I think, for the first time, she *despised* him."

Anne herself made no comment for awhile. It was as though, through her companion's eyes, she gazed upon a rival drama of which she was not the heroine. A drama which she resentfully recognized as being too big for her own tawdry technique. Katherine, of course, had been magnificent. With half her mind and soul, Anne envied her. To be able to respect oneself without reservation must compensate for a great deal, she supposed. "Please God she *has* walked out of his life at last," was all she said.

And so the Legatine negotiations, from which she had hoped so much, came to an ignominious end.

Campeggio claimed leave to return to Rome for the accustomed autumnal recess. Katherine retired to Windsor. And Henry, desirous of leaving London as soon as possible—labouring under the delusion, perhaps, that a man can separate himself topographically from an uneasy conscience—discovered the immediate necessity of a circuit through the Midlands.

And now he and Anne and all the Court were awaiting the Italian Cardinal's farewell visit at Grafton. "And the sooner the better," grumbled Henry, who had been forced to forego a good day's hunting. Never once had he referred to Katherine's trial; but, whatever the bitterness of his disappointment, for policy's sake he could not vent his spleen upon the foreign Legate. An English Legate was, of course, another matter. Cardinal or no Cardinal, Wolsey was Henry's subject, and had not been officially invited.

"There is no room in the house for him, and his ridiculous retinue will incommode our host," objected Anne, when she perceived that Henry would have offered him belated hospitality. "Perhaps our good Hal can find him some accommodation."

And so the great Chancellor of England, who time and again had entertained them all with princely magnificence, was lodged in a local inn. And waiting, he had time to review his grievances.

He had worked harder than any man in the land, spending money and leisure and health prodigally in the king's service. Born in an ordinary unpretentious home, he had by his own endeavours won the regard of princes and theologians, become a Cardinal, and made England a power to be feared throughout Europe.

All winter he had been forced to steer a course between two dangers. Either he must disobey the King or offend the Pope—the authors of his hard-won temporal and spiritual power. And all for the sake of a black-eyed devil of a woman in whom ambition, fed on flattery and family urging, soared obscenely. Like some sudden unnatural meteor she had risen into his cloudless sky, darkening the established rays of his power by the speedy brilliance of her progress. Ambition in other men he had never been at a loss to cope with. But with a woman's white body and tortuous wiles bewitching the King, he was no longer sure of Henry's friendship.

Humbling himself, he had done his best to propitiate this Boleyn wench. At Henry's wish he had gone to considerable trouble to provide her with a house almost as resplendent as his own, hanging her private apartments with arras from his own world-famous collection. On her behalf he had incurred the Queen's distrust and the enmity of Spain. Together, she and Henry had fooled him over that marriage-negotiating visit to France. And when he had come back, there she was, loaded with the King's jewels, laughing at him.

Just as she was laughing now standing between him and the closed door behind which the King was talking to Campeggio. Always standing between him and the King.

The scene was deliberately set for his discomfiture.

But although Wolsey's wisdom far exceeded Spanish Katharine's, he lacked her courage and inherent breeding. Pushing his way into the crowded, improvised anteroom at Grafton, he betrayed embarrassment. Scarlet silk and fine Venetian lace could no longer hide the flabby bulk of his once-powerful body, but served only to enhance the unhealthy sallowness of his pendulous cheeks. His probing, prominent eyes, so accustomed to intimidate, were lowered before the watchful stares of underlings. And he allowed himself to be disconcerted by the impudent popinjays clustered admiringly about Anne, many of whom had learned their fine manners in his house.

From wicked, slanting eyes, Anne glanced across the room and marked him where he stood, a sick and hesitant man. "The wheel is come full circle. If only Percy, my love, were here to see him now!" whispered the devil of vengeance in her mind.

And Wolsey, meeting her hatred with his own, thought, "If only I could break up *this* love affair as easily as I crushed her first!" It was easy enough to make the London people shout "Concubine!" and "We want no Bullen!" when she rode abroad, and secretly to inflame their demonstrations of affection for the young Princess Mary. But if only he could come by some secret knowledge or some fear to hold over her, as she held over him that chance-gotten information about his youth!

Through her satellites, her mocking hostility flowed towards him. No one made way for him, no usher announced him, no single group of persons ceased their chatter—and yet, he felt certain, everyone in the room was watching him and wagering whether the King would receive him or not. Whatever lesser men had suffered awaiting a moment of his own valuable time, Thomas Wolsey suffered now.

"I know the night crow who has the King's ear and misrepresents my every action," he muttered to his bullet-headed secretary, Cromwell; certain in his own mind that, without persuasion, Henry would not have misused him so. And because, in order to cover his embarrassment, he must needs speak to someone, he—the most gifted speaker in all Europe—began a pitiful, pointless conversation with his usher, Cavendish.

"See how cleverly Anne baits him," whispered Jane Rochford.

"Another few moments of this and he will give up all hope of an audience and call for his milk-white mule," laughed Anne.

But she had mocked too soon. In the middle of her excited laughter the door behind her was flung open by a page and Henry's genial voice, together with scraps of his relieved leave-taking, drifted out into the anteroom. And presently Henry himself appeared, accompanying the departing Cardinal. Anne had not counted upon that. Pleasantly, a little absently, Henry stood a few paces within the room, watching him go. And as his eyes followed one scarlet-clad figure they lighted upon another.

Anne tried to intervene, to head Henry off with the preamble of some hastily recalled jest. But he did not seem to hear her. The habit of old friendship was too strong. Wolsey made a pleading gesture, not wholly from self-interest, and seemed to totter a step or two forward. His face was all broken up and working painfully, like a child's that has been shut out. And generously Henry hurried to meet him, all grudges and malicious insinuations forgotten. "Why, Thomas!" he exclaimed, just as if it were the other who had absented himself.

"Your Grace!" stammered Wolsey.

And there before all his abashed enemies, they embraced. Two men who had worked and feasted together, each moulded by the same events, sharing the same memories and tastes, comfortable to each other as a pair of well-worn slippers. Two men who, each in his own way, had just been through a trying time. "I had an idea, now that that foreign nincompoop is gone," began Wolsey, lowering his voice.

"Yes, yes," encouraged Henry eagerly, drawing him into his own room.

"I could act alone, with his Holiness' brief of authority. It included us both—"

"If we can get hold of it—"

Already they were closeted together in the King's room. Anne could see them standing close together in the window recess, Wolsey making confident gestures with his white, puffy hands, and the King listening attentively. She was aware of her uncle Norfolk, craning his neck round the jamb, and of the smothered oath that escaped her father. And then Henry, glancing over his shoulder, snapped his fingers impatiently and someone closed the door, shutting out all jealous prying.

Anne crumpled onto the nearest window seat. It seemed an eternity, waiting there, with her triumphant laughter cold on her lips. All the modish young men seemed to have melted away. And she was glad enough when Thomas Boleyn came and sat beside her. "It is no good losing heart, child," he told her kindly. "All diplomacy has its ups and downs."

Anne seldom saw him alone these days. She regarded him attentively, as if expecting to find him changed. But perhaps the change was only in the growth of her own understanding—perhaps he had always been the same. After all his scheming towards success he looked much the same as during those happy days at Hever—a little greyer, perhaps, but just as suave and handsome, just as unruffled— whereas she—"God must have been with that bloated son of a butcher then! Just a chance encounter and all our work undone," she lamented, feeling suddenly very weary.

The Duke, her uncle, came and joined them. "God will give him over some day. He is getting to be an old man," he observed vindictively. Norfolk had served his country ably by diplomacy and sword, and England had not room for two such proud personalities.

"I heard them say 'If we could lay hold of the Papal brief!' which means that the King would depend upon him more than ever," vouchsafed Anne.

"Then you may be sure Wolsey will leave before noon tomorrow to see Campeggio off in London and persuade him to part with it," grinned Norfolk, showing his unpleasant teeth.

"They will be hand in glove again," she wailed.

"Not for long, perhaps. If you can use those feminine wiles of yours and prevent the King from seeing him in the morning," suggested her father.

Anne sat in ruminative silence, conscious that both men waited upon her cunning. It was a challenge, thrown down at the right moment. Presently she sprang to her feet and faced them with a brilliant smile. "There is supposed to be especially good hunting about here, is there not? And after a day indoors his Grace will be particularly impatient," she said. "I pray you, milords, have our host come to us here. Perhaps between us we can convince him that a fine stag has been seen in these parts. A king stag, that no one can bring to bay. Something almost legendary that his keepers have seen in some distant brake at dawn. And for my part, I will persuade our hostess to have a breakfast carried thither."

"And if the stag should not be oncoming?" enquired Thomas Howard, with caustic amusement.

"Then be sure your niece *will* be," laughed the new Earl of Wiltshire.

What a daughter, this Nan of his! There had been a time when he had feared she would prove sentimental and recalcitrate; but now, removed from Jocunda's fond influence, she appeared to have forgotten all about that callow love affair. She was a wench who accepted no reverses tamely. A wench to be proud of!

ARRIVING BACK AT WESTMINSTER a few days later, Anne had
time to assess her gains. She had prevented Wolsey from
seeing Henry again at Grafton, but she knew that she had
wrought only his discomfiture, not his downfall. And if he obtained
the Papal brief to act for Henry, his influence would be paramount
again. And how much he must hate her!

Seething with anxiety, she dismissed her women and bolted
herself in her bedroom. It was not only her own disappointment.
Her family and her supporters had depended upon her, and their
hopes had been laid low. Before all her admirers, the King and the
Cardinal had walked past her as if she were no more than a tiring
woman, and, as they passed, Wolsey's scarlet cassock had switched
contemptuously against her gown.

"I will make Henry suffer for that!" she vowed. "After all his
fine protestations, his gifts, his kisses, his love letters." And as
she ranged back and forth her eyes rested on the casket in which
she kept them. "Were I to show some of those letters I could
make *him* look a pretty fool!" she thought. Always at the back of
her mind had lain the shameful notion that if ever she found
herself about to be discarded like Mary she could use them. Not
really use them, perhaps; but make Henry afraid that she might.
It would be a mean weapon; but a woman must have some
safeguard.

In her impatience, Anne had sent away the servants who had come to light her candles, and already the shadows were gathering behind the tallboy and the rich hangings of her bed. But by the western window there was still light enough to read a letter. She would refresh her memory, read again the fond, impassioned things that he would hate most of all for other eyes to see. "Would that you were in my arms, mine own darling, or I in yours; for I think it is long since I kissed you," he had written. And then again in some later letter, after he had fondled her more intimately, "Sweetheart, I send you a hart that I have killed in the chase. Hart's flesh from Henry, praying that hereafter, God willing, you may enjoy some of mine. And I would it were now!"

Anne's lips curved into a smile. She forgot her ill-humour. Humming a gay little tune she crossed the room with briskly tapping heels. As she approached her table, she noticed that the casket stood a little awry, showing a thin angle of undusted oak beneath one end. Margaret, who had charge of that and her jewel case, was always so particular. It must be those careless chamberers, thought Anne. She must speak to them about it. But with the tiny key half lifted from her girdle, suspicion assailed her, holding the flowing grace of her movements suddenly taut. After a horrible moment or two she stretched out her left hand, the hand she used so seldom. And the carved lid lifted to her touch. The familiar scent of musk and amber came up to her, making her feel faint. But there was no uplifting of tightly pressed letters.

Panic-stricken, incredulous, Anne pulled the golden thing towards her, carried it to the light and peered in. Search as she would with frantic fingers, only one piece of parchment remained, partly unrolled, at the bottom. "*Forget not yet the tried intent—forget not yet!*" Part of the poet's elegant script was plainly visible. The story of Thomas Wyatt's constant love lay there, mocking her. Something sure and unswerving, which once she might have had. And for the rest the casket was empty—rifled.

The King's love letters were gone!

Anne almost froze with horror. All the raging anger and petty resentment was burned out of her. For an optimistic moment her hunted mind toyed with the notion that Margaret, or that young Savile hoyden, might have played some trick on her. But before she could reach her bell to summon them she knew that they would not dare. Not with the King's letters. Besides they, too, had been away.

Because her legs would no longer support her, Anne sank into a chair and sat staring at the open, empty casket. Trying to think. Of course, this room had been unoccupied, and all her house left in the care of servants while they were all at Grafton backing her to make a fool of Wolsey.

Wolsey!

The man who had owned the house before her. Who must know every nook and corner of it, and who had made such a pother about personally supervising the hanging of his precious tapestries. Wolsey, whose own house, full of spies and agents, no doubt, was hard by. Wolsey, whom she had fooled when he went to France.

"*An enemy hath done this thing!*" The apt words sprang to her lips, hot from the Scriptures which she had been reading, though no longer surreptitiously.

And now she was certain that it was Wolsey who had fooled her. Who else would know about the letters, and be so subtle? It was the deadliest thing anyone could have done to her.

Henry would be furious.

He would never know what eyes were reading his inmost thoughts, what men made merry over the sincere expressions of his private desires. Though it were not her fault, would he not remember that she had been careless before, and that he had long ago urged her to burn his letters? And say that had she really loved his letters, she would have kept the casket near her. Much he might forgive her—but never, surely, would he forgive the person who made him the laughing stock for all the civilized world.

Anne lifted the golden box, shielding it almost furtively with her arms. "I will not tell him," she thought. "I will let him think I have them still. If Wolsey had them stolen he will never dare to produce them. It is only that he wants to have something to hold over me. Something about which I shall never be sure."

A low fire was burning in the grate. She turned towards it with the casket pressed to her bosom. "Better get rid of this, too, in case the sight of it should remind Henry." Her thoughts darted this way and that, and the sight of the warm embers gave her an even more daring idea. "Or could I, perhaps, pretend that letters and all got accidentally burned?"

But even as she stood there, cogitating, the colour came back into her cheeks and the brightness to her eyes, "Merciful God, that I could be so witless!" she cried softly. "If Wolsey would not dare to tell, neither would he credit me with courage enough to accuse him. Oh, my fat Cardinal, at last you have played into my hands!"

She unbolted her door and pealed at her bell. And when her women came running, there was everything to do at once. "Go, one of you, and tell Master Heneage of the King's chamber that I must see his Grace at once; about something which touches him closely. Entreat him that he see me tonight. Here, take the King's ring which he gave me. And someone call for lights, I can see nothing in this accursed gloom. Margot, bring me my jewel box. And fetch Mary Howard, who is so clever with my hair, Arabella, Druscilla, come and make me beautiful! More beautiful than ever before. No, 'Cilla, dear, not the rose pink. Beautiful, mais *un peu triste*."

And then the arrival of Heneage, a short journey in a closed litter, and Anne was facing Henry, alone, in his workroom. Though it was long past supper time, she had found him still busy with affairs of statecraft. But now Wriothesly, his secretary, had been dismissed. Even the handsome French ambassador, who had settled down to discuss something, had been unceremoniously bundled out. And the little gold casket stood on the writing table between the ponderous treatise Henry was preparing about his divorce, and an unsigned death warrant.

He himself was standing with his back to the fire, with perplexity and anger written on his face. "But it is incredible, what you suggest!" he broke out for the second time.

Together he and Anne stared at the empty box, the silence broken only by the pleasant crackling of the logs. And presently

Henry moved to the table to examine the broken lock. "Any rogue with daring enough might have stolen them," he said. "But to suspect Thomas Wolsey—"

"Who knows my house so well as he?" pointed out Anne, looking a picture of injured innocence. "He had duplicate keys and remained here at York House until we were on the point of leaving Grafton. And he is jealous of your love for me."

Henry laughed shortly, although he felt far from experiencing any mirth. "He worked hard for a French marriage, if that is what you mean. But think what you are saying, girl. A man of Wolsey's standing!"

"Stood Wolsey always so high?" she challenged.

Absently, the King had picked up his learned Latin treatise on divorce, and now he banged it down again angrily on his table. "*That* old story!" he scoffed. "At least his people were not butchers, but intelligent landed graziers, who managed to send their son to Oxford. You have been prejudiced against him ever since he did my bidding about that presumptuous Northumberland pup."

Anne was always careful not to provoke him on that matter and in the face of her obstinate silence her maturer lover's pent-up jealousy flared up more generally. "You listen overmuch to the gossip of all those young men whom you encourage," he complained.

"At least my friends are all young men of good family," she flamed back impudently. "How else could I be at ease with them?"

She knew the way to taunt a Tudor. Henry flushed darkly. But insolence was so new a thing to him that he knew not how to deal with it, particularly the oblique insolence of a beautiful woman whom he desired. And Anne was very, very beautiful tonight. Perhaps if he humoured her in this crazy notion she would be kind. "But why should the Cardinal do such a dastardly thing?" he asked weakly.

She came to him at once, all clinging gentleness. "Oh, Henry, Henry, how can we read his tortuous mind? Has he ever really helped us to come together as we wish? And in what way is he better than the rest of us? Churchman as he is, has he ever denied himself the things of the flesh?"

Having been his intimate friend, Henry had no wish to go into that. "He had been a fine Chancellor," he submitted.

"Fine at condemning others," laughed Anne. "Surely you can see that he is no fit friend for you? A man who once sat like any common thief in the stocks!"

Halfway to snuff a guttering candle, Henry stopped abruptly. "The stocks?" he echoed, staring.

"For drunkenness."

Without seeing what he did, Henry laid down the silver snuffers on a pile of exquisitely illuminated manuscripts. Slowly he came towards her. "What is this you are saying?" he demanded dangerously.

Sure of herself in the flattering firelight, Anne stood her ground. "When he was a young parish priest at Limington, in Somerset. I suppose he made a beast of himself at some village fair."

Henry seemed to tower over her, his huge shadow flung grotesquely on the wall behind him. He held himself very still lest he might do her some injury. "You must be crazed to say such things," he growled, momentarily blind to her beauty.

Anne laughed and turned away, pivoting lightly on one heel. "Ask Sir Amyas Paulet if you do not believe me," she suggested, and left him there to think it out while she began turning the pages of his treatise.

"Sir Amyas was my Justice of Peace there," he recalled, speaking more to himself than to her.

Anne only hummed an infuriating little tune.

"A fine shot, Amyas Paulet, with some good West country hunting. Wasn't there something about his being confined in the Temple for heresy? I haven't seen him for years," added Henry on a rising note of anger.

"Perhaps that is why," suggested Anne negligently.

Suddenly his rage burst forth. "Why wasn't I told?" he demanded. "A man swineherds have thrown their refuse at eating and drinking with me as freely as your uncle or Suffolk!"

Anne closed the ornate cover of his book. "Have I not explained that people are afraid to tell things to a King, especially about his friends?" she said. "It is only those who really love him who will dare to do so."

Henry came and took her by the shoulders, turning her to him and searching her face with anxious eyes. "And you honestly believe that Thomas Wolsey stole my private letters?"

"A man with so odd a background might do anything," shrugged Anne.

"Late as it is, I will have him sent for."

That was the last thing Anne wanted. After all, she was not sure. Face to face with Henry, Wolsey might be able to clear himself. Before Henry could reach his bell, her fingers were about his wrist. "If he has your letters he would scarcely dare to keep them here," she hazarded.

"You mean that he might send them abroad?"

"Possibly by Campeggio?"

Henry's ringers slid from the bell. His face seemed to sag visibly. "You mean to Rome?" he almost stammered.

He must have been picturing an assembly of tonsured Cardinals trying to look suitably shocked, and statesmen in Paris and Spain sniggering enviously. Seeing him as a figure of fun because he had been a steady domesticated figure for eighteen years—and now, when he was beginning to put on weight, he had fallen desperately in love like this.

Anne was unfeignedly sorry for him. "If he shows them to the Pope, *mon ami*, there are pieces of them that will not help us very much," she warned.

She could see him trying to recall them. His face was now as red as it had been grey. "Whatever I wrote, I wrote for you alone, Nan," he said, with a kind of desperate dignity. He threw off his short, flared coat the better to rummage through some memoranda on his table. "Campeggio leaves for Dover at dawn, so there will just be time."

Henry's voice was crisp and businesslike, with that little intake of breath it had when he was very angry. As a onetime ambassador's daughter, Anne realized the enormity of the thing he proposed. The unforgivable international insult of tampering with a foreign

Legate's luggage. But Henry would try to get his letters back at all costs, even though his methods put him on a level with the thief. "And there is always the chance that you may find the missing brief," she encouraged.

"The brief?" Henry's sandy brows shot up and his hands stopped busying themselves with instructions for his secretary. "Did I not tell you, sweetheart? I have been so beset by affairs since my return. That wizened rat Campeggio burned it as soon as Katherine's trial was ended."

It was Anne's turn to stand rigid with surprise. "By the Pope's orders?" she asked.

"As like as not. What has Clement ever done but delay and deceive me?"

"Then Wolsey is—" Almost faint with relief, Anne bit back the word "finished" and substituted "of no further use to you?"

"In this matter, no. Nor in any other, if he had a hand in the disappearance of my letters," declared Henry. "Henceforth I will fight for my divorce alone."

Anne looked up at him with shining eyes. "Oh, Henry, it will be better so, though we two defy the whole of Christendom. You are strong enough. And what do the people of this country want with foreign interference and the ecclesiastic rulings of Rome? Most of them have no taste for foreigners."

"Unless they happen to take them to their incalculable hearts," he agreed grimly, thinking of his impeccable Spanish wife. "My people's sense of insularity is at times most inconveniently strong; but it comes second to their unfailing sense of fair play."

He pulled Anne close, and in the warm, log-scented room they stood silent, considering the possibility of some obstacle stronger even than Popes or foreign powers. But after a moment or two she brought him back to gaiety and confidence. "The church would be wholly English, and yourself the head of it," she said. "You could clean up the blatant immorality of some of the convents and clip the power of some of the over-weening bishops. And with some of their wealth, endow colleges for the sons of gifted craftsmen. You could make an abundance of reforms."

"Without taking away any of the beauty of our Holy Offices," Henry was quick to stipulate.

But planning for the future would not bring them back their lost love letters.

Campeggio's party was set upon by hired footpads soon after dawn next morning in Fleet Street. And, since he had but just started on his way, the insult was augmented by the plunging restlessness of the pampered mules he had borrowed from his colleague. In the melee the contents of a dozen trunks or more were scattered over the cobbles and carried by the river breeze from overhung footways to garbage-filled gutters. Sleepy-eyed 'prentices, on their way to open their masters' shutters in Eastcheap roused themselves magically from morning sloth to join in the commotion. Upper windows were flung wide while housewives, half-dressed, indulged with their opposite neighbours in detailed criticisms of the fuming little Cardinal's strewn possessions. "We want no foreigners to manage our affairs!" shouted their husbands derisively, standing stolidly in their doorways. And, gathering their good, warm worsted garments about them, the purse-proud, well-fed citizens of London made merry over the assortment of patched underwear and scruffy soutanes, and the dried crusts and eggs with which the Papal Legate had intended to economize during his return journey to report about their betters. They had no idea, of course, that the group of Palace halberdiers who happened to be passing and stopped to help the Cardinal's Italian servants gather up the litter and restuff the trunks were abroad so early by order of the King. Or that their young captain, apologizing so courteously and chasing a wad of windswept documents as if his promotion depended upon it, was searching for Henry the Eighth's love letters to the accursed Concubine.

But, although the search was unavailing, the secret, shared anxiety wiped out the last of Wolsey's power and brought Anne and Henry yet closer together.

There was that peaceful Christmas at Greenwich, like a brief spell of domestic security set in the loveliest frame. Henry had no wish to look upon a man who might have read his love-making, and Katherine had been sent to some drear, unhealthy place called Moor Park. Even her Christmas gift to the King had been returned, and her jewels sent for to adorn her successor. At first Katherine had refused. She and Anne appeared to be the only two people in all England who had the courage to refuse Henry anything he wanted. But in the end Henry had forced his wife to obey, and her great ruby necklace lay heavy about Anne's neck.

Because he had sent for the jewels and was even contemplating breaking away from the Pope, Anne knew beyond doubt that Henry meant to marry her. And because for once she felt secure, she could afford to be kinder. Outside the Palace lay a white, wadded world, with the Thames partly frozen over and thick wedges of snow framing all the casements. But inside all was colour and warmth. Great logs blazed on all the hearths, and merry servants dragged in boughs of crimson holly to adorn the hall. The painter Cornelisz was making a lovely thing of Anne's portrait, and everywhere there was music. In the King's collection there were seventy-six different instruments, and because there was no hunting or archery, he and Anne had time to learn the peculiar sweetness of them all. Each night there were revels, and every morning the candles were lighted in the Chapel, and Cranmer's lovely voice gave fresh meaning to the prayers. And, best of all, Jocunda had joined her family for Christmas.

Anne tried to forget poor Katherine, shivering sadly in a ruinous, ill-drained house in the depth of such a particularly bitter winter. And, in a mood of contrition, she laid aside the clever tapestry she had been working on as a surprise for Henry, and sat stitching diligently with her women and Jocunda, making warm garments for the poor.

It would be nice, she thought, to be loved by them, like Katherine. To have time to show simple kindnesses and always look serene. But then Katherine had been born royal, and had never had to push and scramble for her place.

The chance to do a simple kindness came before Twelfth Night, when Dr. Butts rode in with the news that Thomas Wolsey was grievously sick. He had come straight from the Cardinal's lodging at Esher, and Henry was all concern at once. "How sick?" he asked, pushing aside the backgammon board and scattering all his winnings.

"Sir, he is sick at heart as well as in body," answered the compassionate physician. "He grieves so constantly that I think he will not live many days unless he has some comfortable message from your Grace."

"Marry, God forbid that he should die!" cried Henry, getting up and forgetting all about the game. "Tell him, my good Butts, that I am not offended with him in my heart for anything, and bid him be of good comfort." He pulled the great ring with his own portrait from his finger. "Here, give him this. He will know it well since he himself gave it me. And when you have eaten and rested, I pray you go back yourself and do what you can for him, sparing your skill no less than if you spent it on my own person."

Anne heard him without resentment. He, too, had regained a kind of normal *bonhomie* since they had been together, with state worries in abeyance, and only Cranmer's unassertive tact to oil the pleasant hours of their regal domesticity. Many a time she had thought, had he been free to take her as his lawful wife, how good a husband he would have made. He came to her now, not ordering or blustering, but soliciting her kindness for a favour that he knew she might find hard to give, but which he earnestly desired. "Good sweetheart, as you love me, send poor Wolsey some token of your kindness," he begged quietly. "And in so doing you shall have my gratitude."

Anne was only too glad to please him, and in her new-won security had no particular desire to add to the sufferings of an old man who was already powerless to harm her. She detached a jewelled tablet from her belt and handed it to her beloved doctor. "Go do as well for milord Cardinal as you did for me when I had the plague," she bade him gaily.

And Dr. Butts did so well for Cardinal Wolsey that he had him on his feet again in a few days.

But, unlike his niece, Thomas of Norfolk had no closed season for hatred. Having seen such proofs of the Tudor's affection, he and his party could not afford to have the two old friends meet again. "If you value your newly curried favour with the King," he told Thomas Cromwell, "persuade your present master that it were better for his health if he retire to his see of York. Then shall we find better prospects for you here. But if he go not speedily, believe me, I will tear him with my teeth."

Chapter Twenty-Eight

MILORD THE CARDINAL IS dead!" announced Cavendish, before he was well across Anne's threshold. His riding boots were spattered with mud, and the emotion in his voice reduced the other four occupants of the room to silence.

George stopped in the middle of a story, Margaret Wyatt sat down abruptly on a stool, Norreys paused with flagon tilted and glass half-filled, and Anne stood resplendent in the rose satin dress she had donned in the glad expectation of meeting Harry Percy.

All four of them had already heard the news, but so great was Wolsey's personality that the panting words had power to shatter their habitual gaiety, draining their minds of present thoughts and hopes.

"You need not be so dramatic, Cavendish," said George, from the cushioned window seat. "My sister and I were at cards with the King when Cromwell's messenger arrived last night."

"Neither do you have to stand there, all white-faced, accusing me with your eyes," snapped Anne, lifting her head defiantly. "Others have been before you. The King sprang up immediately and threw his cards across the table. 'This is your doing!' he snarled at me. 'I would have paid ten thousand pounds rather than lose him.'"

"And went weeping to his chamber," added Norreys, filling up the glass and handing it to Wolsey's favourite usher.

Remembering how Hal Norreys had pitied Katherine, Anne's

glance followed him resentfully. "As if I were God to decide whether an old man succumbs to his loathsome diseases or not," she added. But she spoke half-absently, smoothing back a strand of hair beneath her jewelled cap.

All three men looked at her with covert surprise. A week ago so passionate a reprimand from the King would have rendered her distraught; but she had made the brief assertion unmoved. What mattered one middle-aged man's grief for another when she, Nan Boleyn—more poised and daring than she had ever been—would even now, in a few minutes, be seeing her lover again after seven long years!

Only Margaret, who had dressed her, understood how little her mind was on Henry Tudor. "Of course you could not help the Cardinal dying," she agreed, handing her the necklace she had been about to fasten. "But must you—need you be so—"

"Cruel? Go on, girl, say it," jeered Anne. For how could they know that her own conscience rode her far more remorselessly than any words of theirs.

But Margaret, for all her gentleness, never pandered to her friend's growing importance. "The Cardinal and the Queen stood in your way," she found courage to say. "But the lady Mary's grace—she is but a girl. Must you keep her, too, from Court?"

Anne swung the rope of pearls sullenly. "No, I suppose not. But she is so obstinate. She always has the right answer. Every day, though we keep them apart, she grows more like her mother. Ignoring me. And Henry loves her so."

Anne heard George's light steps from the window behind her and felt his constraining hands on her forearms, his cheek pressed affectionately against her own. "And must you uncurl his fingers from everything he loves, my sweet? From every softening influence that makes him more bearable for us poor Court minions to serve?" he whispered, half-bantering. "Margot is right, you know."

Anne knew that they were both right. That most sane people's eyes accused her. Even while this heady draught of power drove her, she hated herself for growing hard. But whether were it better to sin blindly or to sin and see one's fault, she wondered, envying Henry his self-deceptive smugness. "I make no doubt you are *all* right," she allowed. "And certainly Master Cavendish has every right to feel bereaved. Come and sit you down by the fire, and tell us all that has happened," she invited, freeing herself from her brother's embrace and fastening the famous pearls about her throat. "It was good of you to remember your old friendship with milord Percy and to come to us at such a time; and I for my part will try to remember that although you joined in our levity then, the Cardinal has been your master these many years."

George Cavendish took the stool which Norreys pushed towards him and sat wearily beside the fire, one of themselves, yet a travel-stained figure among so much elegance. "His Eminence was on his way down from York to clear himself before the Council; but by the time he reached Leicester he could no longer sit his mule, and the good Abbot there took him in. Everything possible was done for him, but he knew that this was the end. He was shriven and died soon after cock-crow. 'Had I but served my God as faithfully as I have served my King, He would not have given me over in my grey hairs,' he kept murmuring."

"That was true enough," said George Boleyn. "He always seemed to me more like some great prince, with his wealth and his diplomacy, rather than lovable and saintly like old Warham of Canterbury."

"It is not comparable. Cardinal Wolsey of York was a man who trod the paths of glory, and sounded all the depths and shoals of honour," declaimed his usher, in his flamboyant style.

"Who should know better than you?" agreed George flippantly. "But you can write a book about him later."

"Tell us about his arrest," urged Anne.

"He was taken on a charge of High Treason, of all things."

"I know. But it was nothing to do with me. My uncle of Norfolk struck that final blow." Anne seemed to shrug the matter aside. She stood across the hearth from Cavendish, one hand pulling aside the rich folds of her gown so as to warm a satin-shod foot, the other gripping tensely at the carved moulding of the wide stone chimney breast. Her whole attitude, as she bent towards him, was tense. "I had no part at all in that," she repeated. "All I made my uncle promise me was that when the warrant was signed Harry Percy should be the man to take it and arrest him. Was that done?"

Cavendish did not lift his head to meet the smouldering triumph in her eyes. He just sat there stirring the spilled ashes with the leather tag of his riding whip. "Yes, even that was done," he said bitterly. "As it happened, Percy was coming south about some Border dispute, and he met the Cardinal's party on the way."

"And showed him the King's warrant?" breathed Anne.

"And showed him the warrant." Cavendish's voice was slow and heavy. The sad little scene was still fresh in his memory, and like the rest of them he appreciated what a blow it must have been. But for them it had not spoiled the meeting with a long-parted friend, nor had they been called upon to read the cruel warrant to a dying man.

Anne seemed to have forgotten them all save the tired man with the down-bent head from whom she almost dragged each painful word. Her eyes glittered and her knuckles whitened as they gripped the stone, and her whole body trembled with excitement for the consummation of her hard-worked scheme. "And milord Percy took joy in this chance to repay old debts?" she demanded.

Cavendish shifted his feet uncomfortably, and it was clear that he wished he had not come. "I cannot say, my lady," he answered more formally. "I only know that his hand shook as he pushed the parchment before the Cardinal's fading eyes, and that he ordered one of his men to tie milord's swollen legs to his stirrups, as if he were a common felon."

"He did *that*!" marvelled Anne, scarcely above a whisper.

Cavendish arose, pushing the stool back awkwardly, and glancing imploringly at Norreys as if by some means or other he must depart. "But then Northumberland suffers from an ague these days and his Bordermen are tough," he added, settling his belt and refusing a second glass of wine.

"An ague!" repeated Anne, trying to imagine her robust young lover with shaking hands. "But he still keeps the Border? And he is coming to see me?"

"He is here now, Madame. He has been paying his formal respects to the King."

Anne turned to the others with a radiant smile. "Then, please—" she entreated.

They rose to go immediately. But her brother regarded her anxiously. "It is six years or more," he warned, in passing. And Cavendish, standing by the door which he had opened for Margaret, cleared his throat as if there was something which he must make clear before he left. "I fear you will find him much changed," he said.

"You *fear*! Older, yes, but—" Anne spun round upon him in alarm, then called appealingly to her departing brother. "*How* is he changed? You told me you met him when he rode in."

George paused in the doorway to consider. "Like a man who has lived too long with a nagging wife," he decided.

"Like you," teased Margaret, lingering in the corridor.

He stooped to plant a kiss upon her adorable, tip-tilted nose. "But at least I have not been left to wither without laughter," he reminded her.

Anne watched the charming little interlude and thanked him when he called back that he would find Northumberland; but the moment she was left alone, she flew to her mirror. "I, too, am changed. I am aging and hardening," she murmured, passing appraising fingers down the clear oval of her face. But colour had warmed her cheeks and excitement had given her back that youthful look of happy expectancy. "And I have what Thomas calls my witchery," she reassured herself, glancing sideways at her reflection and pirouetting with hands stretched about her slender waist.

As the great moment of reunion drew near her heart began beating wildly. She had no illusions about the future and the bargained path she had agreed to tread. But this present moment would be hers and Percy's. "Will he forget our obligations and take me in his arms?" she wondered. "Shall we recapture that ecstasy that makes a mock of time?"

Her hands flew to quiet her breast, her eyes shone like stars.

And then the door opened and Harry Percy stood there, leaning against it. Although Anne was prepared for him to be older and a powerful earl, had she not been expecting him, her searching eyes would scarcely have recognized him. Instead of hurrying to her with all his old impetuousness, he just stood there, ill at ease; and through the welter of her racing emotions it stabbed her to the heart that he had not even thought to shoot the bolt.

"Harry!" she breathed softly, some innate pride or wisdom holding her where she stood.

He came to her then and kissed her outstretched hand. Came to her with slow, embarrassed courtesy. All the youthful joy and reckless passion had somehow been worn out of him. "Never again shall I be swept into that passionate embrace!" she thought, and found herself looking into the stern, lined face of a rather querulous man who reminded her fantastically of his own father. He was richly but soberly dressed, more like a soldier than a courtier, and his keen eyes took in the expensive luxury of her apartment.

"I congratulate you, Mistress Anne," he said, the firm mouth she had once loved twisted a little in irony.

"You don't suppose that I love him, do you?" she countered. It had never occurred to her that he might have been thinking all these years that she had gone willingly to Henry.

She motioned to him to sit, and instead of flinging himself down beside her as he used in the old days, he arranged himself and his sword with the preciseness of a man much older than his thirty years. If only one could feel one shred of jealousy in his ironic annoyance! Because she could no longer bear to watch his unresponsive face, Anne looked round helplessly at her familiar possessions as if seeking comfort from the sight of something that had been there just the same, before she was so unhappy—before he came. "But, Harry, I have to play my part," she tried to explain, miserably twisting the rings on her fingers.

"You are cast for a very important part, Nan, and should carry it successfully," he said, noting for the first time the perfection of her toilette. "Your father has achieved an earldom, too, I hear."

Anne could not bear it, sitting close to him, not even touching him. Hard, slow tears welled into her eyes. "But I did not want to be the King's mistress, the grasping way that most women do. I did it all for you, Harry."

"For me?" The almost childish naivety of her words had brought the suspicion of a smile to his face at last.

"To make him suffer as we suffered. Don't you even remember how we suffered? And you don't believe that I have really given him my body, do you? My body has always been yours." Her eyes fell before his incredulous stare. "Though I may have to one day in marriage," she admitted.

"I suppose you were set upon being Queen," he said stolidly.

If she could only make him understand! She caught at the furred lapels of his coat, almost shaking him. "I was ill, desperately ill, all that winter after they parted us. When they made you marry Mary Talbot. I had no means of writing to you. I thought everything in life was over. But when the King kept writing and coming to Hever I saw my way to retaliate. To fool him, and to revenge the way Cardinal Wolsey rated you and let your father dress you down at York House before the servants."

For the first time Percy showed real emotion. "Who told you?" he demanded angrily.

"No one told me. I was there. I saw for myself."

"You were *there?*"

"I sat with the servants and heard what Northumberland said. Saw Wolsey standing there in his scarlet, heartless and sneering. And the way your poor, enraged hands tore at your feathered cap. Harry, I swore then that I would humiliate him as he had humiliated us. For nearly six years I have worked for the downfall of his pride. At first I dared only to drop a word here and there, or to say something with a smile at table which would set him to uneasy wondering. Until at last I had him kept waiting like a lackey, perspiring lest the King would not receive him. How I wish that you could have seen him! What with his anxiety and his swelling sickness he came to such a pass that he began sending letters almost every day to Norreys, imploring poor Hal to let him know whether or no 'the lady' was appeased." Anne's amusement broke out in a trill of musical laughter. "Not the King, mind you—but me, 'the lady Anne.' It seems he had no doubt from whence retribution flowed! And when my uncle had him arrested for treason I made him swear that you should take the warrant. That you should be the man to see proud Wolsey's fall!"

All these years Anne had lived close to the scenes and protagonists of her girlhood's drama. Her nature had never ceased to feed upon resentments which Percy, while allowing them to change him, had in part forgotten. He turned and looked at her curiously. Not at her pearls or her inviting body, but at the sharp intensity of her eager face. He seemed bewildered. It did not occur to Anne that he, too, was looking for the person he had loved so utterly in a Thames-side garden.

"Have you no pity, Nan?" he asked.

Pity! The same word arraigned against her. "I can pity those I love," she said in self-defence. "My heart ached with pity for you that day. Ask my own household if I succour or defend them, and whether my poor fingers are sore this winter with sewing for the defenceless poor." Anne turned them up and looked at them. Such a small, foolish thing. But how could a man appreciate the sacrifice it entailed to abide rough fingers with a rose satin gown?

"But when you hate—" he began remorselessly.

With a harsh swish of silk, Anne stood up and looked him over, almost despisingly. "And what sort of man are you, Harry Percy, who could pity Wolsey, given the requiting task I won for you?" she cried.

"Something still human, I hope. Naturally, I had no liking for the man; but I did it reluctantly, carrying out the King's orders."

"But Cavendish says you tied him like a felon."

"We Northerners are not lily-handed."

"Nor very constant!" flashed Anne, thinking suddenly of Thomas Wyatt, who had bearded the King on his own bowling green. But she sat down again, realizing that she was being but a poor hostess, and asked after Northumberland's own affairs.

"You heard the scandal, no doubt, that my wife left me and went back to her father," he said, dully. "But in the end I had to take her back. Old Shrewsbury insisted upon it. And I had to have an heir for Wressel."

"You would sacrifice any woman for Wressel, would you not?" murmured Anne, remembering how the threat of disinheritance had parted them.

But he scarcely seemed to notice her smouldering resentment. "Women have not meant much to me since you were taken from me," he confessed tonelessly.

"Because you still love me, or because you are a sick man?" Anne asked, almost impersonally.

"Maybe I am sick in mind as well as body. I, too, have suffered," he said.

Anne went to him then and laid her arms about his shoulders, looking searchingly into his face. "Oh, my dear, I am sorry," she murmured.

He was not sure whether she was sorry because he was sick or because of her bitterness and his own indifference. He only knew that she was the most desirable woman he had ever known, and that she had never ceased to love him. And that the poor fluttering spark of his desire was not worthy of one flicker of her tempestuous flame. He did not insult her by a contrived embrace. He kissed her tenderly on the cheek because he wanted to. "You could have any lusty man you wanted; but you, too, have changed," he excused himself.

So this was the end of their reckless love story. For one unguarded moment Anne clung to him, her head pressed in shame against his quiet breast, while he held her with grateful gentleness. Then she pushed him from her and motioned him towards the door. Each of them was too moved for speech.

Anne glanced at the wonderful clock Henry had given her. It was scarcely the fourth part of an hour since her lover came. And now he was gone. Left alone, her mind still held him there, dissecting him more fairly than when he had stood beside her in the flesh. Undriven by desire, she filled in the gap of years. Unlike herself, Percy had been brutally forced into a hateful marriage of expediency. He, who had known the protective tenderness of real love, had begotten his heir in self-loathing. Up in that grim fortress of his he must have tried to live, as George had suggested, without gaiety and laughter. And so, too much alone with men, his strength had hardened into uncouthness. A fine Border Lord. An invaluable servant to the King, no doubt. Filling in love's empty hours with watchful duty, he had become too old for his years; his hands shook with ague, and he had to be careful what he ate.

Not even in the old days had he possessed that sense of artistry common to her other friends—but in youth the need for hills and sunshine essential in an outdoor man had passed for love of beauty. Because he was in love, the flexible willingness to assimilate and to

learn had been there, with burgeoning sensitiveness and selflessness. Matrimony might have been a glowing happiness instead of a
barren goad which destroyed what might have been developed.
Empty-hearted, Anne realized that their passionate interlude had
been but a fierce and tender loving of young bodies—that it had
been allowed no time to grow those enduring roots that blossom
from the mind. And that, though Henry Tudor and the Duchess of
Northumberland might drop down dead tomorrow, she and Harry
Percy could never again be lovers.

Her weeping had been done years ago at Hever. But whatever
might come after, in that quiet room, Anne touched her lowest
hour. Covering her tragic face with both her hands, she drew into
her soul the knowledge that to weep for someone who is gone is
desolation, but to weep for someone who has never really existed is
to lose a part of oneself.

"Why ache, my heart, for what is not there?" she jeered at
herself, groping after courage.

And, when she could stand the loneliness no longer, she lifted
her extravagant skirts above her shapely ankles, and ran along the
corridors to Cranmer. He was on the eve of departure to Germany
to persuade his learned colleagues there to agree upon the King's
divorce; but he was still in the Palace, and his room was as austere
as ever. However high he were to rise, the flamboyancy of the late
Cardinal would never touch him.

He was reading by the fire and before he could rise Anne, in all
her grandeur, was down on her knees beside him. "Is it true that I
have grown so hard that I have no pity?" she cried, her right hand
spread across the book that lay open on his knee. "You, who have
been my confessor, should know."

"Please God it be not so!" he ejaculated perfunctorily. Then,
looking into the distraught misery of her face, he gathered her cold
hands in his and asked, "What is the real trouble, my child?"

"I did not kill Wolsey!" she sobbed hysterically.

"But surely no one accused you?"

"The King last night when Cromwell's messenger came," she
explained incoherently.

Cranmer, so delicately imprisoned, sat consideringly. "The King had lost a friend. Whatever he said, you must not take it too much to heart. This morning when I saw him he did not seem unduly—" Being as yet unaccustomed to meddling so intimately in the affairs of royalty, the King's chaplain left his sentence prudently involved in the throes of a cough.

But Anne sprang up to face him unequivocally. "All the same it is true. I can see that it is true. Everyone thinks me pitiless, even my own friends. But I only meant to discomfit him, to shame him as he had shamed someone I loved years ago."

Cranmer rose courteously, setting down his book and carefully marking his place. By so doing he gained time to choose his words. "Yet you did desire his downfall, did you not?" he enquired blandly.

"Only because in the end I had to. I had made him hate me so much that I dared not let him abide close to the King. Things mount up like that. Do you not see, Master Cranmer? It was either he or I. When I began baiting him I did not mean to hound an old man to his death."

Cranmer had been made by the successful Boleyns. He had seen Anne in a dozen different moods—cajoling, charming, haughty. But this was a new Anne, candid and without artifice, as her friends had always known her. He gazed at her and marvelled. "Whatever may be your faults in the sight of God, self-deception cannot be numbered among them," he murmured.

"I know my brother feels the same," she went on, more quietly. "As if some force, set in motion in our happy youth, pushes us along, further and further from the things we really love. So that in the few moments when we have time to look back at them they seem a long, sad way off."

"It must always be like that where there is ambition, where the mind grows crafty scheming for place," said Cranmer.

Anne took no offence. She regarded his plain cassock and stock, his fine scholarly hands and heavily jowled white face with an interest which momentarily drew her thoughts from her own emotions.

"You are not ambitious—like the Cardinal and Cromwell—are you?" she asked naïvely.

The thin, disciplined lips smiled with singular sweetness. "I have often wished myself back at some quiet University, with leisure for studying," he admitted, matching her candour with his own.

"Then in your heart you must hate being beholden to us?"

"How could I, after all the kindness I have received?"

"It is not kindness," Anne told him in this moment of almost brutal self-revelation. "It is just that we have used you."

The scholarly white hands made a humourous gesture of repudiation. "At least there is no need to pity *me*, whom all men envy. Now that poor Warham is about to die, God rest his soul, have I not the promise of his see of Canterbury?"

"And the King's love."

"Both of which I shall cherish."

"And use to help us to honest marriage, and to the gift of the Scriptures to the people? Tyndale's translation, which I daily read with so much joy?"

"Chanced you to read those uncompromising words of our Blessed Lord's, '*If ye do good to them that love ye, what thanks have ye*'?" Cranmer asked instead of answering her. "I pray you, Mistress Anne, do not think that I am unaware of your many kindly deeds to the poor, and of how your women love you. But real pity should stretch out to people whom we do not like—to those whom we have injured or who despitefully use us."

He seemed to wait while Anne stood in thought. She knew that he spoke of Katherine. But she *could* not be kind to Katherine. Yet there was, perhaps, another way, something which would mean more to the Spanish woman than any olive branch offered to herself. "I will send word to Mary Tudor," she promised humbly. "I will tell her that if she will but cease to be stiff-necked and conform to her father's desires, she may come to Court again, and I will care for her as a mother."

Anne Boleyn stood there, without ostentation, in the glad rose satin in which she had hoped to embrace her lover. She looked like some lovely crushed butterfly, with radiant colour still painted on its motionless wings. "I will try to be kind to her," she promised, with bleak gravity.

Chapter Twenty-Nine

AFTER WOLSEY'S DEATH THE King ruled England himself. It was a new, exhilarating experience. Early and late he saw ministers and foreign ambassadors, attended Councils, or signed important state documents. Tilt yard, tennis court, and bowling alley saw him less and less. And Anne, for weeks on end, saw him scarcely at all.

That he was capable, she knew. And amply supported. Cranmer, who had become his chaplain, was always at hand to encourage and advise; and Thomas Cromwell, daily pushing his ugly feet more firmly into his dead master's shoes, was proving himself invaluable. Norfolk bore all before him as President of the Council—a Council composed mostly of Anne's own menfolk, with Sir Thomas More and Suffolk. And between them, against Katherine's interests, they talked the French ambassador into arranging for a treaty to be signed between the two monarchs at Boulogne.

Directly Anne heard of this, she wanted to go to France. She wanted to see Francis again and, in her vanity, she wanted Francis to see her. By personal bravery in battle he had added excitement to his charm, and from a mere maid-of-honour whom he had patronized, she had grown to be an international figure. 'La Boleyn,' they called her in Paris, like any famous courtesan. Although, had they but known it, her royal lover had never yet enjoyed her. She must tell Francis that; he would throw back his fine head and laugh.

Francis had the wit to appreciate her cleverness. Though probably even *he* would scarcely believe that a woman could dangle the sweets of satisfaction like a jack-o'-lantern before the redheaded Tudor for years, accepting his gifts, yet ever dodging the grasp of his hungry hand.

This subtle power was becoming a heady poison spreading through her blood, compensating for the negation of her one true love. Giving an interest to her bitter restlessness. And Henry had promised to take her. He wanted to show her off to these fashionable Frenchmen. "The Commons are too scared of a Spanish war to grant much of a subsidy, nor will the nobles impoverish their estates to put furs and velvets on their backs as they did for the Field of the Cloth of Gold," he grumbled, striving not to ascribe their lack of enthusiasm to the love and pride they had once felt in him and Katherine. "But all the same we will contrive to go sumptuously."

He had innumerable garments made for her, not the least significant of which was a black satin bedgown lined with taffeta and trimmed with velvet. The price he paid for it would have kept his neglected daughter suitably clothed for a twelvemonth. But Anne would have felt worse about that had not Mary repudiated her effort at reconciliation with a spirited letter in which she thanked the Lady Anne Boleyn for her kind intent, but had no need of her good services at Court since her own mother was still Queen of England.

The one thing Anne hated most was being ignored.

Queen Claude, of the strict ways, had died; and when Anne asked if they were to meet the new French Queen at Boulogne, Henry had blustered uncomfortably about her being Katherine's niece, and said that he had no desire to meet any more Spanish women. That was all very well as far as it went, so long as one could be sure that all the reluctance was on his side. But surely there would be other ladies in Francis' train, thought Anne, choosing her wonderful new dresses—ladies of the French royal blood to whom she had once had to bend the knee. The Queen of Navarre, for instance.

But she, Anne Boleyn, still had no real standing, no title save an over-notorious one.

Henry was as anxious as she that she should be accepted. He made all manner of augmentations to her already honourable coat-of-arms. Besides giving her his wife's jewels he would have laden her with his sister Mary's, had not Anne sent them back with loving enquiries after her erstwhile mistress' health. "Poor Mary will never use them. As you know she lives in retirement in Suffolk, and Charles tells me he does not think she will ever come to Court again," Henry had excused himself sheepishly. And then, in the presence chamber at Windsor, he had Anne created Marchioness of Pembroke, a title which had belonged to his uncle, Jasper Tudor, and therefore seemed to include her in the royal family. At the elaborate ceremony her cousin, Mary Howard, held the coronet, and Henry himself placed it upon her head.

And, for all his passion, that was all Henry could do for her until he was free to make her his wife. Until old Warham of Canterbury should cease to draw his honest failing breath and make room for a more malleable primate, or the obstinate Spanish woman now living in loneliness and poverty at the manor of Buckden in Huntingdonshire, would die.

"But, Pope or no Pope, I will wait no longer. This is to be our honeymoon," Henry insisted, and Anne knew that she could not hold him off much longer.

She, too, was in holiday mood, humming to herself and rehearsing in her mind what she would say to the fine ladies of France. But she might have spared herself the trouble. For when the royal party arrived at Calais, though the King of France sent her greetings and the Grand Marshal sent her baskets laden with fruit, word was brought in from Boulogne that Francis was not accompanied by any ladies. Either by the French Queen's command or by their own desire, they had chosen to ignore the King of England's mistress.

In the humiliating circumstances etiquette demanded that Anne and all her ladies must remain like a clutch of nuns within the boring bounds of Calais Castle, with their coffers of devastating clothes unused, while Henry and his fortunate attendants went hunting through the famous French forests with the susceptible French gallants whom they had hoped to ensnare.

Anne stormed and wept, but all Henry could do was to promise her that he would persuade Francis to return with him to Calais, and that everything should be made up to her then. "And so that the time does not hang heavily, devise some entertainment out of that clever head of yours against his coming," he bade her. "Something that will make Boulogne look like a dunghill!"

With tears of rage in her eyes, Anne watched her father and brother and the rest depart. Not the least of her chagrin was that the Greys, and other highborn English ladies who had been forced to accompany her, were tittering at her expense, and that they would certainly delight her enemies in England with tales of her discomfiture. But Calais belonged to Henry, and she consoled herself with the thought that when the French came for reciprocal entertainment it would be her turn to call the tune. She would be their hostess then with several pretty girls in attendance and, since they had brought none of their own women with them, *tant pis* for the French Queen's moral righteousness! Their jealous wives should have thought of that!

Secretly, Anne had believed that Henry had meant to marry her in France, but now she had the sense to see that, in the circumstances, it would be impossible. And when poor Warham of Canterbury passed peacefully away and Cranmer was recalled from Germany to be inducted as Primate, there seemed every hope that he might sway his colleagues to give his court an appearance of authority, so that the Church of England, without assent from Rome, would ratify Henry's divorce. And even if this should never happen, Anne consoled herself in her more downcast moments, she would not have done so badly—a Marchioness in her own right, with assured succession to her children. At least she would have made a stir in the world and not been fobbed off with a penniless knight, like her fond, pretty sister Mary.

But Anne's thoughts seldom dwelt upon the second-best things, the compensations of life. Her vitality drove her always to take the initiative. She had her women unpack all the trunks and called the Calais servants about her. Upon their Majesties' return, she said, they were going to have feasting and a masque, such as the old castle had never seen. The banqueting hall was hung with silver tissue, and decorated with cloth of gold. Instead of torches in iron wall sconces, branches of silver gilt were suspended from the roof so that the tables might be lighted with modern wax candles. Anne herself visited the kitchens, where she saw to it that some dishes were served in the French manner and some in the English. And on a sideboard of seven stages was set out every piece of gold plate in the town. And when, true to his word, Henry and his guests rode in, they were greeted with loving looks and good English cheer.

"I did well to trust my Nan!" thought Henry. And after supper, when the cheerful music from the gallery changed to sweet dance tunes, the great doors between the serving screens were flung wide to a fanfare of trumpets, and four young girls tripped in. Each, with her unbound hair, was a houri to the men's mellowed vision, and each danced backwards, laughing and beckoning, and leading by multi-coloured ribbons eight masked ladies shimmering in cloth of gold.

The guests rose to a man to greet them, and Henry dug Francis in the ribs with brotherly glee. "Go on and lead the dance! And choose the one with the brightest eyes, look you," he urged, lapsing in his excitement into the Welsh of his forefathers, and assured that after the most cursory glance Francis of Valois would choose Anne.

It was like old times for those two to be dancing together, and when Henry removed all the ladies' masks, Francis, feigning surprise at the identity of his light-footed partner, made gallant reparation for the deliberate insult offered her by his womenfolk. "*Venus etait blonde, l'on ma dit,*" said he, carrying her hand to his heart as only a Frenchman can. "*Mais l'on voit bien qu'elle est brunette!*"

Anne's ready wit and fluent French scintillated that night as brightly as her elusive beauty. Francis enjoyed talking to her so much that he forgot to dance with any of the other ladies, and it was a long time before any of his subjects, who had flirted with Anne in their youth, got a chance to swarm about her. However determined their wives were to ignore her, it seemed that all of them wanted to brag among his fellows back in Paris that he had danced or dallied with the much-talked-of woman for whom the English King had defied the Pope and set all Europe by the ears.

And the more other men admired her, the higher Henry Tudor prized her. He felt himself to be in the pride of his manhood, still young enough for romance, yet experienced enough for mastery. "This night I will have her though I take her by force!" he promised himself, showing his ardour unashamedly before them all.

Both Anne and her brother were at the height of their exuberance. On the spur of the moment their fertile imaginations devised a dozen different mimes, while Jane Rochford and Arabella snatched banners and tapestries and flimsy silver tissues to clothe the performers in impromptu costumes. Androcles and the Lion, they mimed, with Norreys as the handsome Greek and the Grand Marshal of France as the suffering, noble beast, padding round him in a sheepskin floor rug. Paris and the apple, with Anne, inevitably, as the Love Goddess. An absurd burlesque of the Field of the Cloth of Gold in which Will Somers insisted upon impersonating his master, astride a wolfhound bedecked with heraldry. And finally St. George and the Dragon, with Henry, splendid in cloth of gold and armour, as St. George; Anne in white samite, bound to an iron candle sconce as the Damsel in Distress; and a dozen hilarious young gentlemen of England, head to rump on all fours, swathed in dull silver tissue as the Dragon.

"Here, sir! Hack off the Dragon's head with this!" cried Francis Weston, clambering on a stool to reach down a great axe from its hook upon the wall.

But Francis of Valois intercepted him in mock horror. "None of your uncouth English axes!" he protested. "We do things in a more civilized manner in France, where even our blackest traitors get their necks neatly severed with a sword, and my executioner has a sharper blade than any. But here, take mine, Harry, for the easy quittance of so fine a dragon, and forbear to disgust the Damsel with your coarse hackings!"

As soon as the dragon had been more decently dispatched the whole riotous party rode down to the harbour to visit the fleet. Henry wrapped Anne in his own ermine mantle and lifted her, laughing, to the back of his great horse. He led the way down through the cobbled streets carrying her across his saddle before him in the hollow of his arm—a thing he could not do in England, although she often rode discreetly pillion. All the wealthy merchants' houses and the fisherfolk's quaint hovels were lit up, and as they went singing on their way the bilingual English settlers, to whom the injured Queen Katherine was merely a name, ran before them cheering, taking Anne and the great, ruddy King to their hearts with almost Latin enthusiasm for a pair of lovers.

Never would the folk of Calais forget how their Market Square was *en fête* that night, with the gorgeously dressed gallants and lovely ladies, the officers from the English ships, the bobbing lanterns and the prancing horses, and how they all joined in the singing, feeling themselves a part of the land across the sea from which their fathers came. And when at last the merchants and the fisherfolk trailed off to bed, the Castle party turned by the great sea wall and Henry put his horse galloping up the rough dark cliff "to show Nan England." The French knights came scrambling after, full of good wine and laughter, with many an oath for the slippery chalky ground, and Anne, no mean horsewoman herself, thrilled to every effortless movement of Henry's faultless horsemanship. And all the time, in the romantic darkness, his strong right arm held her, his hand crushing her breast beneath the regal white and crimson cloak.

"Look, sweetheart, yon lies your kingdom—yours and mine," he cried, hot with exertion. "See the beacon lit by watchful Englishmen upon the cliffs of Dover!"

And Anne's bright eyes had strained across the twenty miles of dark water towards the familiar little port from which they had embarked in sunlight, and either saw or thought she saw, to please him, a dim speck of fire burning in the night. And Henry had sat his horse in silence awhile, forgetful even of the woman in his arms, gazing through the darkness towards the unseen land that was the very blood of him.

"I would not lose this outpost in Europe for a thousand crowns. And Mary, a woman, might have it wrested from her," Henry whispered in Anne's ear. "So do you not see, my sweet, how surely we must breed a stalwart son?"

And then some woman, less wrapped about in love and ermine, had complained that the northwest wind was cold; and they had all clattered back through the deserted streets again, with boats and nets making a magic, foreign, exciting place of it, and the grim lighted castle before them as a friendly goal.

There had been amicable "good nights"—more genuine, both monarchs felt, because of the Boleyns' crazy escapades than from any long sitting in Council Chambers. A final drink set out by sleepy servants, and a handsome gift from Francis for the English Venus, as he teasingly called Anne. And even while she thanked him, her watchful eye was on the sparkling glasses. She knew that the end of her defiance had come. And that it was true, what Henry had once told her, that in the chase he never let his quarry go. Henry was seldom drunk, but tonight, knowing herself to be no virgin, she would not have him specially sober. The stolid English servants were too slow. But a nod and a captivating smile to Francis' own dapper, quick-witted squire and the half-empty glass at Henry's elbow was unobtrusively refilled, and then filled again. His full-throated, good-natured laughter was echoing to the vaulted roof, filling Calais Castle with the warm assurance that her master was come from overseas again.

And then they had all trooped up to bed. Margaret had been too tactful to offer to sleep in Anne's room that night, and when Arabella had undressed her and brushed out her long hair and gone away to bed, Anne surveyed the room which had been allotted to her and knew that there was no escape. It was a round room built into one of the massive towers in some ruder age. Along the rough stone walls went Anne, feeling carefully beneath the freshly hung arras; but there were no doors except the one through which that giggling jade Arabella had departed, and the only window looked down upon the rocks and a tempestuous sea. The boom of beating waves came up to her and Anne closed the old-fashioned wooden shutter, the better to listen. But she did not bolt the door.

Instead she stood at the bed foot, watching it. By the light of a single candle on a tall iron stand the unfastened black bedgown revealed the alabaster whiteness of her body, making her a snare for any man.

And presently, as she had expected, the door opened quietly and Henry Tudor let himself in. For a moment, he leaned against it breathing quickly, and her mind noted gladly that he shot the bolt behind him. He looked spruce and younger, as he did on the tennis court, in a pair of dark velvet trunks and a silk shirt carelessly open at the neck; and the new French hair crop suited him, showing up the attractive copper lights in his hair. He came straight to her and looked her over slowly, from the aureole of candlelight on her dark head to the white nakedness of her slender feet. It was a very different look from the first lewd survey he had given her at Hever. "You are more desirable than any woman God ever made!" he said huskily.

He took the black bedgown from her gleaming shoulders and flung it across a fireside stool as if it had cost him a mere song. Anne made no protest—only stood there with the sable cloak of her hair about her as she had done years ago when first she knew she was to go to Court, knowing herself, even then, to be more beautiful like that than in any bejewelled dress. But this time instead of shyly seeking her reflection in a simple maid's mirror, she saw it blazing in her royal lover's eyes.

"Like any country wench bedevilled by the romance of a foreign town and the masterfulness of a new man," she jibed softly, hanging on to the remnants of her sophistication even when she was irrevocably in his arms.

"Scarcely a *new* man!" laughed Henry, stopping her feint at cynicism with the hungry ardour of his mouth.

He had known when he had fondled her on his horse that he would have her, and now to his exceeding joy he felt all the long-pent ardour of her desire rising to meet his own. Her white arms reached up to cling, her warm, slanting eyes both promised and invited.

On that old state bed at Calais no phantom lover lay between them. Anne had believed in and waited for her own heart's lover. She had seared her soul to revenge him. And now that there was no such person, it was all too easy to give herself in lust. Rome and England were mere names in some other world. Ambition, cool calculation, her sister Mary's warnings—all were drowned by the hot beat of her blood. Neither coerced nor overawed, Anne gave herself freely that night in Calais, not because her lover was a king but because he was Henry Tudor, a virile redhead who alone could satisfy all her frustrated clamouring of sex.

Chapter Thirty

I T WAS ST. PAUL'S Day in January.

In very different mood Anne stood in a disused attic of the late Cardinal's town house, which the King had taken for himself and renamed Whitehall. A sense of unreality pervaded her as she looked round at the white-washed walls and sloping beams. Such rooms, she supposed, the servants slept in. There was no furniture, no fireplace, and only a small window set deep in the eaves; but a brazier had been brought in to counteract the midwinter cold.

A hastily contrived altar had been set up beneath the sloping roof, and before the lighted candles hovered a group of anxious-eyed priests. There was the new Archbishop, Cranmer, giving instructions, and Dr. Lee from the King's chapel arguing, and an unknown monk who still held the smoking taper in his shaking hand.

For this was Anne's wedding day. Her secret wedding, like Mary of Suffolk's, which in her girlhood she had always envied. And yet how little like! Anne's mind flew back to that spring morning in Paris, with Mary's radiance and the romance of young lovers. Whereas now, somehow the romance seemed to have withered to a kind of furtiveness.

The small, insignificant room seemed full of people. Apart from the Franciscan monk, Anne knew them all—but how different they looked, sleepy-eyed, hurriedly dressed and pulled from their beds at dawn!

On the opposite side of the room from the altar and the whispering priests, stood her own family. They had a wary yet triumphant look. All except Jocunda, who was crying secretly into a handkerchief from which a little nostalgic whiff of country lavender trailed across the ugly room. The Duke of Norfolk headed them, trying his best to appear at ease in such peculiar surroundings. Her father and brother held themselves stiffly, as if determined to support her. And immediately behind her, thrilled to the soul at having been selected to attend her mistress on so venturesome an occasion, Arabella Savile bent to spread the white froth of Anne's simple white train.

It seemed only a moment or two before the key turned cautiously in the lock and the King himself came in, followed by Norreys and Heneage. Henry was dressed in no particular finery and after one hasty kiss upon Anne's cold hand, he joined the whispering, candlelit group about the altar. Even now he was not free, as other men, to think only of his bride; for Anne heard him assuring their troubled consciences that, although his former wife still lived, he held a dispensation for a second marriage. He did not say from whence it had come.

Presently the new Archbishop went to join the other witnesses; for no one must ever bring it up against the Primate of England that he had bigamously abused the sacrament of marriage. Dr. Lee seemed to suspect that it was he, and not the Pope, who had prepared the dispensation. And how right he was, thought Anne, passing proud hands over her still slender hips. For was he not the King's tool, and should he not do something to legitimatize the King's heir. For she, Anne Boleyn, Marchioness of Pembroke, was two months gone with child.

Only yesterday she had told the King and, overjoyed, he had immediately sent her his best physicians. Dr. Butts had confirmed her momentous news, and Cranmer had been told to make plans for this secret wedding. But as yet Anne herself scarcely believed it. It was not as if she were about to bear a child for a man with whom she was passionately in love; and, while fully appreciating her father's reiteration that this was the final steppingstone to success, she resented the sharing and marring of her body which would take from her, at any rate for a time, the personal feminine advantage with which she had always faced life.

Perhaps it was this strong division of feeling which lent to everything within the obscure little room such a sense of unreality. As if she were standing outside herself, objectively watching the untoward proceedings.

She was aware that Henry had returned to her side, and that her cold hand was now firmly held in his comforting warm one, and that it was to be the tall Franciscan monk, who from time to time regarded her with covert admiration, who was to marry them.

"Who is he?" she whispered to Henry.

"George Brown," he whispered back. So commonplace an English name might have come quickly into anyone's mind, and she doubted its authenticity; but at least the Franciscan, whoever he was, appeared to have sufficient fanatical temerity to perform the daring deed.

Although Anne knelt beside Henry and heard his ready responses and, with him, offered at the Holy Mass—although in a vague kind of way she was aware of her father's deep sigh of accomplishment when he achieved the faintly ridiculous status of being the King's father-in-law—her roving mind was never quite contained within the little locked attic of Whitehall. Out through the dormer window, since the room looked eastward up the curved sweep of the Thames, she could see the rosy flush of a newborn frosty day. Away past the little village of Charing, nestling among its trees upon the left bank, rose the imposing roofs and spires of London, and gabled houses of London Bridge spanning the water like a street, and, far as the eye could see round the bend of the reach, the strong, squat white huddle of the Tower.

A prophetic excitement for bigger events rose in her, blotting out the unceremonious, half-shamed present. Out there in her husband's capital she might ride to her Coronation, the unborn child in her womb might one day reign, the Word of God might be free to the people in all those city churches. And who could say what other things might happen? The Future was unwritten history—history which she at this very moment, by marrying the King of England, was helping to fashion.

Henry was helping her to rise, and people were beginning to make polite conversation in little relieved groups again. Well, she had had the secret wedding she had always wanted. In a pearled white dress like Mary Tudor's. And yet—and yet where was the spring sunshine and the reckless ardour? "I have waited so long," warm-hearted, adorable Mary had said. And she, Anne, could say the same. But not for love—the sort of clean-born young love that can make a man and a maid hide letters in secret places, tremble at a touch of hands and, later, give their bodies, each to each, in a kind of dedication. All that had died for Anne, through no fault of her own, although a dozen hardier, more spectacular things might take its place.

"No Fitzroy this time," Henry was whispering tactlessly, as he kissed his new-made bride. And Anne had been thankful that her sister was not present, to add another pinprick of humiliation with the reminder of her sturdy auburn-haired son.

Already there was a snuffing of candles, a grave offering of respects to the bride who was not yet an openly acknowledged queen, a perfunctory kissing among relatives, and a hasty farewell to George who, already booted and spurred, was being dispatched to Paris to bear the good news to "our dear brother of Valois." And then a silent, hasty dispersal from the deserted corridor with instructions to appear, each in his own apartment, as if this day had begun no differently from any other day.

While Arabella unfastened the white wedding dress, Anne pledged the girl's merry tongue to no particular secrecy. As far as she was concerned, she would rather that people knew, as very soon they must—especially Katherine in her new duress at Buckden.

"I am the King of England's wife," she said aloud and, finding herself suddenly weary, she sat to break her fast, dressed in the beautiful bedgown he had given her.

And into the void of her abstracted weariness walked Mary. "Since I was not invited to the wedding, I begged leave of our stepmother to come and wish you well and bring you my small gift," she explained, without any show of resentment.

Somehow the sight of her younger sister, standing serene and unlined in the revealing sunlight, annoyed Anne intensely. "It is kind of you. But you must surely know why you were not invited," she said ungraciously.

"I know that the Duke and our father are angry with me for marrying again without their consent," acknowledged Mary. "Did Master Cromwell plead with them on my behalf as I begged him?"

"Do you suppose I enjoy seeing you, a Boleyn, put yourself into a position where you must needs beg favours of one of my husband's minions?" cried Anne angrily. "And how could you expect the family to feel anything *but* displeasure? William Stafford is a nobody."

"He is an honest knight, which is all the King provided for me before."

"We could do better for you now."

"I thank you. But I love William," said Mary steadfastly.

"How beautiful she is," thought Anne. "And even when that hair of hers begins to grey, she will grow placidly more beautiful down the years." One could picture her training a succession of sons to manhood, training her daughters to be modest gentle-women, and considering all her husband's wishes in some small country manor. And because Anne herself could have had a similar sort of life, and in many a quiet moment her heart harked back to it, she rose from her half-finished bread and honey in a flurry of annoyance. "Have you no ambition, Mary?" she demanded, for the twentieth time.

Undaunted, Mary broke into a little laugh. "If I ever had, I learned my lesson," she countered, without shame.

"You can stand there and laugh now, but you cried then! Do you not remember how you sobbed and sobbed?" retorted Anne.

But Mary only looked at her with a kind of candid tenderness, so that for the first time each of them remembered how she had held Anne from stumbling when she was small. "Having discarded me, the King can do me no more harm," she pointed out.

There was such profound truth in the slowly spoken words that Anne walked away thoughtfully to the window, her expensive black velvet whispering after her. "You mean," she said, thinking suddenly and inconsequently of George, "that only by living humbly can one be safe?"

Mary stooped to rearrange a nosegay of snowdrops that Druscilla had found for Anne's wedding morning. If she had spoken to warn, she had not meant to sadden. Particularly on this day. She began to talk lightly, evasively. "Had I not met William, I should have had to marry someone. For what was I to live on, an impecunious widow, an unwelcome failure in my father's house?"

Anne turned impulsively at once. "My dear! When poor Will died of the plague I wrote to the King at once, as you asked me. But Henry disclaimed all responsibility. Perhaps because at that time we were—because he was wanting me, from the same family." Anne stumbled a little, feeling, as she always did, the embarrassment of the situation. "But he wrote to our father, I know, pointing out that it stood with his honour to provide for you in your extreme necessity."

Anne had always hated speaking of this, because the very words had impressed upon her unwilling mind how callously Henry had rid himself of a woman he had tired of. But now she remembered that she was married. What need had she to heed them now when, before important witnesses, she had been made his wife?

She lifted the insignificant carved mazer bowl which Mary had brought her, and held it appreciatively to the light. "It is beautifully wrought and I shall cherish it," she said gently. And for a moment or two they stood in constrained silence, these twain who had loved each other in childhood and, because of Henry, had drifted so far apart.

It was Mary who broke the uncomfortable silence. "He married you because you are pregnant, I suppose?" she asked.

Once again that sharp prick of anger flamed up in Anne because Mary, looking at Henry objectively as something she had finished with, not only knew him, but could acknowledge forthrightly those things she knew.

"As you must have heard, I went with him to France two months ago," Anne answered obliquely, knowing that the blunt question had been asked without malice.

"A child will be a great joy to look forward to, Nan," said Mary simply, turning to take her leave.

But with her going Anne suddenly felt herself to be losing something comforting and human when she needed it most. She ran across the room and stopped her sister at the door. "Mary, does it hurt horribly?" she asked, in a low, shamed voice.

For a moment Mary's placid face looked merely surprised and uncomprehending; then, seeing the twisting hands, the dark eyes full of apprehension, it changed to a reminiscent, smiling kind of tenderness. "I think without the pain there would be no joy of possession," she said, discounting the suffering in contemplation of her own hard-won happiness.

Anne clutched at her arm. "But I am not good like you," she confessed distractedly. "I have never wanted children like other women. How do you know that I shall love it?"

Although Anne was the King's wife, and in sort a queen, Mary patted her arm and kissed her with that air of achieved womanhood, of faint compassion, which Anne usually found so hard to bear. "The Mother of Christ be with you in your hour," she soothed kindly. "And cease to fret, dear Nan, for babes always bring with them all the love they need."

Chapter Thirty-One

A MAY MORNING AND ALL the bells of London ringing. Ringing for Nan Boleyn, because she was being brought from the Tower to Westminster for her Coronation. Ringing because Henry Tudor had ordered it; because he had cast off the last shackle of Rome and made Archbishop Cranmer declare his first marriage to be null and void. Because Cromwell, the new Chancellor, had threatened the bishops with confiscation of their lands if they refused to acknowledge the King head of both church and state. Because at last Anne was to be Queen of England.

Her eyes were still bemused by the wealth of pomp he had prepared for her. All the way from Greenwich yesterday the Thames had been the scene of pageantry beyond her wildest dreams. The water had been alive with colourful craft. Peacock, the Lord Mayor, had come in his state barge to meet her, followed by fifty barges of the city companies, in all the richness of their ceremonial robes. Before her had gone an armed boat firing culverins and bearing a wondrous dragon belching crimson fire. On her right hand had glided the "Bachelors Barge," from which Fitzroy, her poetical young cousin Surrey, and many of her admirers had filled the morning air with sweet music. While from a flower-decked wherry on her left, her younger maids-of-honour held aloft a golden tree from which bloomed red and white roses, vaunting the strains of Plantagenet blood united by her marriage with the

King. Milord of Suffolk's barge and the Earl of Wiltshire's, with a fleet bearing scores of other nobles, had followed flamboyantly in her wake.

And Anne herself had used Katherine of Aragon's own barge. For her that was the crowning triumph. She had always promised herself that one day she would do so. Secretly she had given orders that the proud arms of Aragon should be hacked off and her own escutcheon painted on the prow.

What mattered it that Katherine's watermen had looked at her with sullen hate, or that half the good Catholics lining the river banks had come out of curiosity to see the "Bullen whore"? Had not the Tower guns boomed and the Governor, Sir William Kingston, welcomed her to the best apartments, and Henry himself been waiting at the landing stairs to clasp her in strong arms?

"What thought you of our welcome, sweetheart? Was it not a brave show?" he had asked eagerly, through the reverberating noise.

Perhaps Anne, who shared his love of the spectacular, had never come more near to loving him. "No one but you could have planned it!" she told him, her eyes wet with gratitude.

"Each day will be better than the last and all entirely yours. To show the world what I think of you," he had promised.

And either because she was touched that for once he should stand aside and leave the centre of the stage to another, or because she had been shaken by that ominous smouldering of hatred hidden beneath all the banners and the fanfare, she had clung to him, realizing that without him she would be as nothing in an unfriendly world.

"Take every care, darling," he had recommended. "For tomorrow you must be up betimes to ride through London for your Coronation. And be sure I shall be watching you. I shall borrow Kingston's barge and go unobtrusively before you to Westminster."

And now the wonderful May morning had come and she stood before her mirror with all her women like a blaze of multi-coloured butterflies about her. They had dressed her in a surcoat and mantle of white tissue trimmed with ermine, with the King's heavy pearls about her neck and a crimson outer robe stiff with gems. Arabella and Druscilla had brushed and scented her hair until it hung in a shining cascade below her knees.

"No need, really, for the cloak, Madame. With hair like this you could ride through the streets nude as Lady Godiva," laughed blue-eyed Arabella.

"It always seems lamentable that her Grace should have to hide so much beauty when she goes abroad," agreed Mary Howard, fixing a coronet of rubies about her cousin's brow instead of the usual pearled cap.

"Well, for one day at least all London will see your tresses, dear sister, as a sign that you went virgin to the King," observed Jane Rochford, with a peal of froward laughter. "And all London seems to be ready and waiting to be so assured," she added, running with her quick, birdlike gestures to push open a casement overlooking the wharf.

Anne looked at her with loathing as she leaned there, wasp-waisted and shrewishly pretty in her daring yellow chequered gown. "I pray you, Jane, go fetch me a spare kerchief," she bade her, sharply.

But although, mercifully, Jane had whisked herself petulantly away, she had left the casement open. And Anne heard the King's voice raised in anger down below. With a small, unobtrusive snapping of her fingers she drew Margaret to the window. Margaret, a Wyatt whose love depended neither upon public rebuff nor royal favour.

"Are there not scores of suitable barges on the river without taking this one?" boomed Henry's voice.

Though they both looked out, neither of them could see him. "He must be directly below," whispered Anne, white as parchment. "Lean out, Margot, and see if you can find out whom he is upbraiding."

"Your Comptroller, or more likely your bargemaster," hazarded Margaret. The diffident murmur of some man's excuses were hard to catch; but not so Henry Tudor's wrath. The barge Anne had arrived in must still be moored there while he waited to step into the Governor's, a contingency which even Anne had not foreseen. And with his quick eye for craft of any kind, he must immediately have recognized it. A thing which had been a part of his family life and was associated in his memory with so many splendid days. Between the shrilling of trumpets and the hiss of fireworks bits of the dressing-down the unfortunate man was getting came up to them. "The gold leaf I had wrought by Cuylders all around the prow, and the arms of Imperial Spain and England. Next after mine, her watermen were the swiftest—she knew them each by name, I tell you." And then, in a final bellow of fury, "How *dare* anyone tamper with my wife's barge?"

Anne's heart almost stopped beating and the child seemed to stir in her womb. "My wife's barge." In his anger, as with many a man who had married a second time, the words he had so vehemently eschewed had slipped out. But Henry's first wife was still alive. And on this day, of all days, that he should have alluded to her so! Anne knew that the furious rating should have been hers; and that, because of the unborn son forever in his mind, she would probably be spared it. But it was a bad omen, more disturbing than all young Arabella's babblings about anti-Protestant pamphlets and old wives' prophecies that she herself would come to some bloody end.

Suffolk's voice could be heard coaxing Henry aboard the other barge lest he be late, and Margaret hastily closed the casement, forbearing to say "I warned you." Perhaps she alone understood how sitting in Katherine's barge had helped to wipe out the humiliating memory of a young, lovesick girl with a voice of gold, being sent ignominiously up the backstairs to mind a snuffling, overfed spaniel, away from all the light and adulation.

But today Anne would have light and adulation enough to turn any woman's head. "The salutes are being fired for me! And women all down the ages will envy me," she told herself, and swept in all her glittering young arrogance from the royal apartments.

Out on the little green before the chapel of St. Peter they placed her in a splendid horse-drawn litter, and although it was May she shivered involuntarily as though, as countryfolk are wont to say, someone stepped across her grave. "A cold, grim place," she thought, looking about her as they bore her through the shadowed archway of the Bloody Tower and past the dark, low arch of Traitors' Gate. And glad to be leaving the fortress in which tradition decreed all English sovereigns must be taken for their Coronation. The gloom put her in mind of the elder Mary Tudor, dying in seclusion in Suffolk. "How can Charles Brandon bear to leave her? And how I would that she were here," were her last coherent thoughts as her palfreys, covered in white damask to their tapering ears, took her out into the sunshine of her triumph. Out to the waiting human tapestry of silk and velvet, heraldry and horses, pageants and Guild banners that seemed to represent the very wealth and power of England.

Anne threw back the weight of her hair, turning her slender neck a little to glance behind her. How lovely Margaret and the other women looked in crimson velvet, "swaying to the motion of their mounts." How sullen the old Duchess of Norfolk, following behind with Suffolk's daughter, Frances, in a chariot! The procession was winding between the tall houses of Fenchurch Street, and the whole city was *en fête*.

There were children with garlands, singing girls dressed as goddesses, and poets reading verses. By the Lord Mayor's orders, all the drinking fountains were running wine. On a platform about St. Paul's were more poets and more singing children. Every balcony and window was hung with rich drapery, and across the streets, stirred gaily by the river breeze, hung compliments in Latin and scrolls of welcome.

It was all flattering, colourful, intoxicating. But after awhile Anne's head began to ache. The morning was getting hotter and the press of people almost suffocating. However careful the grooms at her palfreys' heads, the swaying of the litter made her feel sick. She would have liked to shed the stiff, gemmed cloak; but it was regal and concealed her five months' pregnancy.

And although the appointed musicians played and the conduits ran good wine, the people themselves were silent. With covered heads, close packed and sweating behind the barriers and the halberdiers, they watched her go by. True, there was a certain amount of organized shouting, the open admiration of French merchants, the fervent zeal of followers of the new religion. But

Anne was no fool. She noticed how in places the citizens of London had mocked her, fixing the eagle of Imperial Spain unobtrusively somewhere above her own white falcon.

"'Tis the Boleyns' merchant blood," she heard some old crones shrill when, uncertain what to do, she kept a purse of gold presented to her at Cheapside. "Our good Queen Katherine weren't so niggard mean at *her* crowning."

Anne was not sorry when it was all over. She was overtired. Emotionally and physically, the day for which she had striven so long had proved an ordeal to a pregnant woman.

In Whitehall, Henry's arms were open to receive her. "Well, how liked you the look of our city?" he asked inevitably, just as he had asked her about his splendid water pageant. But this time, for all his eagerness, Anne did not cling with gratitude. "The city was well enough, sir," she answered tartly, jerking the gemmed cloak from her shoulders so that it lay like a thing of no account upon the rushes. "But I saw far too many caps on heads and heard far too few tongues!"

Something savage within her seemed to say it, caring not how much, after all his self-effacing effort, he was hurt. She was not to know how he had had to bully Peacock and his aldermen into spending so much money, nor by what obstinate insistence he had kept his nobler subjects fawning in their places. All she knew was that she had bowed her head graciously until it ached, and that none of those hateful Londoners had cried, "God save your Grace!" as she had heard them do a score of times for Katherine.

When the courtiers had withdrawn and Henry had tried to soothe her, she beat with her fists upon his mighty chest, demanding between hysterical sobs, "Why do you not *make* them cheer me?"

He had ceased to humour her then. "That is something which even I cannot do. The Londoners are a law unto themselves. And you do not always help, Nan, with your haughty ways," he had told her coldly, and sighed and gone his way.

And in the morning, on Whitsunday, Archbishop Cranmer had crowned her in the age-old Abbey. With striped cloths laid all the way from Palace to High Altar, with her aunt the Duchess of Norfolk bearing her train, and the freemen of the Cinque Ports holding the canopy of state above her. With all the monks and choristers of Westminster and their incense, and all the abbots and bishops in their richly embroidered copes. In a tall chair between choir and altar Anne sat, and the Archbishop anointed her and crowned her Queen of England. And, like an incredible dream come true, the glorious *Te Deum* was sung and all the nobility put on their coronets.

But the precious crown of St. Edward was too heavy for her head, just as the inner consecration of the ceremony escaped her sentiency. For her a coronation was something to be grasped at for personal aggrandizement rather than a transmuting acceptance of responsibility. Although she was quicker-witted than Henry, she remained unaware of that deeper obligation which he, with all his faults, accepted. Of that division of personality which made him daily more uneasy because he had produced but a daughter. No woman had ever worn that golden symbol in her own right, and to be really Queen of England a woman must be great enough to lose herself in part. To identify herself not only with all that glittering, symbolic ceremony but with the very earth of England. No matter what her personal loves, to *be* England. Pulsing to England's pride and vulnerable to her wounds. Transfused, dualized to part divinity, by solemn anointing.

When they had taken the weight of gold from Anne and set a lighter crown about her brow, she went, holily resolving, to Mass. And afterwards—a richly dressed maumet, a graceful puppet Queen—was led by her proud father, to the feasting in Westminster Hall.

Such was the grandeur of ceremony in that exquisite and traditional place that even Anne was awed. The most powerful earls in the land were her carver, her steward, her pantler, and her cupbearer. The Mayor of Oxford kept the buttery bar. While right into the hall through shafts of sunlight rode Suffolk and the Lord William Howard, her younger uncle, their chargers caparisoned to their fetlocks in crimson and purple. Anne knew that the King was watching from the cloisters, showing off his woman and his wealth to some of the foreign ambassadors and, deeply as she had delighted in the long-awaited triumph over her enemies, she wished with all her heart that Henry were at table beside her, to ease the ceremonial pomp with his experienced geniality.

And then, while silver trumpets heralded the first dishes, someone knelt before her holding a golden bowl of scented water between fine, strong hands; and, turning to freshen her fingers, she found herself looking into Thomas Wyatt's eyes. For a brief, swooning moment all the pomp and ceremony swung away and the birds were singing again at Hever. Instead of some exotic fragrance, in nostalgic memory she smelled the aromatic scent of freshly clipped yew, the lingering sweetness of gilly flowers. "Tom!" she breathed, with eyes closed against giddiness.

"For your Grace's fingers," he said formally, reminding her that the Tudor's small keen eyes were watching.

Anne dabbled her ringed fingers, seeing his handsome, down-bent head through a sudden haze of tears. "Thank you, good cousin," she said, as formally.

Gracefully, Wyatt rose. "Forget not yet," he whispered daringly, as he bowed himself backwards from her side. And Anne knew that, married or single, he loved her still.

And so, at last, the long day ended. The day of which she had dreamed for years. Tomorrow there would be tilting and a wealth of festivities in her honour. But this night she must sleep—and think no more of Hever nor of Wyatt's poet's eyes.

"At last I am Queen of England," she said, stretching her limbs between the sheets of the great four-poster, and longing for the time when her body would be her own again.

She watched Henry shed his furred bedrobe and stand for a moment or two in pink, muscular nudity; and noted the serious contentment on his face, as he leaned to snuff a candle. "And what should be still more important to both of us is that, after me, our son will be king," he said sententiously.

In spite of her weariness, Anne began to giggle in the darkness.

"What cause is that for mirth?" he asked, clambering into the great bed beside her.

"None, God be praised," smiled Anne, turning to his hungry embrace. "Only, my great zany, you always seem so certain that the child will be a boy."

"But of course it will be," he assured her, and fell to twining her dark hair about her little, pointed breasts. "All that is over, hinney, about my sons dying. It was a curse because Arthur had her first."

"Please God you be right!" prayed Anne, knowing that he really believed it. Knowing that so much depended upon it.

Chapter Thirty-Two

W ILL THAT OBSTINATE OLD woman never give in? Can she not see how obscene it is to keep clutching at a man who had been tired of her for years?" groaned Anne, staring out at the dispiriting rain. She was living at Hampton in apartments that had been Queen Katherine's, for she and Henry had taken possession of the Manor they had always coveted; and since their return from France, workmen were busy making improvements everywhere.

"This new Spanish ambassador, Chapus, puts fresh heart into her, I think," observed Will Brereton, who had come to Anne's rooms to while away an idle hour with his lute.

"The King is very agreeable to Chapus," sighed Anne.

"He cannot afford to be otherwise," George reminded her, glancing up from the sheets of music he had been looking over for his friend. "After all, have we not been living in fear of a Spanish war for years?"

"All the same, I overheard Chapus complaining bitterly that when he went to Buckden he found the King had sent secret instructions before him that he and his Spanish party were not to be admitted," volunteered little, dapper Francis Weston, who always managed to overhear everything.

"My new stepson by Blount was telling me something about Katherine and her women appearing on the battlements like a lot of sex-starved harpies to be serenaded in their native tongue with a romantic flourish of feathered hats," said Anne maliciously.

"Young Fitzroy was so doubled up with laughter when they were talking about it at supper that for once he forgot to ogle our haughty Howard cousin, Mary," confirmed George.

"But the Queen won the next trick," said Brereton.

Anne stamped her foot at him and would have turned them all out of her room, so uncertain was her temper these days. "*Must* you go on calling her 'the Queen'?" she cried.

Big, broad-shouldered Brereton caught George's eye and sighed resignedly. But before he could gather up his lute and music, Anne had swirled round and kissed him to make amends. "Oh, Will, forgive me! My nerves are all shred to ribbons these days," she apologized immediately. "What with the people reviling me in the streets and those self-righteous Grey girls telling everyone that none of those hateful women would meet me in France."

"But, Nan, you never stood so secure. Our father, Uncle Thomas, everyone belonging to our party, says so," remonstrated George. "It is only because these other women envy you." He glanced around at the sober, magnificent furnishings of the apartments which Wolsey had always set aside for the use of Queen Katherine. "We thought your having 'the Lady Anne's apartments' wonderful once, do you remember? And then your very own house at Westminster. And look at you here, in the Palace you always wanted. Cardinal Wolsey's Palace. And his Grace almost rebuilding it for you!"

Anne joined him at the window above the King's privy staircase, and together they looked down at the new gilded fountain in the inner courtyard, at the masons working beneath sodden sacks upon the scaffolding within which the new Great Hall was rising, and the labourers who took it in turns to work at double wages all night so that the tiled floor might be laid and the slender pinnacles bear aloft proud little gilded weather vanes, and so that her initials and Henry's might be graven, entwined, on the fan vaulting of the great doorway. What other woman in England could have such solid tokens of a man's enduring devotion? The sight of them restored Anne's confidence and painted a proud smile upon her petulant lips.

"I must be overtired, I think," she yawned, turning from the rainswept window. "If the King gluts me with palaces, he starves me of sleep." She treated them to a comically lewd grimace which set them all laughing, and went to join Margaret, who sat quietly sewing beside the hearth. "Well, then, let us hear about the Queen, Francis Weston," she invited, spreading out her full stiff skirt with exaggerated matronly effect.

Like most rather vain men, Weston loved to hold the floor, once he had the chance. And he told a story well.

"I had it from Suffolk himself who is but now returned from Buckden," he began, anxious to impress upon them upon what favourable terms he stood. "What with his wife's sickness and the reception he got in Huntingdonshire, the poor Duke looked quite worn out, and Norfolk and milord of Wiltshire were reviving him with some good strong Malvoisie."

"And they bade you stay," interpolated George impatiently. For was it not common knowledge how high the Westons stood in the King's good graces, since he had prudently bought from them the ground lease of Hampton before spending money on the place?

"The King sent Charles Brandon there to dismiss the woman's household and bring her to reason. How long can he be expected to keep three royal establishments?" flared Anne, not choosing to remember that it was she who urged him to keep mother and daughter apart, or to compare the lavishness of Hampton with the meagre households at Hatfield and Buckden.

"Like me, Charles has always had to earn his status. A brother-in-law is a useful sort of relation," observed George, who had missed a couple of good tournaments through having to go to France.

"I happened to see them start out from London. The King sent five hundred men with Suffolk to intimidate one woman," remarked Brereton, bending to admire Margaret's embroidery.

"And much comfort he had of it!" scoffed Weston.

"You mean she still defied him?" asked Margaret, looking up with poised needle.

"Even though he called out all the local gentry, armed with weapons of Bosworth vintage, to give him countenance."

"Tell me just what happened!" cried Anne, feeling that she must know the least detail about her rival, though the hearing of it might give her no particular pleasure.

Weston was well into his stride, perched on a table, telling his secondhand tale with so much vigour that they forgot he had not actually been there. "It appears that the Duke of Suffolk saw the—the lady and told her in his blunt way that she must submit to Archbishop Cranmer's decision, and abandon her everlasting appeals to Rome; and that she and all her household must take the new oath of allegiance to the King."

"Which was as good as to acknowledge me his lawful wife," put in Anne, gleefully.

"And himself as head of the church," added George.

"Or else, he told her, she must lose all those devoted servants of hers and go to Fotheringay or some other pestilential place," went on Weston. "I had had to look out all the most unhealthy fenland manors on the map before he set out."

"Well?" demanded Anne, lifting her chin proudly lest any of them should think she had suggested it.

"The Duke is not, as you know, the type of man to stand any nonsense from underlings. He made short work of the English members of her household, dismissing them all in floods of tears. Though in actual fact it was their mistress bade them leave her sooner than take the oath."

"One would think that out of pity for them she would capitulate," began Margaret.

"I suppose Suffolk must have counted upon that, too. And considered his odious task half done. But the lady knew what she was about; for there and then, before his eyes, the wives of the local gentry came out into the driving snow with pack horses and cloaks and took her people into their houses."

"And what about the Spaniards?" asked Brereton.

"There the poor Duke had yet more trouble, for they pretended not to understand English and protested that without a trusty interpreter it was against their consciences to subscribe to any oath which might perjure their immortal souls. And when, hating himself for it, he gave orders for her frightened women to be dragged from her, Katherine of Aragon only stood on the damp staircase, pulling her furs closer about her, and swore that it would make no difference. That if her husband chose to treat her so, she would neither eat nor undress, but stay alone in her room until it pleased the Almighty to take her. So that in very pity Suffolk let the women and her aged priest and apothecary stay."

In the face of such epic defiance even the well-favoured, well-fed young men and women gathered around the new Queen's fire had no word to say. It was as if the stark loneliness of Buckden penetrated their happiness, giving their unwilling eyes a glimpse into the torment of the forsaken woman's soul.

"After that," Weston's voice went on, "she retired to her room and would talk only through a draughty arrow slit, so that Suffolk had perforce to shout up to her, which he must have hated because he is precious of his dignity and could hear some of the locals and soldiery tittering behind his back. 'Think upon all his Grace's past kindnesses which you and I well remember from our youth,' he besought her, being reduced to try persuasion. 'And consider how deeply you have worried him all these past months, putting him to endless expense and setting him at enmity with all his neighbours both at home and abroad.'"

"It must have been like spreading a bright tapestry of bygone days before her," murmured Brereton, who was older than the rest of them and could remember her sharing in the laughter and glamour of life with the King and Brandon and her sister-in-law, Mary Tudor. "How did she answer, Francis?"

"By setting her mouth rigidly in the way she does, and telling Suffolk that if the King suffered from the enmity of his neighbours it must be the outcome of their sense of justice. Because, for her own part, although she was a foreigner, her neighbours had always loved her."

"It is as if she cannot keep her tongue from saying the thing which most annoys him," commented Anne.

"But she has more courage than us all," said George Boleyn, wondering if his own licenced tongue would ever dare to wag one half so defiantly in self-defence against the King.

"Then the Duke, torn between exasperation and admiration, it seems, tried another approach, speaking, I think, in genuine concern for her safety," said Weston. "'If I return without your submission, his Grace will but send again someone, perchance, who has no love for you, Madame,' he reminded her. 'You have many a time complained of this place, but Fotheringay or any of the other houses that have been mentioned are slow death.'"

"Surely that moved her?" said Anne, in a low, shamed voice. She had so fervently hoped that it would because, for all the cruel things she said in her anxiety, she did not want death again upon her conscience, even indirectly, as in the case of Wolsey. If only the woman would give in and allow herself to be hounded quietly into a convent!

"Not by a hair's breadth!" declared Weston, leaning across the table to pour himself some wine. They waited, all of them with lifted faces, while he swallowed the drink he must have needed. "Prompted, perhaps, by the allusion to neighbours," he went on, patting his lips fastidiously with a napkin lying near, "the Princess of Wales, as the King would have her called, came down the castle stairs again, leaning upon the arm of De la So, or whatever her apothecary's name is. Beckoning Suffolk and the Captain of the Guard to follow her, she walked with difficulty to the great open doorway of the Manor. From where she stood she must have seen the tall shining pikes of the King's soldiers surrounding the moat; but her eyes and heart went to the little groups of Huntingdonshiremen, standing around their little bivouac fires within the courtyard. Homely little groups of country squires and farmers, in furbished-up breastplates, and even the humblest cowman armed with a riphook or a bullprong. As everyone knew, they had been called out to augment the royal pikemen, or at least to lend countenance to the proceedings; but at sight of her a great shout went up, and everyone among them doffed his cap in passionate loyalty. That must have been what Queen Katherine had counted on. She turned to her husband's brother-in-law then and smiled. 'Take me now,' she challenged. 'But I warn you that before these honest men, you will have to carry me over the threshold by force!'"

It was a long while before anyone in Katherine's usurped presence chamber spoke. Although she was not there, she shamed them. "And there had been nothing in the King's orders about force?" suggested Brereton at last, for the sake of something to say.

With a wary eye on his hostess, Weston slid down from the table. He had let his gift for dramatic eloquence carry him away again. He had let himself be more moved by the telling than he had intended—more moved, perhaps, than was safe. "So Suffolk and his five hundred men marched back again," he concluded, trying to speak indifferently. "'There never was a more obstinate woman!' he told the King."

To his surprise, Anne, the unaccountable jade, rose suddenly to her feet without rebuking him. "Nor a braver one," she admitted bitterly. The words were wrung out of her, torn from her inherent integrity; and, covering her face with both hands, she stood before the fire and wept. More, it is true, because her rival's courage was greater than her own, than for the other woman's unhappiness. And partly from exasperation because, for all her own wit and witchery and the King's child already stirring in her womb, she *still* could not win.

Swiftly, Margaret laid aside her sewing and went to comfort her. "That woman is my death or I am hers," moaned Anne, from within the loving shelter of her arms.

"Come and lie down awhile," coaxed Margaret, making a sign across her mistress' shoulder for all of them but George to go. "It is so bad for you to excite yourself just now."

"But I will see that she does not live to laugh at mine!" cried Anne shrilly, before George could put a warning hand over her mouth. They were dangerous words—words which might be brought up against her—and the others scarce out of the room. Anne herself must have realized it, for she let them quiet her almost at once. "You are right, Margot, darling," she said. "I carry England's heir within me and I must rest. And try to stop thinking. To stop thinking."

Disengaging herself gently from her friend's arms, she stood for a moment with fingers pressed to throbbing temples, trying to calm herself. "A while since you spoke of war with Spain. If Spain is going to send her ships, I pray she will send them now," she said with sudden earnestness.

"During our lifetime, you mean?" they asked, in accidental unison.

Anne nodded, lifting her eyes to a slim, golden shaft of sunshine piercing the heavy clouds. "So that we who have provoked war are the ones to suffer. I would not have my poor child—"

"Your poor child!" scoffed George, seeking to tease her back to gaiety.

But Anne was in serious vein, and thrilling to a new thought. "He will be neither half-French, nor half-Spanish," she mused, holding proud hands in a kind of wonder against her side. "But purebred English."

Her brother clapped her on the shoulder as he might have clapped Norreys or any of his men friends who had scored well at the butts. "And believe me, Nan," he encouraged, "if he grows up anything like you, with half your wit and spirit, he will know what to do about the Spaniards when they come!"

Chapter Thirty-Three

ALL EYES AND THOUGHTS were centred on a room in the
hushed Palace of Westminster where the new Queen was
brought to bed. To a gorgeous French four-poster, part of a
King's ransom, which rumour said she had chosen as being the only
bed fitting for the birth of her son.

Sweating, shuddering from a devastating wave of pain, Anne
clutched the sheet and seized a moment's respite from her travail.
Beyond the half-drawn bed curtains the room seemed full of
people. Relatives, apothecaries, an Archbishop and a Chancellor
—all muddled together in her anguished mind. Their subdued
whispering was but an unsubstantial background to the comings
and goings of her women, bearing innumerable strange burdens
and bowls of steaming water. And, in spite of everything, Anne's
lips had to widen in the similitude of a smile because, as George
had prophesied, half the physicians in the land appeared to be at
her bedside.

As a fresh pain wracked her, the familiar face of Dr. Butts,
detaching itself from the rest, swam before her, close and reassuring.
Anne clung a moment to his clever hand. He had been so kind to
her when she had the plague. But, Mother of Christ, would that he
had let her die of it, if this be bearing an heir for England!

Obediently, she crouched as he told her, knees to swollen belly.
Though the labour was growing harder she bit her lips until the

blood trickled to her chin, sooner than let out a sound. There were women there, she could swear, who grinned to see her suffer.

Someone was leaning over her, delivering a message. Enunciating each word very clearly as though to catch the consciousness of someone already far away. "Master Heneage from the King. His Grace sends you his loving assurances in your hour."

His loving assurances. Rows of blue and gold fleurs-de-lis wavered drunkenly on the embroidered tester before Anne's starting eyes as her whole being shuddered to another pain. If Henry, or any other man, had to produce a living child from his body, how soon the human race would become extinct! "Is it always like this?" she whispered towards the vague blackness where it seemed Butts had been standing.

"A long and hard delivery, your Majesty."

Anne knew it in her body that all women did not suffer so. She saw it in the hurrying panic of her women and in the hard faces of people like Jane, softened to pity. And all the value of majesty was wiped out because even a Queen must lie and suffer crudely as a cow—and die perhaps, as Mary of Suffolk had just died.

Hurt beyond endurance, Anne heard herself scream. "Harry! Harry!" she cried, and mercifully they supposed it was her husband upon whom she called. In the privacy of the curtains they were all gathered about her now. Jocunda was holding her. Holding her back from death, perhaps. In hot agony something was being torn from her loins. For what seemed an endless space of time she was the blind, mindless reservoir of all agony. Then down, down, into some merciful oblivion where there was only darkness and no more pain.

Long before Anne opened her eyes again, she was conscious of muted voices, of people's hands doing things about her body. A body which felt so light and detached that it might float away, and yet so weary that it must sink through the feather softness of the bed. She felt the warmth of a charcoal pan at her feet, and tasted the hot sweetness of the cordial someone held to her half-responsive lips. But in order to hug this blessedness of relief from suffering she kept her eyes shut still.

"It is all over, my poor darling," someone was whispering against her cheek. Margot, it must be, whose cool hands were wiping the sweat from her brow. And the loving kindness in her voice drew hard tears to lie hot upon Anne's cheeks. It was over, the agony was over. Gradually, thankfully, Anne savoured the return of her own identity. For awhile her thoughts went no further than that. Then, tentatively, she moved a hand beneath the bedclothes, felt her body and found it bound and flat.

The half-swallowed cordial was making her drowsy. If only she could sleep! If only all those important people beyond the bed curtains would go away! If only they would go away forever, leaving her to lie in her own bed at home without any golden crowns or fleurs-de-lis, as her sister had been content to do! Mary, who had not been such a fool after all. If only they would stop *talking*.

Through the annoyance of their urgent, agitated whispering, Anne became aware of yet another sound. A small, shrill, insistent sound, disturbing and unfamiliar. In her lassitude she lay listening to it for awhile before realizing that it was the vigorous wailing of a newborn child. Her child. The reason of all this ceremonial commotion of which, in spite of all her suffering, she herself was but a necessary part. The culmination of years of frustration. The heir for whose existence half Christendom had been turned upside down.

The whole extraordinary pattern of her life came back to her. Slowly, heavily her eyes began to open. Through thick, wet lashes she could see the wooden cradle on its rockers; and over by the fire a group of women clustered about the midwife who, sitting wide-kneed upon a stool, swathed long white bands about something in her lap.

Even then, Anne would have turned her head away wearily to sleep. But suddenly the thought of Henry charged into her mind. Wildly, she tried to raise herself. "Is it a boy?" she croaked.

They all turned from the babe to look at her pityingly, she thought. She began to understand the uncertain, half-frightened hush that had fallen upon the room. "For the love of Christ, say *something*!" she entreated.

Chamberlain, the King's chief physician, cleared his throat and tried to tell her. But he was old and slow and pompous. In charity, Jocunda forestalled him. "It is a daughter, Nan, darling."

A daughter!

All Anne's pride, all her security, were shattered like brittle glass. For the first time something, something completely outside her own control, had defeated her. She had known that it might happen, but Henry had been so sure! "Has someone told the King?" she faltered.

"Even now, your Grace," Butts assured her.

And now they were bringing her her daughter. Holding her out on a crimson cushion. Placing her on the great bed beside her. A bundle of expensive silks and laces with a tiny, reddish face and perfect waxen hands. Anne stretched out a shaky finger to push back the ornate bonnet, touching a soft fluff which promised to be red-gold. She sighed, oddly comforted, even in that deflated hour, because the girl child had at least her own tapering hands and Henry's hair.

"Children bring love with them," her sister had said. Yet, in the aftermath of hard travail, Anne felt nothing. "Am I an unnatural monster?" she wondered, simulating pleasure for Jocunda's sake. All she knew was that her heart was desolate and blank, and that the whole weary business would be to do again—the dull months of carrying, the unsightliness, the stabbing agony.

And then all the company beyond the curtains seemed to part and bend like a swaying field of corn before the sickle. All lesser figures in this drama of birth melted away into shadowed corners. The curtains at the foot of her bed were jerked apart peremptorily, and her husband stood there. Anne liked to remember afterwards that his eyes went straight to her. "They say you called for me in your hour," he said, touched to the core of his masculinity.

Anne lay like a colourless ghost, and did not gainsay him. Even she did not understand what had made her call aloud upon the name of the only man she had ever loved, the man to whom she had once pleaded that she might bear his child. Particularly since, in a sense, he no longer existed. "They have told you about the babe?" was all she could find to say.

Poor Harry Tudor, who had spent so many anticipatory hours preparing with his own hand the proclamation for a prince! But at least he must have experienced many similar disappointments; and for Anne's sake he made the best of it. "We shall have to have the clerks add an 'ess'," he said.

Anne felt grievously sorry for him. Although he tried to speak negligently, all the pride and excitement had gone out of him. He came round to the side of the bed, he who hated sickness, to lift her hand and kiss it. But even while his lips were pressed against it, his glance strayed from her pallid face to the shape of her body, flat and slight again beneath the freshly-smoothed coverlet. "We are both still young and lusty," he encouraged. "We must do better next time, eh, sweetheart?"

"Next time," echoed Anne, as he turned away to look at their child. Only a man, surely, could say that at such a time, after such bitter labour.

"Another daughter!" Henry was muttering, as he explored the beribboned bundle in the midwife's arms.

"She has Tudor hair," came Anne's weak vindication from the curtained depths of the bed. And because she seemed to be excusing the helpless mite's existence, for the first time a faint wave of possessive tenderness swept over her.

Like most big, outdoor men, Henry liked children.

With exaggerated care he took his newborn daughter, cushion and all, into the crook of his mighty arm. And instantly, as if aware of her warm security, she stopped wailing, while her minute hand ceased waving aimlessly and curled with extraordinary tenacity about his signet finger.

Henry laughed aloud, delighted as any ordinary father.

"A high-stomached little rogue!" he exclaimed. "And, but for the family red, the living spit of her mother!" He turned about and faced the crowd of enthralled spectators as if for the first time aware of them. "And depend upon it, milords, like her mother before her, she will always get her way!"

"What shall she be called?" asked Cranmer, who was already calculating how he could make less lavish arrangements for the christening.

Henry brought the child to him for a blessing before handing her back to the midwife. It did not occur to him to consult his exhausted wife. Faced suddenly with the necessity of choosing a name for a mere girl child, his thoughts flew immediately to his adored Plantagenet mother. "We will have her christened Elizabeth," he said.

"And we will have your bastard Mary hold her train," decided Anne voicelessly, in the grips of that evil demon that leapt upon her so violently these days.

After the King and all his gorgeous minions were gone, she turned on her side and slept. Slept and waked and slept again all through a day and night, while wise old Butts guarded her against a dozen different stimulants suggested by his colleagues. Slept until she was refreshed enough to bear the combing of her matted hair, and to receive her more intimate friends and relations.

"Where is Mary Howard?" she asked, missing her cousin from the ranks of her other ministering ladies.

But no one answered her directly. "She is sick, perhaps," suggested Druscilla soothingly. But days passed and her cousin did not appear to perform her usual duties. "When I feel strong enough I will speak to her father," thought Anne, preferring not to refer the matter to the King.

By the time the Duke came to pay his respects, she was strong enough to sit out of bed, but there was a surly jauntiness about him which put her on her guard. "Is Mary become too high to wait upon me these days?" she enquired negligently, when she had made civil conversation about his health.

"Mary has no need to wait upon anyone these days," he told her rudely. "The King has betrothed her to Harry Fitzroy."

It was ever his way to blurt things out like that, and because Anne was not yet quite strong, it took her some time to appreciate the full import of his news. "You mean because he did not get the son he hoped for?" she deduced at last, gripping the arms of her chair and staring into his shifty countenance. On account of the cast in his eye, she was never certain whether he was laughing at her or not.

"He thought to make sure," said Norfolk.

"But uniting his by-blow with the highest ducal blood? And you allowed it! Why, but for your wicked machinations, he himself would not have dared suggest it to a Howard."

Norfolk did not gainsay her. "It is not good for you to excite yourself," was all he said.

But Anne had risen to her feet, pulling her velvet bedgown about her. "I believe that you yourself suggested it—slyly, over the card table or a game of bowls, to gain favour," she accused; and had the satisfaction of seeing the red creep to his sallow cheek. "It is what that fox Campeggio said about marrying Fitzroy to young Mary Tudor that must have put it into your aspiring head. But you would do well to rein in your hopes, milord; for though my child be but a wench, the English will never accept a bastard son!"

"You underrate the King's power," snarled Norfolk. "The time may come when my dutiful daughter is of more service to me than my insolent niece."

If Anne had been in full strength she would have struck him. "Did you not hear what he said after the birth? That we are still young and lusty?" she cried, clinging to the chair back and shaking in her weakness and anger. "And next time," she panted, out-facing him with crazy confidence, "I will see to it that it is a boy!"

"Best bestir yourself then to make sure there *is* a next time, ere your husband swings like one of those gilded vanes towards a blonde," smiled Norfolk sardonically, and bowed himself out, calling to her women to come and care for her before she fell. But Anne waved them away and stared after him. She could believe anything of him now. Even what backstairs gossip said—that he had rolled, armed and spurred, upon his naked wife to cure her of her shrewishness.

With dreadful clarity, Anne saw what she had done. Now that his rival Wolsey was gone, Norfolk had become the most powerful man in England. And now he was no longer her ally, looking to her meteoric rise for that extra balance of power he had once needed. He had become her vindictive enemy, leading some thin, chancy hope of his own.

"But the people would never tolerate it," she argued, after her women had put her back to bed, where she lay tossing far into the troubled night. "Sooner than bend the knee to Bess Blount's boy, they would clamour for Catholic Mary. And even if it be true that Henry tricked me with Norfolk behind all his show of gentleness, even though I should never give him the wedlock son he craves, I will fight like a vixen for Elizabeth!"

Chapter Thirty-Four

DEAR LORD, HOW THE day dragged at Hampton! The day when Anne and her ladies stood around waiting for Katherine to die. "She is sick unto death," the messenger from Huntingdonshire had said, and Henry had ridden immediately to Westminster. Hastily, before mounting his horse, he had given the order for Court mourning. "Heneage will get you and your ladies whatever is needful," he had told his wife, his mind full of other things. Such things as a tactfully worded letter to the Emperor, a special Council meeting, and arrangements for a dignified funeral well away from London. Peterborough Cathedral, perhaps.

Normally the accounts for Anne's extravagant clothes were kept by the Comptroller. She hated Heneage. He knew too much. But a personage like Henry must have just one underling like that, she supposed. A person with sealed lips, more like a eunuch than a man; someone whose mind didn't recoil from knowing even the most intimate things in other people's lives. Someone who would bundle a pretty baggage up the backstairs as impassively as he would whisper to the Queen if his master were coming to her bed. Or alternatively fail to appear at her elbow after supper if the King were otherwise minded. And that was when Anne really minded Heneage most. When he was *not* there. It was a new kind of message for her to accept.

Restless as a caged tiger, she trailed up and down her windowed gallery in the new wing at Hampton. Bleakly she considered the prospect of a Court in hypocritical mourning, with Twelfth Night masques and all other dancing abandoned, and thought how well sombre black would suit a nameless fair-haired rival whom Jane Rochford had maliciously hinted at during her own lying-in. Like Henry, she was suffering now from the overlong frustration of a passion that should have been enjoyed in full bloom. Her nerves were at breaking point.

She paused by a window to stare absently at the moribund January garden. Well, if the brighter blooms of summer seemed dead beneath the frost, at least Katherine was dying, too. Only why, why couldn't she have done so years ago? And saved so much effort, so much scheming and cruelty? Effort that no one must ever know—not even the women who dressed Anne when she felt sallow and tired. Scheming from which she now hoped to be able to rest, so that she could be kinder to Henry who, with the first flush of passion spent, must be feeling the strain of all his mighty efforts for its assuagement. And cruelty? When Mary Tudor had fallen sick and Katherine had written beseeching the King to let her nurse their lonely, fifteen-year-old daughter in her own bed, Henry would have allowed it. But had not Anne persuaded him that it was only a dangerous plot to spirit Mary away to form a focal point of opposition in Spain? Being now a mother, Anne understood how unspeakably cruel she had been.

"I must have been sick in mind," she thought, continuing her restless pacing. "But for being her mother's daughter and a bigot, there is something about the girl I always liked. She has an honesty, a freshness, an avidity for love that I, too, used to have."

But Anne had learned insidious fear, and fear bred cruelty. It had begun, she felt, on that day when she had been borne through the streets of London and felt the people's hatred; and their awful justice.

"Even when the Spanish woman is dead, in the minds of half England, I suppose it will be *my* daughter who is the bastard," she exclaimed bitterly.

"But the King has declared Mary so," Jane reminded her. "If the country will stomach a queen at all, Elizabeth is safe for the succession."

"Until I bear a son," agreed Anne.

Bearing Henry a son was becoming an obsession.

Back and forth again she paced, promising herself that once Katherine was dead she would relax. Then suddenly deciding that she must work at her tapestry. Anything to keep her fingers occupied and kill the lagging hours! At her sharp command pages came running to set out the frames, and her women began sorting out their silks. Anne was an expert needlewoman. Before touching the delicate white and gold altar cloth she had been working upon, she called for water to rinse her hands. And just as Sir Richard Southwell was holding it for her in one of Wolsey's priceless golden bowls, the long-looked-for messenger from Westminster arrived.

All present waited in profound silence, arrested as they sat or stood. They could hear the swift hoofbeats of his horse across two courtyards. It seemed to Anne he had been half a lifetime coming. And before ever he reached her, the news he brought spread through the Palace like lighted straw—through the beautiful, homely Palace where Katherine had spent so many carefree hours as Wolsey's guest. Seeping through gracious archways where she had walked, and into the gilded chapel where she had worshipped. Sobering the older grooms and cooks and ushers who could conjure up happy memories of Hampton, secure and serene, in the great Cardinal's heyday, when the swish of stiff Spanish velvet and pontific scarlet had whispered together amicably along the garden paths. And now neither Queen nor Cardinal would ever grace the place again.

For Katherine of Aragon was dead. Dead at last!

Anne had it direct from the messenger's lips the moment he reached her gallery. "Here, keep the bowl, Sir Richard, keep it for yourself!" she cried, pushing the gleaming thing with reckless generosity into Southwell's hands—laughing, crying, dancing, flirting her wet fingers in the air so that all who stood near her were sprayed as by an arc of sweet-scented rain.

"How did she die?" enquired the astonished knight, when he had done thanking her.

The man the King had sent was the same who had ridden down from Huntingdonshire, a stocky yeoman, abashed by such elegant company. "They say she willed herself to live till sunrise, to take the Body of our Lord," he told them, in his slow, broad speech. "The Lady had made her will, and all her people were remembered. When the chandler be come from embalming her, he told me that though she was a queen, begging your Grace's pardon, she wore a nun's hair shirt beneath her velvets an' such. And there was a little reliquary she always wore—a thing of no value in itself, they say—that she begged might be given to her daughter." The man was obviously a devout Catholic. He stood stirring the scented rushes with his mud-caked boot, and swallowed hard. "Because the poor lady had no jewels left."

Anne ignored the thrust. "And what did she leave to the King?" she prompted.

For the first time the man made so bold as to meet the eyes of the imperious young Lutheran Queen. "To his Majesty she wrote a letter. 'Twould not be for our eyes to see, Madame. The last words that ever she wrote, on her dying bed, were to his Grace. Her clerk left her room in tears."

"And he told you?"

The man nodded. "While he wrote the message for me to bring to Westminster. You see, there was no one else to—to care. Except her friend, who was Donna da Sarmiento before her marriage, and who had forced her way in without permission, to be with her at the last."

"Tell us what she wrote," commanded Anne.

Silently, her women gathered closer. Avidly, they listened. How had the late Queen parted from her husband when she came to die? Now that it no longer mattered what she said because she was beyond human vengeance. Haughtily, as a daughter of Imperial Spain? Self-righteously, as she had often done? Had she died upbraiding him, as she, of all women, had the right to do?

The travel-stained countryman screwed up his eyes in an effort to remember. "Concluding her letter to the King she said, 'more than anything in this transitory life mine eyes desire the sight of you'."

There was silence in the long gallery. For the last, the final time, the indominatable spirit of Katherine had silenced spite and ridicule, tearing down their modern lyrical pretensions with the most beautiful, elemental words of all.

"Then she really loved him through everything," said Anne slowly.

And because she herself had not, and yet had filched him, she stood condemned in her own eyes and shamed in the sight of God.

"I will do penance. I will be kind to Mary. I will protect the poor. Most of all I will work for our new, reformed religion," shrieked her soul wildly. But for the moment, for very pride's sake, she must pursue her heartless ways.

"Reward this good man and see that he is fed, Sir Richard." She forced herself to say the words naturally, pulling herself back from some irrevocable abyss of remorse.

And when both men were gone, she picked up her skirts and executed a new dance step invented out of her own jubilation. There was triumph in every movement. "Now am I Queen indeed!" she proclaimed, and laughed until a fit of coughing choked her.

"What shall we *do*, Madame?" asked Arabella, holding some water to her mistress's lips.

"Do?" questioned Margaret.

"To make specially merry," explained the volatile wench.

"Merry!" scoffed Jane lugubriously. "With all the Twelfth Night revels in abeyance and the seductive dresses for the Queen's masque mouldering among the sewing maids! Why, look, even now they are bringing a boatload of black draperies from the watergate!"

"The Lord be thanked, we do not have to attend the obsequies!" shuddered Jane Seymour, the new maid-of-honour who had been appointed in place of Mary Howard.

"My pretty Bella is right. We must do something," agreed Anne suddenly, stretching her shapely arms above her head as if to shake off dull care. "It is intolerable that on this day, *my day*, I must languish here of boredom because Katherine is dead. Is there no note of music in all the manor? Are all the King's musicians gone to swell her requiem at Westminster?"

"There is Mark Smeaton," suggested Arabella who, though recently betrothed, had still an eye for a good-looking lad.

"Where?" asked Anne, who loved the clear alto of his voice.

"Down in the courtyard. Did you not know, Madame, that his father is one of the master carpenters finishing off the panelling of the new Hall? Mark told me he was to have been apprenticed like his brothers had not the King paid for him to be one of the 'singing children' at Windsor."

"Well, have him brought up," said Anne indulgently. Her eyes were sparkling, and suddenly she looked young and gay again. "We will have that masque after all, tonight, here in my gallery."

"You mean the one that you and milord Rochford wrote, about Circe and the men she turned into beasts?"

"But what if the King returns tonight?" said Margaret.

"I overheard his Grace tell Heneage that the matters he had to attend to would take at least two days," volunteered Druscilla.

"And is it not a joyful occasion for him, too?" Anne reminded them. "We can at least rehearse it. And if it is very good perhaps the King will let us have it after all on Twelfth Night."

"Oh, Madame!" they cried in unison, and clapped their hands.

Instinctively, Anne looked round for her brother, whose spirits made the success of any party. But, of course, he must have gone in attendance upon the King.

"A masque without men," scoffed her sister-in-law.

"And why not?" challenged Anne, for the sake of gainsaying her. "Besides, we have Sir Richard Southwell and half a dozen gentlemen ushers and the Comptroller's young son."

"And Mark and Heneage," encouraged Arabella eagerly.

"No, not Heneage," frowned Anne.

"Well, for the rest, some of us could dress as men."

"Arabella!" breathed the sedate Seymour girl, being recently come from the seclusion of her parents' manor in Wiltshire.

"What matters it, Mistress Modesty, since we are alone?"

retorted Arabella. "Oh, Madame, Madame, let me wear the lovely slashed suit with antlers made for milord Rochford!"

The Queen pinched her dimpled cheek. It was her animation and her initiative that Anne had loved since they had first manoeuvred their way into Wolsey's town house years ago. "Go tell the sewing maids to bring all the costumes, and we will sort them out," she bade her. "Druscilla is tall and should make a doughty partner."

Soon the Queen's gallery was bespread with fantastic yellow costumes and the stuffed heads of animals, all of which the busy, laughing seamstresses allotted to the ladies they fitted best.

Anne looked ravishing as Circe. Margaret had unbound her tresses beneath a wreath of laurel. The tight yellow satin suited her, looped as it was with bronze serpents about her breasts. But—when she looked closely in her mirror—there were telltale lines about her eyes, a hard, determined secrecy about her mouth. A woman who would keep a King's passion hot for years must expect to bear the mark of it, she supposed.

But with this morning's news the main burden of her struggle had fallen from her shoulders. She was the King's wife indeed. She felt young again, completely recovered from that terrible childbirth. The old gay laughter bubbled to her lips. Tomorrow, next week, sometime she would rest—ask Henry if she might take her child to Hever, perhaps, where Jocunda's quiet love would cure all ills. But now she must have lights and music. Katherine of Aragon was dead.

It was only then, when she had sent someone for the words and music of the masque, that she noticed Smeaton standing half-hidden by the open door. A handsome, well-grown youth, dangling a beribboned lute. A youth whom much royal notice had matured too quickly for his years. Anne had been wont to think of him as a mere singing boy; but, seeing the look upon his face, she was aware that he must have been standing there all the time Druscilla and the rest were dressing her; for so, with incipient lust, had a world of grown men looked at her.

"Come here, Mark, and see if you can read my score and transpose it to your lute," she called to him sharply. "It is but a rehearsal and we have no proper musicians."

He came eagerly. Unabashed and efficient, he was quick to comprehend her wishes. He even had ideas of his own. A whole new golden world opened before him, wherein he was called upon to serve both his beckoning Muse and the seductive Queen, whose romantic reputation had fired his imagination.

Anne had him in her music room, working for hours towards the perfecting of her brother's verses and her own settings. It was work she loved, and none of her gifted friends was there to share it. And Mark, with eyes as black and warm as her own, was full of creative fire. Because he was neither gentleman nor servant, she found it all the easier to talk to him informally about their mutual art.

And after supper the Queen's gallery was filled with music and laughter—all the more light-hearted and abandoned, perhaps, because only girls and men of lesser birth took part. Because the King was not there, all were good-natured, without rivalry. Smeaton proved himself invaluable, like a very young Master of the Revels, here, there, and everywhere. And such men as were left about the Palace on that momentous day had come right willingly to participate so unexpectedly in the gaiety of the Queen.

All except Heneage, whose closeness to the King made him accustomed to being pandered to, and whose peculiar mind saw nothing debased in spying. Heneage, who had spent a dreary day doling out lengths of black sarsenet to the servants.

While the rest of the Palace remained in decorous gloom, the Queen's gallery glowed out into the darkness, betraying to a censorious world how much she must have felt herself to be a usurper until her rival's death.

"'Tis the loveliest masque you ever devised, Madame!" cried Arabella, handing her mistress gallantly in the dance, a charming chit of a boy in the beloved Rochford's finery.

And now it was time for her to don her antlers, for the Queen, leaving her bevy of saffron-gowned maidens, was beginning to lure the men dancers within the magic circle Smeaton had chalked upon the floor, turning them, by her lascivious dancing, into beasts. Through the noise they made, the stamping and the laughter, they did not hear the commotion of the King's unexpected arrival; the baying of hounds, the clap of sentries springing to attention, the hurrying of grooms. They heard nothing until a sleepy, tousle-headed page rushed in and piped, "The King has come back from Westminster."

"Already?" stammered Margaret, with foreboding at her heart.

"Then he will be able to see me as Circe after all," cried Anne excitedly. Henry, who so loved a masque. Who must be as excited as she. Who would come presently and fold her in his arms, glad to be home to mingle his relief with hers, and to see something cheerful after his lugubrious day. This beloved Hampton was their *home*, where neither of them need appear in public nor pretend. Time enough tomorrow to think of creeping about in decorous mourning.

In the sudden silence Anne heard his step upon the stair. "Quick, open the door, someone!" she ordered, standing exultantly among her saffron-decked maids. And Mark Smeaton, swift in his adoration, ran to throw it wide.

Henry stood there, blinking in amazement. In his short swinging coat and prodigiously puffed sleeves, he seemed to fill the wide archway, so that his followers remained almost out of sight.

Anne's gasp could be heard in the sudden stillness.

From velvet cap to rolled, slashed shoe, he was clad in black velvet, with only a plain silver dagger hanging from his belt. She had never seen him in black before. It was slimming, and suited his warm fairness. But at the same time made him appear a stranger, severe and unapproachable, wrapped apart in a semblance of personal grief. Or was it only a semblance? Anne noticed that his eyes were puffed and red.

"The hypocrite!" she raged inwardly, knowing how he could be moved to facile self-pity; and stopped halfway towards him, her fond greeting frozen on her lips. Surely this bereavement could mean nothing to him compared to the death of his beloved sister Mary, for whom he had mourned sincerely in silence!

"I saw the lights of your orgy," he said, his blue eyes no longer blinking, but flicking like a whip over everybody present and taking in every frivolous detail.

Anne knew that he couldn't have done so from the courtyard, and the crop still clenched in his hand testified to the fact that he had not come by barge. Heneage must have made it his business to tell him. Heneage, whom she had not invited.

She stood mute while Henry strode into the gallery. "Did milord Chamberlain neglect to issue my order for Court mourning?" he enquired with cold and terrible politeness.

"N-no, your Grace," admitted Anne, glancing down at the offending yellow silk skirt folds extended so dramatically between her shaking hands.

"Then why are you and these women mumming the night away in unseemly, atrocious yellow?"

Anne stared at him, too amazed for speech. There was that small, sharp intake of breath in his voice which betokened that he was furious. With one contemptuous word he had torn the beauty of her best masque to shreds. He might never have begged her love, never have tried for years to be rid of Katherine, nor, in his impatience, laid himself open to excommunication from the Pope.

"Answer me, some of you!" he burst out, seeing a Boleyn for once tongue-tied before him. "Why do I return from arranging about my wife's funeral to find you all indulging in ill-timed festivities like a troupe of cold-blooded mountebanks?"

It was Anne's turn to be furious. She let the offending silk rustle to the floor and went to face him, head high. "Your *wife!*" she challenged indignantly.

"My late wife," he corrected himself.

She went and laid her hands against his unresponsive breast. "But, Henry, I thought . . . Have you not said a hundred times . . . Have we not prayed for this moment?"

In her genuine perplexity she looked, to all who watched, more beautiful than ever. But for the first time Henry did not seem to care whether she were beautiful or not. "Take off that unseemly dress," he ordered sharply, "and go pray for some sense of fitness!"

He went out and slammed the door behind him. Anne was still standing where he left her when she heard him calling for his horse again. He was not going to sleep at Hampton after all. But at some other of his palaces where his late-coming would drag the unfortunate servants from their beds and where everyone would mumble round in black and treat him as a bereaved widower. And show a sense of fitness!

Anne screamed aloud to relieve her feelings, and then turned everyone from her disordered gallery. Most fiercely of all, that impudent, staring gut-scraper Smeaton, who had dared to look sorry for her.

Bolting her bedroom door against her women, she tore off the yellow dress, ripping the costly silk from shoulder to hem. "The hypocrite! The self-righteous hypocrite! Let him go to his dead wife's bed to warm him," she raged.

But was it all hypocrisy? What was it Tom Wyatt had once said in the beloved Kent garden. "After all, he has lived with her in amity for eighteen years." Was that, with men, the substance, and all their hot amours the shadow? And what was it Mary had said? "From the moment he had his way with me my power was gone." As Anne lay in bed the room seemed full of warnings. They came at her like jabbing knives through the darkness. And her heart was cold with fear.

Though she played at being Circe, for the first time her power over a man had failed.

"He has had a surfeit of my body. I have given him everything I have to give. Except, of course, a son."

In the grip of some nameless terror Anne raised herself like a white wraith between the hangings, hand to throat as if she strangled. "A son!" The husky words became a prayer. "Merciful God in Heaven, send me a son for my security!"

Chapter Thirty-Five

THE GUST OF HENRY'S anger was soon over, and Master Heneage at Anne's elbow again. But while she was more careful than ever to preserve her beauty, she strove also to live more decorously.

She would pore over the Gospels as earnestly as over her mirror, and—knowing that poor Mary Tudor had been brokenhearted at her mother's death—Anne wrote to her again, assuring the girl that if only she would acknowledge her illegitimacy, she would be welcomed at Court and excused the hated indignity of carrying the train of her baby sister's robes. An invitation which that stubborn and courageous wench declined.

Instead of using all her gifts on arts and pageantry within her husband's palaces, Anne tried to bring enlightenment to his people. Especially she wanted the poorer sort of people to be able to read, against that great day of which she and her friends so often talked, when the Bible would no longer be a forbidden book in the hands of priests, but open for all in the churches. As yet Henry was but half-persuaded, and she often risked his displeasure by trying to protect the Dutch merchants who were constantly smuggling copies of the Bible into the country.

Anne wanted to be beloved as Katharine had been; to be looked upon as a benefactress. And, apart from the complete divergence of their religious views, unconsciously she began modelling her queenly years upon those of her former mistress.

Surprisingly she found herself thinking more and more about Katherine. Being rid of her had proved by no means the easing of life for which she had hoped. It simply meant that she herself had taken Katherine's place, and found it less enviable than she had supposed. Unquestionably, now, she was Queen. But she was also the woman possessed and in possession, lacking that element of excitement that blooms on all forbidden fruit beyond the matrimonial pale.

And now, as the secure, uneventful months slipped by, she found herself, like Katherine, lying depressed and listless, recovering from a miscarriage.

The King had sent one of her Boleyn cousins, Madge Skelton, to be with her; but no one could make up for Margaret, who was at Allington. Merry little Arabella had leave to visit a sick mother, and Jane Seymour, her new maid-of-honour, although gentle and mannerly, was not particularly interesting. During the past unhappy weeks there had been only Jane Rochford, of her old entourage, left. And only propinquity and lack of distractions could have brought Anne to confide in her.

"I never dreamed this ignominious mischance could happen to *me!*" she marvelled incredulously for the twentieth time, listening enviously to the brisk footsteps and careless laughter of those who passed beneath her window. "Although it is true I have had grave illnesses, Jane, I have always been so full of life."

Jane ceased her restless peeping from the open casement in search of the partner of her latest amour; which, after all, had lost much of its savour because her husband did not even pay her the compliment of trying to find out about the furtive little affair. "Perhaps it is nothing to do with you at all?" she suggested, drawing a stool to Anne's side.

Anne, too, had considered that unmentionable possibility. At least, Jane's mind worked as daringly as her own, and her jealous tongue had been less venomous since the others were gone.

"Of course, there can be no truth in what people are beginning to say," went on Jane tentatively.

"And what are they beginning to say?" enquired Anne, with the idle curiosity of sickness.

"That now the King is putting on years and weight he grows impotent."

Anne could have boxed her ears. "Obviously not," she replied curtly, shifting her weary body significantly on the cushioned pallet.

For a minute or two her sister-in-law allowed herself to be silenced by the snub. But Anne could feel her curiosity rising like an unpleasant miasma. And presently Jane glanced cautiously over her shoulder at old Lady Wingfield, who was sewing quietly at the other side of the room. Poor Wingfield who had once assisted the Mistress of the Queen's Wardrobe but who was now growing deaf and senile, and whose presence Jane decided to dismiss as negligible. "Tell me, Nan, now that for once we are alone—what is he really *like* as a lover?" she asked, just as Anne herself, devoured by curiosity, had once asked Mary.

It was the thing that half the women in England would have given their ears to know. Plenty of them, one way and another, had tried to find out.

At any other time Anne would have resisted such crude persistence; but it was a matter about which she had often longed to speak to someone, if only to relieve her own bitter disappointment. With a movement suggestive of accumulated irritation, she succumbed. "He is not the great lover you women suppose," she said, half angrily. "When it comes to the point he has not half the verve of which his courtship and his kisses give promise. Let me warn you, Jane—in case your own affairs should pall and you should be tempted to try for more exciting game—there is many a lusty squire might serve your turn better."

"You mean—" persisted Jane, round-eyed.

"I mean," said Anne, tossing all caution aside, "that Henry Tudor is considerably less clever in a bed than in the saddle. *En cas de se copuler avec femme il n'a ni vertu ni puissance*," she explained, because it seemed less embarrassing to say it in French.

"Neither power nor aptitude for giving pleasure. Oh, my poor, poor Nan! And you, as you say, so full of life," laughed Jane, literally hugging herself for having wormed out the biggest bit of scandal in the land. "Listen, sib, you must lure him again, soon, before the *puissance* goes completely."

Anne squirmed beneath the stifled mirth that underlay her sister-in-law's solicitude. She raised herself on the pallet, hand to mouth. "I did not say that he was becoming impotent!" she protested sharply, wishing that she had not spoken at all. And to Jane, of all people!

"No, but it is what you are afraid of," affirmed Jane.

In full health and spirits, Anne would have denied any such fear indignantly. But Jane had a way of speaking with real concern at times. After all, she was one of the family, and Anne felt that she must voice the ugly thought to *someone*. "What I am really afraid of is that if ever I should have *another* miscarriage, that conscience of Henry's will persuade him that the same curse lies on *me*."

"A curse?"

"The same as on Katherine; because our wedlock was not legal."

Anne was loath, even by the oblique implication of such words, to compare her slender body with Katherine's stumpy one. But lying there, she knew for the first time what Katherine must have felt, dragging herself tight-lipped and uncomplaining from one Court function to another, from one ill-fated pregnancy to the next. Gradually seeing state, pleasure, life and love slip from her, all for the want of a son.

Brought home by Jane's crude advice, a terrible possibility confronted Anne. What if her witchery were really waning? Suppose when she got up she found she could no longer entice and hold Henry? Suppose, even now, as her enemies suggested, he were sniffing round some other woman's skirts; while she kept her room, pallid and undesirable? A swooning nausea overcame her. For now she saw it all. What had Katherine ever been to her but an unwilling protection? Why, why had she ever wished the woman dead? For as long as Katherine reigned, had Henry tired of his new love it would have been easy enough to rid himself of a subject whom even his own jester called "the bawd." Even when the bawd became his wife and Queen of England, as long as Katherine lived even Henry's convenient conscience could not have disclaimed his second marriage as illegal without admitting to the righteousness of the first. But now, standing in Katherine's shoes indeed, Anne found herself open to danger such as humble Mary Boleyn had never known. And none knew better than she what drastic measures a King must take to rid himself of a guiltless Queen who cannot give him sons.

Suddenly, stark unreasoning fear gripped her. How right was Jane, saying that she must lure Henry soon! Swaying with giddiness, Anne slid her feet to the ground, driven by some crazy notion of finding him. But as the room began to go dark about her a merciful Providence appeared to have sent succour. The door had opened and someone had sauntered, singing, into the room; and then, all in a moment, George was striding across the room to catch her.

"Save me! Oh, my dear, my very dear, save me!" she cried incoherently; but whether from falling or from some awful inexplicit fate was a jumble in her troubled mind.

"Why, Nan, my poor precious!"

Oh, the comfort of George's voice and the lovely security of his arms! It was like being a child again at Hever, and shedding all this regal anxiety. Almost at once Anne was calmed. Reassured by tender endearments and compassionate kisses, she sank back against her pillows, sane again. With regained clarity, she saw Jane standing watching them, her face momentarily contorted with envy. She even wondered if it could be possible that in some strange, twisted way Jane loved him. Whether it might be agony to her to see him throw himself eagerly across another woman's bed, though that woman be but his sister, just as she had always resented not being able to enter into the charmed affection of their circle of friends? If it were so, Jane controlled herself admirably. "I will leave you two alone. You understand her better than do the rest of us, George," she said gently, with a light hand on her husband's shoulder.

She smiled at Anne meaningly, it seemed, as if to remind her of their recent intimate conversation. Then turned to deal with the agitated and hovering Lady Wingfield, showing far more patience with her than usual. "You heard her Grace call out, didn't you? And couldn't hear what it was all about, poor soul! It was just that she was distressed and called upon her brother to save her—yes, to save her!" she repeated, raising her voice close to the nodding grey head. "But milord will know how to comfort her. We had best leave them alone."

"Why disturb the old lady?" remonstrated George, hurrying to gather up her scattered possessions.

Agnes Wingfield peered at him short-sightedly, but her memory was still good. She had been wont to give him sweetmeats when he was a child, and he was still her favourite of all these restless, extravagant younglings at Court. "Marry, save us, if it isn't my gallant George bothering with an old woman," she chuckled, well pleased. And, seeing that she was willing to go, he let his wife coax her from the room. After all, here at Court it was a rare treat for him and Anne to be alone, particularly since she had become Queen.

"What grieves you, my sweet, besides this unfortunate miscarriage?" he asked, lounging back to stretch his slender length across her feet and helping himself to an apple from her dish.

"Oh, mercy me, it is only that I grow foolish with some childish fears."

"Our brilliant Nan afraid?" he jibed, setting strong teeth upon the rosy fruit.

Anne sat up and hugged her knees. "Not afraid of anything I *know*, George. But some fear comes at me these days, some shuddering fear of I know not what."

"Don't look at me like that, with your eyes all fey, or you will have me believe you are a witch again," he complained, discomforted beneath his laughter.

"You *did* believe it, didn't you, when we were small?" smiled Anne, distracted momentarily from her troubles. "And often the King has said that I bewitch him."

"Then what cause have you to call upon a mere viscount to save you?"

There was so much they had to talk of. It was one of those golden, undisturbed hours stolen from the crowded ceremony of Palace life. A time in which to speak for once of their secret fears and hopes; to discuss the position of their party, and the growth of the religion of which they dared not speak in public. They fell to discussing Norfolk's defection and the significance of Fitzroy's marriage with Mary Howard. They spoke of Mary of Suffolk's death, and their sister's humble, happy marriage. Of everything from the news of Percy's increasing ill health to Tom Wyatt's latest rhyming, and of the way their younger cousin, Henry Howard, sang his praises. "According to young Surrey, if Wyatt should die Nature will have lost the proper mould to make a man," laughed George, coaxing his sister back to gaiety.

"And now, too late, I know that I agree with him," sighed Anne.

"But Jane is no fool, Nan, if she told you to stop moping here," George advised more seriously, knowing perhaps more than either of them. "I will tell you what we should do for Michaelmas. Revise that Circe masque we made. It has some good stuff in it. And I will see that you, as Circe, have scope to do all the luring you need and so bewitch the King afresh!"

And so he left her bright-eyed and confident again, with all her worries dismissed as sick imaginings; and strode forth singing as he had come, almost colliding with Jane Seymour and Druscilla Zouch outside the door.

"Forgive me if I have kept you from your duties, poppets," he apologized airily, realizing the lateness of the hour by the sound of the chapel bell.

His sister's new maid-of-honour dropped him a shy curtsy. "Milady, your wife, was at pains to tell us you were with the Queen and bade us in no wise disturb you," she explained primly.

So he had his wife to thank for that happy hour with Nan. "Would she were more often so considerate," he thought, kissing Druscilla casually in passing, and hurrying along stairs and galleries lest he be late to attend the King to evensong.

Cheered and refreshed, Anne took up her life again; going to visit her little daughter at Hatfield, playing with her spaniels and her great hound, Urian, in the gardens and, as autumn drew on, playing backgammon in the evenings. Henry hawked and hunted with her, and was affable and kind; but the weeks went by and he did not seek her bed.

It was the day when the new French ambassador presented his credentials at Hampton that she stumbled upon the reason why. Her beloved Margaret was back at Court again and had helped to dress her with the utmost care in the pearls and clinging black velvet which so became her, and which a Frenchman of taste was sure to admire. Never, perhaps, had Anne looked so intriguingly romantic, with a faint air of delicacy still about her. She felt warmed and confident. "Perhaps the King will come tonight," she thought, turning from her mirror to take stock of her maids-of-honour and wondering which of them she should take to attend her.

All of them looked lovely, like a field of flowers in the variety of their coloured dresses. But, alas, so much younger than herself! Not in years so much as in a kind of unlined serenity; rather like nuns, for whom all worldly calculations are arranged. "Why eclipse myself with a whole bevy of youthful beauty?" she decided. "Just one, perhaps, would be effective. Which one shall it be?" Druscilla, though deeper bosomed, dwarfed her height. Anne did not want Margot to watch her at her wiles, while Jane Rochford would appreciate them all too accurately, with that embarrassing spark of stifled mirth. Anne's eyes lighted upon Jane Seymour, sitting on a cushion apart from the rest, industriously embroidering a kerchief. This Jane was a year or two older than herself, quiet, well-mannered, inconspicuous, and colourless, except for the honey-coloured hair drawn back beneath her beaded headdress. The perfect foil. Anne caught sight of her own dark, sparkling reflection in the mirror again. What man in his senses would even notice a Seymour when a Boleyn was by?

"Come with me, dear Jane," she bade the girl in passing, giving her no time to prink. And Jane, reared as a gentlewoman if ever there was one, rose obediently, without commotion. "After all, whatever she did, poor girl, nothing would flush her cheeks or ruffle her quiet composure," thought Anne, with last-minute compunction.

Down the Palace stairs they went together, dazzling Queen and inconspicuous maid-of-honour—down to the newly finished Great Hall, with a blaze from the central hearth illuminating the lofty hammerbeam roof, and a tall oriel window aglow with heraldic colours lighting great tiles of Tudor green. The long side tables were already filled with cheerful guests, augmented, as it always seemed, by the richly dressed, life-size figures worked in the wall tapestries behind them. Servants in royal livery were beginning to bring the dishes from behind the carved serving screens, while above them, in the musicians' gallery, viols, rebecs, and hautboys started up a selection of the King's own songs.

And on the dais stood Henry receiving Gontier, the new ambassador, with her father, Norfolk, Suffolk, and other notables grouped about them. Henry was always at his best when entertaining. He had just that touch of bonhomie which sets a hall full of divers guests at ease. He turned immediately to present the ambassador to her, and Anne felt warmed by his courteous attention, glad to be back in the midst of all the amusement and splendour again.

After supper the fiddles struck up a favourite dance tune; but the ambassador was elderly, and Anne's cough and giddiness still assailed her at times. She smiled and shook her head when Henry gallantly offered her his hand. "If it please your Grace I will entertain our guest while you choose another lady," she excused herself. Yet Henry, who loved to romp through a square dance, made no attempt to dance either. It was kind of him, she thought; and emulating his consideration, she sent her mouselike maid-of-honour to foot it with the rest.

After King and Queen and ambassador had sat chatting for a while, the talk turned upon Gontier's young French secretary whose brilliance had impressed Henry.

"I shall have to meet this paragon and match his wits against those of my cousin Wyatt and our other budding diplomats," laughed Anne.

"I will find him and bring him to you, my dear," offered Henry, rising impulsively and stepping down between dances into the thronged body of the Hall.

While he was gone, the French ambassador talked on and on. Anne sat there, bored and flagging, automatically making the right answers, while her gaze and thoughts strayed, willy-nilly, over the gaily dressed company.

There went Henry, the genial host, threading his way between them, his broad-resplendent back inclining this way and that as he greeted a foreign guest, remembered a subject who had done him some service, or paused to chuck a pretty wench under the chin. Henry, who was so much a part of England because no amount of ceremony could hedge in his personality or prevent him from doing all the human, exciting things of life for himself.

And there was George, Heaven bless him, balancing a full glass of Rhinish on his head and trying to persuade a still sober Wyatt to walk on his hands like one of the paid acrobats; while Jane, his wife, ogled one of the Frenchmen.

"*Mais, non, non! Oh, oui, vous aveu raison,*" she kept murmuring at appropriate intervals, stifling a yawn as the long-winded ambassador went on airing his views on the Spanish situation.

Surely Henry would be back soon to relieve her of this incredible bore! But there was no sign of either him or the brilliant young secretary. And then the fiddlers struck up again, and as people moved to take the floor, Anne caught sight of her husband standing close to a woman down by the buttery hatch; talking to her long and earnestly, not just inviting her to dance. The woman herself was hidden by Henry's bulk. And when the other couples began to dance he still stood there, one hand seeming to imprison her as it rested against the panelling behind her head. Imprisoning and persuading. How well Anne knew his every gambit! She leaned forward, completely forgetful of the man beside her, moving her head as the prancing couples shifted between her and the object of her gaze. If only they would stop obstructing her view! If only she could see who the woman was! The sly blonde bitch people were whispering about, no doubt. Now, now, as the dance was about to stop, when they turned round, at last she would know.

But they did not turn. Anne saw Henry slip a coaxing hand beneath the woman's arm and bundle her through the opening in the serving screen. So neatly that none of the excited dancers noticed, and Anne herself had time only to observe that her rival was young and fairish and about her own height and build.

Anne was worlds away, watching the familiar kind of little drama which often she had figured in. She had no idea that the French ambassador was still talking to her. She only knew that the players in this particular drama were making for the flight of steps which led, by way of the kitchen passages, back to the private apartments behind the dais. And as the last fluted pleat of Henry's rose satin coat flicked from sight round the screen, suddenly, uncontrollably, she burst out laughing. Laughed and laughed and could not stop.

She knew that heads were turned, and that presently the violence of her coughing choked the violence of her laughter. That the hall was a hot blur of shifting colours, and that the French ambassador had risen in profound dudgeon.

"Madame, is there anything so particularly risible about me? Or the matter of which I speak?" he demanded.

"No! No! I assure your Excellency," panted Anne, who had not the least idea of what he spoke. Someone had brought her water, and she was sipping it. And growing calmer. Jane Seymour, she supposed, had gone to fetch the rest of her women. "It is only that the King, my husband, went to fetch your secretary to me, did he not? And now," in spite of herself a fresh spasm of laughter shook her, "and now he has met some lady by the way, and forgotten all about it!"

Poor Gontier stared at her as though she were possessed. "And is *that* so very amusing?" he persisted.

"Yes. No. By the living God, I really do not know," Anne stammered in confusion, stretching out a hand in some attempt at apology.

It all depended upon how one looked at it, she supposed. Perhaps, after all, it *was* a jest—a better jest even than any of her laughter-loving brother's or of poor, hard-working Will Somers'— if one could but see it that way. Katherine and herself in the old days. And now some other woman philandering with Henry—and Nan Boleyn, the King's "own sweetheart," weak from a miscarriage, sitting here on the deserted dais in Katherine's place.

Chapter Thirty-Six

ALTHOUGH ANNE WAS BEGINNING to taste the gall of being in Katherine's place, she had the advantage over her predecessor. She was still seductive and comparatively young. She had the sustaining loyalty of gay and gifted friends about her. So that, unhampered by Katherine's conscious goodness and impediment of pride, she could put up a fight.

"I will make Henry forget all the blonde women in the world," she swore, inviting him to take part in her masque. Now that Cromwell was taking over more and more of the government, Henry had leisure again for the amusements in which he delighted. And never had masque been more cunningly devised, nor his musical, dancing Queen more in her element. Never had those slanting, almond eyes of hers glittered so dangerously, or her every movement been so seductive. He supposed that, ogling other women or keeping his eyes too long on state papers, he must have forgotten just how desirable she was.

He, of course, must be given the best part. He must be the lion when all the men dancers were transmogrified by Circe's lure to various beasts. Without question he donned the maned and tawny pasteboard head. In the heat and excitement of the dance half the other men, Anne knew, had forgotten their wives. But not so Henry. Dancing wildly, sinuously in the midst of them, Anne was aware only of her brother, the graceful, high-leaping, antlered stag, executing a triumphant and knowing little *pas seul* on the edge of the mystic circle he had prepared, and of Henry, the tamed lion, well within it, almost slobbering with desire against her gold-clad knee. For this King of Beasts alone she sang and postured, until he was incapable of seeing any other woman in the world. Until, a hot-breathed beast, he concluded the masque with an unrehearsed incident—throwing off his disguise, and carrying a thinly draped, white-limbed Circe off in his arms.

"At thirty-three I can still do that!" thought Anne, feeling his passion as urgent as that first night in France. "I can fight that unknown, fair-faced thieving cat whose sleek body has probably never been marred in childbirth, and win my husband from her."

And that night Anne took back her own. Neither for love nor lust, but from sheer necessity. That she might bear him a son.

And all through the months of that winter she stepped happily, knowing that within her quickened the seed of England's heir. The terrible memory of Elizabeth's birth was resolutely thrust behind her. The physicians had told her that she would never bear children easily, as did women of more placid type. But no matter what suffering lay ahead, once it was over she would be safely established, serene and invulnerable. Having learned some of Katherine's hard lessons, Anne made no doubt there would from time to time be other lights-o'-love; that as Henry grew older many a young girl might snare him by her very freshness to an amorous clip—but she, Anne the Queen, would be the mother of his son. With beauty enough to call him back, when she would, for the begetting of more sons. For, supine and satisfied beneath Henry's crazed, recaptured ardour, Anne wondered how she could ever have said what she had about the wreck of their long-frustrated passion. Recovered from that too-long celibacy enforced by her, released from all the tension of the divorce proceedings, the man had acquired a new confidence, a new virility for breeding.

"In truth, I believe that you really did bewitch me, Circe," he would say, regarding her half-fearfully, as her brother used to do, and half-resentful of her power. Anne knew that he was no longer in love with her, but believed that he had forgotten the woman with whom he had been dallying.

Together, companionably, they would go to visit their child at Hatfield, Henry on his tall roan and Anne riding obediently in her coach. "No taking chances as you did last time, hawking when Butts had advised you not to," he told her.

It was good to feel precious, to be delivered from her enemies, to know that her father was satisfied and George and Jocunda safe. Anne had no false illusions about the stability of greatness; for had not she herself manoeuvred the downfall of a man like Wolsey? But so long as she gave Henry a son no one, neither scheming Norfolk nor jealous Suffolk, could claw her down from that high place in which she stood. Henry himself, in whose hands they were but as pigmies, would be her protector; and neither Mary Howard nor Suffolk's semi-royal daughters would be within grasping distance of the throne.

Unless she vastly deluded herself this less urgent, child-bearing phase of married life, during which she and Henry would take time to enjoy shared interests and gradually merge physical ardour into companionship, could be mighty pleasant. And perhaps, as the years passed, she would be able to damp down her gusty fires of sex and look no longer enticingly at men. Travelling in good company to Hatfield, discussing plans for the enlargement of the royal nursery, Anne saw stretching before her an era of contentment and security such as she had never known.

She felt the promise of it warm in her arms when she lifted her little daughter from her cradle. In the child's enchanting smile of recognition, Anne saw the promise of profound and joyful participation in the growth of a new generation. "By the time Henry is old, Elizabeth will be a grown person," she discovered, her mind bound by the absurd conviction of personal immutability.

She surrendered Elizabeth to him and watched him proudly carrying the pretty two-year-old in his arms, showing her off to all his friends and followers, no longer minding that she was a girl— because, come springtime, his wife had promised him a son. For this time Anne was as certain of male issue as he himself had been before. She felt it in every fibre of her being, and in the memory of his forceful mating. In the spring all those pompously-worded proclamations about a prince would be heralded forth indeed, and all the bells would ring again. And although the inner dedication of a crowning was still a hidden thing to her, Anne was yet aware that the anticipation in her husband's heart was all bound up with that of his subjects; that it was something implicitly shared with them. Because, however culpable they might have found him in the matter of his divorce, an heir would be born to them too, to carry on their traditions and save them from internal strife and from the strange, chancy idea of a woman ruler, whose state marriage might put them in hated bond to France or Spain.

For all her ambition, Anne's personal reactions were simpler. Looking out upon the flat Essex landscape blanched by a light fall of snow, she saw the good brown earth beneath, churned and pitted by their horses' hooves. The brown fecund earth. And told herself that in a few months' time the sun would be warm again and the flowers in bloom. It would be May time, the loveliest season in all the year. With greening trees along the grassy rides at Hampton, and pleasure skiffs flitting on the Thames. The month of her triumphal Coronation. Her own particular month, for which she waited now.

Sharply, she called herself back to the present. Before they left there were instructions to be given to Mistress Ashley, the faithful nurse. And Henry, she perceived, had tired of playing with the babe and, with his usual boundless energy, was beginning to fidget round in search of fresh distractions. Another minute and he would be sending for Mary, who was nineteen and intelligent enough to converse with any man in almost any language. The girl with whom he was displeased, but whose happy, loving, radiant image he had never been able to erase from his heart. And once he saw her—who could say?—he might be inviting her back to Court, where she would break up their new-found contentment with her stiff, resentful ways, and become a constant bone of contention in this new phase of security for which she, Anne, had laboured so hard and prostituted her enchantment!

This was what she had been afraid of when she came. What she had written about in that letter sent privately to her aunt, Lady

Skelton, telling her to see to it that during the King's visit his elder daughter should keep her room. The very reason why she had put a relative in charge of Hatfield.

After all, it seemed, one could not safely relax. Even now one's mind must keep one move ahead of Henry's.

Anne's eyes sought Alicia Skelton's; and after a sly glance at the King's scowling face, the Princesses' governess nodded reassuringly. And although Lady Skelton had reported that Mary often held her helpless half-sister to her love-starved heart in private, Anne knew the proud piece well enough to rest assured that she would have obeyed only too readily; to escape the polluting presence of her stepmother and the ignominy of waiting upon her bastard! Anne knew just how Mary Tudor must have looked, saying it, with her back rigid and her beautiful Spanish eyes half blind with hurt arrogance. In rankled imagination, Anne could almost hear her.

And then, while still thinking of her, Anne had cause to hear her in reality. All of them could hear her. Playing on the virginals, with all the doors and windows flung wide; purposely, no doubt. And with that sweet, trained touch which was sure to catch the King's ear. Playing, by all that was impudent, a melody of the King's own making to which she had many a time danced before her parents!

Anne rose and kissed her child good-bye. "If it please your Grace, I think we should be on our way. The days shorten, and for the boy's sake I would be home before nightfall," she urged, feigning a shivering fit which was yet not all counterfeit; and perceiving, to her relief, that Henry was as anxious as she to get away. For what was there, after all, that he could say to a perspicacious grown daughter whom he had so grievously wronged? He liked to pose as a bluff, benignant personality; and, as Mary Boleyn had once pointed out, he had a way of leaving all the unpleasant interviews to underlings.

But as they mounted their horses the music stopped. Mary had yet another trick to play. She must have left her virginals and decided to take the air, for she was there on her terrace as they rode out; a small, upright, self-contained figure in a rich, dark brocaded dress of damasked black, with gold kirtle and sleeves. Save for a single pendant cross she had no jewels, but for sheer cut and good taste the severity of her dress made Anne's pearl-crusted one look trashy and flamboyant. Grief, vicissitudes and ill-health had stolen from Mary Tudor her first fair promise of beauty, and she made no effort to hide the ravages of bitter years from their curious gaze. But when she saw the resplendent figure of her father riding forth, in spite of all his ignoring, she curtsied to the ground with all the grace of her small-boned body and all the grandeur of her birth.

The challenge of that lonely, perfect figure, outlined against a scene as wintry as her fortunes, was breath-takingly poignant. It was as if in her own small person she showed her mother's wrongs to all the world.

As she rose again and surveyed them quietly, Anne, the Queen, lowered her eyes. And Henry, to his credit and her chagrin, pulled his great horse up short and stayed the following company with an outflung hand, while he bowed low and doffed his plumed velvet cap as if to the highest lady in the land, so that his entire company, perforce, followed suit.

Once out on the open road, he spurred on ahead immediately so that none should speak with him, and Anne could not see his face. And never once did he refer to the incident. She could only suppose, like all the rest, that he was moved by courage when he saw it.

For Mary it must have been a signal victory over a bog of legal verbiage, a silent acknowledgment of her rightful place. The sort of thing which Anne, another woman of spirit, might have staged. But Mary was but a chit, with no one in the world. "When I can afford to I will try again to win her to accept some kindness," resolved Anne. "Once my son is safely born and she but a marriageable pawn."

Christmas and Twelfth Night slipped by with all their Holy Offices and feasts and revels. And as the new year wore on, Anne spent most of her time at Greenwich, the Palace officially chosen for her lying-in. Henry was often closeted with Cromwell or in

London gathering into his own hands the rich church lands which had accrued to him since Wolsey's downfall; but whenever he was at Greenwich he visited her apartments more assiduously than during her other pregnancies.

"Put your feet up and let our son grow strong," he would admonish, whenever departing upon his state or sportive occasions. And Anne would let gentle Jane Seymour bring her a warm wrap and set her pillows just right. Jane who was always so deft of hand and quiet of step, and so anxious that she should rest; and whose quiet efficiency was ousting even Margaret who, even if for no other cause, had reason to dislike her.

"This girl must be with me at the birth, Henry," said Anne, one afternoon when the first pale rays of spring sunshine brightened her room. "Do you not think she would be invaluable in a sickroom?"

"Or in any other bedroom, come to that," teased Henry, with his boisterous laugh, trying to make the shy chick lift her downcast lashes. For he always seemed to take a special delight in shocking the Wiltshire wench's demure modesty.

And Anne had laughed, too, and sent the girl packing. "Go take the spaniels for a run in the garden and get some roses in your cheeks," she told her, feeling that perhaps she had selfishly kept Jane indoors too much.

Henry had bustled away, too, full of plans for the tournament with which he wanted to impress some foreign visitors he was inviting to the christening.

But that afternoon Anne could not doze contentedly as usual. Perhaps it was the tempting sunshine, or the distant hammering already going forward down in the tilt yard. She had a sudden longing to be out-of-doors herself. She rose and looked from her window.

But there was no sound of Henry's voice booming instructions to the carpenters, and no yapping of small dogs along the paths below. She decided to go down and take a turn or two in the gardens. "Bring me my warm cloak with the miniver," she called to Druscilla, who alone remained in attendance.

But willing Druscilla fumbled and scolded the wardrobe maids and could not find the cloak.

"I wore it but yesterday, and soon the afternoon sun will be all gone," complained Anne irritably.

At last the thing was found and brought. "But, your Grace, is it wise?" remonstrated Druscilla, all fingers and thumbs at fastening it.

"Is what wise?" demanded Anne, with mounting annoyance.

"To—to go out there. Your Grace should know what the King said about keeping your feet up."

"And your Pertness should know when to mind your own business!" flared Anne, slapping Druscilla's agitated face.

So often afterwards she remembered how, with the tears welling to her eyes and a hand to her burning cheek, the poor fond girl still tried to stop her. "Wait at least until I call Margaret," she had beseeched, as if for some reason Margaret's being there could help or her tongue reason more effectively.

Anne pushed Druscilla Zouch aside and opened the door herself, not waiting to change her soft fur slippers for the leather shoes which the weeping fool held ready in her other hand. Poor 'Cilla must have had a quarrel with that devoted husband of hers, or something. But whatever lunacy had taken her, Anne would go down into the garden alone. Out into the April sunshine. To smell the violets in bloom and play awhile with her dogs. And then stroll round to the tilt yard, perhaps, and find Henry, and see some of the preparations for herself.

But Anne did not have to go into the garden to find Henry. She came upon him, close at hand, in a little room giving off her antechamber. Sitting on the cushioned window seat with Jane Seymour on his knee.

At sight of them, she stopped short as if some invisible sword had struck her, and the King's son turned in her womb.

There was nothing shy nor shocked about the way Jane was abandoning herself to his kisses, with those deft hands locked behind his florid neck, and the grey of her gown draped intimately across his white hose.

Anne's slippered footfalls must have been very soft, for Henry did not raise his mouth from her maid-of-honour's until she spoke his name.

After that, in her rage, Anne had no idea what she said. Her whole body trembled with indignation, less because of the physical betrayal than because she had found herself so insultingly duped. Her husband tumbled the wench from his knee and stood there, looking sheepish. But Mistress Seymour offered no word or cry, holding herself in Henry's shadow with amazing aplomb. The sight of her well-nigh maddened Anne, who had shown her scores of kindnesses. "So it was you, that night the French Ambassador came—when I supposed that, in your concern, you had gone to summon the others!" she accused, ignoring Henry as if he were some irresponsible groom. "*You*, who slunk down the kitchen stairs like any Bankside bawd to huddle with another woman's husband! You mealy-faced, smooth-tongued mopsy!"

To cover his discomfiture Henry pshawed and strutted where he stood. "Anne! Anne!" he remonstrated, "I would have you remember it is our good friend Sir John Seymour's daughter you revile, as virtuous a lady as ever came to Court."

"When she *came*, perhaps! Upon my troth, she looked virtuous, with skirts all spread across your jewelled peascod!"

At that he calmed into self-righteousness. "Anne, you know you lie! Many a time you have seen me clip one of your maids without this pother. We went no further than that, I swear! Neither now nor at any other time."

Knowing him as she did, Anne thought his protest was probably true, but her laughter shrilled through the anteroom. It brought Margaret running, with Druscilla still hand-wringing and explaining in her wake. "Why then doesn't your innocent honeypot beshrew me, or deny it—or only have the common humanity to *speak?*" Anne demanded, beside herself with exasperation.

Jane swept her the correctest of curtsies. "By Our Lady's Body, Madame, I promise you I am as much a maid as when first I came."

"For lack of opportunity, then. That I can well believe," countered Anne, glad to see the blood mount to Jane's cheek at last.

At any other time Henry's immense vanity would have been tickled at the sight of two women of good birth quarrelling over him. But it was the Queen who was behaving like a fishwife. And exciting herself. In her transport of anger she would have done the Seymour girl some bodily harm had he not put himself between them. He held Anne's wrists firmly, but without hurting her, and spoke quietly. "Be at peace, sweetheart, and all shall be well," he promised her, already regretting his own careless folly which might well bring about such dire consequences. "I promise you the fair honeypot shall be sent back to her father's house, and all shall be as you wish."

"Would that I could believe it," moaned Anne, dissolving into bitter tears in Margaret's supporting arms. The sudden discovery had been a cruel shock; but upon reflection, she supposed that he would probably keep his word, at least for the time being, since she knew that all the women in the world were as nothing to him compared with the well-being of his heir.

Weeping and sick with anger she let her women get her to bed.

"Nan, my love, you really must control yourself! Remember how it is with you," exhorted Margaret. And already Anne was remembering. Already the swooning nausea was creeping on her. She would lie still, resolved to fight it with all her strength. By sheer will power she checked her shuddering limbs. Not a second time should her enemies exult over a miscarriage. Never again would she let Jane Rochford's bright eyes mock her nor her Uncle Norfolk step stealthily nearer the glittering throne.

"Dear Margot! Let me hold your hand awhile and dream myself back at Hever until I am cool and sane," she murmured. Then, after a time, when she could laugh again, she grinned across the coverlet at her lifelong friend. "You know, Margot, if he sends that Seymour trollop away it will not be for love of me. I warrant you right now he is sweating with fear lest, with my vile temper, I bring forth an idiot!"

Chapter Thirty-Seven

For weeks Anne saw nothing of Henry in private, but in spite of her bitter resentment she joined in her ladies' cry of delight when one morning he clanked into her room in full armour.

It was a new suit of shining gold, sent him by Katherine's nephew, the Emperor, in token of renewed friendship; and before practising in the lists, Henry could not resist showing himself off in it. He had brought Norfolk, Suffolk, and a crowd of friends and competitors with him and, judging by their animated conversation, it would be difficult to say with which Henry was the more pleased, the gift or the consummation of his political endeavours.

"You look like a sun god!" breathed Anne, walking round him, forgetful of past dudgeon in her admiration of both man and craftsmanship.

"I *feel* like a suffocating felon clamped in the stocks," he laughed ruefully, passing a finger round the top of the heavy gorget.

"Now your Grace knows how we women feel in our leather stays," giggled Anne's cousin, Madge Skelton, mischievously.

"But you don't have to hold in a plunging sixteen-hand destrer and couch a fourteen foot lance," retorted Henry, making as if to pinch her rosy cheek with his mailed fist. But once he had bent his comely head so that his squire could fit the great ceremonial heaume upon his head, the conversation became as muffled as it was technical. "Does it not seem to you, Charles, that this joint is riveted a shade too high?"

"And I would have them ease the left gauntlet, Harry, so as to give the rein hand more play."

"The vizor needs a drop of goose grease, sir, lest it stick."

"Here, Norreys, let them see to it down in the armoury as milord of Suffolk and my squire say, and have it ready for me presently at the barrier."

Unbuckled and unbraced, Henry took a deep breath and limbered up his muscles, flexing and unflexing his mighty biceps. "God's teeth, 'tis good to be tilting again," he exclaimed.

"Your Grace should take it gradually, having laid aside sport for work of late," warned Norfolk. And all knew that he spoke sourly because his interests lay, not with Spain, but with France.

Henry turned and landed him a good-natured thrust in the doublet. "Tush, Thomas, you old raven! D'you suppose my limbs are rusted? For all your croaking, I can make my destrer rear more dangerously than anyone's, and though it be but showmanship, that is what the spectators like! And yesterday, in the preliminary trials, did I not overthrow our coming champion, Brereton, there? Not so bad, eh, cousin, at our age."

Anne knew it for a gallant mixture of obstinacy and vanity, and hoped he had not strained himself. Knowing how a woman clings to her armour of feminine wiles, she realized that once Henry, the great athlete, was forced to give up sport, some good part would die in him. She called to Madge for scissors and cut a ribbon from her sleeve. "Will your Grace wear this for me, since I shall not be there to see?" she invited.

Always, even in informal practice tournaments like this, he had been wont to wear her favour; but this time, either from embarrassment or from preference for another, he had not asked for one. And as he took it and put it to his lips as custom demanded, both of them knew that the scrap of gay silk was a peace offering. An effort to efface his faithlessness and her anger in their quarrel about the Seymour girl. "It should look well in your new gold helm," smiled Anne, only too thankful that he had accepted what once he had so humbly sought.

For a moment or two he stood with her apart, while the others jeered and jested over the laying of their wagers. "Truth to tell, Nan, when it comes to actual combat I would as lief wear my old, dented steel," he confided, with a little less confidence than usual. "It may not look so fine, but it has seen me through many a fray. I am at home in it."

"And, best of all, you like to feel at home," answered Anne gently. She was thinking how spurious his few love adventures had been and how at heart he was a home-loving man. And how, in his homelier moments, she liked him best. Then, and when he was pulling that great, wide-nostrilled charger of his to its haunches. Even if a woman were not in love with him she could get a thrill out of seeing him do that. "I wish I could be there to see you ride," she sighed involuntarily, and for no particular reason found herself in memory back on the wooded hill at Hever, a young girl again, and Henry bestriding a dead stag, with the ruddiness of beech leaves on his face. And somehow, just remembering, her breath was caught with all the old, mad stir of the senses.

"So do I," he was saying in a matter-of-fact way. "But it is only a little while now, and we must be sensible. All the excitement would be bad for you, sweet, and there might be some hideous accident." Since she had caught him philandering with Jane Seymour he had not spoken to her so pleasantly; but already the trumpets were shrilling and he was champing to be up and doing. "You shall come and Queen it at the real tournament with all our foreign guests; and bring the boy!" he called back to her with his great boisterous laugh.

With his cropped head rising from the golden gorget he looked eager as a boy himself. As always, when engaged in open air sport, more braced and young. "At least our son should be virile," thought Anne.

A flatness fell upon the room when King and courtiers were gone. "Surely it could not hurt me more to watch from one of the towers than to sit moping here," she thought, half-minded to disobey him. But remembering how malevolently both ambitious Dukes stared at her now she was *enceinte* again, she thought better of it. A month or two more and she would be able to Queen it at any tournament in Europe. To ignore black looks at home and meet the Queen of France on equal terms. Better to be bored now than barren later!

Her brother and Brereton were already down in the lists, preparing for combat. Anne had given Jane Rochford leave to watch George tilt; but Norreys and Weston stayed as long as they dared to cheer her. And when they, too, were gone, she saw Mark Smeaton waiting moodily by the window. "Why do you not go, too?" she asked irritably.

"I am a musician, Madame, not a courtier," he answered; sulking, no doubt, because, being but a craftsman's son, he had no call to change into armour or to attend the King.

"That is no reason why you should moon about me until your eyes are like dark-rimmed platters," she retorted. But her women were all agog at the windows watching the crowds and competitors come past, and Smeaton, when he forgot his amorous pretensions, was good company. "Well, how shall we pass the time, Mark?" she sighed.

"Very well, I wager, now they are all gone."

Anne could not help laughing. "Marry, what a spoiled coxcomb it is. Why should you be so glad that all the gay company is gone?"

Smeaton came and stood close beside her, his eyes smouldering jealously as they had that night when Henry had lifted her in his arms after the Circe masque. "Because you never look at me nor speak to me when they are here," he blurted out.

Of a truth, the youth was making himself ridiculous, with this notion that he could be her swain; spending most of the money the King paid him on modish silks and velvets in which to prink himself for her presence! "But, Mark, they are my friends, and gentlemen," she tried to explain kindly. "You cannot expect me to draw you into the conversation when they are by."

"Then you love me only for my voice?"

"I do not love you at all," Anne told him coldly, amazed at his effrontery. "But you may sit at my feet and sing. And I will pay you for it."

He dragged a cushion to the floor before her chair, but made no attempt to sit on it. Lifted out of his own world and spoiled with flattery, he must have been living in some hallucinatory realm of romantic fantasy. "Everyone knows that I would die for you," he dared to say, lowering his voice so that the women at the windows could not hear.

"You mean, everyone about the backstairs?" mocked Anne.

"And everyone *shall* know it," he went on wildly, "from the King downwards!"

"The King would make short work of you," yawned Anne, half despising herself for arguing with such inflated lunacy. "Already he has complained that you are always under his feet, hanging about me."

"Then he has noticed?"

"Mark Smeaton, you must be mad!"

Anne was really angered now, but in his crazy passion he went down on his knees before her. "Have mercy, Madame," he implored. "Whatever my birth, I am a man the same as all those others whom you jest with and touch so easily. And because of our music there is an affinity between us. Consider the way our minds worked as one over that masque. I know when your Grace is perplexed or sad, and my songs can soothe you. I do not want to go gallivanting to every sport, but am always happy here at your feet. Is it not true that you like to have me here?"

"So long as you stay there—with my dogs."

"The dogs are often in your arms."

Anne sprang up as if to spurn him with her foot, so that he sprang backwards; but still he stood there, glowering and defiant, with his oiled dark hair and petulant, libidinous lower lip. "What have I said that those others do not say?" he demanded. "Only last week I heard Sir Francis Weston say the same."

"I tell you they are men of breeding who can say these things with a kind of unmeaning lightness."

"While I, a carpenter's son, must only let the thought sear my heart?"

Even Smeaton's speaking voice was deep with light and shade and he had a pretty turn of phrase. He looked so sulkily handsome standing there that Anne had not the heart to send for the

Comptroller of her household and have him whipped. She allowed leniency to overcome wisdom; partly, perhaps, because the persistent urgency of men's love, which once had been her daily portion, was now growing rare. "You go too far," she warned wearily, sitting down again with a sigh. "Now for God's sake, sing or go!"

As Henry so often said, there was magic in the young man's voice. And he knew her loneliness, and how to choose a song. He had jerked his cushion closer so that as he sang his head rested, as if by accident, against her knee. Anne was vaguely aware that Margaret and Druscilla were talking in anxious whispers at the other end of the room, hating the youth's persistence and fearing for her indiscretion. But she closed her eyes and rested, and after awhile, when all the shouting and clamour from the tilt yard seemed to have died down, she looked idly around for her lute.

As if reading her desire, Mark Smeaton turned and put it into her hands. Better than anything in the world, he loved to sing in harmony with her. But she had scarcely plucked a note before the door was thrown open and her uncle and sister-in-law burst into the room.

"Why have you both come back so soon?" she asked, looking up in amazement.

But they did not answer. Jane came running and threw her arms about her protectively, whimpering and weeping. And Norfolk just stood there, cap in hand, wiping the sweat from his brow and panting as if he had been running. His swarthy face looked all broken up with agitation. Anne was aware of Smeaton slithering as unobtrusively as possible from his self-appointed place against her knee, and of Margaret Wyatt coming to her side.

"Oh, my poor Nan!" cried Jane Rochford against her shoulder.

Only then did Anne realize that their news concerned her, and that it must be of vast importance for the first Duke in the land to come running. Only then did she notice the ominous stillness outside, where all had so recently been excitement and clamour.

She got to her feet, the absurd lute still in her hand, her other hand instinctively groping behind her in search of Margaret's. "What is it?" she asked.

"The King—" croaked Thomas Howard, coming closer.

"Yes? Yes?"

"He—"

Anne stamped her foot at him because he looked like a frightened, grimacing monkey. "Go on, will you!" she whispered, thinking that she shouted.

"He took a fall—against Sir Edward Seymour—it was that cursed Spanish armour."

The lute fell to the floor and broke as Anne made an impatient, groping gesture. Through the heavy stillness she could hear men's voices giving instructions in unnatural undertones, and their footsteps echoing heavily, direfully across the paved courtyard, carrying someone, or something, with great effort. "He is not dead?" she asked, and her voice sounded like a stranger's, coming from a long way off.

"Not yet, I think." Norfolk was speaking more coherently. "You know his weight, Nan, even without the armour. His horse rolled on him and crushed his leg. Broke open a vein. The doctors cannot stop it. Charles is with him now. They say he is bleeding to death."

Anne tried to picture her husband as she had seen him but an hour ago—a great, handsome, ruddy giant—now lying in a colourful pool of gold and blood. Lying quite still, and never laughing any more. And in that moment she understood the truth of Thomas Wyatt's words about the tie of marriage. Whether she had loved Henry or not, she had been married to him for the best part of three years. And they said he was dying. It would be his boisterous laughter she would miss most, and his protection.

For without Henry Tudor what was Anne Boleyn?

"There might be some hideous accident," he had said, fearing lest his child be marred. And so there had been. But in spite of the fact that Anne's only hope of personal survival from her enemies lay, even now, in the birth of that son, her whole instinct was to go to Henry. For all his self-deception and egotism, there was something about the man. She broke from Margaret and Jane, ran a step or two towards the open door, then stumbled over Smeaton's discarded cushion and fell, unconscious, at her callous uncle's feet.

Messengers galloped madly from the gateway and pandemonium reigned within the Palace.

For hours Henry's life hung in the balance, and there were weeks of sickness and commotion before Anne's child was born, although it came before its time. Henry, from his sickroom, sent her messages of encouragement and reassurance. Henry, who was too tough to die; whom Chamberlain and Butts had so skilfully bound up that already he could transact urgent business, sitting with his injured leg stretched out before him on a cushioned stool. And when her hour came, he spared her both physicians. But it was of no avail. All the suffering they had predicted was there, but not the living breath. The child was born dead.

"And none of you need tell me it was a boy!" raged Anne, returned to cruel consciousness and staring straight and unseeingly before her.

There were no salvoes and proclamations, and no more messages from the King. People of importance, hastily gathered for the event, seemed to slink away from the luckless Queen. "It was all deliberate malice," she said tonelessly, when her father, in common humanity, came to visit her.

"Diabolically clever malice," agreed Thomas Boleyn, Earl of Wiltshire.

"They were clever in seizing the opportunity."

"And because it can never be brought home to them, for many who were in the lists at the time believed the same. That the King was dying. Even those of us who carried him in."

"Yet it had to be Thomas Howard and Jane Rochford who came to tell me!"

"Defend me from vipers within my own nest," muttered Wiltshire, already calculating how much of the wreckage of their hopes he could by cunning save. Standing by the bedside, he regarded his most brilliant child consideringly. "You really think that Norfolk—?"

"When first I learned that Mary Howard was betrothed to Fitzroy, after my miscarriage, he taunted me. 'Best make sure there is a next time!' he said looking, with that sinister squint of his, as if he would perform any villainy to prevent it."

"You and your husband are still young," Wiltshire suggested halfheartedly, unconsciously quoting his master.

"And I have cheated him twice, or so he will say! That first time, horse riding; and now my enemies are sure to tell him the child was already dead, and he will say I killed it with my crazy temper when I caught him dandling that Seymour bitch upon his knee." At the bare thought of her, Anne dragged herself up in bed. "But I can get me another son," she cried wildly. "Bring me my mirror, some of you! Though I look like a raddled drab now, I can be groomed sleek again. I can win men when I want them. Always, since I was a slip of a wench, I have been able to bewitch them and they come. I will get the King back, I tell you!"

But in spite of her frenzied boasts, her father had no more heart to console her. He put out a pitying hand and touched her dishevelled head. "Not this time, Nan," he told her gently.

"And why not?" she snarled at him. "Am I unshapely or poxed?"

"I make no doubt you will be alluring as long as you live, whenever it pleases you," he smiled ruefully. "But by the time you are about again in all your gewgaws and a trailing velvet gown it may well be too late."

"Too late?" Anne's fingers flew to her blanched cheeks, her pain-sunken eyes enquired of his. "You mean that Seymour strumpet?"

Wiltshire's fine hands worried at his black beard. "Unfortunately, she is no strumpet. Say, rather, the new figurehead of our enemies' party," he explained bitterly. "For she returns all the King's gifts. His amorous advances shock her modesty, and she declines to be his mistress."

"God help me, has it come to that?"

Wiltshire nodded reluctantly. "Yet she lives discreetly with her relatives, and it is the jest of the Court to see the King visit her so virtuously there. A jest at our expense."

"You mean she thinks to play her cards as shrewdly as I played mine? That nothing less than a Queen will do for her? That girl whom I thought so meek and stupid!"

Her father took his leave warily before the gathering storm of her rage. "I thought it best to warn you, Nan," he said, hurrying away because it was no longer politic to be seen visiting the Queen.

Anne was warned indeed, so that fear overcame her anger. "I beseech you, give my love to my lady mother and to Mary," she called after him, with great slow tears welling from her eyes.

No wonder her erring maid-of-honour had remained so unruffled! No wonder everyone seemed to have forsaken her! Almost in an apathy, Anne lay there, considering Jane Seymour's cunning. Or could it, in truth, be virtue, as her own reluctance had been in part? But cunning or virtue, what difference would it make in the end? Gradually Anne's listless thoughts slipped from Jane to people and places that she loved. Back to Harry Percy and Thomas Wyatt, to Jocunda and the long summer evenings at Hever, with the rooks cawing in the elms.

And then before she could comb her hair or paint her face, it was evening, here and now at Greenwich, and the King himself had come.

Anne had heard him coming along the gallery. No longer striding with that light, masterful tread; but shuffling with the help of a stick, and though many came with him, they came in silence, without the customary chattering. By the time he reached her bedside, Anne realized that even the short distance from his apartments could have been accomplished only by sheer determination. Bandaged to the thigh and furious with his own ungainliness, he waved back his anxious followers with an oath. She had never seen him look anything but the picture of robust health, but now he was grey with pain. "Oh, Henry, I believed that you were killed!" she blurted out.

"I told you to keep away," he snarled.

"I did. I obeyed you. But they came and told me—"

"And like a woman you believed the first set of cursed busy-bodies you heard!"

She tried to tell him that it had been done purposely, and he called her a fool for her pains. When she shouted Norfolk's name she was not sure that it penetrated his rage or whether he disregarded it as incredible. In spite of her weakness, he had dragged himself there to upbraid her, to blame her for the loss of his son.

"I, too, was nigh unto death, and am not yet strong," she pleaded.

But because of his own bitter disappointment, he could feel no shred of pity for her. At first she tried to cajole him, but there was no weapon left in her armoury with which to cajole—neither beauty, wit, nor self-confidence. She knew only too well how drawn and haggard she must look; and that even had she looked radiant, his desire could not be reawakened because it had passed elsewhere.

Even the most curious eavesdroppers had withdrawn, and it seemed that they two were alone in the room, quarrelling as crudely as any married couple in the land, knowing each other's most vulnerable spots and trying to hurt them.

"It was that day in the anteroom. With your hell-cat temper you destroyed my son."

Anne's spirit remained unbroken. "If that were the cause of it, and not my misfortunate fright for you, you have only yourself to blame for it, huddling shamelessly with my maid!"

"Doesn't a man need a change sometimes? Some relief from haughty ways and nagging? Some change to peace and gentleness?"

"Say rather, from dark beauty to fair insipidness! Must your conscience still find fair names for the snare of the flesh?"

"That you of all people, should prate of snaring flesh! For the lustiest years of my life you kept me living like a monk and then, when at last I was satiated, with your infernal mumming you bewitched me back. I say you bewitched me. For two pins I would have you burned!"

Secure in her womanhood, Anne was sure that he would not. But he stood over her, brutal and gigantic, shaking with rage and pain. Pain such as she was accustomed to, but which was to him a completely new experience. Yet even now she found it difficult to believe that he was impervious to pity. That—cajole, plead, or rage as she would—nothing could make any impression on this new brutal personality. That her power was completely gone. "How can a wife who is no louse accept such betrayal and make no struggle?" she faltered, envying her predecessor's still dignity of pride.

"You will have to learn to accept these things as your betters have done before you, Madame!"

"Meaning Katherine?"

"Keep your glib tongue off her name." For a moment or two his bluster died down in shame. "But for you I might not have let her die forsaken. Even her last words to me—"

"Everyone knows what they were!"

"And that she loved me."

Finding herself in the unhappy situation she had created for Katherine, Anne clutched at the sheet like a cornered thing. Hurt in her vanity, all her desire was to destroy his. "Did that make you think that *all* your discarded women loved you? That my poor sister did? Do you suppose that *I* ever really loved you?" she spat at him, in an agony of humiliation that knew no salve but cruelty. "Ever once in all those years when you wrote such beautiful letters and restrained yourself because you really cared, or even that night when you held me in your arms upon your horse in Calais? Pff! It was just your vain imagining!" Anne saw him wince and knew that the shaft had gone home; knew that as long as he lived the memory of her and that ecstasy of his senses would come back to him, like a perfume of lusty youth drifting across his middle age. At last she had silenced him. But because there seemed nothing more to gain or lose, in her insane fury she must needs strike deeper yet. With black protruding eyes and a hand holding her slender throat lest she suffocate with her own emotions, she went on baiting him. "Do you believe I ever really gave myself to you, as I have done in love?" she laughed scornfully. "Are you so simple as to believe that no man ever had me before you? You must have been drunk that night in Calais!"

Shocked by some change in Henry's face, Anne's mind sent her hand flying from throat to mouth. Too late, both hands clamped down on her betraying lips. But at long last the crazy words were said, and nothing could unsay them. Peering from her bed, she realized that only Henry could have heard them, and, understanding his inordinate vanity, she knew that no power on earth would ever draw them from him to confess himself a woman's fool. But they would always be there, in his mind, dimming his self-esteem. They would be cause enough for that woman's undoing.

His rampant stance had become stilled. His small blue eyes went cold and unforgiving as a snake's. For a moment the two of them stared at each other in a land of horror, the scales of glamour fallen from their eyes, incredulous that they could have come so long a way from the roseate days of courtship, wondering how they could ever have turned England upside down in order to lie legitimately in each other's arms.

And Anne, with awful clarity of mind, perceived how through the years of their intimacy he had changed. When she had first known him his egotism had been nurtured upon unlimited power and flattery, but he had always been likeable, and generous to the call of those who loved him; whereas now he was behaving like an insensate brute. And Anne knew that it was she herself who had schooled him to shut up his compassion against his family; she, who through years of trickery and sex enslavement, had made him what he was. And that now she was hoist with her own petard, as he would say of his soldiers when they bungled, breaching some city wall.

Fear was mingled with sincere remorse as she stretched out a beseeching hand to him. "Oh, my husband," she faltered, "could we not, even now—"

But the words died before his basilisk stare, and when at last he spoke it was with that dangerous, hissing intake of his breath. "You will get no more sons by me!" he vowed roughly and, although he had not raised his voice, the cruel, inflexible words must have reached her women, cowering against the wall.

He shuffled from her room without another word. Some obsequious hand closed the door behind him, and Anne heard the angry tap of his stick receding through the rooms, and fading gradually into a diminuendo of shutting doors. Tomorrow, she supposed, he would leave the Palace and be borne in dudgeon to Westminster or Hampton; and the relentless doors would have shut her out of his glittering personal life forever.

When Margaret and the rest would have tried to comfort her, Anne waved them away. "Put out the lights!" she ordered wearily.

And as the long fingers of shadow reached out from the four corners of the room to entangle her, she turned her face to the pillow, tasting through salt tears the bitter gall of her ambition's golden sorrow.

Chapter Thirty-Eight

THE GRAND TOURNAMENT WHICH had been planned for June was held instead as part of the usual May Day celebrations. People flocked to Greenwich by road and river, the banners waved bravely in the sunshine and children who had been amaying in the meadows brought their garlands to deck the royal stand, against the moment when the Queen should step forth into the public gaze again after her illness and take her place at the King's side.

By the time her women had finished working upon her, Anne was sleek and attractive as ever. Suffering had lent a new interest to her features, but, although she was barely thirty-three, all the radiance of youth had gone from her forever. The long weeks of a dispirited convalescence had been spent playing with her dogs in the deserted gardens at Greenwich, or resting in her own apartments while Mark Smeaton sang to her. For Anne herself seldom sang any more. She only watched and waited, wondering what the rest of her life would be like without Henry's favour. She had no illusion about his ever forgiving her.

Glad to put off the moment of meeting him, she had paused on her way to the tilt yard to watch Mark Smeaton mount a restive new horse he had bought. Arabella and Madge Skelton were shaken with laughter because, for all his finery, he was such a poor horseman, and even Anne herself was smiling. She found it easier to relax with these lovable girls now that they were all relieved of the presence of the two Janes. "Why, Mark, whither away in all the new May Day garments?" she teased.

"To Secretary Cromwell's, to dine," he had answered, puffed up with self-importance.

"And since when have you been on such terms of friendship with Thomas Cromwell that, although he is too busy to attend anything as frivolous as a tournament, he should put himself to the pains of entertaining you?" enquired Arabella, wickedly.

"He has guests, 'Bella, and needs someone to sing," joined in Madge. "That is how our songster can afford a new horse."

But Smeaton, red in the face, drew a well-thumbed letter from his pouch and, in spite of his equestrian difficulties, leaned down to dangle the Secretary of State's seal beneath their noses. "He has perhaps heard that I have been much in the Queen's company of late, when others have deserted her," he suggested complacently, eying Anne adoringly, and starting off for London with a flourish.

The women looked after him and laughed, and Margaret muttered something about a dangerous, swollen-headed coxcomb. "Will Brereton says everybody is asking where he gets his money from," added Madge. And because they were all making fun of him, Anne remembered how sensitively he had helped her through the dragging hours. "Poor foolish lad," she sighed, touched by his devotion, and through her own suffering, grown more kind.

But soon maids-of-honour and musicians were forgotten. Holding herself regally as she approached the royal stand, Anne tried to control her nervous tremors at thought of meeting Henry. Would he begin upbraiding her again, or shame her publicly? But she need not have worried. Although he never once smiled at her or gave her a personal word, he went through all the ceremonial motions of greeting, answered her enquiry about his health, and made formal enquiry for her own, then seated her at his side; so that no one save their personal followers could have suspected that there was anything amiss. Anne, the Queen, was there—Queen of the tournament. Pale from her illness and grievous disappointment, but elegant as ever. Later on, perhaps, she would be more fortunate and the bells would ring again. "Serve the witch right for making a tyrant of a good King," growled her enemies. But she was bearing her misfortune with such dignity that, on the whole, the women's hearts were softened towards her.

Once the fanfares were sounding and Norfolk, as Grand Marshal had declared the lists open, Anne tried to concentrate on the festive scene and to forget the massive, surly figure by her side. She could the more readily do so because Henry paid her no attention and seemed engrossed in some low-toned conversation with Suffolk; or, whenever competitors charged and thrust at each other across the barrier, sat moodily staring down into the lists where he would never pose and fight and rear his horse again. She knew how the sight of men with half his skill enjoying the daring rush of combat must madden him, and how the mockery of the occasion and the loss of his longed-for heir gnawed at his heart.

But Anne's compassion for him was dead.

She turned from him to gather what entertainment she could. The pomp of trumpets and the reckless thunder of hooves had always been as the breath of life to her. It was good to Queen it over such pageantry again; to watch all the colour and movement, to see her brother and Brereton smile up at her encouragingly as they rode past, and Norreys, in his master's place, wearing her favour; all of them trying, as far as they dared, to assure her of their friendship and to make amends for the King's neglect. "These, and my women, are no fair weather friends, dependent upon the sun of royal smiles," she told herself, and found herself laughing, pointing, wagering, picking out possible winners; so that she was carried out of herself, and clapped as vigorously as any when her gallant young champion charged and thrust and won a splendid bout against her brother. And by the time Hal Norreys drew rein immediately beneath her stand, she had momentarily forgotten the King's displeasure.

Norreys bade his squire help him off with his heaume, so that he might cool himself and, flushed with exertion and enjoyment, he looked up and saluted her. "How good to have you back, Madame!" he panted informally, his horse being so close. Like old friends, they had smiled into each other's eyes; and, seeing how the sweat ran down his face, Anne tossed him her handkerchief. It went fluttering down into the lists above the halberdiers' helmeted heads and, laughingly, Norreys made his horse rear so as to catch the wisp of gaudy silk, and, without any attempt at gallantry, mopped his brow with it.

The sun shone warm upon them and it was all like a light-hearted fragment from her old life, so that in her momentary happiness Anne scarcely noticed that the King had risen. That his face, flaccid from lack of exercise, was nearly purple. And only when Margaret had touched her on the arm did she become aware of the commotion occasioned by some messenger breaking his way through the throng of gaily dressed nobles.

"He has brought the King a letter."

"It looks like Cromwell's nephew."

Scraps of speculation drifted about her. And then Anne saw Henry show the letter to Suffolk, and limp down the steps of the stand leaning on Will Somers' shoulder. Together with his brother-in-law, he hurried back to the Palace, calling to his gentlemen to follow him. Even Norreys and Brereton were wanted and had to change quickly from their armour. And with no word of explanation the tournament was broken up.

The King, it seemed, was riding to London, taking most of his suite with him.

"Cromwell must have sent him news of a Spanish invasion." The old, unfailing rumour beat round among the credulous and the timorous, easing the Marshal's task and dispersing the disappointed crowd to their homes quicker than any body of halberdiers could have done.

"Better go back to your apartments," Norfolk told Anne curtly, as he, too, followed after the King. If he was aware of any reason for his Grace's extraordinary behaviour, he refused to speak. But both he and Anne knew Henry well enough to be sure that he would have told his subjects, and rallied them to go with him, had it been the Spaniards.

Wondering, waiting, worrying, Anne and her ladies lived through the rest of the day, and as soon as it was dark George Boleyn came back from London in a hired skiff. He bribed a page to tell Margaret he was waiting beneath the willows down by the river to see the Queen. He came with the utmost caution, for in London his movements were being watched. And by similar contrivance the two cloaked and hooded women found their way to him through the deserted gardens.

There was no time for waste of words. "Nan, the letter concerned you. It is the end of everything," he told her instantly, in urgent, guarded tones.

"Concerned *me?*" Anne stopped short with a hand clasped to her racing heart.

"All our friends have been arrested, and for all I know, I may be added to their number in the morning. The King and all our enemies are determined to trap you and hunt you down."

"But how can they? What have I done?"

"It is not what you have done, but what they will pin on to you." He took her cold hands in his, speaking against time, fearing that at any moment they might be disturbed. "Cromwell, Norfolk, Suffolk and all of them are with the King now, concocting their foul slanders. Anything to discredit you."

"My own husband! I knew that he is angry, but I cannot believe—"

"They will accuse you of adultery."

Anne let out a stifled cry, and he drew her further into the shadows, where she sank down upon a low garden wall. "But never once have I been unfaithful to him!" she protested.

"He is afire for Jane Seymour," Margaret reminded her. "If it is true that he wants to marry her, then he might agree to anything—as he did before."

"With whom do they say that I—that I—" began Anne, piteously.

"It seems you played into their hands when you tossed your handkerchief to Norreys this morning."

"You mean, that because of a handkerchief—"

"My dear, you should know this weather vane Court as well as I do."

Anne was horrified. She could not bring herself to believe it. "But Hal's sweet friendship has lightened all our days. Ever since we came, he has been like a brother to us."

"That would not save him," jeered her real brother, with intense bitterness.

"This must be terrible for him, too."

"All the way to London the King pleaded with him, promised him every sort of pardon and reward if only he would confess to it, and so ease the path of dalliance. It was even put to him that if only he would say you had once tempted him—"

"Oh, dear Christ, the wickedness! And Hal, what did he?"

"What do you suppose, sweet idiot? Hal was bewildered, horror-stricken as you. But right to the gates of Whitehall he protested your innocence."

Anne lifted her drawn face to the stars. "After all, the world is still beautiful," she said softly.

"But he is not the only one they mean to accuse!"

Anne stared incredulously at the white, featureless disc of her brother's face outlined against the dark cascade of willow branches. "What! Would they make me a common bawd?" she stammered. "I know, none better, that to climb is to augment the venom of one's enemies; but who else, for pity's sake, must be endangered because of me? With whom else have I fouled my husband's bed?"

"Will Brereton and Francis Weston."

"George, it is incredible!" protested Margaret.

But Anne's agile mind, goaded by fear, was already seeking for some loophole in the snarers' net. "Will, I think, would not betray me. He is brave and strong like Hal," she calculated, her eyes wild pits of desperation, "But Francis Weston, with his boastful bawdy stories and his scented shirts—"

"It is possible that his imaginative tongue might unwittingly destroy you," admitted George.

"But how can even the King's fawning curs substantiate these things?"

"There will be plenty of jealous tongues, I fear, to swear that these men are frequently in your apartments."

"Yet everyone knows that Francis, for all his brazen compliments, comes to see my cousin Madge."

"Besides, all three of them have the sense to come in company or when we maids-of-honour are present," pointed out Margaret. "So what can they prove against Nan?"

"The Crown can usually produce plenty of glib witnesses, dear Margot," answered George sadly.

It was so true that it reduced them to silence. "Is that all?" asked Anne presently, in a stricken voice.

It was some moments before George could bring himself to answer. For Margaret's sake he would have omitted the name of his best friend. "There is also Tom Wyatt," he said.

"Tom!" cried both women, aghast. And Anne sprang up in fury, all weakness forgotten. "I know it is common knowledge that the King was once jealous. But you know how careful Thomas has been never so much as to cross my threshold, forswearing my company sooner than put me in suspicion! I thought I had proved it to Henry long ago."

"And may yet again, dear Nan," soothed Margaret. "It is all too, too fantastical. If they be sent for trial, surely, George, my brother will be cleared?"

"I think they might all have been cleared for lack of evidence," said George gloomily, "had Smeaton kept his cursed mouth shut."

"*Smeaton!*" Anne's angry movements were stilled. The very word was a gasp of incredulity. "God in Heaven!" she cried. "Does anyone outside Bedlam seriously believe that I would stoop to huddle with that little common runt? Even if there were no men left on earth?"

George laid a warning hand upon her mouth. "He was always crooning round you, and the King himself has had occasion to boot him out." In his anxiety lest they be overheard, he spoke more roughly than he intended.

"George! *You* cannot suppose—"

"No, I cannot, with your fastidiousness and his greasy love locks," he laughed shortly, convinced by her indignant horror, and hating himself for even such momentary doubt. "But you must see that he, of them all, is the easiest to bring evidence against, to make people believe evil of. For one thing, he has no family backing. And so my lady wife makes it her business to tell Cromwell that the day she and our illustrious uncle came back unexpectedly from the tournament they found Mark Smeaton with his head against your knee. Damn her ugly soul in hell!"

Anne and Margaret turned to each other instinctively in the darkness. "So that was why Cromwell—"

"They say Smeaton's vanity was tickled by an invitation to dine. He was trapped into Cromwell's house. Pleasantly, over strong wine, that one-time creation of Wolsey's tried to worm evidence out of him—a jumped-up singing boy who even when sober, needs no encouragement to brag about the hours he spends comforting the neglected Queen! Cromwell pretended to admire his fashionable new doublet, his well-fitting hose, asking awkward questions about how he came by the money to buy them. Questions that everyone is asking! Until even the poor fool himself must have perceived his danger."

"*His* danger!" breathed Anne.

"Your own, dear Nan, cannot have weighed with him overmuch for all his gusty protestations. Cromwell sent for two stout fellows waiting outside the door, no doubt, and had him tortured. Down in some cellar from whence his shrieks could not be heard."

"They tortured him?" Woman-like, Anne pictured him as the boy whom Henry had first brought to her, the boy with the golden voice.

"They knotted cords about his forehead and wound them tighter and yet tighter with a couple of sticks," went on the relentless voice from the shadow of the willow tree. "'No more, Sir Secretary! I will tell the truth,' he cried. 'It was the Queen who gave me the money.' And as the cords pressed tighter, tighter even than Cromwell's horrid mouth, God knows what more the whimsical coward confessed. His imaginary dream about being your lover, no doubt."

Anne crouched on the wall again, with Margaret's arms around her. She covered her face and rocked herself in horror. Even then she could not wholly blame someone young and lovesick, unversed in the evil ways of Machiavellian statesmen, who, like herself, had been raised to dizzy, unfamiliar heights; and who had then been tortured. "After this, people will believe anything," she kept moaning. "Oh, that Thomas and Hal and the other two should stand in danger of—of I know not what for me!" In an agony of love and self-reproach she stretched out a hand and caught at Rochford's. "Thank Heaven, you are my brother, George! At least, such shameful accusations cannot endanger *you*!"

George freed himself gently, and stood staring silently across the dark, moving stretch of river. And in those quiet moments Anne allowed her shocked mind to look upon the reality of danger in which her friends stood. In Henry's present mood it might mean death for them. For Hal, whom even the King could not cease loving; for quiet, sturdy Will, and mercurial, amusing Francis, and for Thomas.

For all of them the Tudor's grasping for a new woman might mean a sudden cutting off of all their splendid gallantry, their vivid creative minds and carefree jests. Yet even in her grievous anxiety for them, Anne was shamed at finding herself silently thanking God that she had been born a woman. That the unfaceable thing—Death—would not happen to her.

"Do you think that he will put me in the Tower?" she faltered, remembering her instinctive horror of the place.

"If they can concoct a charge of treason," answered George, looking down at her pityingly.

In her utter misery Anne wished that he would take her in his arms and comfort her; but for some reason he did not touch her. He seemed suddenly older, as if something had shocked all the impulsiveness out of him. And yet, as he stood motionless beside her, she felt the strong, sustaining weight of his sympathy; as if he shared this tragedy as no one else could. As if the shadow of death hung about him, too.

Before he slipped back through the willows to his waiting boat he turned and took Margaret in his arms and kissed her with lingering passion, the frustrated love of a lifetime upon his lips.

"The King, more than any man, appreciates Tom's gifts," he tried to console her. "In any case, there is nothing you can do for him. And rather than anyone in the world, I would have you with Nan now."

"Whatever happens, I will never leave her," promised Margaret, with the starlight reflected in her steadfast eyes.

And in the morning, before they had finished breaking their fast, Norfolk came with a company of halberdiers to take Anne to the Tower.

"Of what am I accused?" she demanded, facing him bravely.

"Of adultery," he told her.

"The King does this monstrous thing but to try me," she said, with a lift of her little, pointed chin; utterly grateful to George because this time Norfolk's blunt news was not the devastating shock he had hoped, and she found herself able to meet it with some kind of dignity.

"Be that as it may, niece, he would have you come at once, while the tide serves."

"But her Grace is all unprepared. I pray you wait while I pack her clothes," Arabella defied him gallantly.

"She will not need her gewgaws there—only a warm cloak against the damp and cold," he laughed, with his odd, perverted sense of humour.

"Then we will come at once," said Margaret, with a new quiet dignity.

But even that, it seemed, was to be denied them, and this was indeed a blow for which they had not been prepared.

"But how can I dress and who will serve me at table?" demanded Anne, as Katherine of Aragon had done before her.

"Women will be provided for you," said the man who hated them all. "Your aunt, Lady Boleyn, and a Mistress Cosyns."

"Both of them my mortal enemies who spy on all I do!" cried Anne, on the point of swooning. But when they were come to the watergate Margaret and Arabella stepped into the barge, defying him, so that it swayed perilously as his men pushed off. "Unless you carry us ashore or throw us into the water, Mistress Savile and I will lodge in the Tower, too," vowed Margaret, remembering how Queen Katherine had defied the Duke of Suffolk.

"Come if you will," he allowed grudgingly, in the face of the grinning crowd that had collected. "But I warn you the world is a sweeter place outside. And these women the King has chosen have their orders. They will not let you speak with her alone."

Up river towards London they went as Anne had gone three short years ago, with so much pomp, to her Coronation. "If only I could see the King! If only I could speak to him! I pray you, good uncle, have me taken to him!" cried Anne, as the gracious roofs of Westminster came into view.

But the easy, rhythmic dip of oars bore her inexorably from all hope and gaiety and laughter, from family and child, and from the heady stimulant of admiration which she, of all beings, had so fiercely loved! Never, surely, had barge skimmed so swiftly or tide flowed so fast. Never, it seemed to Anne, had any journey been accomplished in so short a time.

Perhaps she had really believed that they would take her on to Westminster, that she would see again the familiar rooms and gardens where Henry moved in pitiless self-righteousness. For when the barge began to slacken speed by Tower wharf she threw herself upon her knees, beyond control or care. "Then it is true—true that his Grace, whose child I bore with so great agony, will let me go to that terrible place!" she moaned, with tears streaming down her face. And then, as the thought of Mark Smeaton's torture came to her, she screamed aloud, "Uncle Thomas! Uncle Thomas! What will they do to me there?"

"Madame, I cannot say," answered Norfolk, turning away his eyes for very shame.

Chapter Thirty-Nine

"D O I GO INTO a dungeon?" Anne asked, as the turgid tide bore her through Traitors' Gate and the iron-toothed portcullis clanged behind her.

Kingston, the Governor of the Tower, took her by the arm to help her up the slippery steps and, after her uncle's rough contemptuousness, his voice sounded comparatively kind. "No, Madame, to your lodgings, where you lay at your Coronation," he assured her. And, weeping and recalling with hysterical laughter how differently she had been received that other May three years ago, she had suffered him to lead her there.

The torture of her imprisonment was slow and subtle. Although no one laid a hand upon her, within two weeks Anne had drunk to the dregs the cup of grief and fear and indignity. She knew now, past hope, that the King himself had ordered this savagery. At times she was able to rally herself to a kind of gay defiance, but at others, with no privacy or chance to speak to anyone she loved, this half life stabbed with stark terror became a jumble of emotions in her mind.

Sleeping or waking, she knew herself to be spied upon. Margaret and Arabella were lodged in some distant apartment. At night, when from very weariness she might have snatched relief in sleep, she lay moaning and tossing rather than risk babbling in her hideous dreams; because she knew that, beyond her curtains, her jealous aunt and Mistress Cosyns took turns at listening. And during the dragging hours of daylight they would ply her with impertinent questioning, dragging in the name of every man she knew; over and over again until her resistance broke and she would blurt out some foolishness which their hatred could twist and turn against her. And yet, in her anxiety for her friends, she could not keep her tongue from begging news of them.

"Smeaton is in irons," Cosyns had said with relish.

"All five of them are here in the Tower. They are to be taken for trial by state prosecution in Westminster Hall," her aunt had told her. "And that is as good as to be found guilty."

"Guilty of what?"

"Guilty of treason. Treason against the King's person."

Treason. That meant they would be executed; all except Smeaton, who, because he was not of noble lineage, would be hanged, drawn, and quartered. For the others there would be a block and axe. Every night in her vivid imagination, Anne saw the flashing blade come down through the darkness; and Norreys' handsome head rolling, the strong column of Brereton's neck gushing blood. One after the other, in the darkness of the night, she died the death of each, shuddering and moaning. Until she came to Thomas—and then she would scream aloud. Scream, and stifle it too late; and they would be at her again with their questions. "It is only that I was thinking my cousin Wyatt will make no more ballads about me," she would lie, crouching there, muttering about things that mattered nothing, like a mad woman.

And then, in the morning, for the twentieth time, she would ask the question that she could not hold back. "Where is my father?"

"Trying to keep himself safe," they would scoff.

And always, the insistent enquiry. "Where is my sweet brother? Master Kingston, has no one seen milord Rochford?"

"Do not distress yourself, Madame," Kingston's wife would lie kindly before Cosyns could open those thin, cruel lips of hers. "I do assure you my servant saw him a while since in the garden at Westminster."

And in the midst of this nightmare of grief there had been one moment of unexpected joy. Margaret had contrived to meet her alone and give her the good news. "Thomas is safe! We saw the others taking the air by the Lantern Tower, and he was not with them. He has never been here at all, Nan. Almost as soon as he was arrested the King ordered his release." In the darkness of the passage to the privy she and Margaret had clung to each other, thanking God that at least some part of their prayers had been answered.

Strengthened, uplifted, Anne had called for lute and pen that she might pass the time composing songs. Kingston seemed to fear that she would bedevil some of his men into smuggling notes to her friends. That they would even make some attempt at escape. But Anne, in high spirits again, laughed, and teased him for his caution, pointing to the thickness of the walls. "People who come in by Traitors' Gate do not get out again—unless it be by the King's pleasure!" she said.

By the King's pleasure.

She herself, her wit, her voice, her body, had been all the King's pleasure once. Would he not for the sake of past pleasure given, forgive her now? What if she wrote him a letter? At least it was worth trying. Cromwell was coming that very day. Would he dare to seem her friend by delivering it?

Sitting in the Governor's garden, under pretence of making a roundelay, Anne wrote it hurriedly while Cosyns, somnolent with so much eavesdropping, nodded in the afternoon warmth. Because she had no time to finesse with phrases, the words came straight and fearless from her heart. "Your Grace's displeasure and my imprisonment are things so strange to me that what to write, or what to excuse, I am altogether ignorant. If, as has been hinted to me, by confessing my grievous faults of artifice and pride, I may obtain my safety; then with all willingness and duty I will obey your command. But let not your Grace ever imagine your poor wife will be brought to acknowledge a fault of which no thought existed. Never a prince had a wife more loyal in duty and in true affection than Anne Boleyn, with which name and place I would willingly have contented myself had your Grace been so pleased." One by one, between cadences plucked on the lute, the impassioned sentences were added. "Good your Grace, let not any light fancy urge you to this infamous slander." And finally, "If ever I have found favour in your sight, if ever the name of Nan Boleyn has been pleasing in your ears, grant me this request—that myself only may bear the burden of your Grace's displeasure, and that it may not touch the souls of those poor gentlemen who are in imprisonment here for my sake. Try me, good King, let me but have a lawful trial, and let not my sworn enemies sit as my accusers and judges."

Whether the King had received her letter or whether Cromwell hid it away among his other papers, Anne never knew. Any more than she would ever know for certain how the King's stolen love letters had come into the hands of the Pope. All she knew was that there had been no royal mercy for her friends.

Hope rose again when Archbishop Cranmer came to visit her. Cranmer, who owed her gratitude and who would have helped her if he dared. He talked with her as a friend, but Anne soon found out that the King had sent him to worm from her some reason for proclaiming their marriage invalid from the first, so as to make Elizabeth a bastard in favour of any children Jane might bear him. Perhaps if she would do this, Cranmer hinted, even were she found guilty of the charges now being brought against her, she would be allowed to live peacefully abroad.

"His Grace will always acknowledge the Lady Elizabeth as his natural daughter," he assured her, as if it were some magnanimity on Henry's part.

"Because she will be a useful marriage pawn," scoffed Anne, who had often heard her husband bargaining with foreign powers about Mary.

But Cranmer had not come to bandy words and dared not go back empty-handed to his royal master. "If only your Grace will suggest some means to make your marriage void," he almost pleaded.

"The marriage which you took such pains to make," mocked Anne. "Well, Thomas Cranmer, what is to prevent you from unmaking it again? The King's conscience could always veer round like one of those little gold weather vanes at Hampton, and make him feel that after all Katherine of Aragon really *had* been his lawful wife."

"That would only leave the lady Mary Heir Apparent instead of Elizabeth," pointed out Cranmer, too worried even to rebuke her treasonable levity.

"The same objection about marriage within prohibited degree might serve again," she suggested. "For as you must surely have heard, my sister Mary was once his mistress."

But, being the very argument they had used to get rid of Katherine, it would make the King look faintly ridiculous, and he must always come out of everything with righteousness.

So Anne laid down the last remnants of her pride, prepared to appeal to a man whose love for her had languished. "There is milord Northumberland," she reminded the Archbishop.

Again Cranmer only shook his head reluctantly. "I have approached him more than once, for your sake. Proof of a pre-contract might save you. But he would not acknowledge it. And now he is a very sick man."

"You have seen him?" asked Anne pitifully, diverted for a moment from her own desperate plight.

"Yes, I have seen him. And it may well be that he thinks to serve you best by his silence, like all the rest," probed Cranmer.

Anne returned his searching look unwaveringly, making no attempt to deny his suspicions. Since he was the King's confessor, it was even possible that he already knew the truth. "You know as well as I, milord, that his Grace would never allow such a thought to be made public," she murmured.

But Cranmer was scarcely listening. He had got what he came for, and rose with a profound sigh, thankful that his hateful task was done. "I have only to swear before God that you have confessed to me some secret matter which is sufficiently grave to have made your marriage void from the first."

"And once it is annulled?" interrupted Anne eagerly.

"It will make no difference, my child, if that is what you have been hoping," he told her, as gently as he could.

"Make no difference?" Anne withdrew her pleading hand from his sleeve as if such duplicity scorched her. "No wonder he sends you crawling to me secretly! Is there no justice left in England?"

Panting, furious, superb, with hands and skirts pressed back against the wall as though his very presence contaminated her, she flung each indignant word at him. "In any impartial court of law you would be confounded. And you both know it! For if my marriage never was legal, then how can I be convicted of adultery?"

"It would make no matter," muttered Cranmer. "To come to the King unchaste can be accounted treason."

"It would make no matter!" Anne flamed at him. "Though honest men lose their lives! When I alone might have borne the burden of my iniquities!"

Cranmer's face was white as parchment. He tried in vain to calm her. But Anne was past caring now. "Go tell the King from me that I thank him for the way he has raised me up from a plain knight's daughter, happy in her home at Hever," she cried. "Raising me first to be a Marchioness, and then a Queen, and now—God's truth—a martyr!"

She swept the silenced Archbishop from her presence with a scornful curtsy, then burst into jangling laughter. "And tell the Tudor, too, that whatever fate befalls me, I have already half forgotten him," she called after. "But that though he should kill me and take a score of wives, I wager he will never fully enjoy one of them for remembering the pleasure he had with Nan Boleyn!"

Chapter Forty

A ND NOW, IN THE Tower Keep, they were trying her on a
charge of adultery and treason; trying her for her life. Her
own uncle was presiding, with Suffolk, Fitzroy, and twenty-
four other lords to support him, and the great hall packed to the
doors with their henchmen and the chief citizens of London
summoned to witness her humiliation. Anne knew that most of the
nobles had been chosen for their undisguised animosity; all but her
young cousin Surrey and her onetime lover, Northumberland, whose
faces showed that they had been forced to attend against their will.

Only her father, it seemed, had been spared the ordeal. Or was
it that, fearful for his own neck, he had deliberately stayed away
sooner than speak a word in her defence? Yet once he had loved
her. "Wily Wiltshire, still hunting the King's deer at Windsor, whilst
his curs hunt me here!" thought Anne bitterly, looking round upon
a sea of hostile faces.

If only George could have been there to support her! Coming
into the crowded hall, her first hope had been to find him. But
either he must be sick or they had prevented him.

Summoning every shred of wit and personality she possessed,
Anne stood alone and faced them all. Whatever her past sins of
pride and cruelty, she fought courageously for her virtue and for the
lives of the four men still accused with her, casting substantiated
truth in the teeth of paid false witnesses, so that again and again her

accusers were proved liars and her judges discomforted. Especially for Weston she strove, because she had misjudged him. For however freely he talked, however lively his imagination, he had refused to speak one word against her. "You say that he was frequently in my apartments, bandying bawdy compliments. Then I pray you call my cousin, Mistress Skelton, to witness, that she may tell you whom he came to see," she invited.

When chamberers, tempted by her enemies' gold, perjured their souls by giving time and place at Hampton, Greenwich, or Westminster for the adulterous acts to which they testified, her quick mind dealt effectively with at least one of them, thus laying the rest open to suspicion. "How can it be said that I was guilty of betraying my lord the King with Norreys on the sixth day of October, in the year of Grace 1533, when at that very time, as Dr. Butts will tell you, I was yet in my lying-in bed after the birth of my daughter, the Princess Elizabeth?" she cried indignantly.

And when one of the Seymours passed round the court Mark Smeaton's written confession of adultery, she challenged Cromwell's confidential servant, Constantine, to deny that the signature was obtained by torture and under promise of pardon. Why, she demanded, was he not brought into court that she might question him face to face?

Finding her no easy game to trap, Suffolk stood up and solemnly accused her of conspiring with Norreys to kill the King. His absurd charge was concocted on the flimsy grounds that some groom had overheard her teasing Hal about putting off his marriage so that he might step into a dead man's shoes, and Anne laughed in his face. "Good milords, and you city merchants from whose stock I come, I appeal to your common sense!" she cried. "Where should I, Nan Boleyn, have been with Henry Tudor dead? Gather your wandering wits, if you would bring some plausible charge against me! For was it not the cruel shock of milord Norfolk there pretending that the King was killed on May Day that deprived me and all of you of England's heir?"

And, so, carrying the attack into the enemy's camp, Anne prevented them from entangling her. She could feel that the people pressing against the barriers, who had come to gloat over her down-fall, were already sympathizing with her, and that several of the lords were beginning to think all these trumped-up charges were a travesty of justice. Their hard-won, grudging admiration warmed her to life and loveliness, lending her power to sway them. If only one among them would speak for her now, declaring honestly what he thought, the rest might dare to defy Cromwell and the King by bringing in a verdict of "Not Guilty"! Imploringly, her gaze turned upon Harry Percy. If only he would rise up courageously, vindicating her, and restoring her faith in him! But he just sat there with his head resting upon his hand, looking desperately sick and ill at ease. And presently, sooner than put his hand to any warrant of her guilt, he stumbled from the court.

And so, after all her strenuous defence, Anne's moment of hope died. And Norfolk, becoming aware of the dangerously changing atmosphere, hurried on with his brutal business. "Call the accused, George Boleyn, Viscount Rochford," he shouted to the heralds.

Anne turned in amazement to find her brother standing behind her. And suddenly, as he smiled at her, the grim building seemed full of radiance. "You are here—in the Tower!" she breathed forgetting everyone else.

"Foolish baggage," he bantered. "Did you not know that I have been here all the time? Or remember my promise that whatever happened I would stay with you?"

And that for the moment seemed to suffice.

But Anne's joy was short-lived. The buzz of excitement died down, and the crowd craned their necks in peculiar, expectant silence. Two tall halberdiers marched George to his place, and the charge was read.

A charge of incestuous adultery between George and Anne Boleyn, son and daughter of Thomas Boleyn, Earl of Wiltshire.

This was the culminating horror. Norfolk's trump card, played to tear the last shred of pity from the Queen and transfer it to the King. And, as he showed his hand, even hardened court officials gasped.

It was minutes before Anne could take in the purport of the appalling words, though as understanding gradually came to her, she realized that when George had come to warn her at Greenwich he must have had some inkling of what was being planned against them. Shocked to the soul, she sank back onto the chair provided for her, and sat staring down at her own shaking hands. She felt as if the two of them stood in some monstrous pillory of shame, with the libidinous curiosity of all men's gaze burning them. As if slime had suddenly been smeared across the fairest page of life.

How, in God's name, would he meet so foul a charge? Cautiously, Anne raised her eyes. George was standing in the centre of the hall, composed and debonair, with a long shaft of sunlight from one of the narrow Norman windows spilling light about him; gilding his fair, handsome face and tall, lithe figure, picking out the jewels on his best white brocaded doublet so that he looked the only lovely thing in a mire of drabness. In spite of the loathsome mire, Anne's lips quivered into a smile. It was so like George to put on his finest clothes to meet a difficult occasion! To stand there nonchalantly pulling a sprig of pink may through a buttonhole of his modish velvet!

At first she was too shamed to meet his eyes. But when she did, he looked at her across the court as if they two were alone, with that faint air of mockery and one quizzically raised brow. And Anne accepted his unspoken challenge and rose again to face their slanderers as instinctively as if he had reached out a hand and pulled her to her feet. She was no longer alone. At last there was a man to defend her. A man who had promised to stand by her to the end.

George let his excited enemies talk themselves to a standstill; then, succinctly, irritatingly, he pulled their case to pieces until even to the trial lords it began to look ludicrously poor. Never once did he let them taunt him into an indiscreet word about his royal brother-in-law, and only those who knew him intimately were aware of the anger like steel beneath his easy manner. At times he had the court tittering. Yet he was no longer the George Boleyn who had laughed and quipped his way through Court, lifted high by his father's insatiable ambition; but rather a man strengthened and sobered by a sincere searching of the Gospels, a man who had learned to hide a travesty of marriage and a disappointment in love beneath a show of badinage.

There were people present, he pointed out, who had known him from childhood, who would bear witness that he had always been on terms of the utmost affection with the Queen.

"We have it on oath that the aged Lady Wingfield testified on her deathbed that some nine or ten months ago you asked to be left alone with the Queen in her bedchamber," began his accusers.

"So inconsiderate of her to die just before I needed her," murmured George. "For she was my friend and always spoke the truth, *in toto.*"

"Mistress Druscilla Zouch was kept waiting a whole hour outside the door."

"With another maid-of-honour who appears to have grown tired of waiting."

"We are not here to speak of her," snapped the King's attorney hurriedly, as a snicker went along the barriers. "Mistress Zouch will bear witness."

"Very unwillingly, I think. But there is no need to call her. The Queen was in distress and I stayed to cheer her."

"Distressed about what?"

"She had been in poor health and spirits since her miscarriage."

"That would be about nine or ten months ago, would it not?"

"Probably."

"Lady Wingfield particularly recalled that the Queen called to you to save her. To save her from what, milord Rochford?"

"From falling in a swoon, so far as I recall."

"Was she not distressed because of the King's neglect?"

"Heneage would be able to answer that question better than I."

"I put it to you, Rochford, that she was calling upon you to save her from the stigma of bearing no son?"

"And I put it to you, milords, that that is an insult to the King!"

Enraged, they pressed him harder. "Yet you said openly and lewdly among your friends that the dead child that was afterwards born to her prematurely was not the King's."

"Never!"

"Is it not true that before the calamitous birth you were heard to boast among your friends that you were responsible for the Queen's being *enceinte* again?"

"Assuredly, it is true," George Boleyn admitted. And then, when all his enemies were a-tiptoe and agog, he deflated their nasty triumph by adding negligently, "For did I not arrange the masque which lured the King's wandering fancy back to her Grace? Have I not played my part in trying to provide England with an heir? And less clumsily, I flatter myself, than my illustrious uncle played *his* in destroying it!"

Proud Norfolk was never popular with the people, and the Boleyn charm was difficult to resist. "This rambling evidence of a dying old woman which you have used against me," George went on thoughtfully. "Obviously it must have been culled and twisted by a third party. And delivered as a well-arranged nosegay to Secretary Cromwell. Could the third party be said to be disinterested? Ah, my own wife! Who, as your witnesses had already been at pains to point out, is so jealous of my affection for the Queen's grace. Since milady Rochford had taken so active a part in collecting the evidence, would it not be simpler if she made her accusations face to face?"

And so the final outrage had been perpetrated which had reduced the charge to absurdity in most men's eyes. Lady Jane Rochford giving evidence against her own husband. Lady Jane Rochford, whose marital infidelities were a byword. And in the end all that she could swear to was that he had stayed a long time in his sister's bedroom, that he had embraced her and had been left alone with her, lying across the foot of her bed.

"Munching apples, Jane. Do not forget the apples," George jeered at her. And some of the city merchants had had the audacity to laugh out loud. For whatever they might think about the Queen, surely no man with Rochford's shining grace and sense of humour could be such an unnatural monster!

"Oh, what matters all the rest so that he go free," thought Anne. And free he would be any moment now. The judges and the lords had retired to discuss their findings. All round her people were whispering that he would surely be acquitted. Would that her own life hung on this accusation alone! Or, indeed, upon any accusation.

If only Henry would send her to some convent now, how willingly she would go! Or banish her abroad. Surely, surely public opinion would not suffer a Queen to be put to death! Death was so easily spoken of in a sonnet or a song; so different when, for the first time, one came to understand what the fear of dying meant.

Norfolk was coming back, with all the others trooping after him. Their lagging footsteps seemed to seal her fate. Their faces had a stunned, blank look. Norreys, Brereton, Weston, Smeaton—all of them were condemned to die for her. And now everyone was looking at her; save her accusers, who could not. Were they about to condemn a woman to death? Could it be possible that Henry would really let it happen, that it was going to happen now? That Cromwell's hands were shaking, and that there was pity at last in Norfolk's eyes?

She heard the sum of her foul iniquities told over in her uncle's harsh, familiar tones; and then the fatal words, "Anne, Queen of England, to be burned or beheaded at the King's pleasure."

To be burned alive. The most terrible death of all, reserved for heretics and witches. And how often, in loving sport, had Henry threatened it! Even in the terrible, awe-struck silence Anne could not really believe it, As the rows of upturned faces blurred together and her world went black she was really listening to Henry's voice, musical and persuasive against her ear, "Nan, Nan, my witch, I should have you burned for so enslaving my senses! Nan, there is no woman's body I could ever desire after enjoying yours."

In bare humanity Cromwell was telling them to take her back to her room. But with a supreme effort Anne waved women and ushers aside. As long as she could see and stand she must stay and hear what they did to George. Surely they had taken vengeance enough, surely they would acquit him now!

But it seemed they had not finished with him yet. Incited by the lascivious interest of the day, egged on by Norfolk who, after so much zeal on the King's behalf, must have been anxious to know how his daughter's slender chances stood, there was still some question they wanted to ask. But no one dared to voice it.

"Is it true that your wife sometimes repeats to you things which, in the performance of her duties and the closeness of their relationship, she might hear the Queen say?"

"As you have heard, she has a serpent's tongue." George, white as death, had eyes only for his sister and seemed to brush the question aside as though he scarcely heard it.

Remembering what she had said to Jane, Anne longed to call out and warn him that there are things which it is treason to know. Intimate things, which touched the King's pride.

But Norfolk was writing something on a piece of paper. Shame-facedly, it was folded and handed to George. "Did Lady Rochford ever repeat to you the words that are written there?" The faces of the two dukes whose children stood nearest the crown were working with excitement.

Forgetful of her own fate, Anne watched her brother's fine swordsman's fingers unfold the thing fastidiously. Heard his contemptuous apology as he held it to the light. "Your pardon, milords, the Duke writes a villainous hand!" And then as he stood there reading, Anne watched the devilish grin dawn upon his illumined face. She could guess what was written on the paper, and through the close mental link which bound them she could almost read his thoughts. She knew that it was almost as if someone had thrust into his hand a weapon wherewith to achieve his purpose and to avenge his family wrongs. Her life was already forfeit. His was his own to play with. He had only to say Yes or No, and burn the secret paper, and he would go free. But instead, assuming an air of bland, inane misunderstanding, he read the words aloud, before his horrified judges could stop him.

"That the King is well-nigh impotent? No, milords, I do not recollect—"

Norfolk had packed the hall with spectators so that they might hear the Queen's shame and go home and talk about it. Now they would have something still more interesting to talk and titter about, to spread through the taverns of London. Something for which another Boleyn death warrant would be signed, but for which the King would never forgive their haughty ducal kinsman.

Chapter Forty-One

IT WAS ODDLY STILL in the Queen's lodgings. The crowds had been dispersed, soldiers and heralds had clattered away, and there was no need to concentrate and use one's wits any more. No more need to hold oneself watchfully before all those staring eyes, or to swing alternatively between hope and despair.

Anne found herself standing by an open window with a tiny nosegay of pink-tipped daisies in her hand. Vaguely she remembered stooping to gather them as she crossed the green, and how her silent entourage had waited patiently while she did so. No one had attempted to stop her. Perhaps they, too, had remembered that it would be the last time she would be able to gather flowers.

Already the people who stood about her or brought her food were shadowy beings, with whose thoughts and aims she was no longer concerned. Even the two women who had spied upon her tripped over each other to offer her small, propitiating services. The dignity of death was upon her so that, condemned, she was immune from hatred.

"Queen Katherine died slowly. But is this much worse than what you urged him to do to her?" her aunt and her own conscience had asked a dozen times.

"But Katherine had her righteousness to keep her company. For my brother and those others, I would willingly suffer many deaths," she had said bravely enough, over there in the court. How easy it had been to say it, keyed up by an audience! But when it came to dying *one* death—sinking to the floor, crazed with fright, faced with unknown eternity, Anne wept and screamed unrestrainedly, blind for the time to any plight but her own. In vain the women tried to quiet her, and when, fearing that she would go mad, they sent for Kingston, Anne reached up and clung to him. "Will the King really burn me?" she asked with shaking lips, letting out at last the words which had been beating at her brain all day.

Since he would have the arranging of it, Kingston devoutly hoped not. "Not *that* for a Queen," he mumbled.

"Then it will be the axe?" Anne pulled down his warm hand between her two cold ones, watering it with her tears. "I have heard it said that the executioner has sometimes bungled."

But there must be mercy somewhere; and one must not go out unprepared. She rose with what dignity she could muster, eased by the wild escape of words long leashed by pride. "Good Sir William, I pray you fetch me a priest so that I may have the Body of our Lord in my oratory," she begged, turning spontaneously, in her extremity, to the religion of her childhood. And when he had done so, she knelt for hours before the Host, saying over and over again old familiar prayers and every now and then punctuating the familiar, soothing words with passionate personal cries that broke from her over-burdened heart.

"If my poor Jocunda, who has been more than a mother to me, could see me now!"

"Oh, that I could see Mary Tudor and ask her forgiveness before I die!"

"Dear Christ, as Thou didst bear the cross, help me, help me, to meet the axe. Oh, if it be Thy will, let the extraordinary dread of it pass from me!"

For Anne understood only too well now what had been the un-comprehended, nameless dread which had at times come upon her, blacking out her most glittering triumphs and sending her hand to her suffocating throat.

When at last she came from her oratory, she made Lady Kingston sit in her own chair. "I would have you pretend to be the

Princess Mary so that I may publicly beg her pardon as I would if she were here," Anne entreated.

In an agony of remorse, unheeding what they thought, Anne knelt humbly before the Governor's wife and confessed with tears every petty oppression which she had devised against her step-daughter and every cruelty towards her to which she had persuaded the King. "And I charge you, before God and as you shall answer for it at the Judgment, that you will go to the lady Mary's grace and kneel down on your knees to her as I have to you, asking forgive-ness for the wrongs I have done her. For only so will my troubled conscience know quiet."

And as if in answer to her passionate prayers, when Anne rose from her self-imposed penance, she found Kingston standing there with news that some part of her sentence was to be alleviated. Francis of Valois, he said, was sending his executioner from Paris; the one man with a sword sharper and more expert than his own.

There was to be no clumsy, bungling axe.

Instantly, Anne's thought flew, glad and warm, to Francis. Here was a source of succour of which through the long sleepless nights, she had not even thought. But Wyatt, perhaps, had. Since state business had frequently taken him there, he had no doubt been able to send a message through some friend. And Francis, who could neither interfere nor deflect Henry from his purpose, had remem-bered the masque of St. George and the Dragon in Calais Castle, and once again had offered Henry a civilized sword with which to do his butchering. It would be the Valois' last, strange gift to her.

Francis had always admired her. He had never seen her drawn and despairing, nor struggling back to vivacity after childbirth. He would be thinking of her as he last saw her, utterly desirable, with the aura of Henry's love about her, and the admiration of other men enhancing her elusive beauty. A dark Venus, he had called her. Even now the bare thought of him brought a little secret smile to Anne's lips. Her eyes glinted and narrowed, as of habit. But she checked herself abruptly. Of what profit now to dwell upon things of the flesh? Now, when one's body was about to be mutilated. One must thank God humbly, and think only of the King of France's kindness.

"So it will not hurt much after all," she managed to say, smiling at Kingston. "And my neck is very small. See, I can almost span it with the fingers of one hand!"

Fooling gently, she tried to draw her companions with her to a quickly changing mood of defiant gaiety. It was her flickering effort after courage.

Among the awful, dragging hours one day stood out, when the sun shone brilliantly from early dawn to tardy dusk. When the loveliest month was at her zenith and England drenched with the scent of early summer flowers. When Anne's beauty-loving senses saw nothing of the transient pageant, nothing but the torment in her own soul.

The day when five men must die because of her. The day when her brother must die.

All day long she and Margaret knelt, hand-locked, in prayer— prayer broken only by foolish recollections and little heartbroken sentences. Though the crowds gathered as soon as it was light on Tower Hill, their own hearts and minds were often back at Allington and Hever. Until there came the solemn beat of slow marching feet across the flagstones, and the droning Latin of an intoning priest. And the unbolting of a gate. Then their lips stopped moving and their ears followed the meaning of every sound. The murmur from a mass of people awaiting the spectacle of death, a shocked murmur more awful than any shouting. The occasional crack of a sharp order, the complete silences more poignant than any sound. And then the salute of a gun, echoing from wall to wall. Five separate times a salute broke the ominous silence, and each time Anne seemed to crouch a little lower, to die a little in herself. Until at last, shrouded by a dusk more human than her enemies, a cart creaked mournfully back across the draw-bridge and into the courtyard. A cart into which they dared not rise and look.

But the bodies of the dead were least of all.

Out on Tower Hill youth and grace and virile beauty had been slain. There had been an insentient cutting off of gifted promise, of laughter, enthusiasms, and loving plans. And somewhere out in the country the last pale streaks of sunset were leaving to darkness ancestral homes made desolate by the death of eldest sons.

"Let me go! Let me go and make my end with these, who for my grasping ambition die!" Anne had begged. "For looking into their eyes I shall be brave."

"It is no sight for a woman," her keepers had said.

And yet sometime she would have to go out onto Tower Hill before all those staring eyes. Tomorrow, perhaps. Oh, cruel, that she must wait and go alone!

It was Arabella who made eyes at the Captain of the Guard and so managed to bring news of their passing. "The Westons are so rich, and Francis was so beautiful. His widowed mother offered as ransom all the money the King had paid for the grounds of Hampton—even their lovely home Sutton Place," she reported. "But they would not spare him."

"Tell us what they said on the scaffold," Margaret bade her.

"All of them acknowledge sin in the sight of God; but denied guilt of the specific charges. And lest their families should suffer, they spoke no evil of the King."

"And Mark?" enquired Margaret.

"He alone called out, 'Masters, I beseech you to pray for me, for I have deserved the death!'"

"What, with the noose about his neck and nothing more Cromwell could do to him, would he not clear me of the shame he brought upon me?" cried Anne indignantly.

"I suppose he could have meant that by his betrayal he deserved to die," suggested Arabella, in his defence.

"Then he should have made it clear in men's minds," said Anne. "But it is not for me to condemn him." And dismissing him with a pitiful sigh, she asked the thing which lay nearest her heart. "And what of my brother, 'Bella?"

"Milord Rochford?" Arabella's wide, generous mouth parted in a little, loving laugh, the kind of tribute he would have liked best. "He stood and looked the crowd over, I am told, cocking an eyebrow as he so often did. 'What would you have me say?' he asked, knowing well that they were all agog with prurient curiosity.

'I am come here to die, not to preach.' And die he did, forgiving his enemies and warning his friends not to rely upon fortune's smiles—gay and fair and gallant to the last!"

It was Margaret who broke down and hid her face in Anne's lap. "Oh, Nan!" she cried, between stifled sobs, "Terrible as it is for you, at least you and he will be together afterwards. Whereas I must go on living somehow without you both!"

"You will have Thomas," Anne reminded her gently. And Arabella thrust a sheet of paper into Margaret's hand. "See, hinny, here are some verses my amorous Captain found in their cell, and I bought them for you with a kiss. The jailors say that last evening Rochford was singing some gay ballads to keep the others' spirits up. But this one, which he was writing at dawn long after they were asleep, shows a little what was in his own heart."

Together the three of them bent over the crumpled sheet. It seemed like a tender farewell, seeing George's familiar script again.

> "*Farewell, my lute, this is the last*
> *Labour that thou and I shall waste,*
> *For ended is that we began;*
> *Now is the song both sung and past,*
> *My lute, be still, for I have done.*"

Outside, as if outraged, Nature joined their grief, a wild gale was blowing up. Rain lashed the casements and the warning calls of watermen echoed fearfully from the wind-tossed river. To cheer the condemned Queen, and because even in summer the Tower could be cold and dank, some kind hand had kindled a fire. And far into the night Anne and Margaret and Arabella sat over it, listening to the wind, praying, even laughing sometimes, and talking of old times.

Chapter Forty-Two

"Is he COME, GOOD Kingston? The executioner out of France?"

"Madame, consider the storm last night. Perhaps his ship could not put in at Dover."

"But this morning the storm is past and over. Listen how the birds sing!"

"He is probably somewhere on the Dover road, and that a quagmire."

Anne pictured him. A Frenchman with a sharp broadsword, riding headlong through a strange country, hurrying to behead her. Hurrying mercifully.

"Oh, will he never get here? Suppose, Sir William, that he had not enough English to ask his way, or his horse stumbled and threw him. You all said that it would have been over yesterday. I had thought to be out of my pain by now."

"Cromwell sent an escort to meet the man. It is supposed that he may be here by noon."

"What makes you think so?"

"A detachment of the new Honourable Artillery Company has been sent from Westminster with orders to stand by for the firing of a salute."

"You deafened all London with salutes when I came for my Coronation. But why do me that much honour now?"

The Governor of the Tower stood silent, with bowed iron-grey head.

"Ah, I see," said Anne, on a long-drawn sigh. "So that the King may know the moment it is done."

When Kingston had gone, she raised her arms above her head in a gesture of renunciation—the lovely arms which Henry had so often covered with kisses—and went to an open window, her clinging black velvet swaying and soughing after her. Out in the little privy garden sunlight lay upon the grass and drew a drowsy sweetness from the box borders of prim little flower beds. A linnet carolled from its cage beside a doorway. High above the tall city wall the last wrack of the storm scudded in small white clouds across a sky of summer blue. And from somewhere behind the Keep came the cheerful echo of workmen's shouting and hammering as they went about their ordinary daily work.

Or was their work so ordinary?

"'Tis but the carpenters fixing up extra stabling by the guard-room," lied Arabella, a shade too negligently.

But Anne had already guessed what the workmen were doing. They were putting up a scaffold. And each ringing blow fell not only upon the nails but upon the quivering consciousness of the woman for whose destruction it was being built. "I hear it is to be very low," she said, passing her tongue across dry lips.

"So that the people outside on Tower Hill will not be able to see the Tudor's shame, and tear you free," muttered Arabella passionately, pulling her mistress into strong young arms.

Anne was thankful to rest there for a minute or two, comforted by the warm impulsive love of friendship in which, of late, she had found herself to be so rich. "What will they do with me afterwards?" she asked in a broken voice, as the hammering went on.

For Margaret's sake, Arabella was trying to silence her. "That, darling Nan, will be *our* grief," she reminded her.

To pass the heavy time, and so that she might no longer harass them with her secret thoughts, Anne went to her writing table. Humming softly to keep her teeth from chattering, she pulled a sheet of paper into position and took up a pen with that one-handed gesture so familiar to those who watched her. Because it did not seem worth-while to sit down, she remained standing, absently stroking the goosequill feathers against her pale cheek while she collected her thoughts. Setting herself a test of courage. For if George could be so master of his mind as to write verse on the brink of death—why, so would she.

Firmly, her quill began to move.

> *"Defiled is my name, full sore,*
> *Through cruel spite and false report,*
> *That I may say for evermore*
> *Farewell to joy, adieu comfort."*

"Do you write a last bequest, that I may see to it for you, Madame?" asked Lady Kingston, touched by the divorced and crownless prisoner's true repentance, and anxious to be of service.

"Why, no, I thank you. I write verses to pass the time," answered Anne, trying to achieve something of her brother's nonchalance.

But a tear splashed down onto the paper as her pen moved on afresh.

> *"Oh, Death, rock me asleep,*
> *Bring on my quiet rest,*
> *Let pass my guiltless ghost*
> *Out of my careful breast."*

"What kind of verse *can* you write at such a time, Nan?" whispered Arabella, coming to peep over her shoulder.

"A lullaby, dear 'Bella."

"Her last thoughts for her baby daughter," murmured Lady Boleyn, raising sanctimonious eyes to Heaven.

"No, for myself!" Anne corrected her crisply. And hearing the tramp of approaching feet, she turned sharply, leaving the half-finished lines there for all to see; to see and to puzzle over as they would probably puzzle over the whole enigma of her life.

She knew that the end was come. That there was no longer any hope of the last-minute reprieve for which, in her weaker moments, she had prayed. How often had she seen a death warrant lying on

Henry's table! With his own hand, he must have signed hers. Through the open doorway she could see Kingston bringing a priest and a posse of official-looking people. Before going to meet them she stood for a moment or two watching the sands filter through the slender waist of the hourglass on her table. "Strange that I should have been striving to pass the time, who have so little time to spare," she thought, almost dispassionately.

The executioner had arrived at last. It would not be long now, they assured her. But first he and his assistant must eat. How strange, thought Anne again, that they *could* eat! But of course, they had ridden hard; and it was a trade to them like any other. They would be ready by noon, Kingston said. Ready to put her out of life.

Someone brought her a glass of hot spiced wine; but she set it aside, untasted. Suppose in their new concern for her they had mixed in it some poppy seeds or bryony to drug her senses? No, she would go clear-headed to her death suffering all to the uttermost rather than fail to proclaim, by word and behaviour, the innocence upon which rested her own fair name and the honour of her friends. She would look her best and go proudly.

With that quiet authority which she could assume at times, Margaret Wyatt turned them all from the room. For this last half hour they would be alone; Arabella, herself, and Nan.

"Make me more beautiful than ever," ordered Anne, making them laugh shakily, because it was what she had always been wont to say before any special occasion in the past. So they dressed her in her favourite black damask which parted in front to show a rich crimson kirtle. As carefully as if she were going to a masque or a tournament they brushed out her long, dark hair. Only now they dressed it higher and caught it up from the whiteness of her neck beneath a jewelled coif. If the pins slipped now and then from their trembling fingers, or they dropped a comb, all three of them pretended not to be aware of it; and there was no one there to see. Only from time to time one or other of them would give voice to some little half-finished sentence, making it sound as casual as she could.

"If it had not happened that you wanted to get into the Cardinal's house that day, I might never have served you."

"You must marry and be very happy, 'Bella."

"I shall go straight home to Allington and tell Thomas how brave you were."

"Tell him, rather, dear Margot, that having had you with me all these years has been a little like keeping something of him."

All too soon the escort came for them. For a hasty moment Anne clung desperately to each friend in turn. Their cheeks were cold and wet; but because she had yet a drama to play out in the sight of men, Anne herself could not afford to weep. At the last moment she picked up a little book of devotions which her step-mother had given her long ago when life had been a string of happy days. It was so small that she could encircle it with her hand. It would be something of Jocunda to take with her.

"*Yea, though I walk through the valley of the shadow of Death, I will fear no evil; for Thou art with me,*" she read, because the golden covers fell apart at that familiar page. But she could not really see the words. Her eyes were too blind with unshed tears.

"Do not grieve for me," she managed to say, as the door opened and Henry's creatures came for her. "George and the rest are now, I doubt not, before the face of a *true* King, and before long I shall follow."

At thought of them a strange peace possessed her. A lifting of all fear. She felt their goodly company about her, as though they tarried for her, and was sustained by a great longing to join them. Lifting the pearled crimson kirtle a little, she almost ran down the stairs, humming a snatch of song, for all the world as though she were hurrying out to meet them in the garden at Hever.

Suffering had softened all her hard haughtiness. Never had she looked more beautiful, with her proud head held high, nervous strain painting colour on her cheeks, and her great dark eyes glistening with emotion. Men and women, stepping aside to make way for her to pass, could not take their eyes from her face. For the first time, perhaps, some of them understood how their King had been bewitched.

"It has been my lot to see many people executed, but never one went more gaily!" marvelled Kingston, waiting to conduct her out through the Palace gate to the little green behind the Keep.

But once out in the noon sunshine, Anne's composure began to break. At sight of the scaffold she stopped abruptly, drawing a breath which seemed to stab her side.

There were no vast crowds. Only a group of well-dressed persons around the finished scaffold, and the Lord Mayor and sheriffs in their scarlet robes, standing at a little distance. And, raised above them on the straw-strewn platform of the scaffold, the two most important protagonists of all—except herself. A tall man with a little pointed beard and a shock-headed youth. The executioner and his assistant.

So the scene was all set, much as she had pictured it; with the grim white walls of the Keep rising up on one side, and on the other the sad little church of St. Peter-ad-Vincula, where the men-at-arms and grooms and jailors worshipped. All just as she had steeled herself to face it.

But to die on a May morning, while one was yet comparatively young! While the gilly flowers were drenched with sweetness, and happy hawking parties went galloping across gorse-gold heaths, and the sap of love and laughter still rose in one's blood. To give up all warm, human loves and the comfort of familiar, earthly things. To moulder in some warm dark grave. At thirty-three a woman wanted a man's love, and children—laughter, gowns, and gaiety—not a Heavenly crown. But of what avail to think of such things now, when one was already shriven and prepared for death?

After that first recoiling, Anne forced her reluctant limbs to walk on. The way was so terribly short. No time to gather daisies now. She had only to walk a few short steps across the green and mount those four shallow wooden steps. And then life's journey would be done.

Sir William Kingston went up first so as to give her his hand. With a swift, imprudent movement his wife, at the scaffold's foot, bent unobtrusively to kiss her flowing sleeve. Margaret and Arabella followed up the steps.

Once upon the scaffold, Anne was able to look down upon the lines of upturned faces. She heard their involuntary gasp, and knew that, though she was no longer a Queen, she could still stir the hearts of men. Until the moment when they struck off her head she would be able to bemuse theirs with her strange, fatal beauty. The knowledge warmed her, giving exonerating reason for all that she had ever done. For everything which had happened since that day when Simonette had called into the stillness of the garden, "Nan, Nan, it is your turn to come to Court!"

Cromwell, she supposed, was the one man present unmoved by feminine appeal. Norfolk's absence was attributable, she hoped, to his disgrace. But surely there was one of Jane Seymour's brothers? With just enough decency left to try to hide his splendid height behind a line of steel-helmeted halberdiers. Suffolk stood immediately below her, with his chance resemblance to the King and his determination to have a front place; and by his side her Howard cousin's bridegroom, Harry Fitzroy. Probably it was the first execution young Fitzroy had ever witnessed in his pampered life. In spite of all his swagger and finery, he looked greenly nervous. Anne hoped that he would vomit and disgrace his manhood. But, alas, she would not be there to see!

From the grievous contemplation of foes and forsworn friends, Anne lifted her eyes to the unpolluted sky, only to see the King's gunners standing at the ready by the cannon on the wall waiting to proclaim her passing. So that Henry could hear it at Westminster and know that the final price of their furious loving had been paid. And rejoice that he was a widower again. And get on his great horse, no doubt, and ride to his new marriage bed.

But why picture Henry in all his lusty attractiveness? Would to God she had never seen him!

Kingston was at her elbow, reminding that she might speak from the scaffold—that people were expecting her to.

But what was there to say, save to reiterate her innocence of treason, adultery, and incest? And to yield herself humbly to the King's will, lest more ill befall their child. Standing there, with her own clear voice echoing strangely back to her from the surrounding walls, Anne could not curb her thoughts from going forward into time with Elizabeth. How would the new Queen treat her? "As I treated Mary?" she wondered. Or would gentle Jane be kind, so that the child would learn to love a stepmother, as she herself had done? But whichever way God willed it, Elizabeth would be taught that Nan Boleyn had been a harlot, and would remember no mother save as a thing of shame.

"I pray God to save the King, for to me he was for many years a good and gentle lord," Anne said steadily, coming to the most difficult words of all. And then, her short speech done, she turned impulsively to Margaret and Arabella. "And to you who have never forsaken me, through good fortune and bad, what can I say—" What could one give in return for a lifetime of devoted friendship? Beyond speech, they looked into each other's eyes, and Anne pushed Jocunda's little golden book into Margaret's hand.

And now, although the noonday sun still shone and the birds sang, there was nothing more left to do. Nothing but kneel down and lay one's neck upon the block. For the first time Anne allowed herself to look down at the sinister, hollowed out square of wood, well scrubbed from the last victim's blood. At sight of it her heart began to race so that it seemed everyone must hear it in the solemn hush. What would they do with her afterwards, she thought hysterically for the hundredth time. With her stiffening body and her gruesome, bleeding head? Would they wait until it was dusk—a summer dusk which she would never see—and throw them into a cart, like those others, to creak mournfully across the courtyard?

Arabella, holding herself from swooning, would have tied a scarf about her mistress' eyes, but Anne pushed away her shaking hands. Up to the last moment she must see what they were going to do.

In a frenzy of dumb terror her gaze slid round to Kingston who was standing gravely behind her waiting to give the fatal sign. And then to the executioner on her right. Save that he was coatless and wore a narrow velvet mask across his eyes, he might have been one of the spectators. His brown leather jerkin was belted above long, elegant brown hose. There was no sign of a sword. Had he hidden it somewhere in the deep piled straw? Even at such a time Anne's practised eye noticed that he was handsome in a dark, sinister sort of way. And because he was a Frenchman, and somehow apart from all the pother of her guilt or innocence, almost involuntarily she looked at him through lowered lashes from those enticing, almond shaped eyes of hers. In the way that other women called wanton. And because it was a May morning and she was the most desirable woman he had ever seen, his dark, glittering eyes smiled back at her from behind the black velvet. She knew that he wished her well. That he would go back and tell Francis that she had made a good end—that she had been as brave as she was beautiful.

He went down on one knee and asked her pardon for what he must do. Henceforward he was the one man left in her life. All the human help she could expect must come from him. Though she did not even know his name, only they two existed in this tense half world between life and death. It was he who guided her gently to her knees—but it was for her to bend her proud neck to that dreadful hollowing in the block. And that she could not bring herself to do.

She began to fidget at her coif. It would be in the way, she imagined. But both Margaret and Arabella had turned away their faces. She must move it aside herself.

"Give me a moment more, kind Kingston," she entreated. "Dear God, give me strength!"

And then, trying to compose herself, she closed her eyes. "*Miserere mei, Deus. In te, Domine, speravi.* Into Thy hands I commit my spirit!" she prayed over and over again, through rigid lips, still kneeling upright.

But though she tried desperately to fasten her hopes on Heaven, her senses were sharpened to the sound of every movement behind her.

A stealthy rustle in the straw, an approaching footstep. Quick as a warned, defensive cat, Anne swung round to her left from whence the sound came. But only the shock-headed young assistant stood there, empty-handed, advancing close upon her in feigned action, obedient to his master's sign. Anne's eyes, protruding with terror, stared up into his. Her brain recorded a vivid picture of his callow, countrified face. Momentarily, her head was turned, her attention distracted.

And in that moment, mercifully, the French executioner swung his sharp sword and struck.

The End

Reading Group Guide

The enigmatic Anne Boleyn comes to life in this charming, brilliant portrayal by acclaimed British novelist Margaret Campbell Barnes.

The infamous love of King Henry VIII and the mother of Queen Elizabeth I, Anne Boleyn undertook a rocky journey from innocent courtier to powerful Queen of England. A meticulous researcher, Margaret Campbell Barnes immerses readers in this intrigue and in the lush, glittery world of the Tudor Court. The beauty and charms of Anne Boleyn bewitched the most powerful man in the world, King Henry VIII, but her resourcefulness and cleverness were not enough to stop the malice of her enemies. Her swift rise to power quickly became her own undoing.

The author brings to light Boleyn's humanity and courage, giving an intimate look at a young woman struggling to find her own way in a world dominated by men and adversaries.

1. Anne Boleyn has come to be depicted as history's favorite vixen. How is she portrayed in *Brief Gaudy Hour*? How does Margaret Campbell Barnes help us to see her in that way? At what moments in the book did you identify with Anne?

2. Anyone who has taken any world history course knows the story and fate of Anne Boleyn. And yet, Margaret Campbell Barnes still manages to create and maintain a level of suspense and surprise throughout *Brief Gaudy Hour*. How does the author use irony and

foreshadowing in combination with the reader's presumed fore-knowledge to give the story this propulsion? What were some moments in the story that had you on the edge of your seat?

3. Early in chapter 1, Anne stands naked before a mirror and examines herself. What purpose does this scene serve? How does it help the reader connect to Anne?

4. What would you say is the turning point in the relationship between Anne and Harry Percy? Anne takes out her anger mostly on Cardinal Wolsey, but who do you see as being most at fault in the end of their relationship? Why? What did you think of Harry's betrayal of Anne? Did he have any other choices?

5. In chapter 15, Anne says to Jocunda, "Would I could make the King suffer and humiliate the Cardinal as he humiliated my love that day!" How does Anne get her revenge on the Cardinal? Is his final punishment fair in relationship to his offences against Anne? Does she get her wish for the King?

6. Anne works very hard to keep King Henry at bay for more than half the book. What were her motives in doing so? How does this serve to increase her power over him? In what ways does it lead to her eventual downfall?

7. In chapter 28, Anne tells Cranmer, "I did not kill Wolsey!" Is she in some way responsible for his death? What does her sense of guilt over the issue say about her character? Why do others accuse her?

8. In chapter 32, Anne says of Queen Katherine, "That woman is my death or I am hers." What role does Anne play in Katherine's death? What role does Katherine, or the history of Katherine, play in Anne's death?

9. Also in chapter 32, Anne makes an unknowingly prophetic speech about her unborn child, whom she calls "he," and a war with

Spain. We can now understand the irony of Henry and Anne's anxieties over Henry's female, and lack of male, children. Why was it so important to Henry? How does our knowledge of the outcome of the situation give Anne's speech significance?

10. What is the turning point in the "brief gaudy hour" of Anne and King Henry's relationship?

11. When Henry is injured in the tournament in chapter 37, Anne fears losing him, "for what is Anne Boleyn without Henry Tudor?" Might we also ask, what is Henry Tudor without Anne Boleyn? What would England be without Anne Boleyn?

12. Based on the character of King Henry VIII which Margaret Campbell Barnes has portrayed here, do you think Henry believes any or all of the charges brought against her? What does his absence from the trials and Anne's last days say about him?

13. Margaret Campbell Barnes is careful never to pass judgment on any of her characters. But it is scarcely easy for us as readers to remain impartial in the light of such events, especially bearing in mind their verity. Based on the evidence Ms. Barnes presents, what verdicts did you as a reader reach in regards to characters such as Anne Boleyn, King Henry, Harry Percy, Cardinal Wolsey, etc.? What led you to reach these verdicts?

14. Margaret Campbell Barnes's writing career first took off in the years following World War II. She published 10 books of historical fiction between 1944 and 1962. She was a volunteer in the ambulance service during the war and lost her eldest son in the battles in Normandy. How might these things have influenced her writing of this particular story? Are there moments in *Brief Gaudy Hour* where this is apparent?

Reading Group Guide written by Elizabeth R. Blaufox, great-granddaughter of Margaret Campbell Barnes

About the Author

Margaret Campbell Barnes lived from 1891 to 1962. She was the youngest of ten children born into a happy, loving family in Victorian England. She grew up in the Sussex countryside, and was educated at small private schools in London and Paris.

Margaret was already a published writer when she married Peter, a furniture salesman, in 1917. Over the next twenty years a steady stream of short stories and verse appeared over her name (and several *noms de plume*) in leading English periodicals of the time, *Windsor, London, Quiver,* and others. Later, Margaret's agents, Curtis Brown Ltd, encouraged her to try her hand at historical novels. Between 1944 and 1962 Margaret wrote ten historical novels. Many of these were bestsellers and book club selections and were translated into foreign editions.

Between World Wars I and II Margaret and Peter brought up two sons, Michael and John. In August 1944, Michael, a lieutenant in the Royal Armoured Corps, was killed in his tank, in the Allied advance from Caen to Falaise in Normandy. Margaret and Peter grieved terribly the rest of their lives. Glimpses of Michael shine through in each of Margaret's later novels.

In 1945 Margaret bought a small thatched cottage on the Isle of Wight, off England's south coast. It had at one time been a smuggler's cottage. But to Margaret it was a special place in which to recover the spirit and carry on writing. And write she did. All together, over two million copies of Margaret Campbell Barnes's historical novels have been sold worldwide.